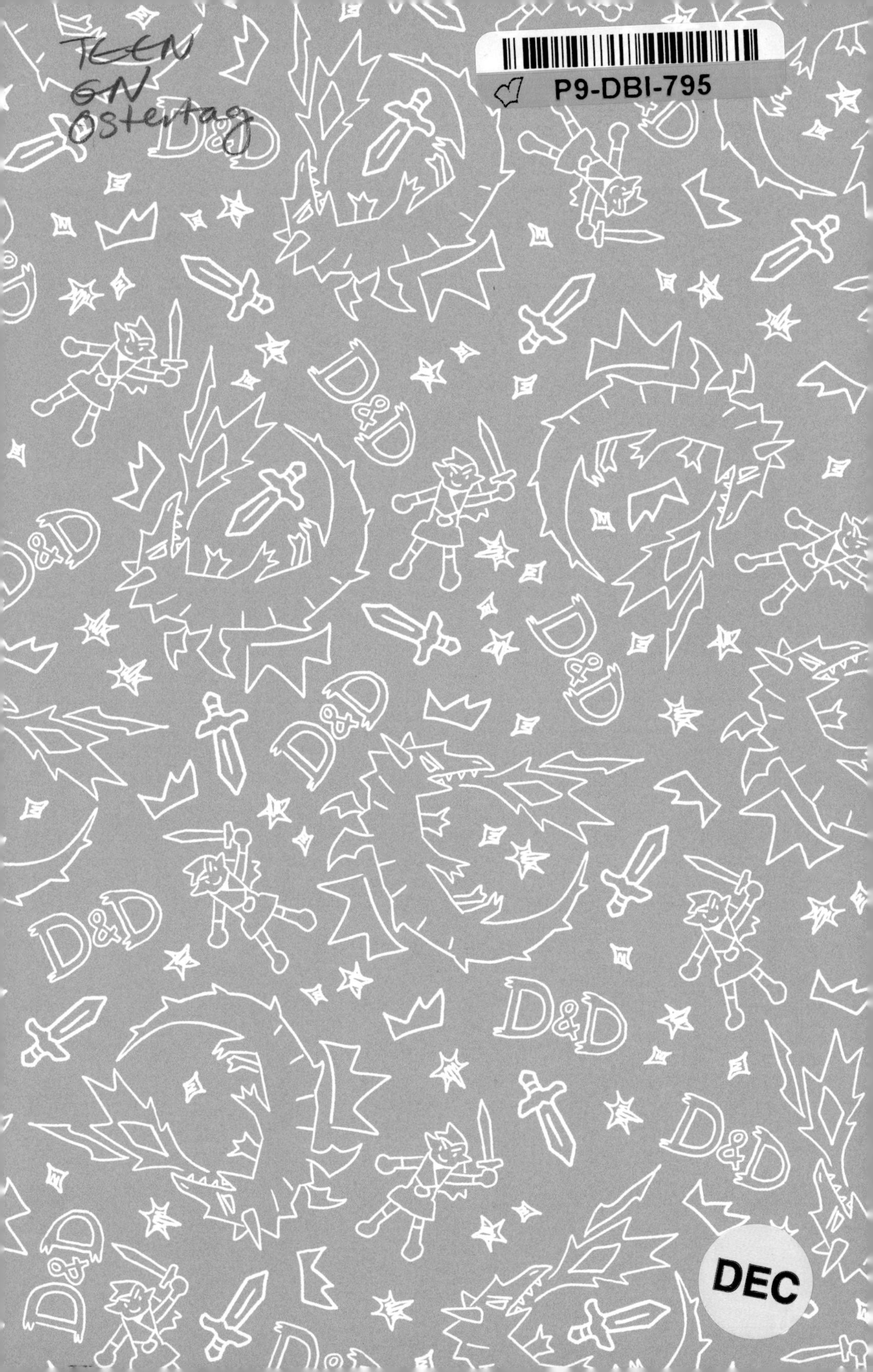
D&D

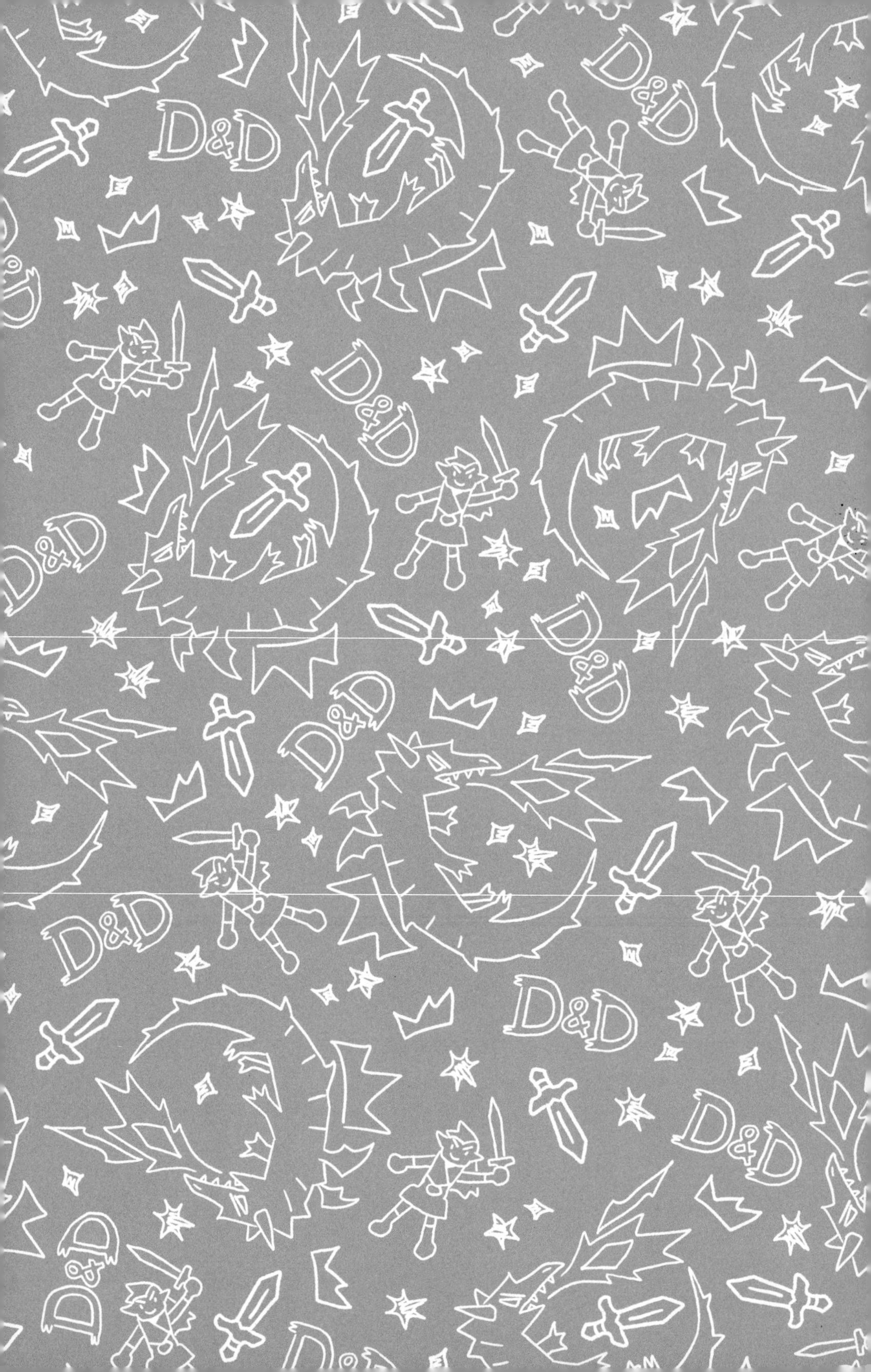
D&D

D&D

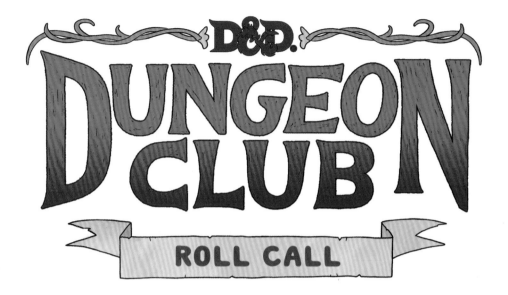

DUNGEON CLUB

ROLL CALL

18
20
8

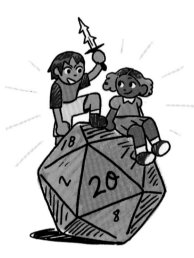

Molly Knox Ostertag

Xanthe Bouma

HARPER alley

An Imprint of HarperCollinsPublishers

WIZARDS OF THE COAST
OFFICIAL LICENSED PRODUCT

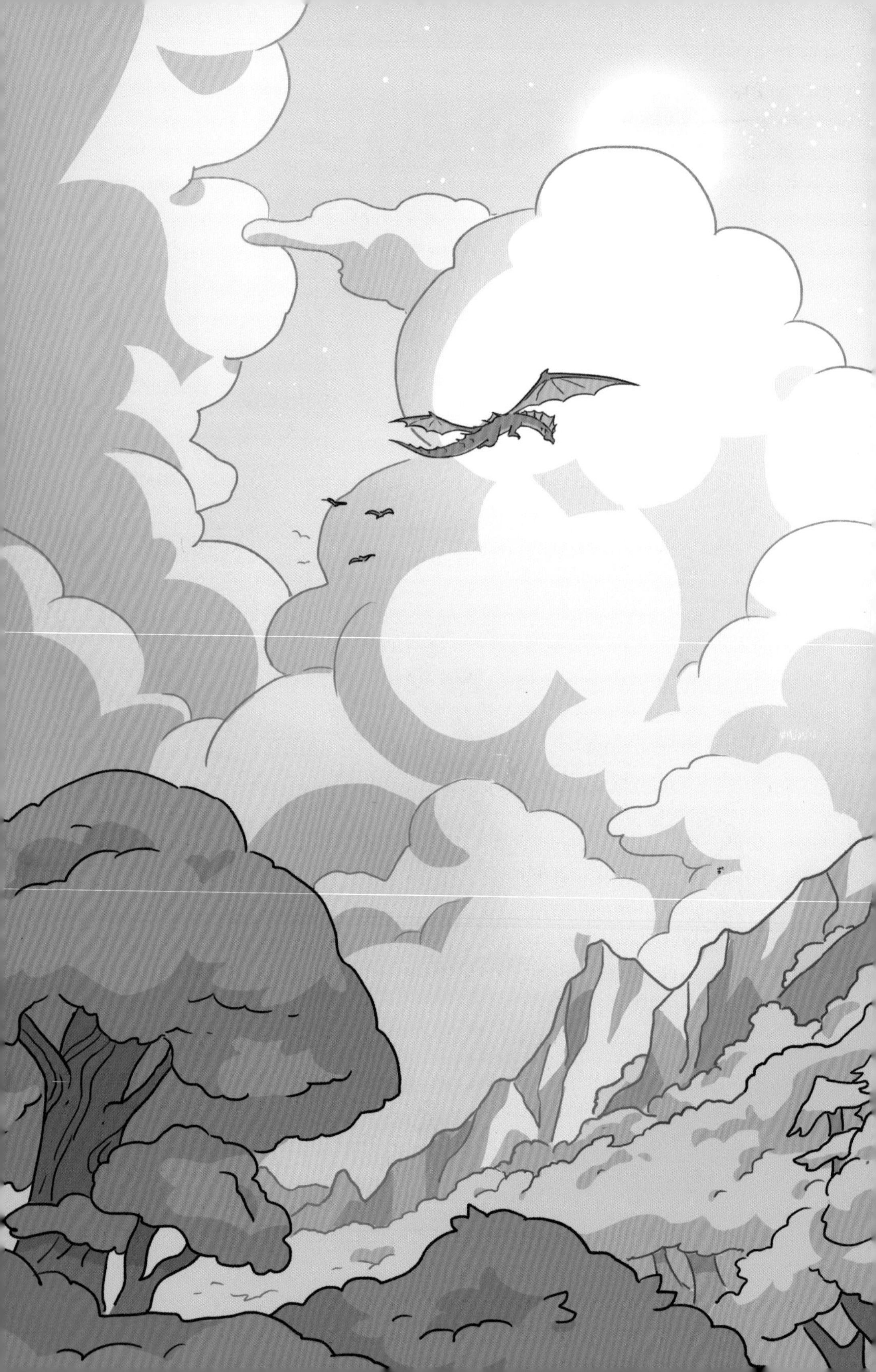

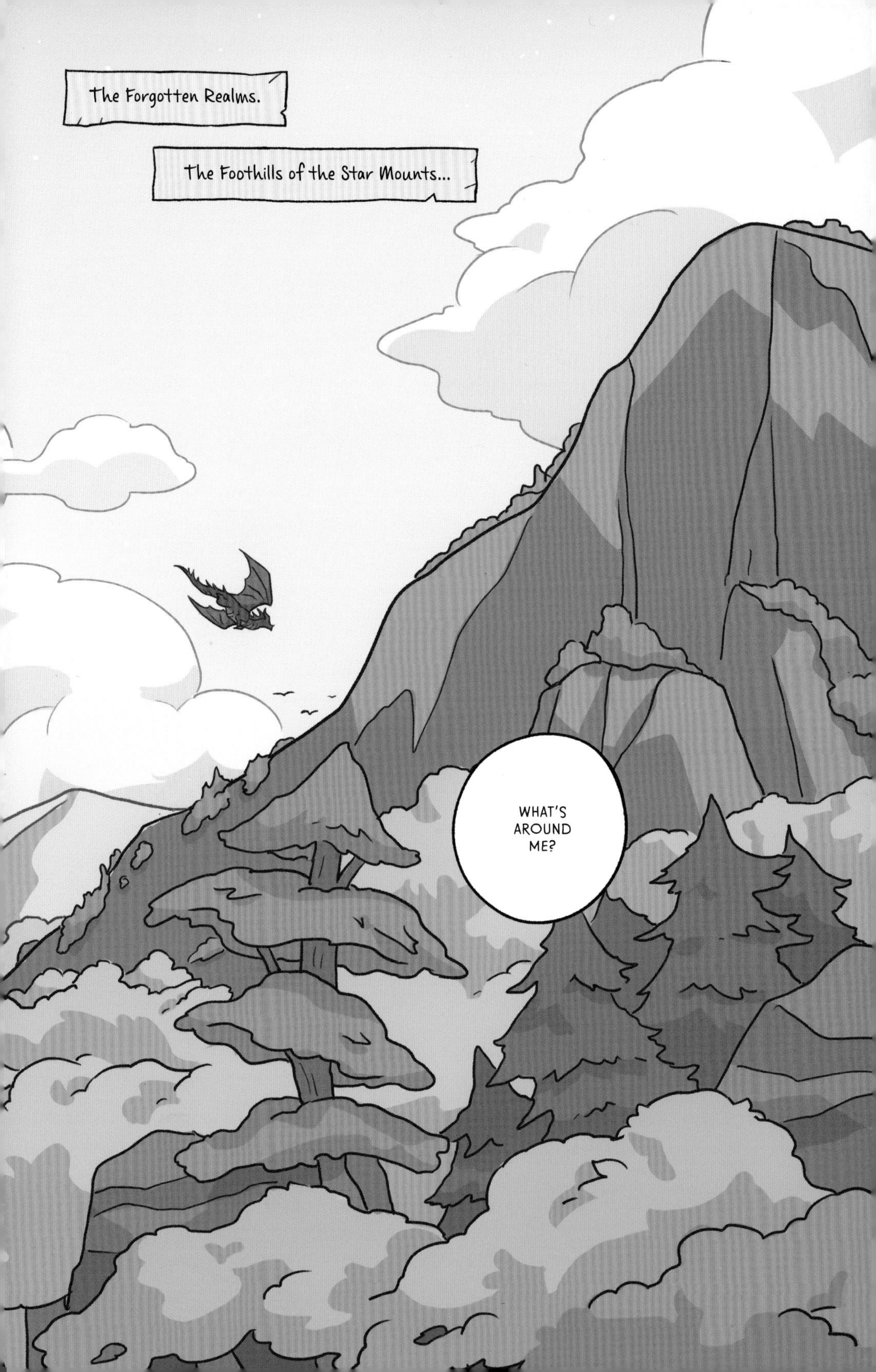
The Forgotten Realms.
The Foothills of the Star Mounts...
WHAT'S AROUND ME?

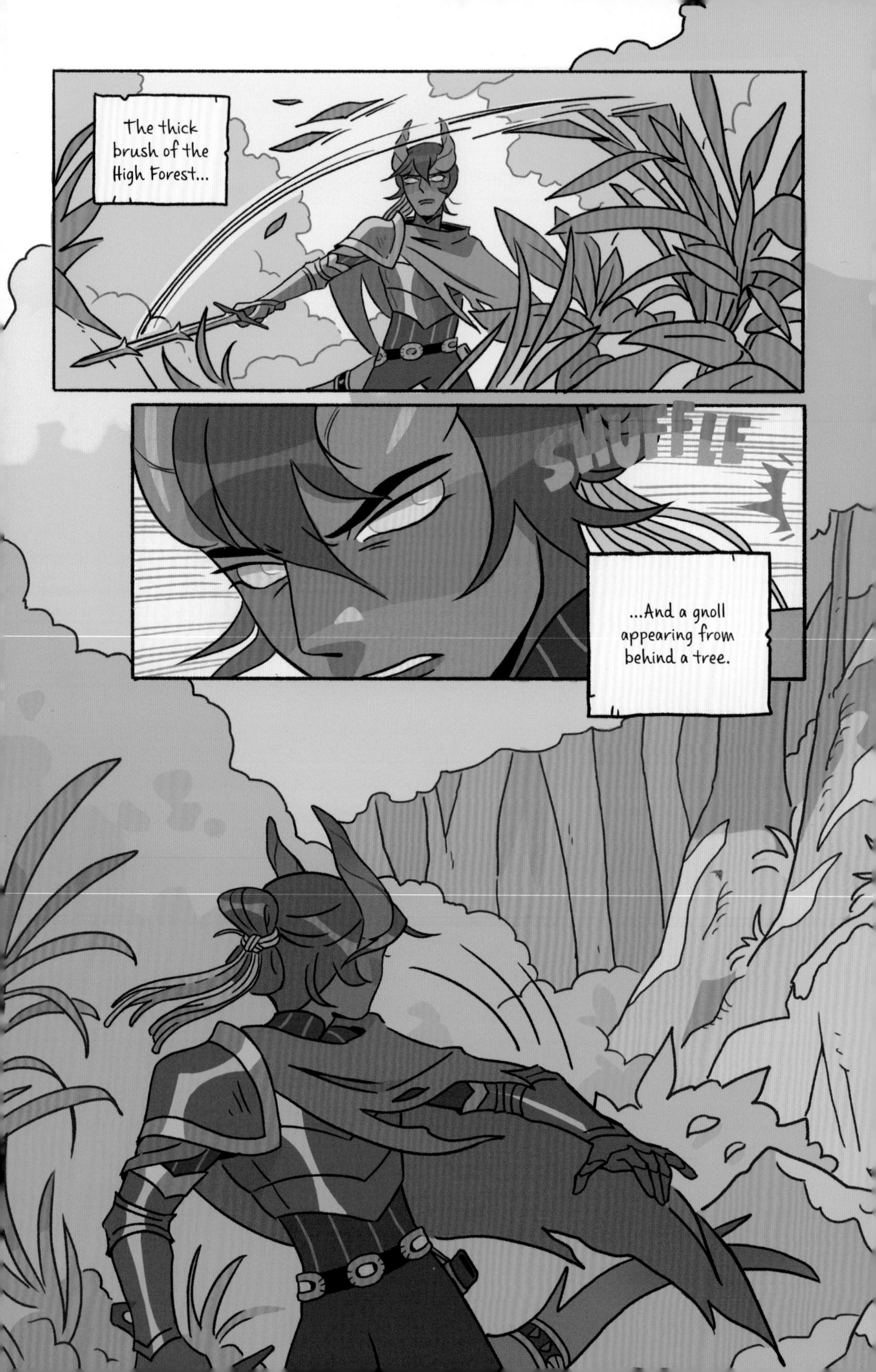

The thick brush of the High Forest...
SHUFFLE
...And a gnoll appearing from behind a tree.

Gnoll

Medium Humanoid (Gnoll), Chaotic Evil

Armor Class 15 *(hide armor, shield)*
Hit Points 22
Speed 30 ft.

STR	DEX	CON	INT	WIS	CHA
14 (+2)	12 (+1)	11 (+0)	6 (-2)	10 (+0)	7 (-2)

Actions

Bite. *Melee Weapon Attack*: +4 to hit, reach 5 ft., one creature. *Hit*: 4 piercing damage.

Gnolls are feral, hyena-headed humanoids that attack without warning, slaughtering their victims and devouring their flesh.

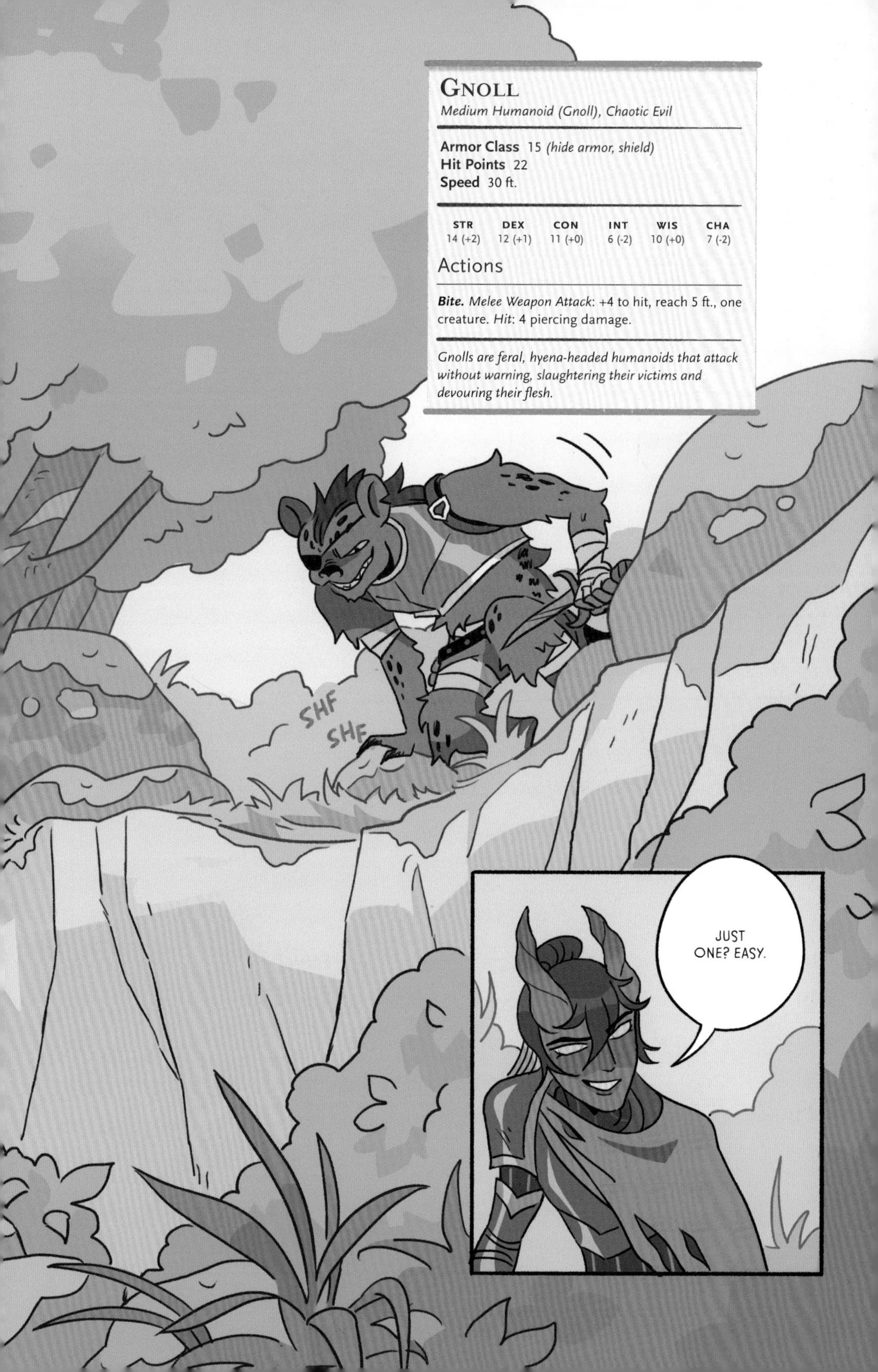
SHF
SHF
JUST ONE? EASY.

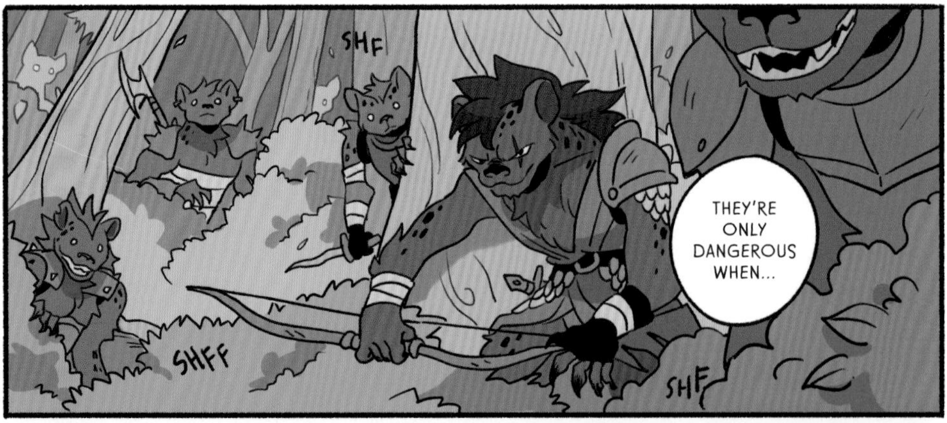
SHF
SHFF
SHF
THEY'RE ONLY DANGEROUS WHEN...

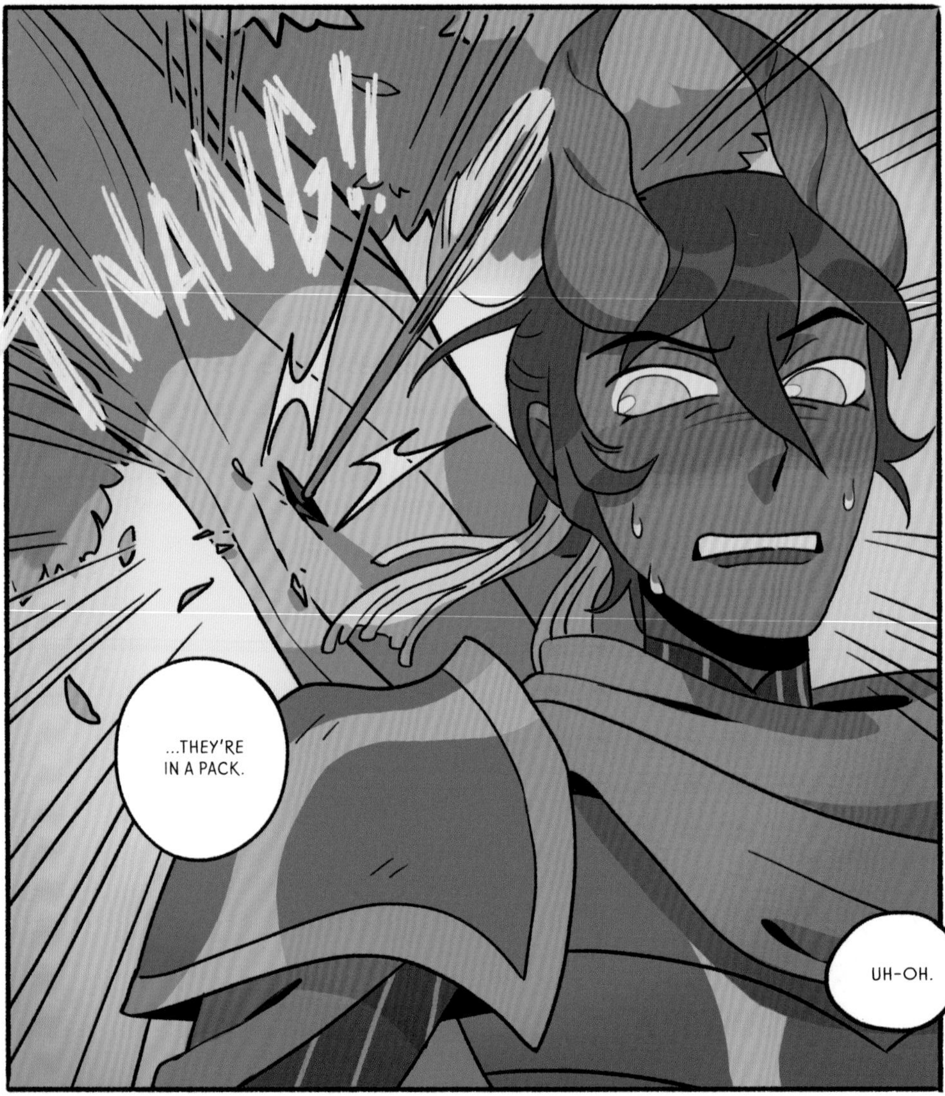
TWANG!!
...THEY'RE IN A PACK.
UH-OH.

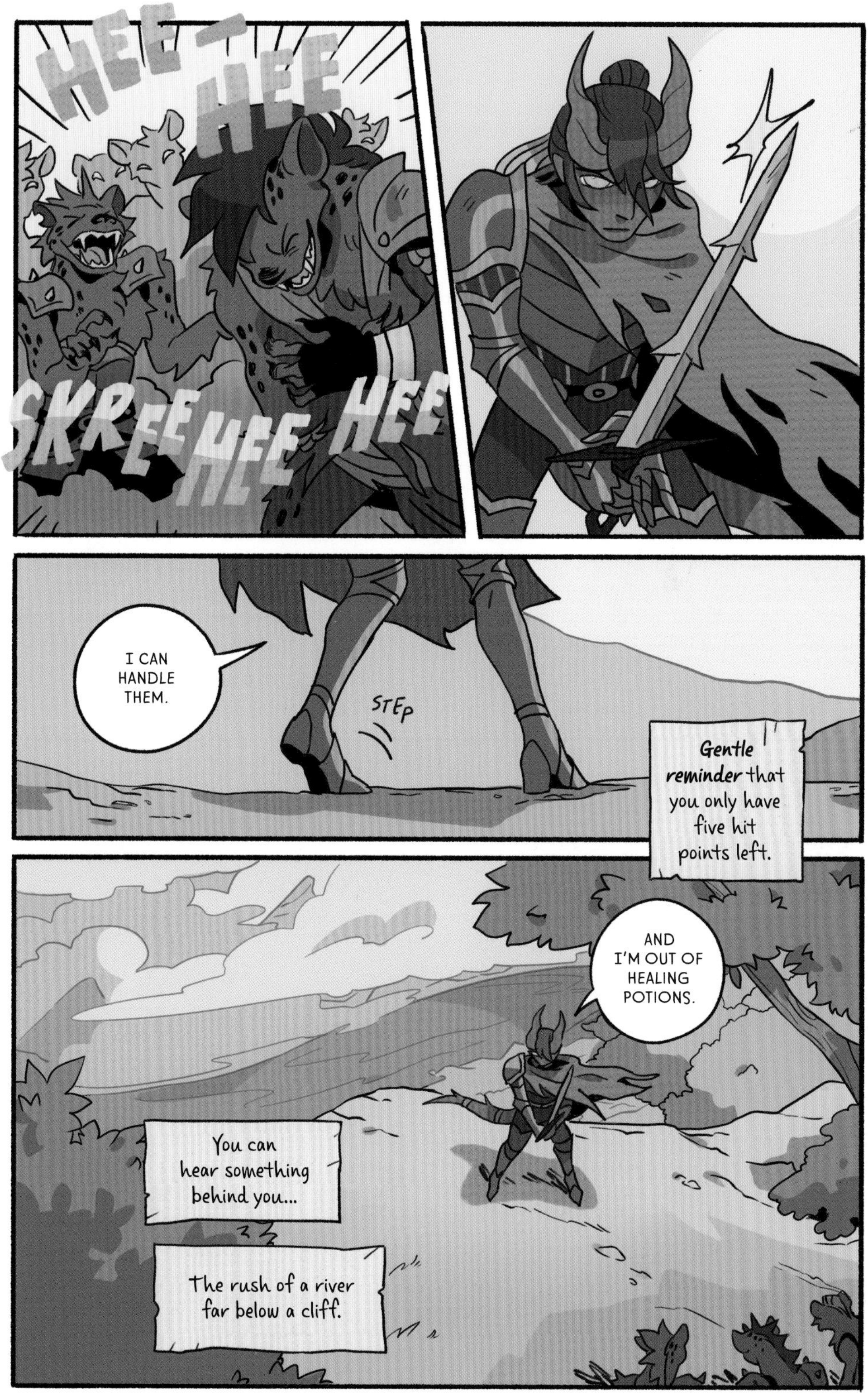
HEE-HEE
SKREE HEE HEE HEE
I CAN HANDLE THEM.
STEP
Gentle reminder that you only have five hit points left.
AND I'M OUT OF HEALING POTIONS.
You can hear something behind you...
The rush of a river far below a cliff.

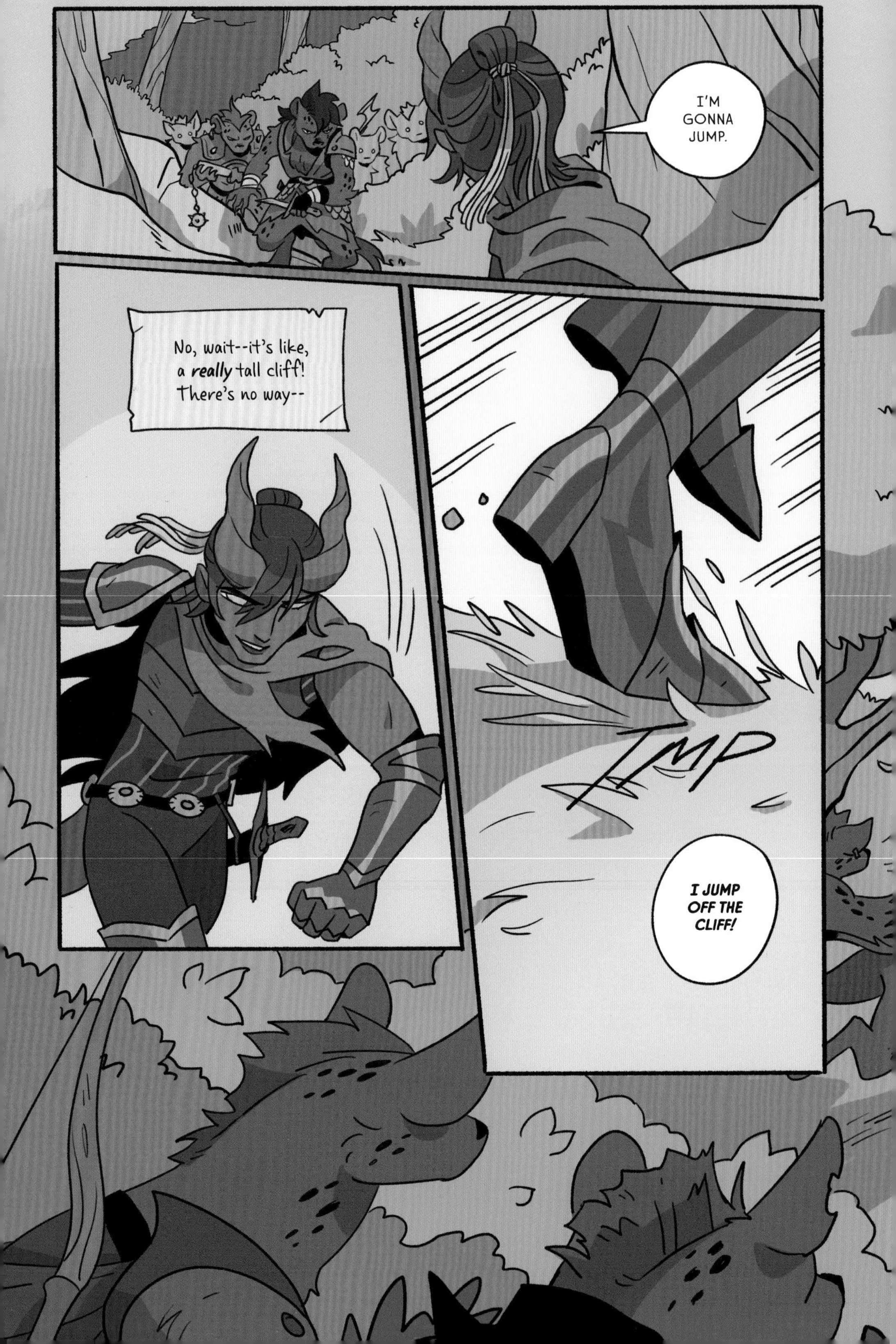

I'M GONNA JUMP.
No, wait--it's like, a *really* tall cliff! There's no way--
TMP
I JUMP OFF THE CLIFF!

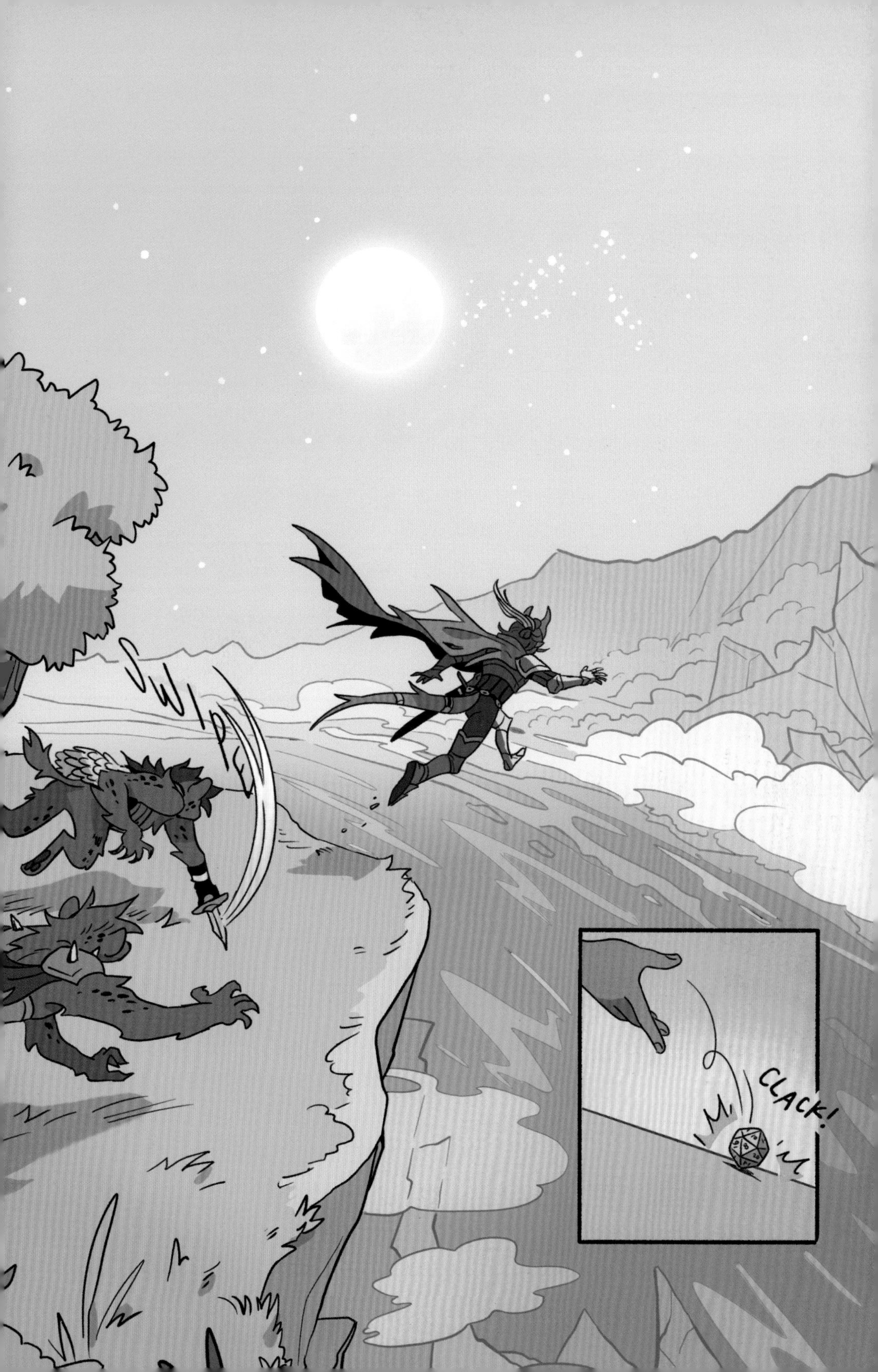
SWIPE
CLACK!

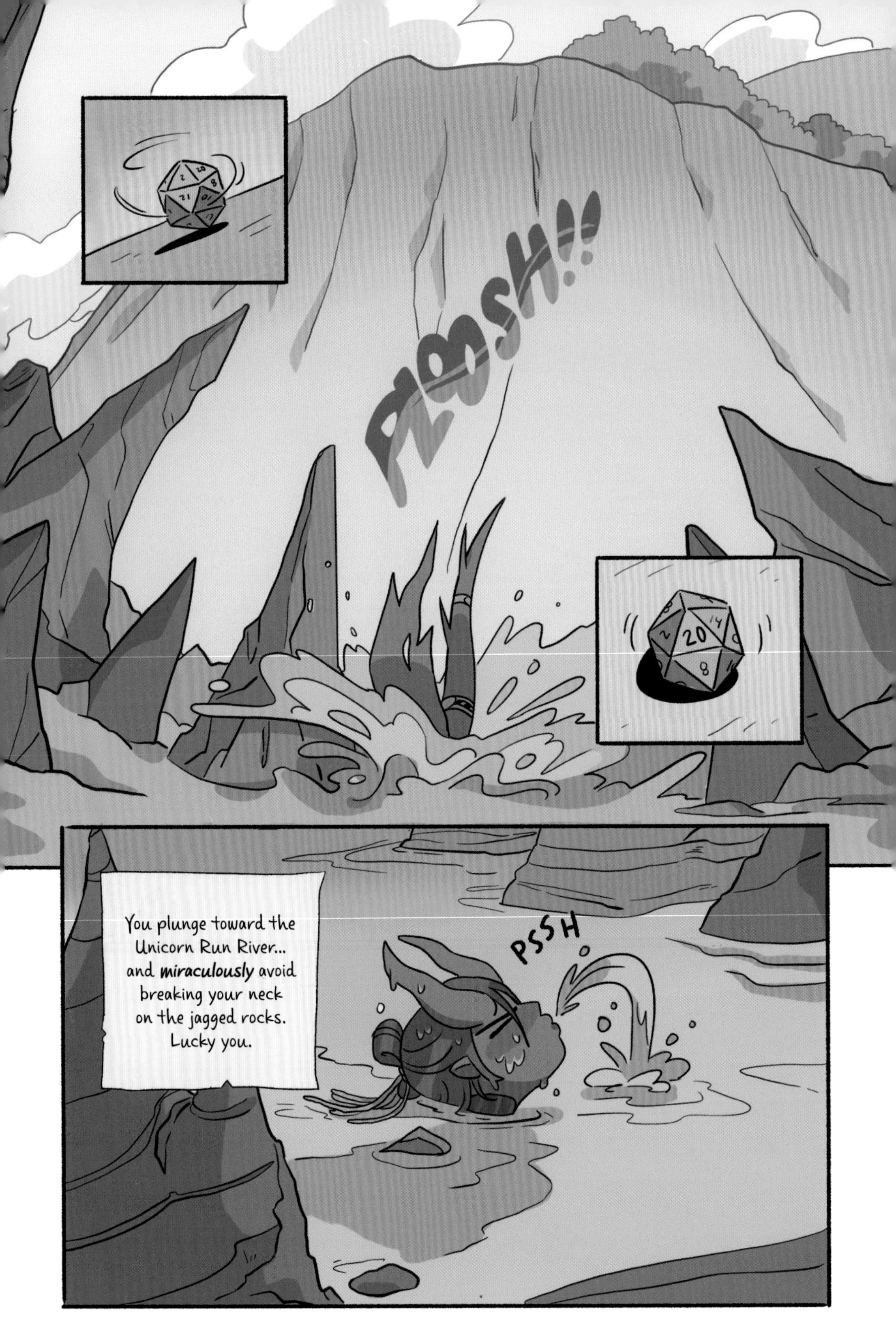
PLOOSH!!
You plunge toward the Unicorn Run River... and ***miraculously*** avoid breaking your neck on the jagged rocks. Lucky you.
PSSH

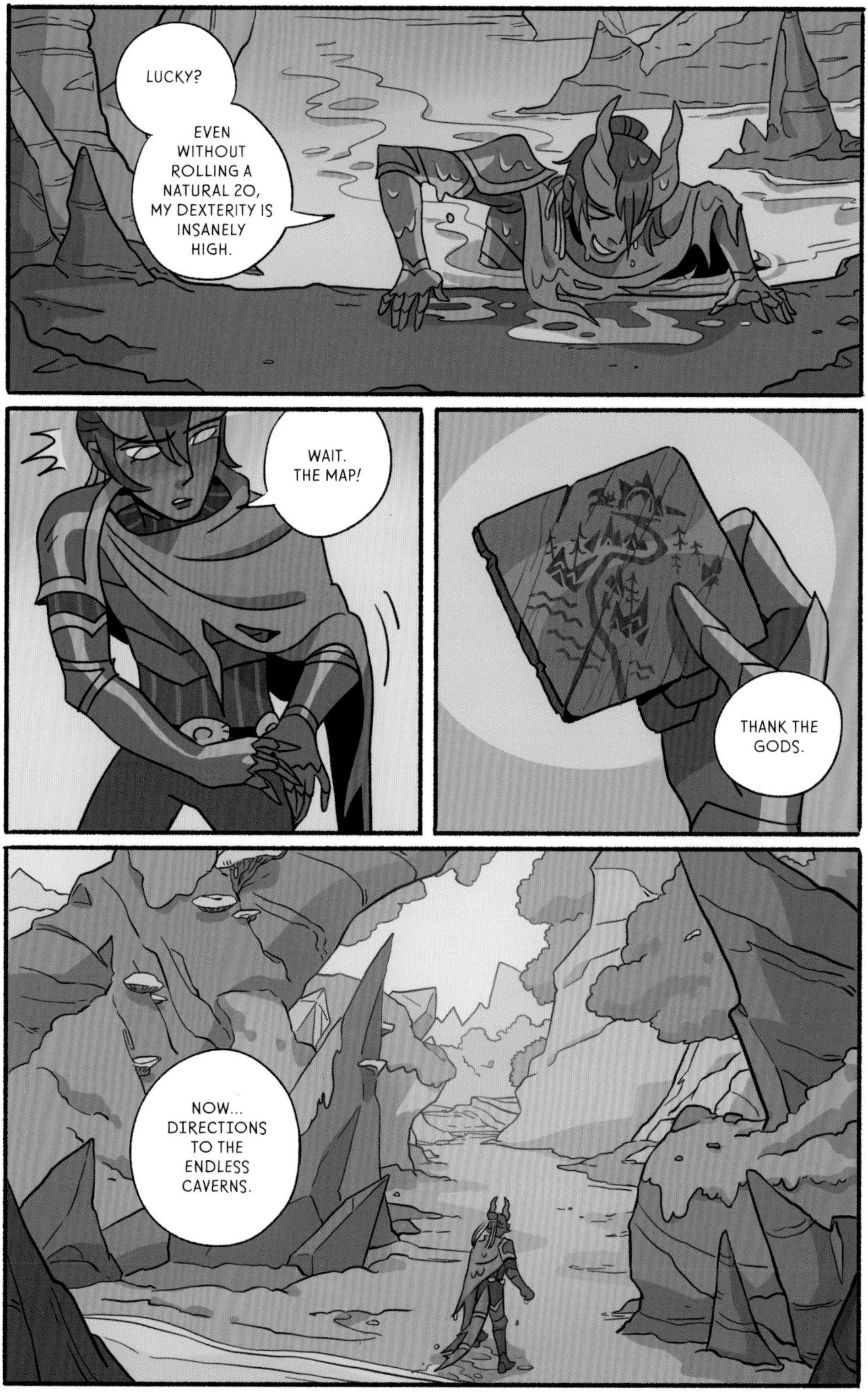
LUCKY?
EVEN WITHOUT ROLLING A NATURAL 20, MY DEXTERITY IS INSANELY HIGH.
WAIT. THE MAP!
THANK THE GODS.
NOW... DIRECTIONS TO THE ENDLESS CAVERNS.

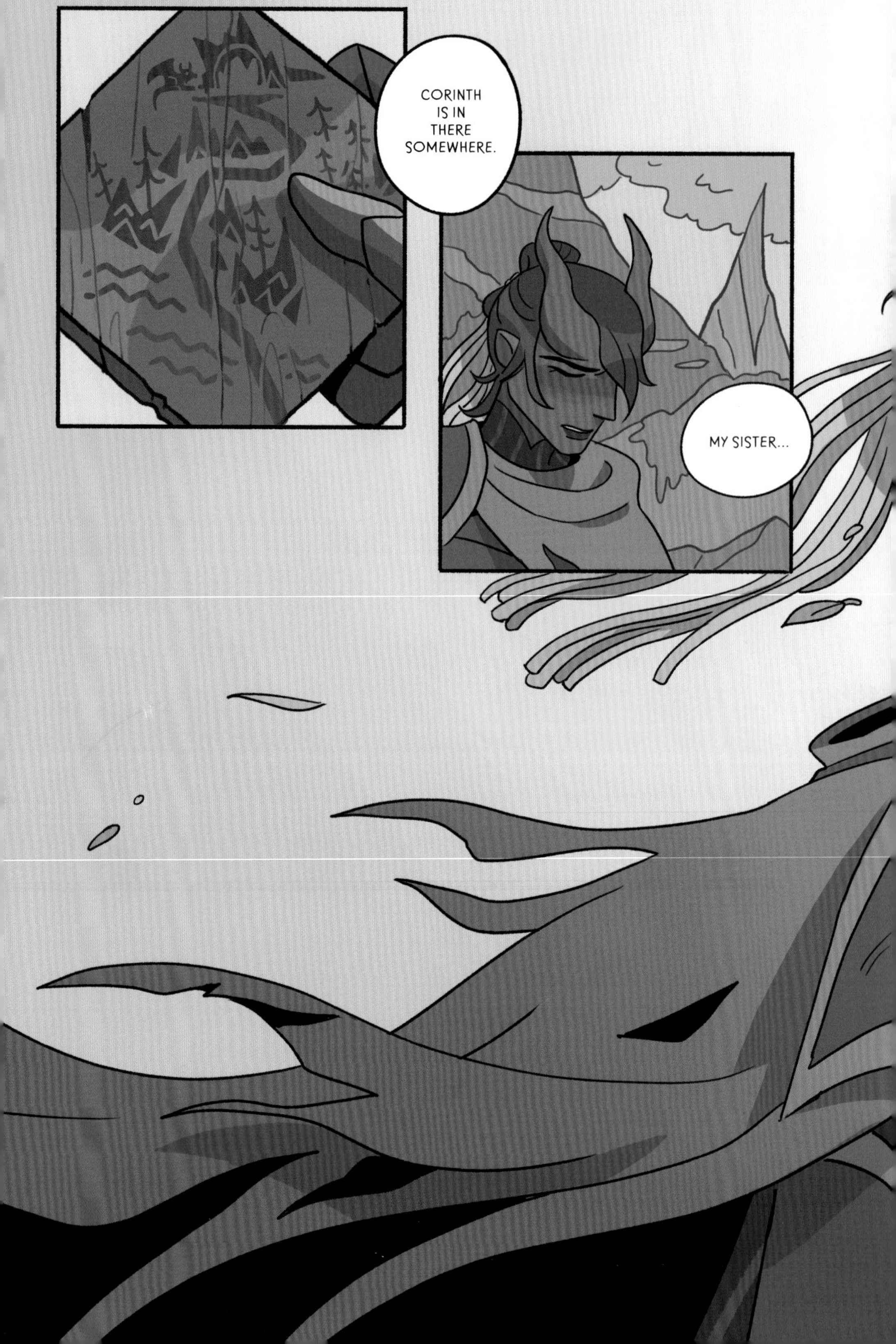
CORINTH IS IN THERE SOMEWHERE.
MY SISTER...

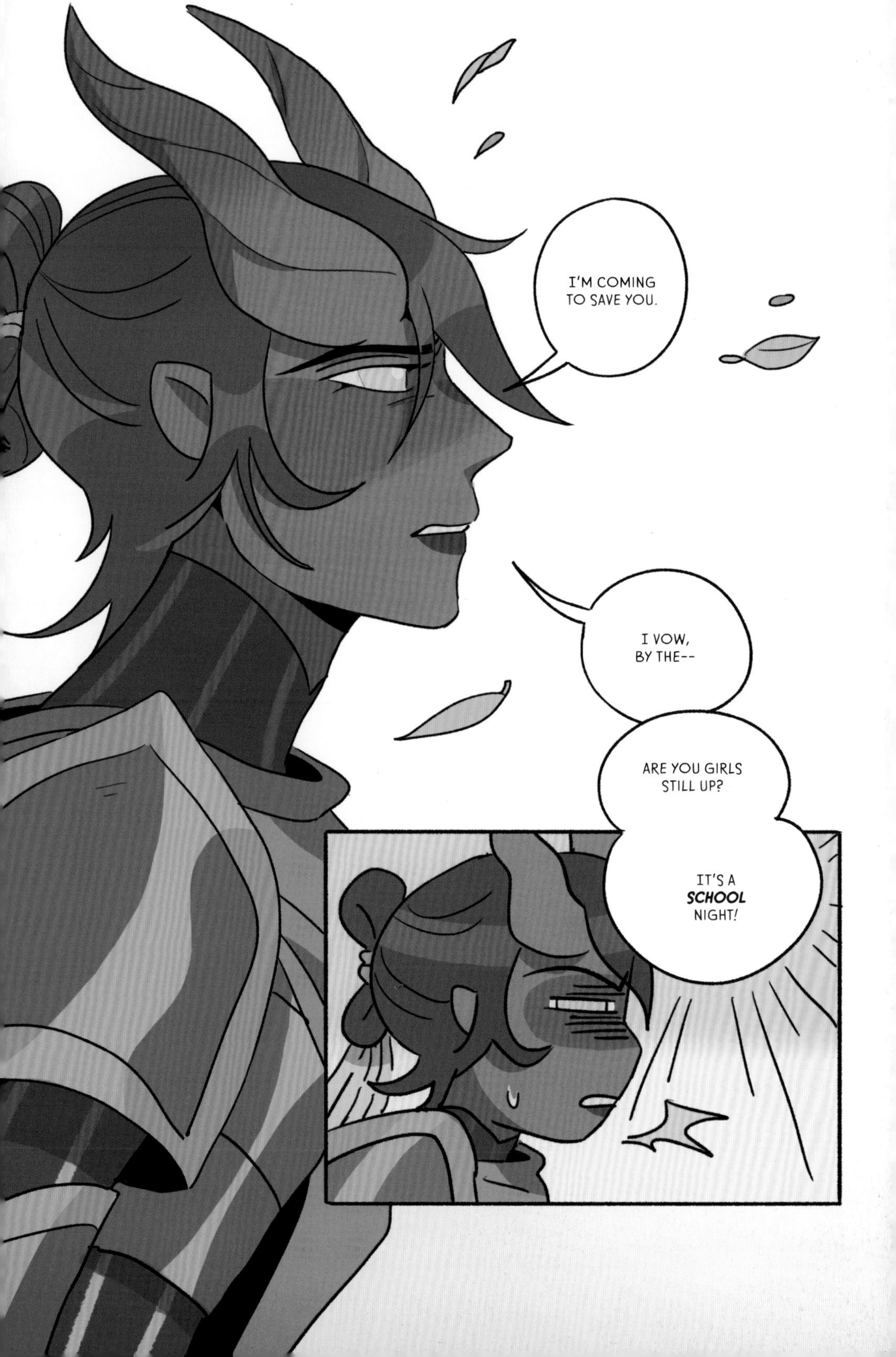
I'M COMING
TO SAVE YOU.
I VOW,
BY THE--
ARE YOU GIRLS
STILL UP?
IT'S A
SCHOOL
NIGHT!

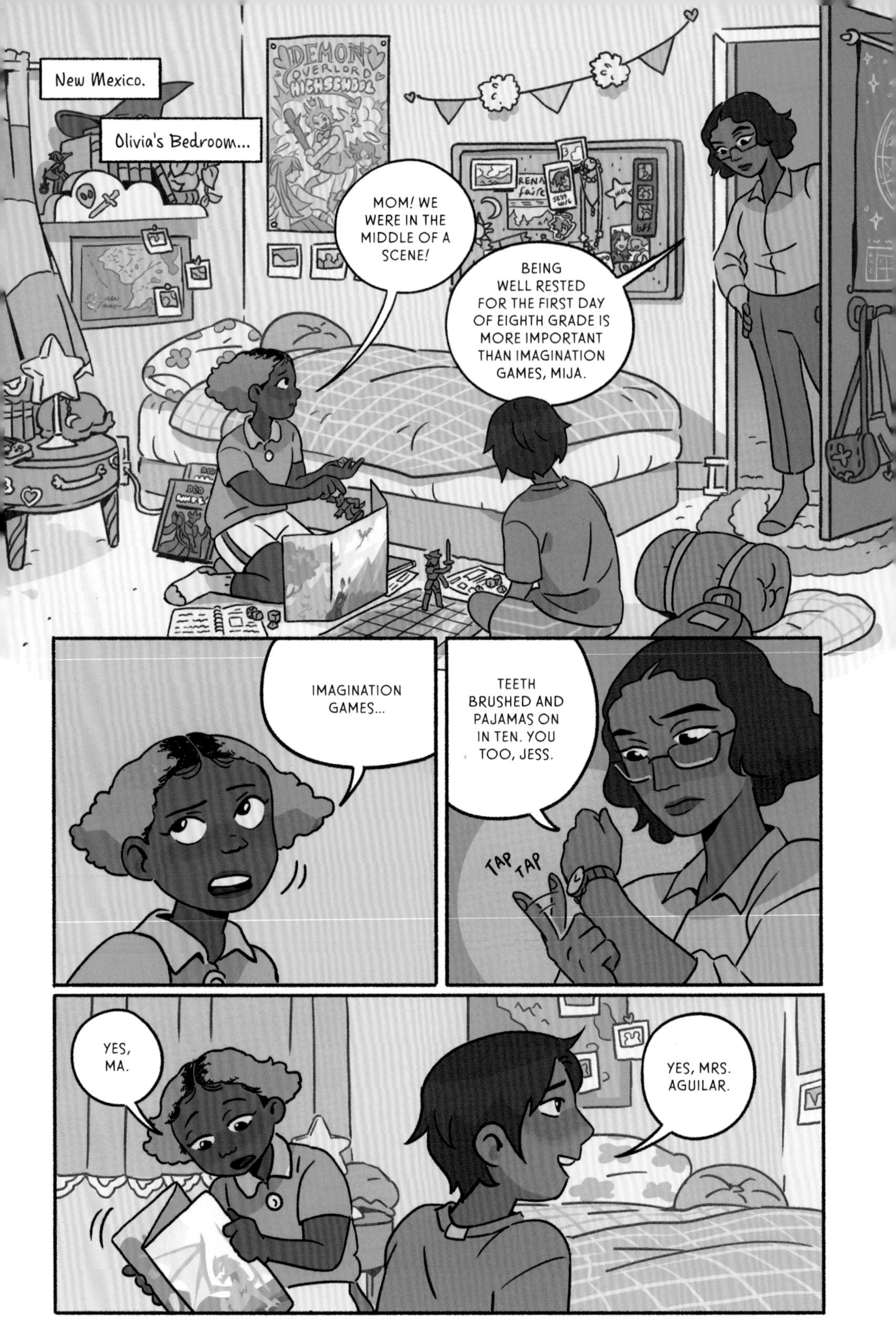
New Mexico.
Olivia's Bedroom...
DEMON OVERLORD HIGHSCHOOL
MOM! WE WERE IN THE MIDDLE OF A SCENE!
BEING WELL RESTED FOR THE FIRST DAY OF EIGHTH GRADE IS MORE IMPORTANT THAN IMAGINATION GAMES, MIJA.
IMAGINATION GAMES...
TEETH BRUSHED AND PAJAMAS ON IN TEN. YOU TOO, JESS.
TAP TAP
YES, MA.
YES, MRS. AGUILAR.

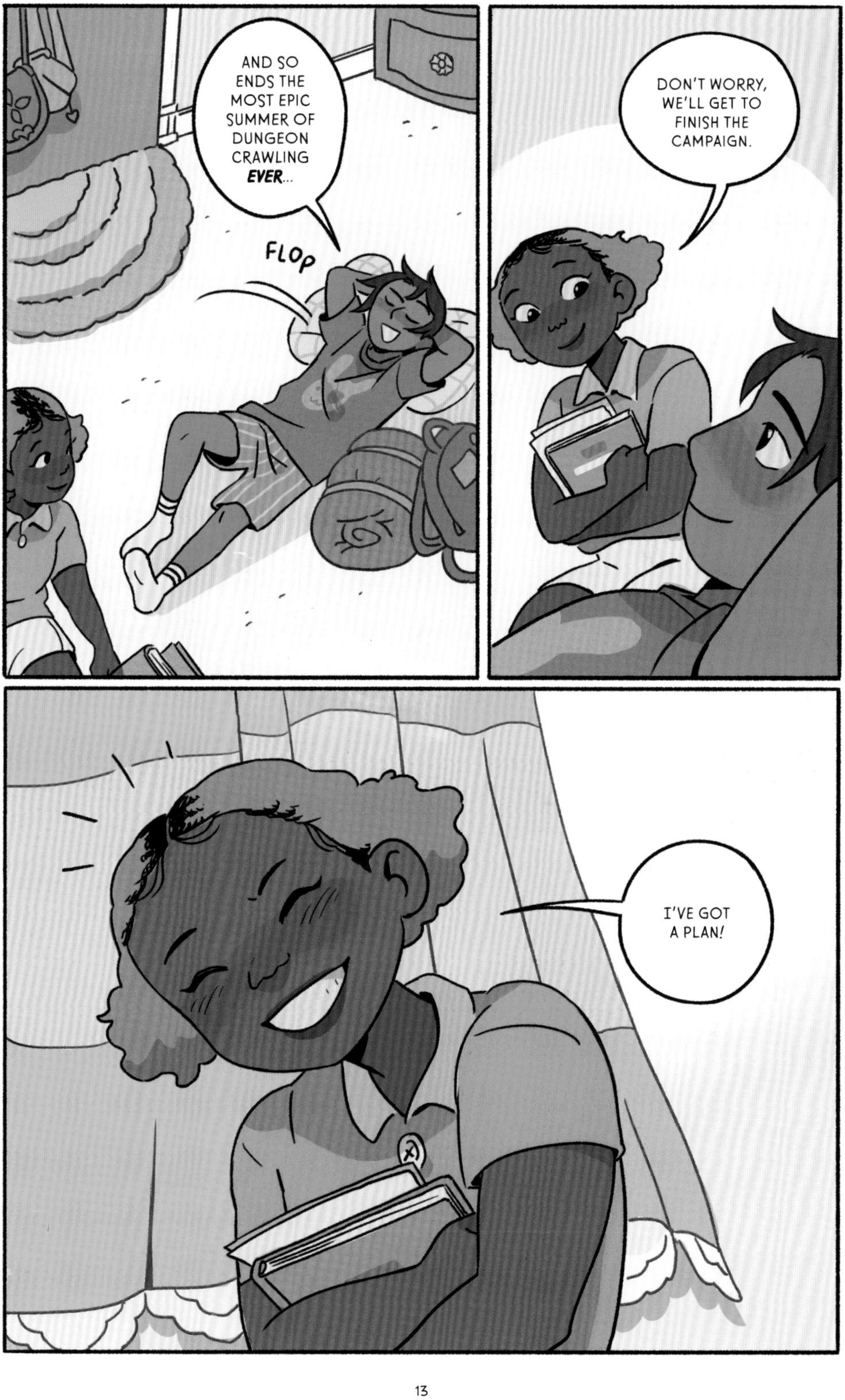
AND SO ENDS THE MOST EPIC SUMMER OF DUNGEON CRAWLING **EVER**...
FLOP
DON'T WORRY, WE'LL GET TO FINISH THE CAMPAIGN.
I'VE GOT A PLAN!

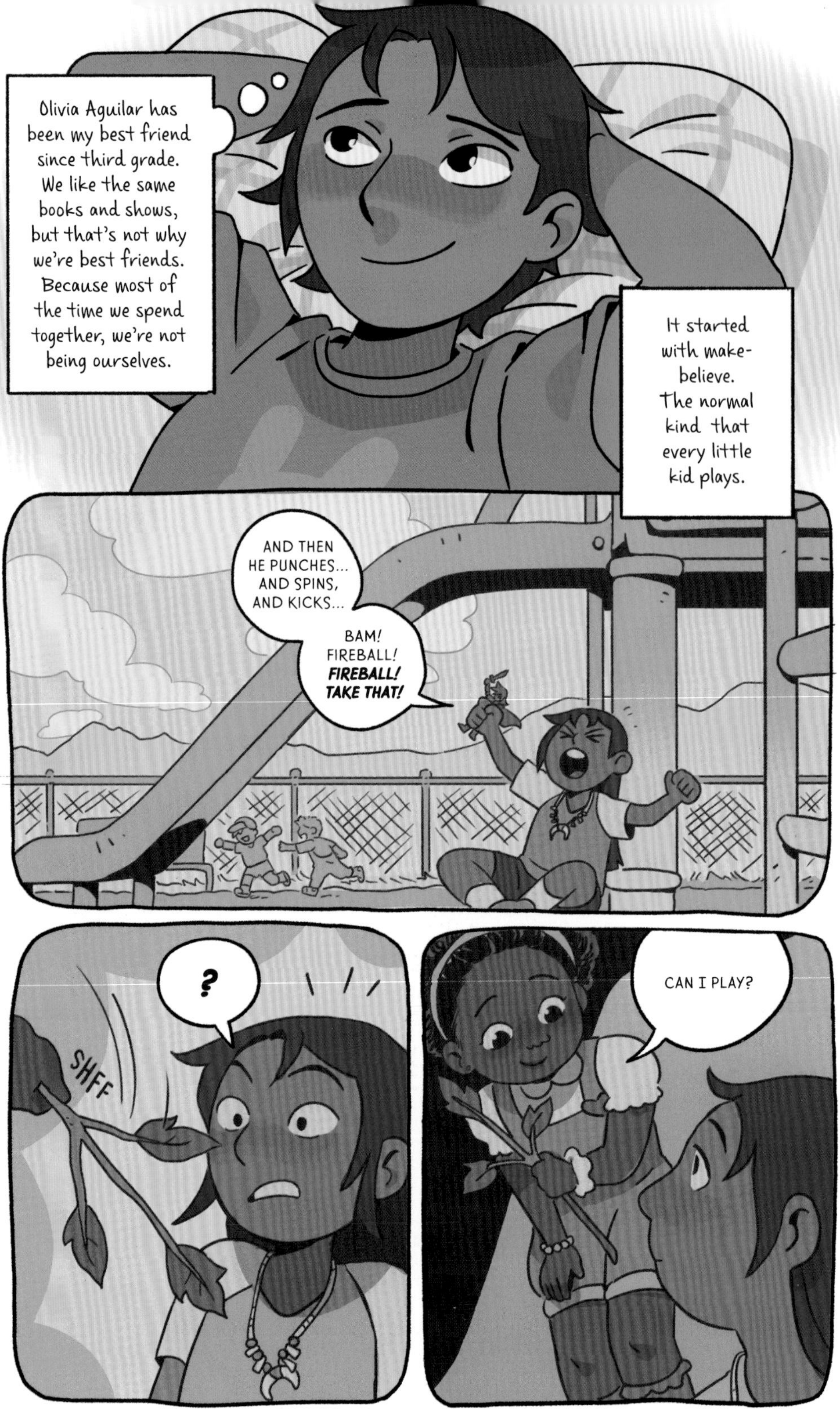
Olivia Aguilar has been my best friend since third grade. We like the same books and shows, but that's not why we're best friends. Because most of the time we spend together, we're not being ourselves.
It started with make-believe. The normal kind that every little kid plays.
AND THEN HE PUNCHES... AND SPINS, AND KICKS...
BAM! FIREBALL! FIREBALL! TAKE THAT!
?
SHFF
CAN I PLAY?

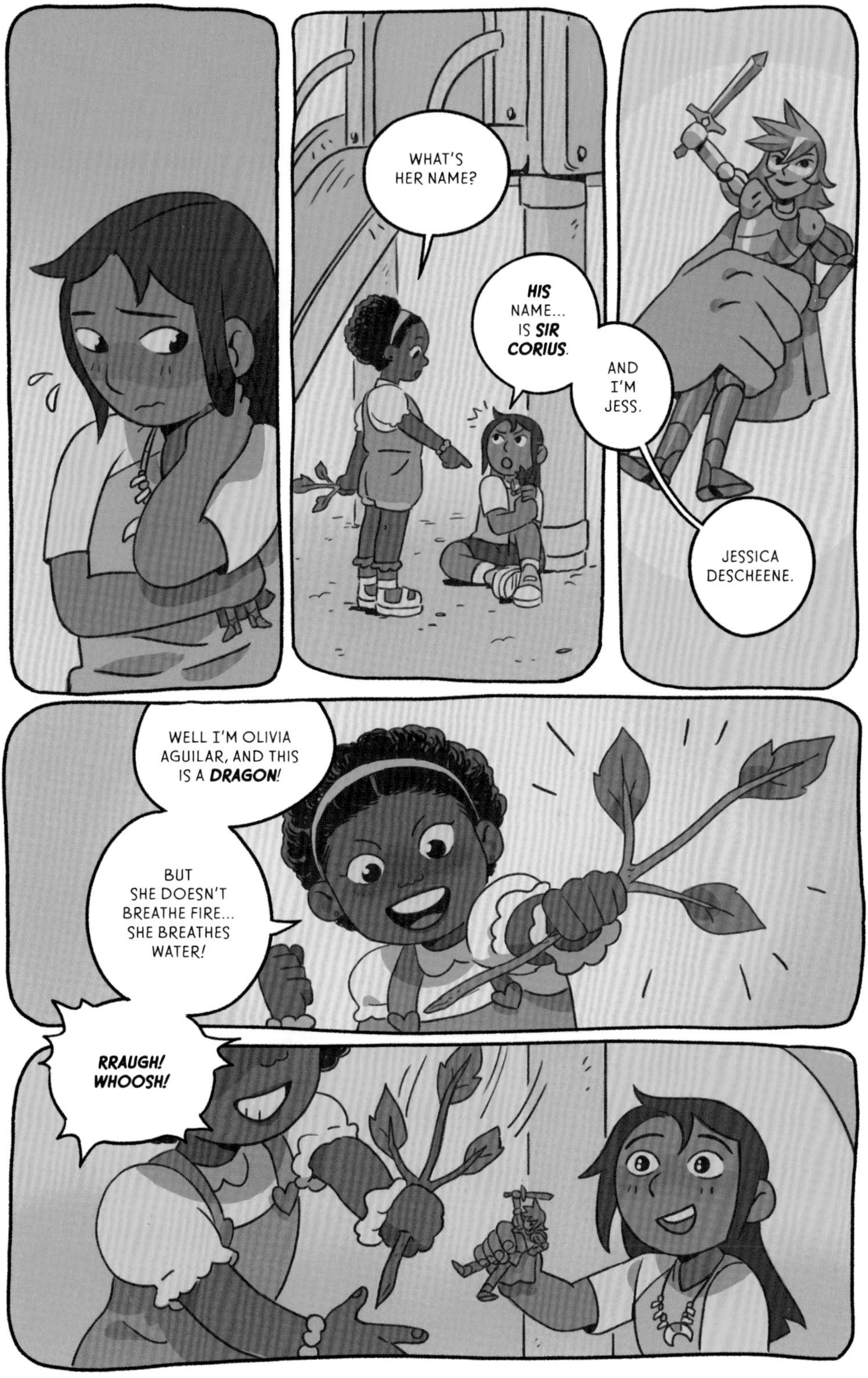
WHAT'S HER NAME?
HIS NAME... IS SIR CORIUS.
AND I'M JESS.
JESSICA DESCHEENE.
WELL I'M OLIVIA AGUILAR, AND THIS IS A DRAGON!
BUT SHE DOESN'T BREATHE FIRE... SHE BREATHES WATER!
RRAUGH! WHOOSH!

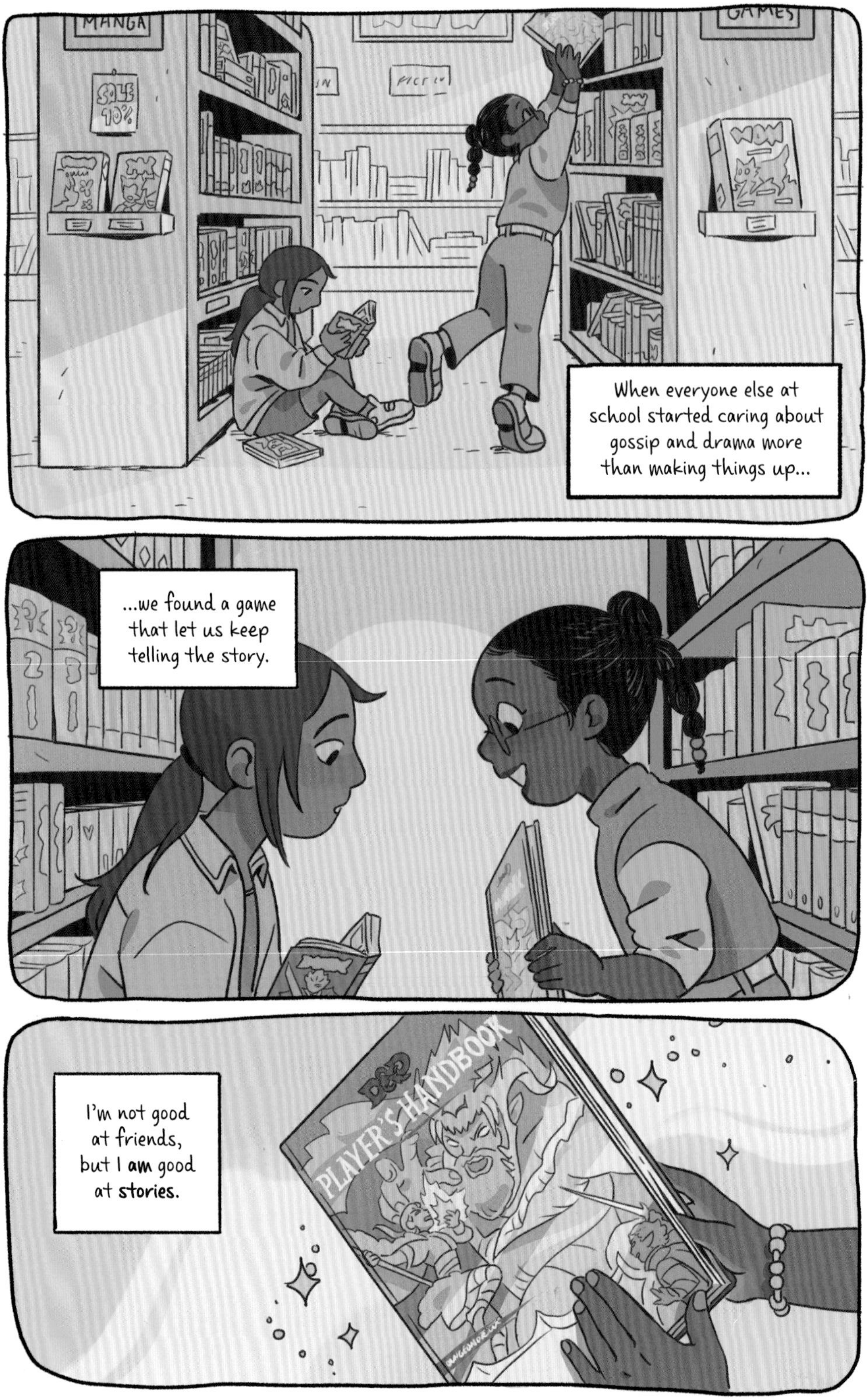
MANGA
SALE 10%
GAMES
When everyone else at school started caring about gossip and drama more than making things up...
...we found a game that let us keep telling the story.
I'm not good at friends, but I **am** good at **stories.**
PLAYER'S HANDBOOK

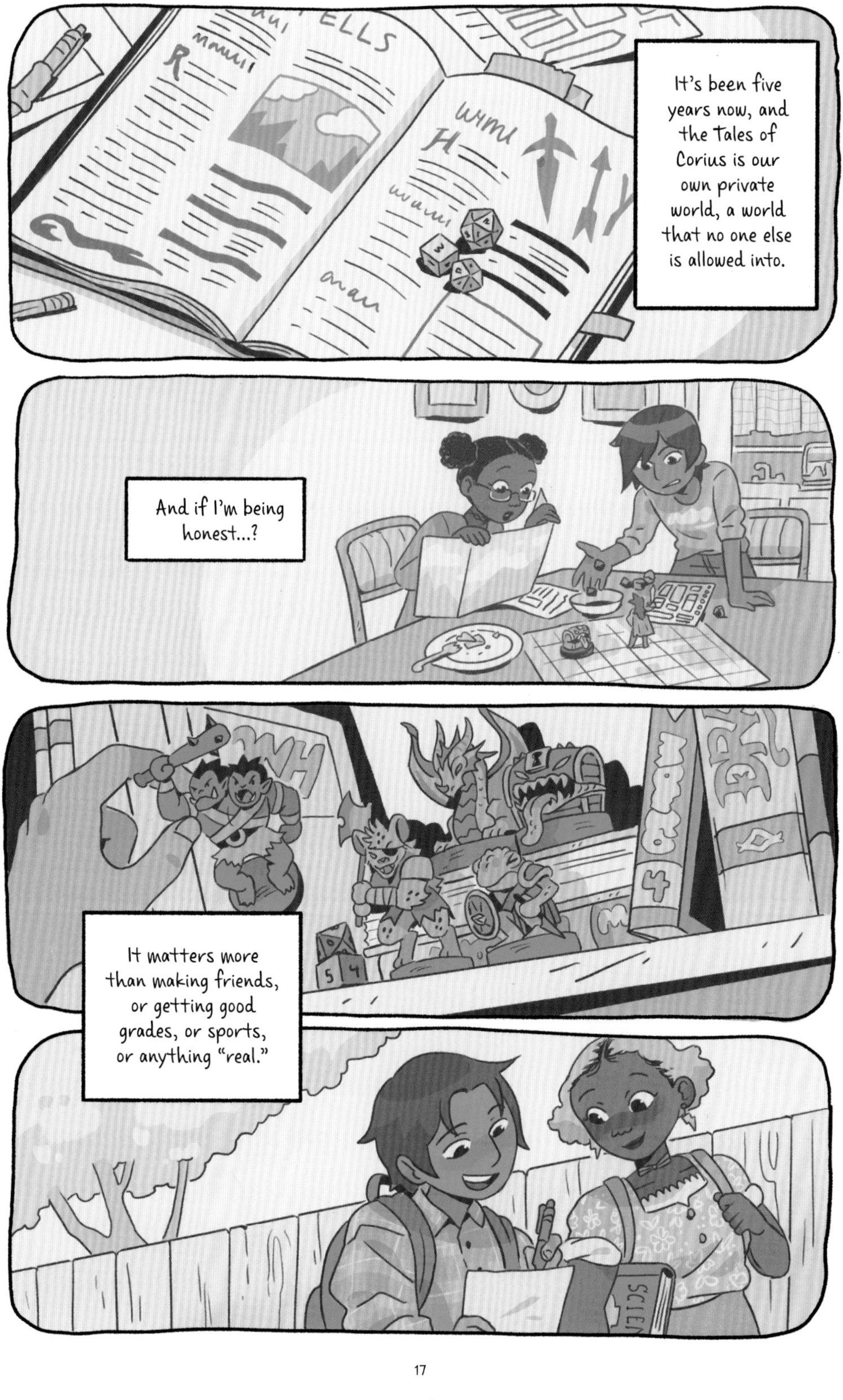
It's been five years now, and the Tales of Corius is our own private world, a world that no one else is allowed into.
And if I'm being honest...?
It matters more than making friends, or getting good grades, or sports, or anything "real."

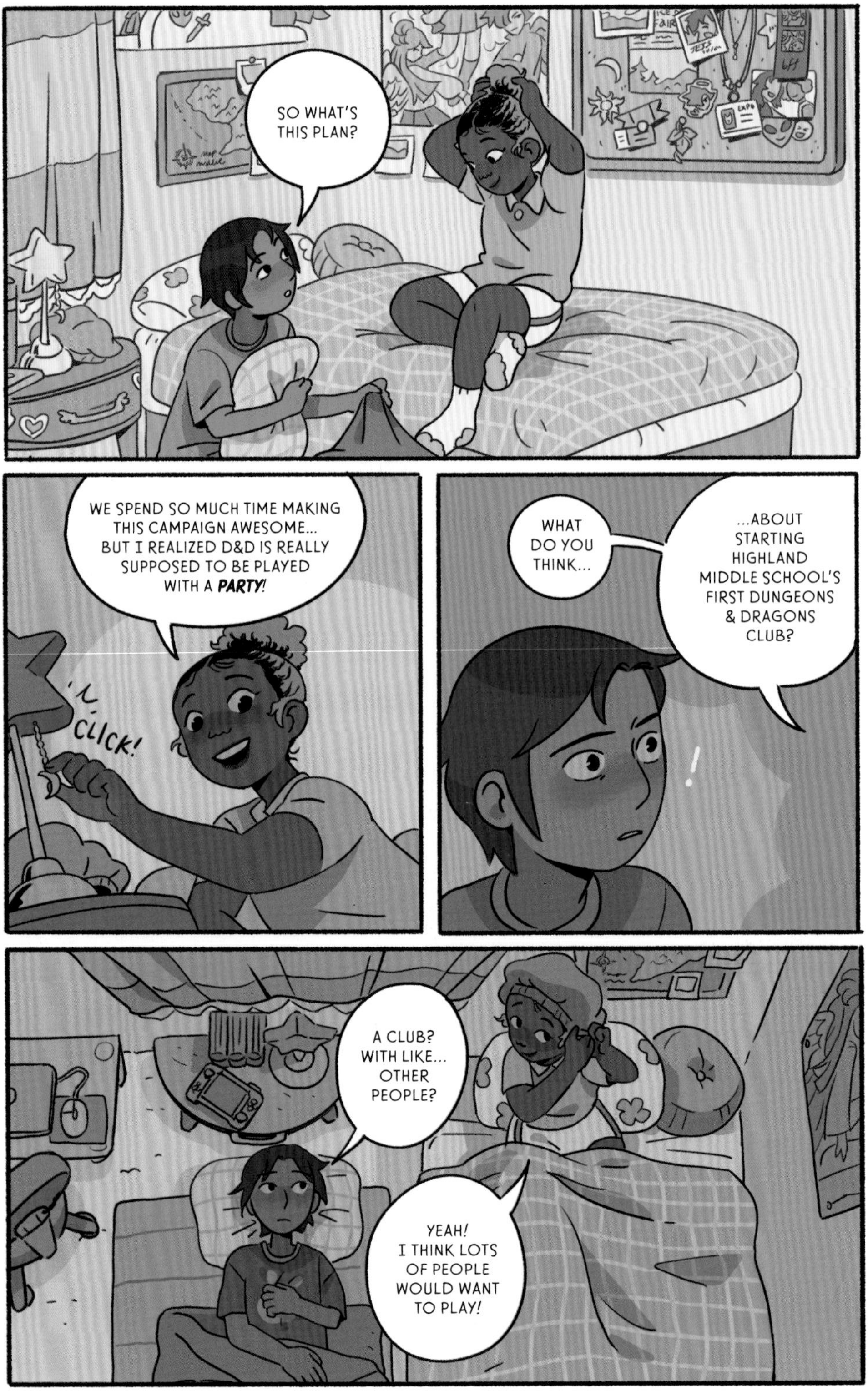
SO WHAT'S THIS PLAN?
WE SPEND SO MUCH TIME MAKING THIS CAMPAIGN AWESOME... BUT I REALIZED D&D IS REALLY SUPPOSED TO BE PLAYED WITH A **PARTY**!
CLICK!
WHAT DO YOU THINK...
...ABOUT STARTING HIGHLAND MIDDLE SCHOOL'S FIRST DUNGEONS & DRAGONS CLUB?
!
A CLUB? WITH LIKE... OTHER PEOPLE?
YEAH! I THINK LOTS OF PEOPLE WOULD WANT TO PLAY!

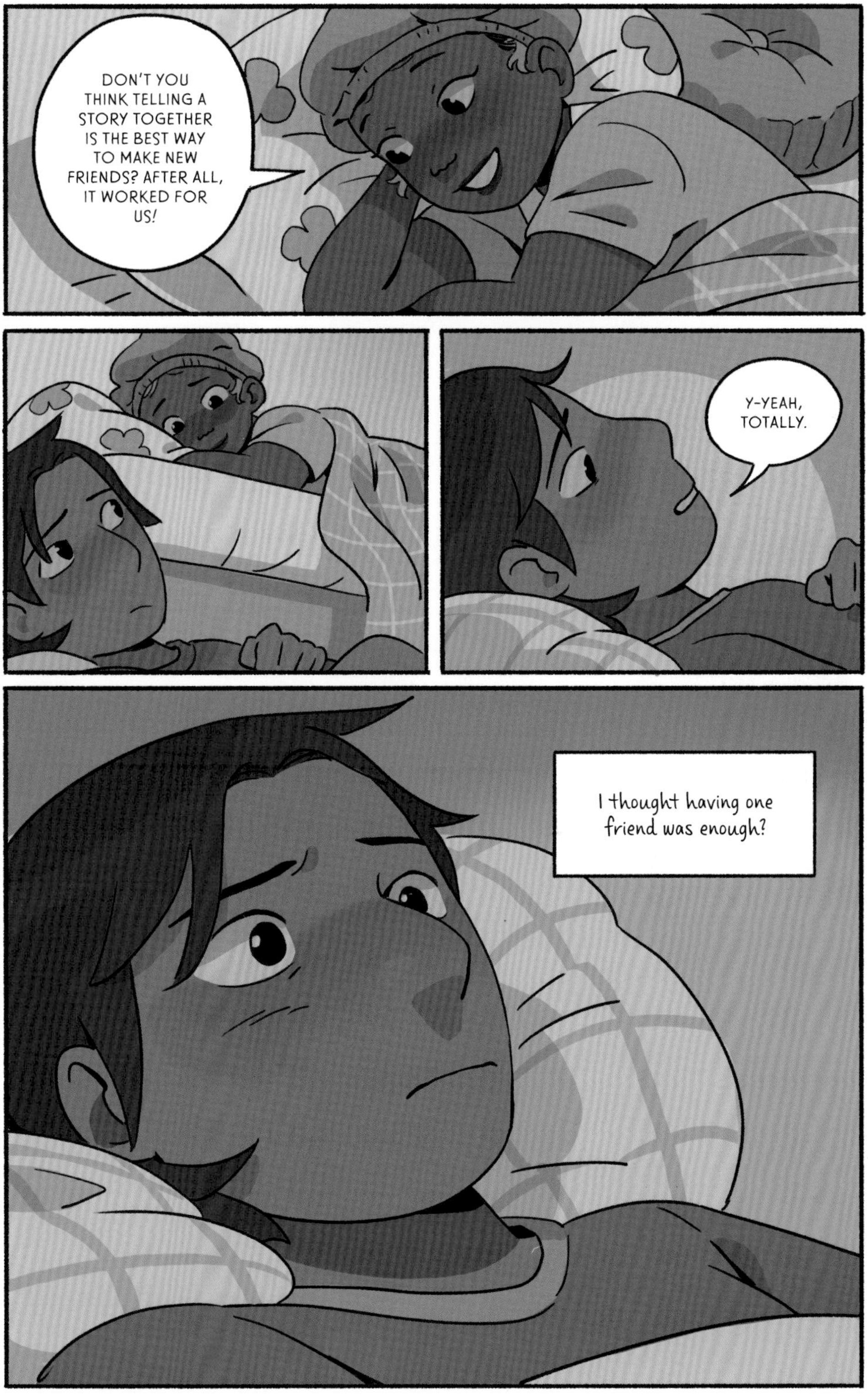
DON'T YOU THINK TELLING A STORY TOGETHER IS THE BEST WAY TO MAKE NEW FRIENDS? AFTER ALL, IT WORKED FOR US!
Y-YEAH, TOTALLY.
I thought having one friend was enough?

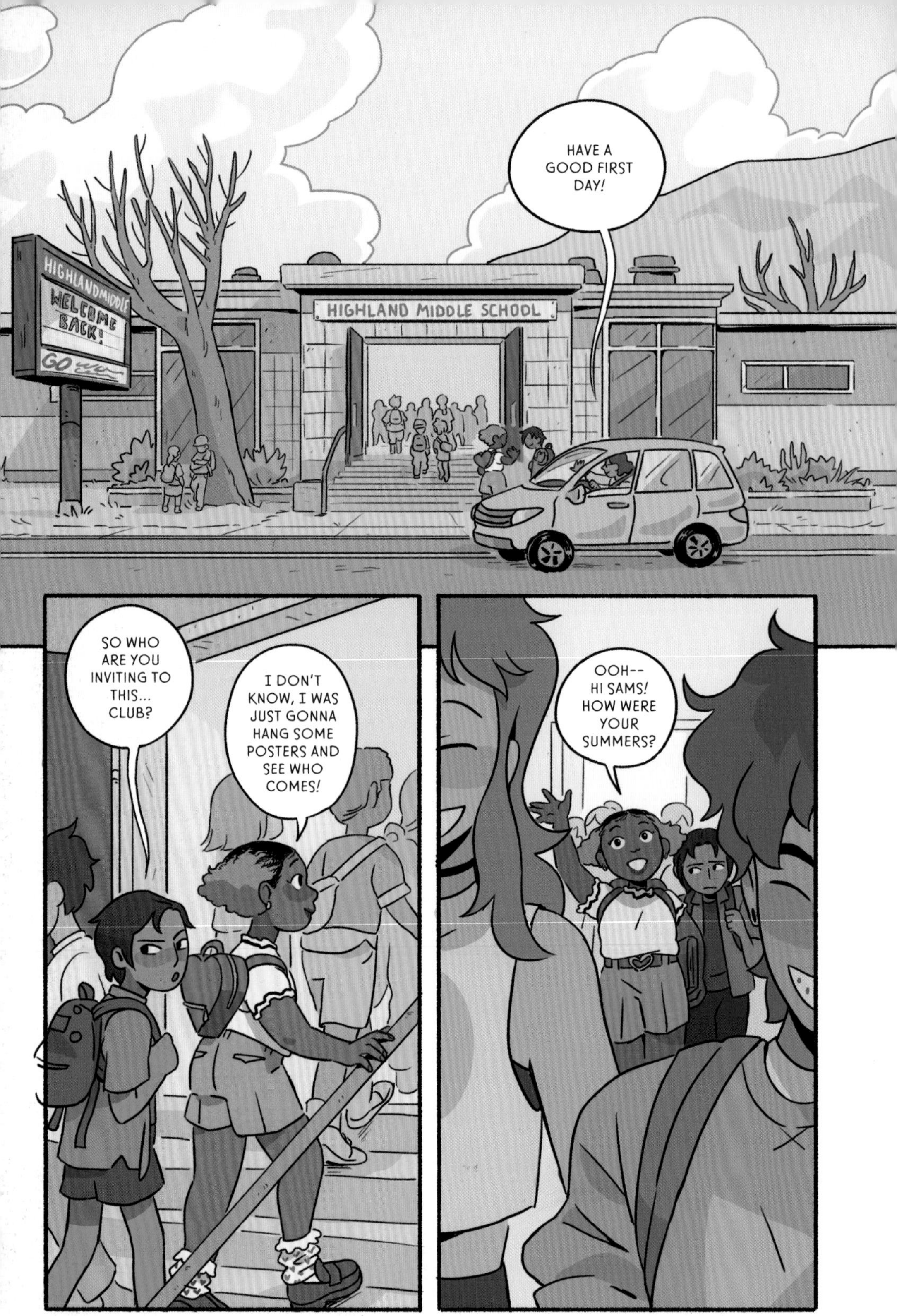
HIGHLAND MIDDLE
WELCOME BACK!
GO
HIGHLAND MIDDLE SCHOOL
HAVE A GOOD FIRST DAY!
SO WHO ARE YOU INVITING TO THIS... CLUB?
I DON'T KNOW, I WAS JUST GONNA HANG SOME POSTERS AND SEE WHO COMES!
OOH-- HI SAMS! HOW WERE YOUR SUMMERS?

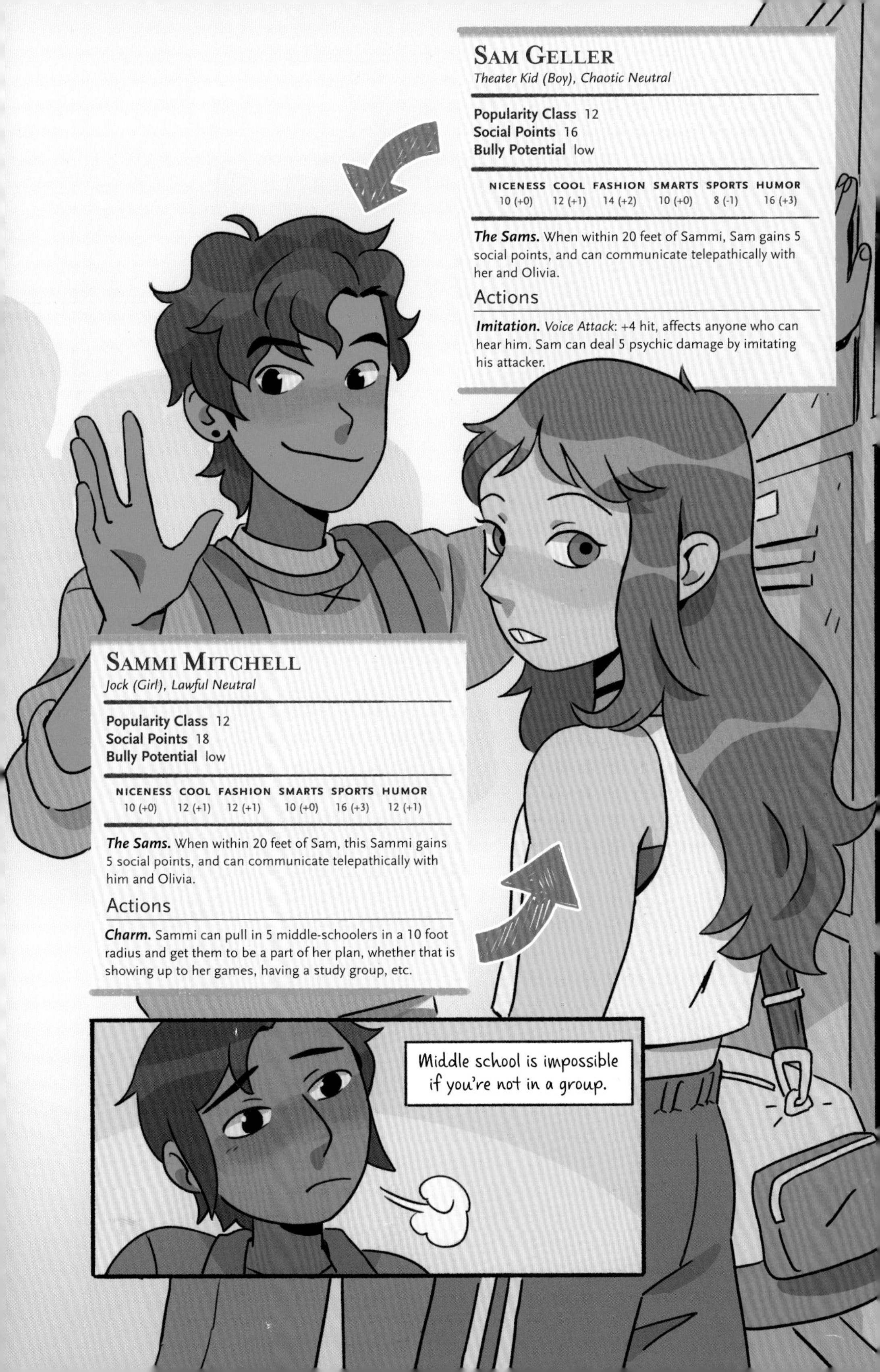

Sam Geller

Theater Kid (Boy), Chaotic Neutral

Popularity Class 12
Social Points 16
Bully Potential low

NICENESS	COOL	FASHION	SMARTS	SPORTS	HUMOR
10 (+0)	12 (+1)	14 (+2)	10 (+0)	8 (-1)	16 (+3)

The Sams. When within 20 feet of Sammi, Sam gains 5 social points, and can communicate telepathically with her and Olivia.

Actions

Imitation. *Voice Attack*: +4 hit, affects anyone who can hear him. Sam can deal 5 psychic damage by imitating his attacker.

Sammi Mitchell

Jock (Girl), Lawful Neutral

Popularity Class 12
Social Points 18
Bully Potential low

NICENESS	COOL	FASHION	SMARTS	SPORTS	HUMOR
10 (+0)	12 (+1)	12 (+1)	10 (+0)	16 (+3)	12 (+1)

The Sams. When within 20 feet of Sam, this Sammi gains 5 social points, and can communicate telepathically with him and Olivia.

Actions

Charm. Sammi can pull in 5 middle-schoolers in a 10 foot radius and get them to be a part of her plan, whether that is showing up to her games, having a study group, etc.

Middle school is impossible if you're not in a group.

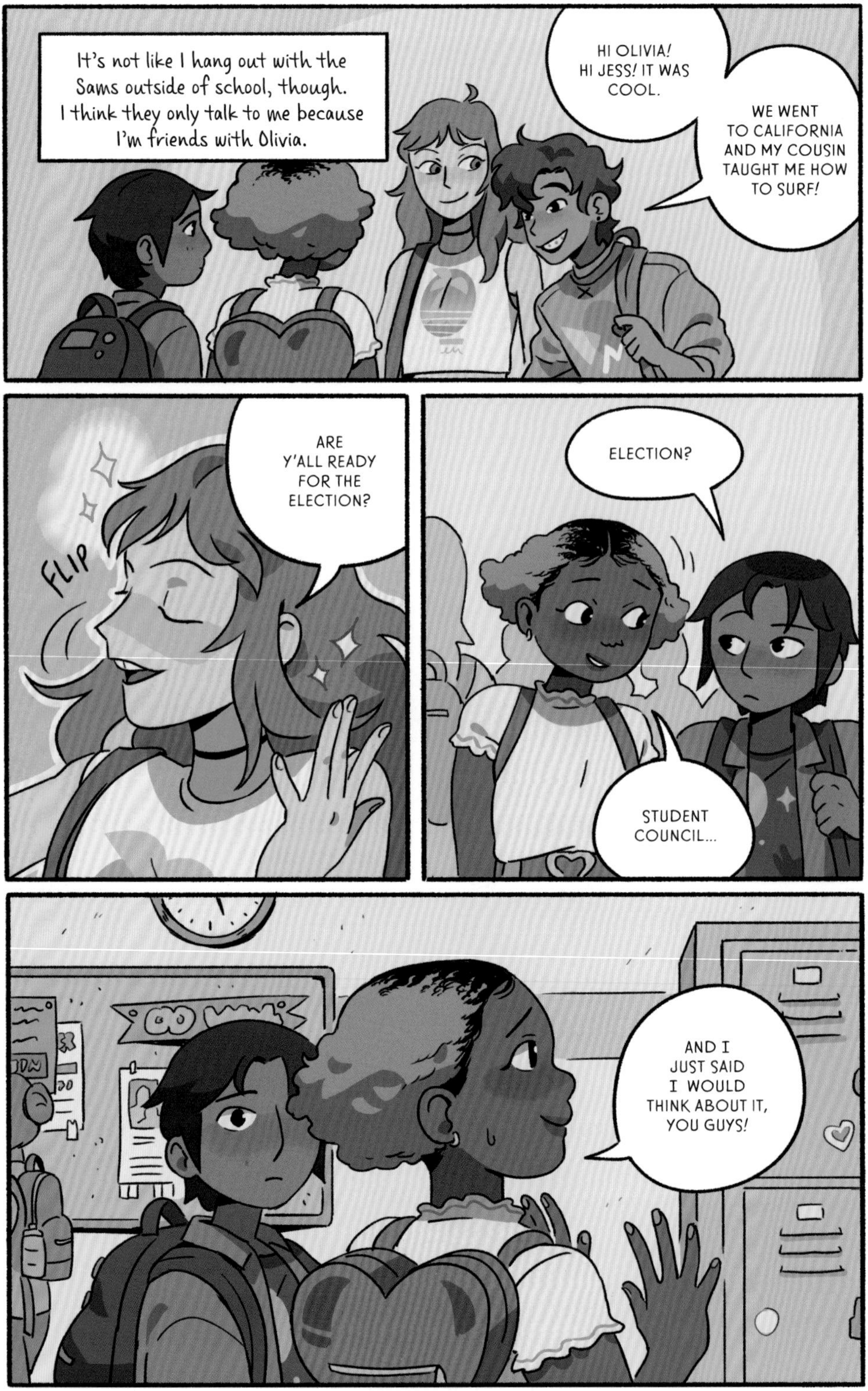
It's not like I hang out with the Sams outside of school, though. I think they only talk to me because I'm friends with Olivia.
HI OLIVIA! HI JESS! IT WAS COOL.
WE WENT TO CALIFORNIA AND MY COUSIN TAUGHT ME HOW TO SURF!
FLIP
ARE Y'ALL READY FOR THE ELECTION?
ELECTION?
STUDENT COUNCIL...
AND I JUST SAID I WOULD THINK ABOUT IT, YOU GUYS!

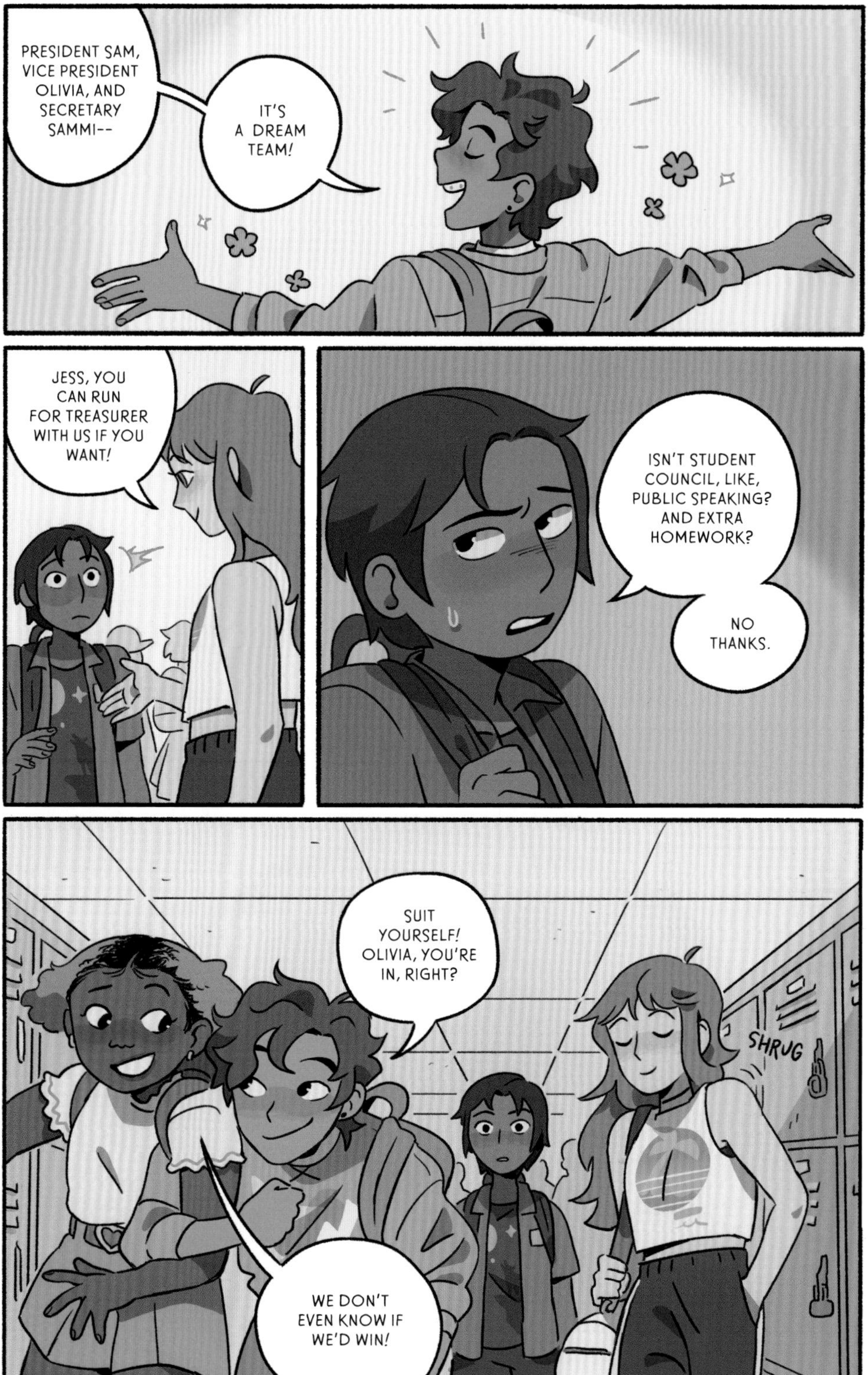
PRESIDENT SAM, VICE PRESIDENT OLIVIA, AND SECRETARY SAMMI--
IT'S A DREAM TEAM!
JESS, YOU CAN RUN FOR TREASURER WITH US IF YOU WANT!
ISN'T STUDENT COUNCIL, LIKE, PUBLIC SPEAKING? AND EXTRA HOMEWORK?
NO THANKS.
SUIT YOURSELF! OLIVIA, YOU'RE IN, RIGHT?
SHRUG
WE DON'T EVEN KNOW IF WE'D WIN!

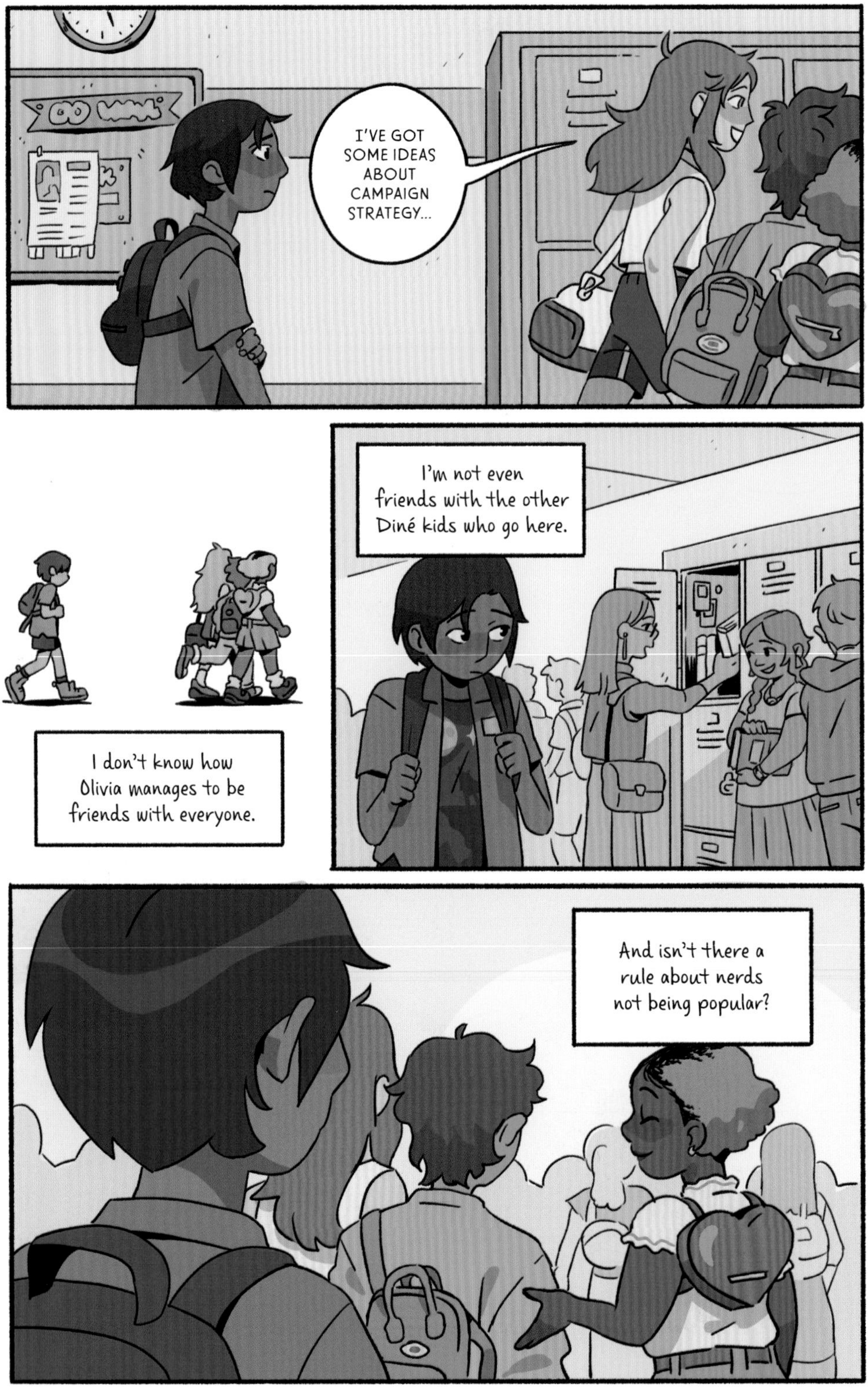

I'VE GOT SOME IDEAS ABOUT CAMPAIGN STRATEGY...
I don't know how Olivia manages to be friends with everyone.
I'm not even friends with the other Diné kids who go here.
And isn't there a rule about nerds not being popular?

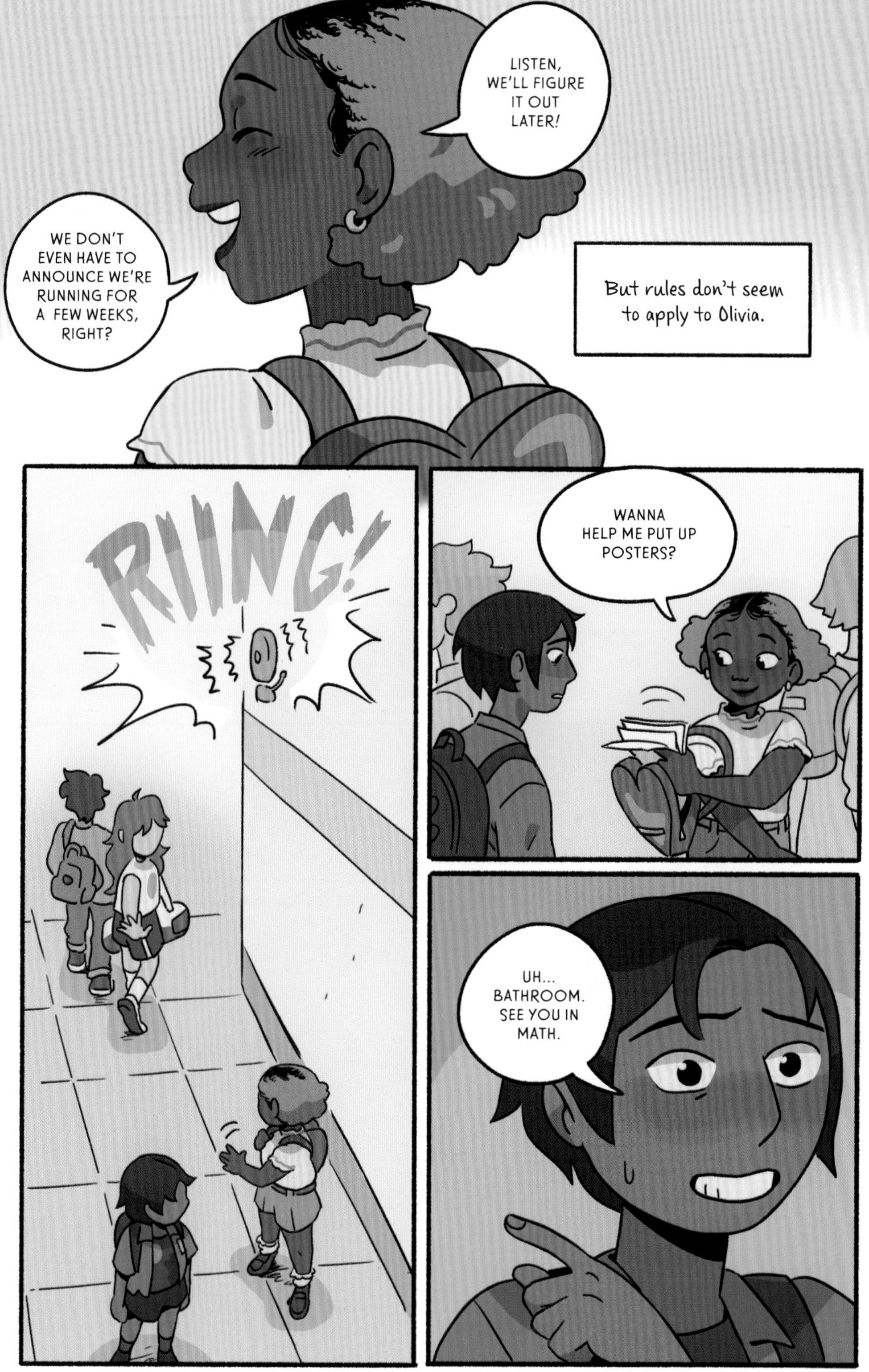
LISTEN, WE'LL FIGURE IT OUT LATER!
WE DON'T EVEN HAVE TO ANNOUNCE WE'RE RUNNING FOR A FEW WEEKS, RIGHT?
But rules don't seem to apply to Olivia.
RIIING!
WANNA HELP ME PUT UP POSTERS?
UH... BATHROOM. SEE YOU IN MATH.

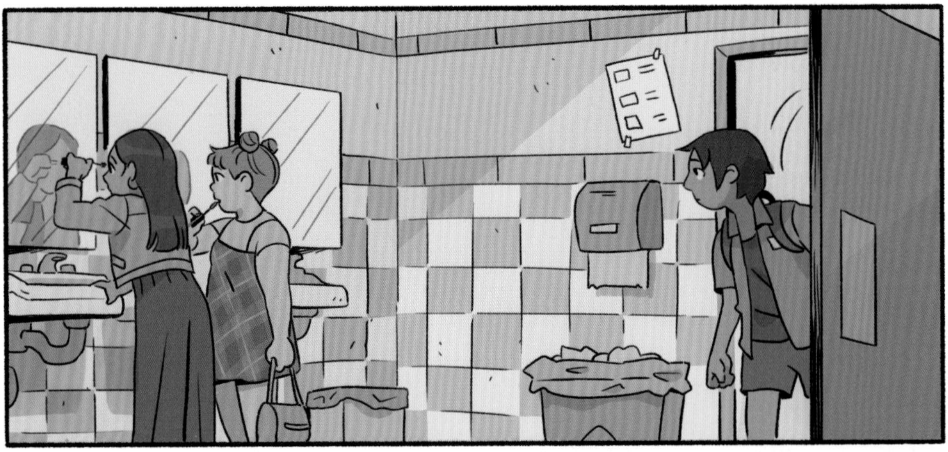

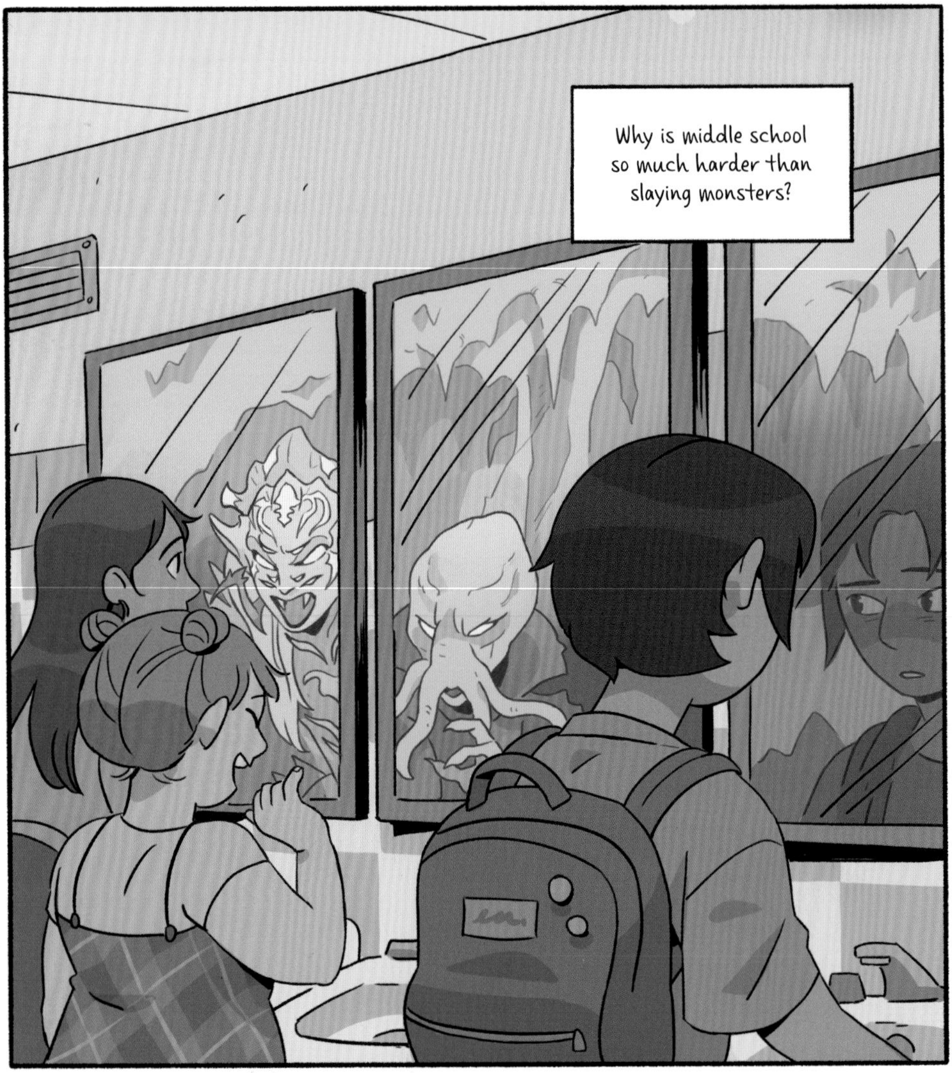
Why is middle school so much harder than slaying monsters?

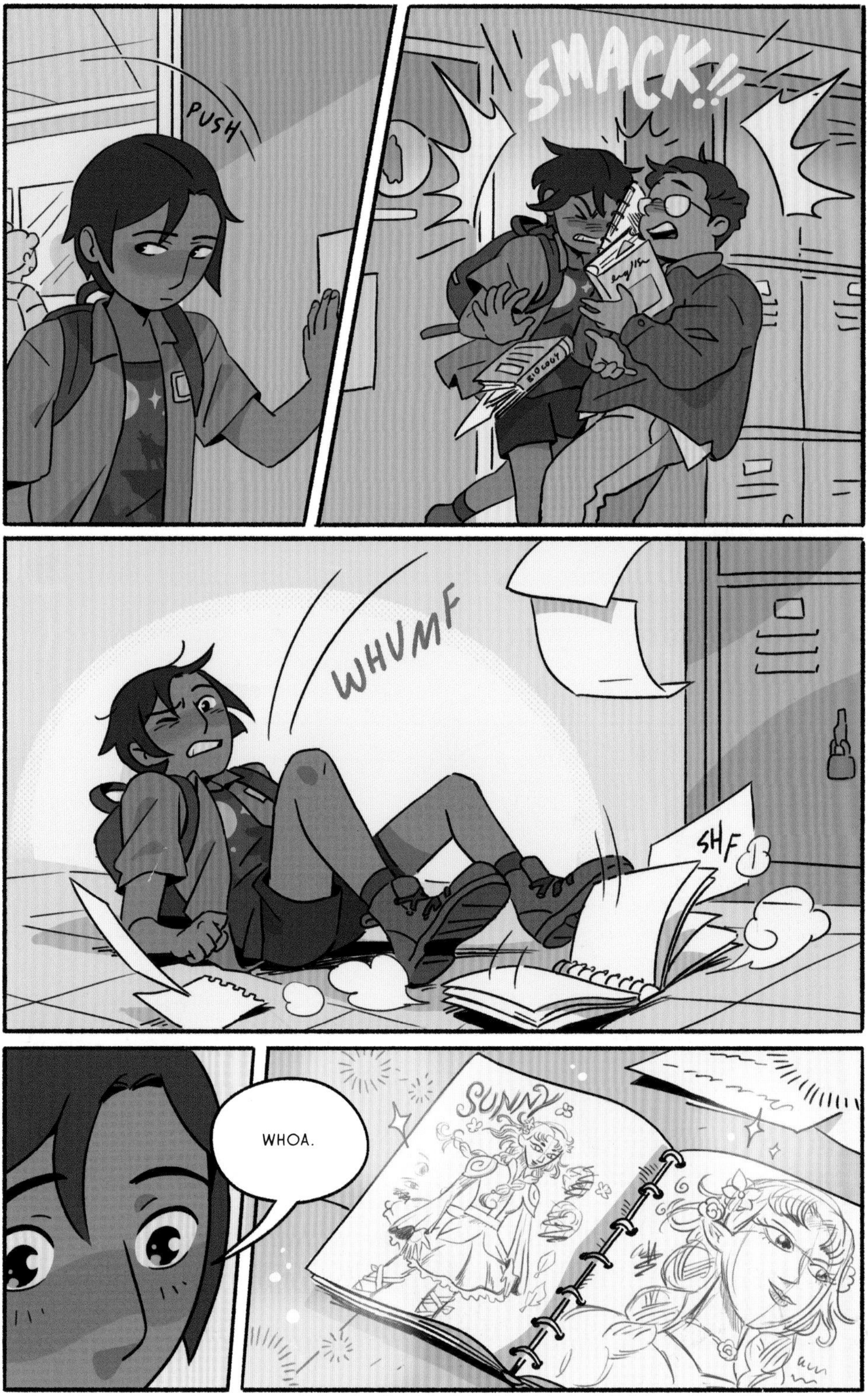
PUSH
SMACK!!
WHUMF
SHF
WHOA.
SUNNY

Tyler Rubio

Weirdo (Boy), Chaotic Neutral

Popularity Class 2
Social Points 4
Bully Potential very low

NICENESS	COOL	FASHION	SMARTS	SPORTS	HUMOR
10 (+0)	2 (-4)	5.25	14 (+2)	6 (-3)	10 (+0)

Contrast. When within 10 feet of Tyler, other middle schoolers automatically gain 5 social points.

Actions

Rumors. If Tyler claims to be connected to another middle schooler, they must succeed on a Difficulty Class 12 Cool-saving throw or automatically lose 5 social points for the rest of the week.

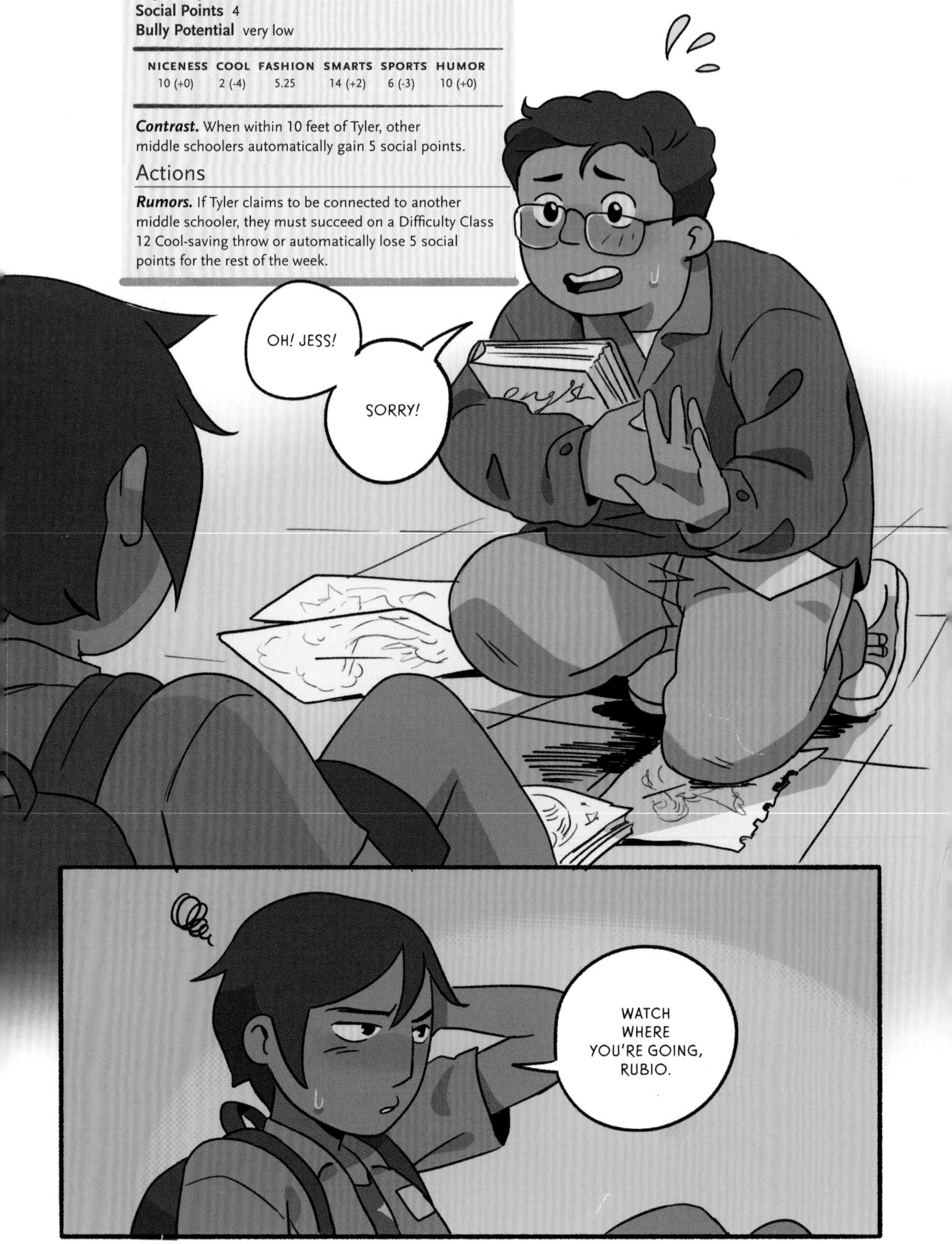

OH! JESS!
SORRY!
WATCH WHERE YOU'RE GOING, RUBIO.

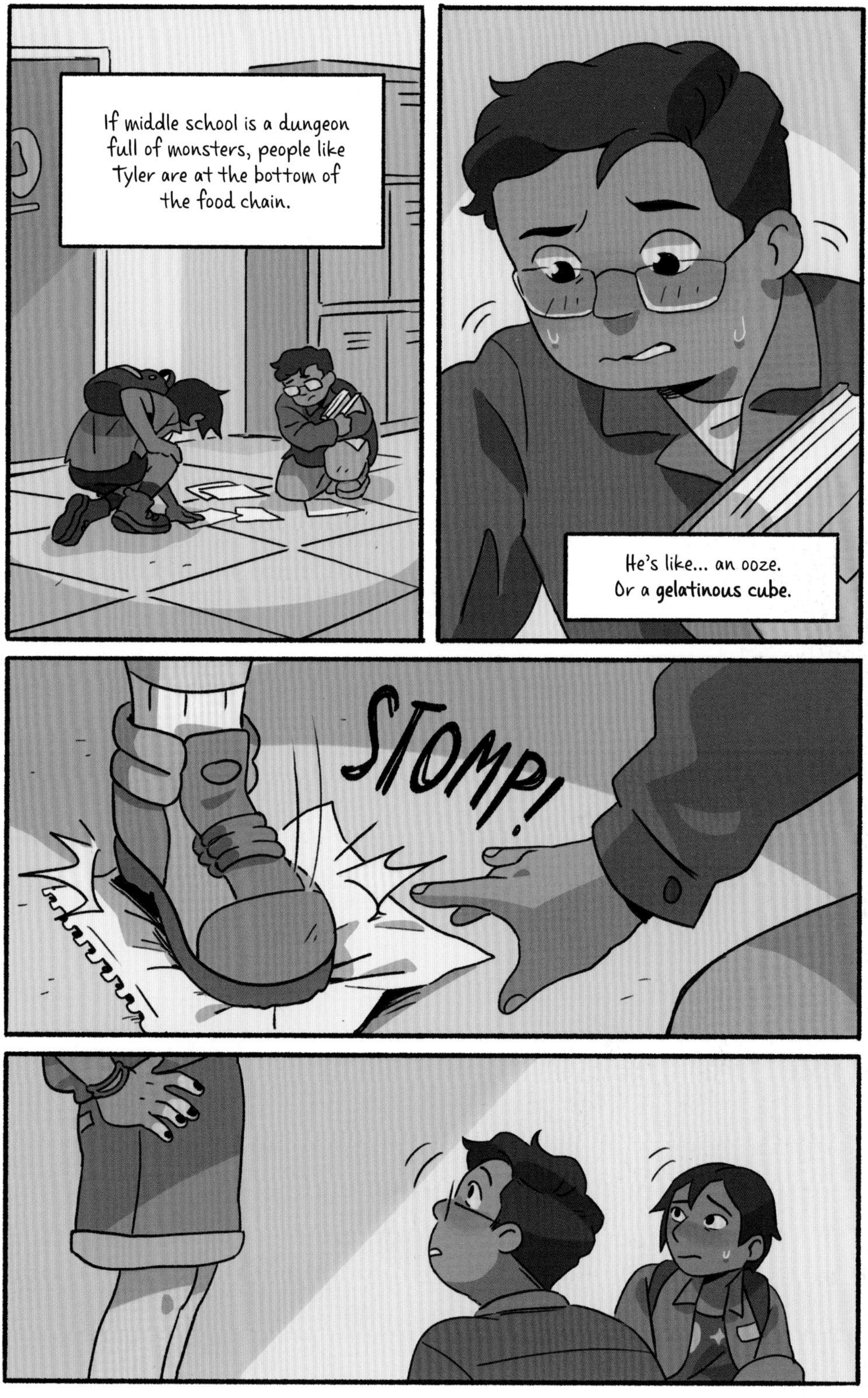
If middle school is a dungeon full of monsters, people like Tyler are at the bottom of the food chain.
He's like... an ooze. Or a gelatinous cube.
STOMP!

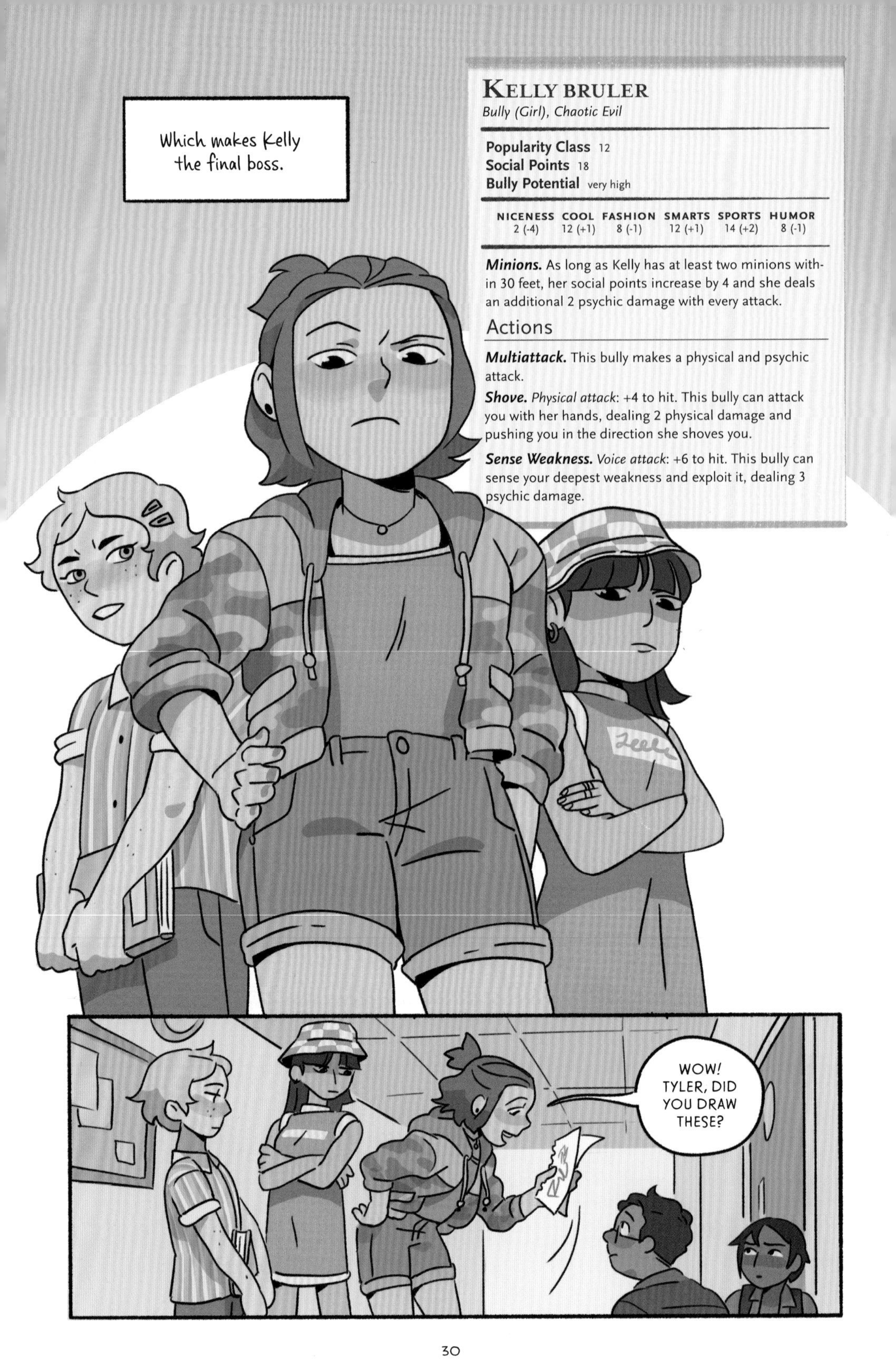
Which makes Kelly the final boss.
KELLY BRULER
Bully (Girl), Chaotic Evil
Popularity Class 12
Social Points 18
Bully Potential very high
NICENESS 2 (-4) COOL 12 (+1) FASHION 8 (-1) SMARTS 12 (+1) SPORTS 14 (+2) HUMOR 8 (-1)
Minions. As long as Kelly has at least two minions within 30 feet, her social points increase by 4 and she deals an additional 2 psychic damage with every attack.
Actions
Multiattack. This bully makes a physical and psychic attack.
Shove. Physical attack: +4 to hit. This bully can attack you with her hands, dealing 2 physical damage and pushing you in the direction she shoves you.
Sense Weakness. Voice attack: +6 to hit. This bully can sense your deepest weakness and exploit it, dealing 3 psychic damage.
WOW! TYLER, DID YOU DRAW THESE?

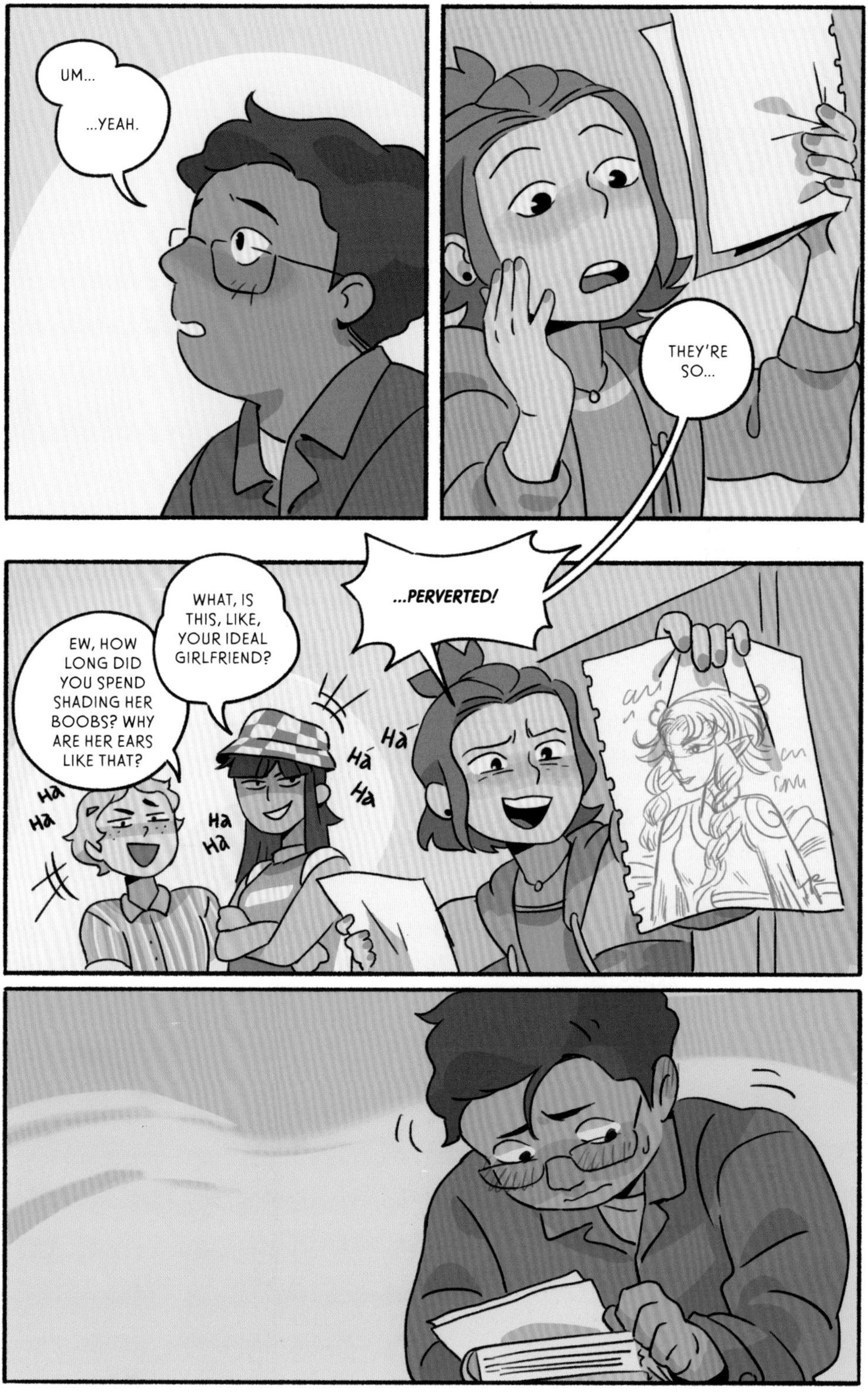
UM...
...YEAH.
THEY'RE SO...
...PERVERTED!
WHAT, IS THIS, LIKE, YOUR IDEAL GIRLFRIEND?
EW, HOW LONG DID YOU SPEND SHADING HER BOOBS? WHY ARE HER EARS LIKE THAT?
Ha Ha
Ha Ha
Ha Ha Ha

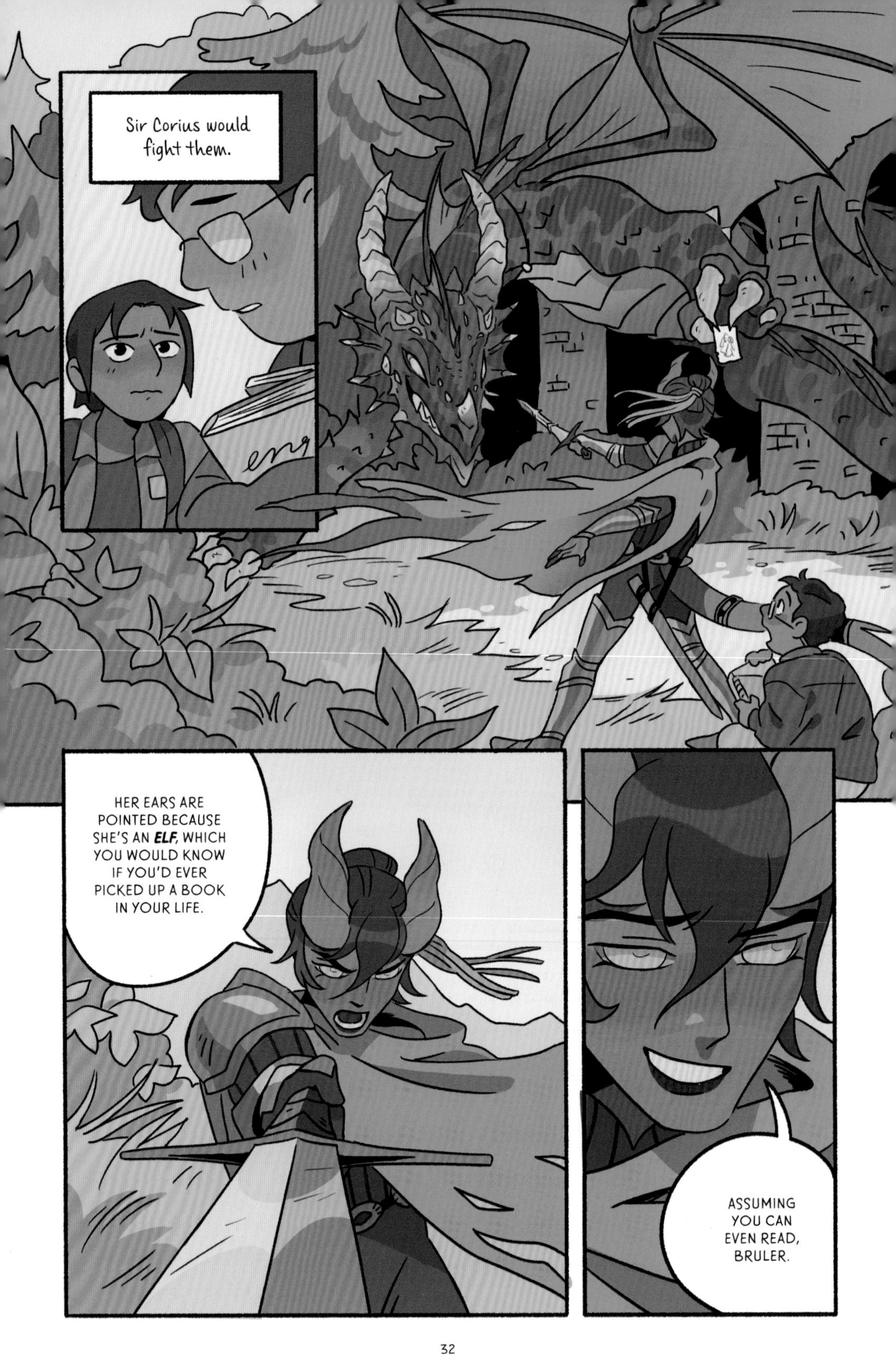

Sir Corius would fight them.
HER EARS ARE POINTED BECAUSE SHE'S AN ***ELF***, WHICH YOU WOULD KNOW IF YOU'D EVER PICKED UP A BOOK IN YOUR LIFE.
ASSUMING YOU CAN EVEN READ, BRULER.

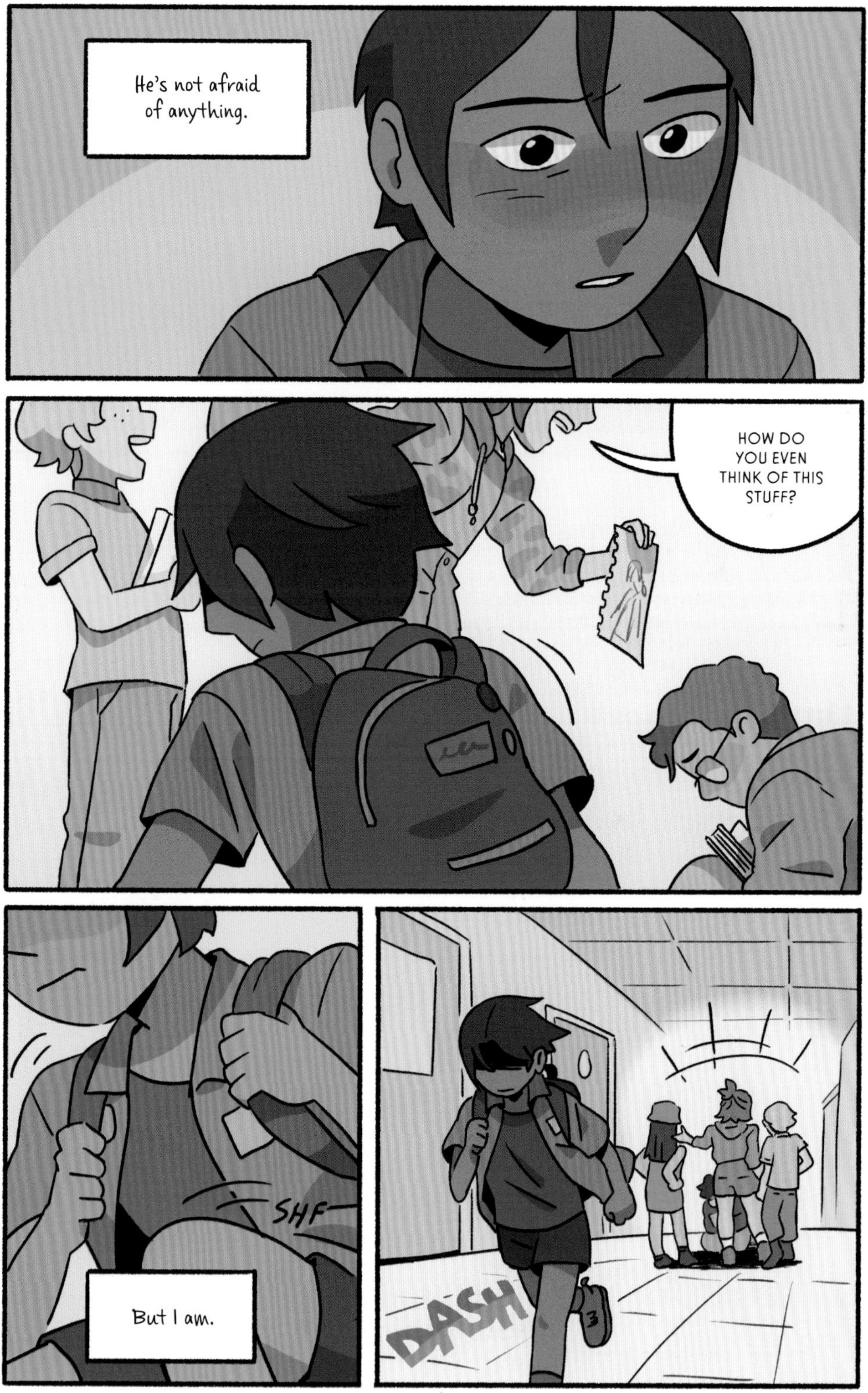
He's not afraid of anything.
HOW DO YOU EVEN THINK OF THIS STUFF?
SHF
But I am.
DASH

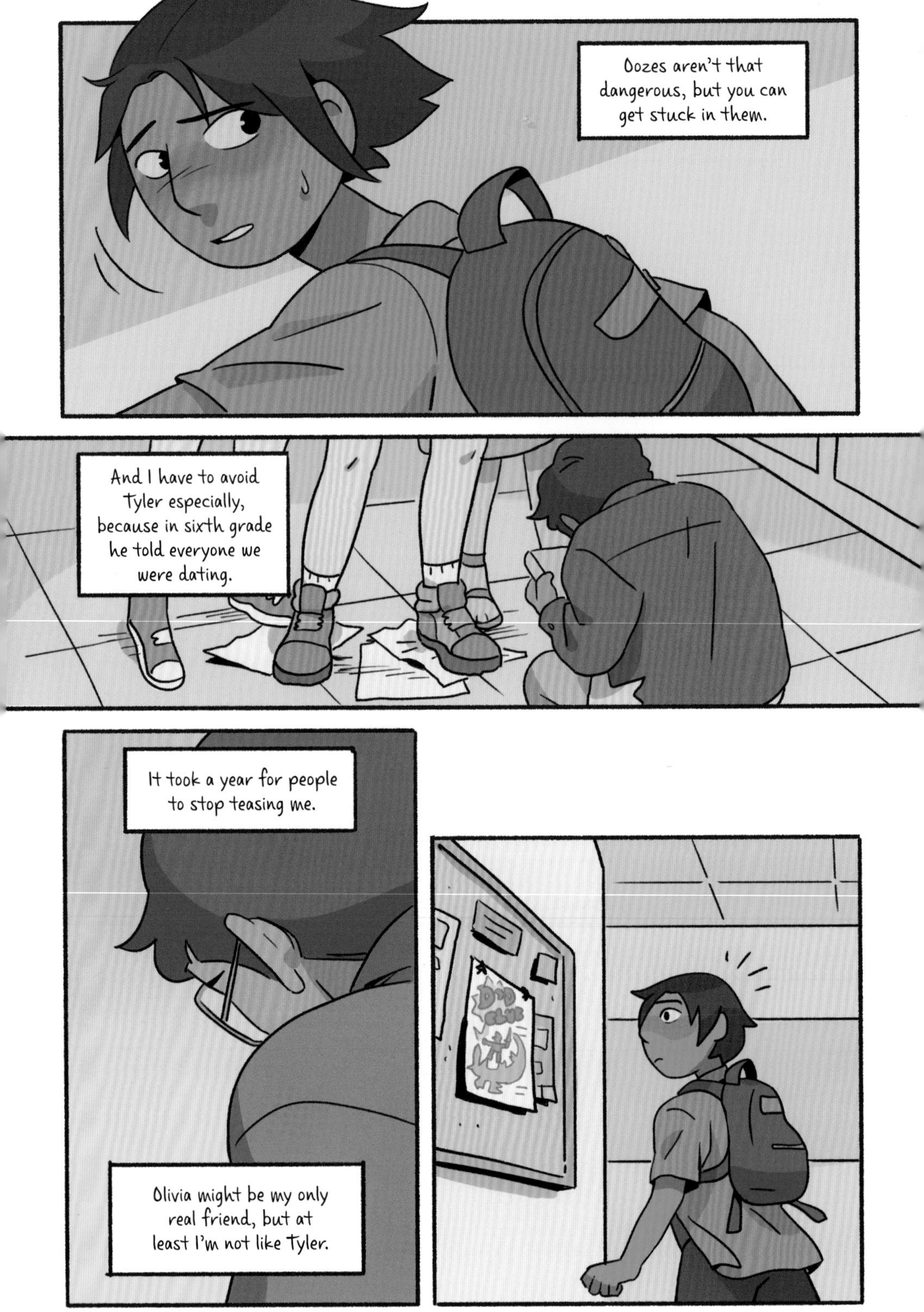
Oozes aren't that dangerous, but you can get stuck in them.
And I have to avoid Tyler especially, because in sixth grade he told everyone we were dating.
It took a year for people to stop teasing me.
Olivia might be my only real friend, but at least I'm not like Tyler.

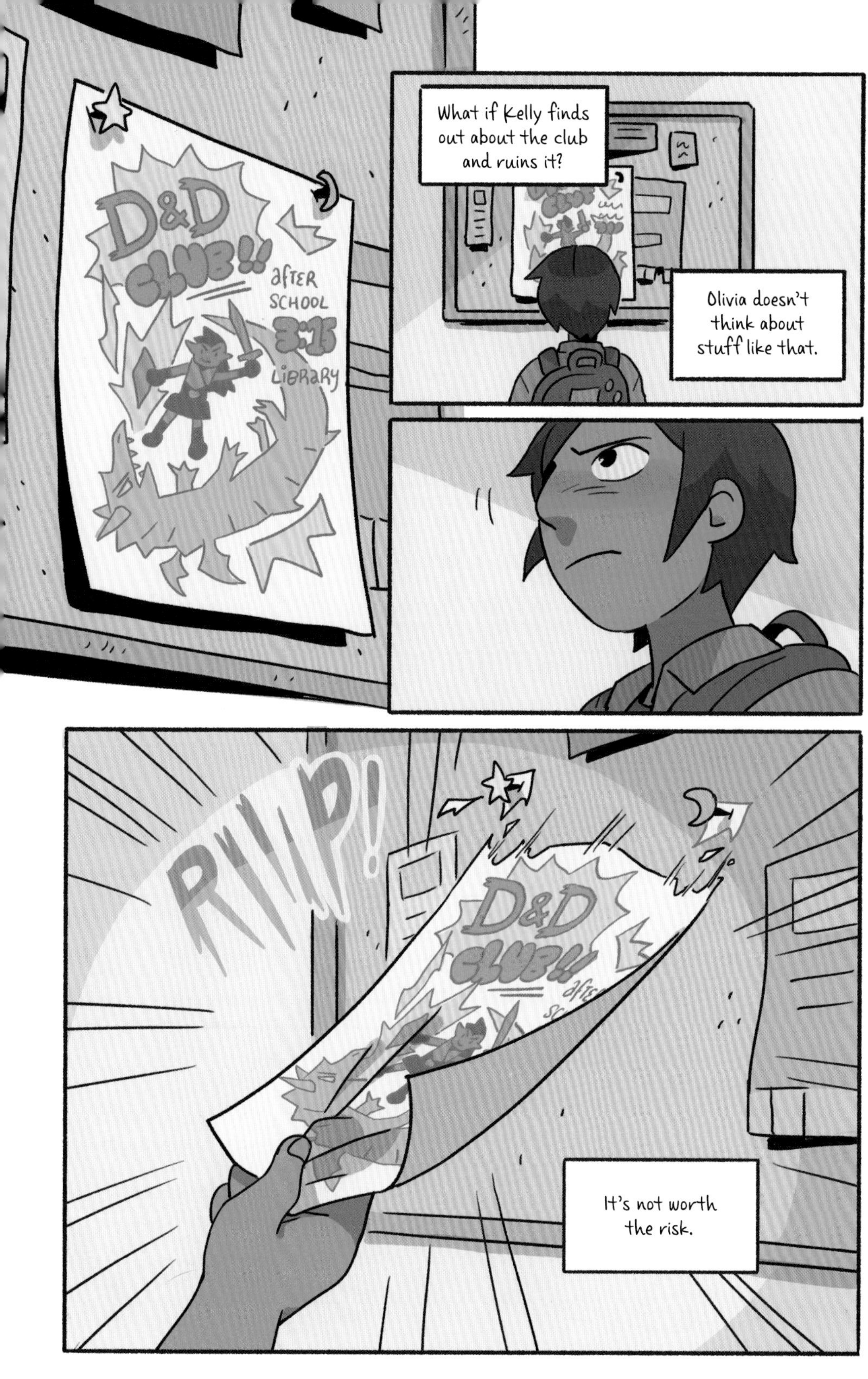
D&D CLUB!!
after SCHOOL
3:15
LIBRARY
What if Kelly finds out about the club and ruins it?
Olivia doesn't think about stuff like that.
RIIIP!
It's not worth the risk.

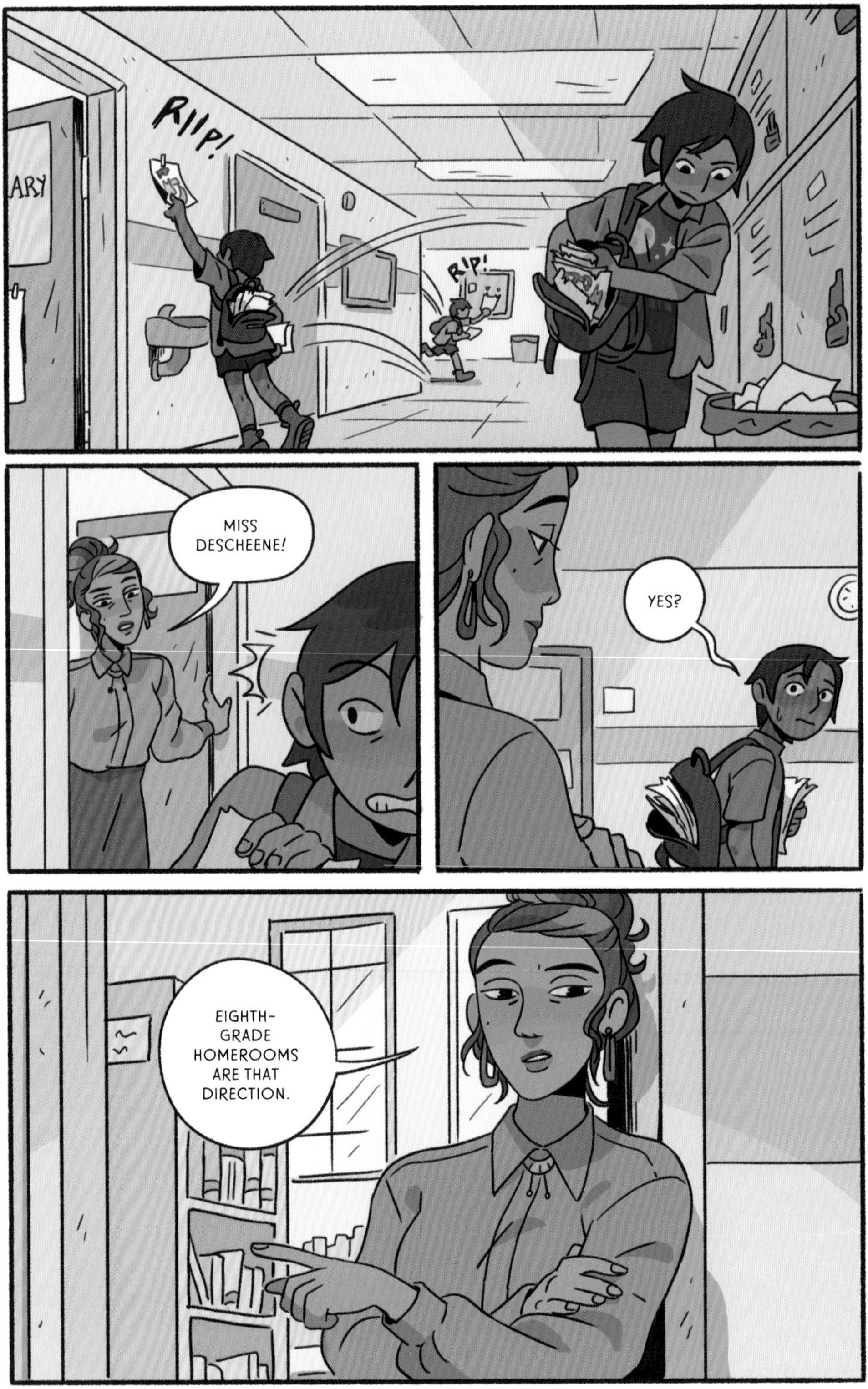
RIIP!
RIP!
MISS DESCHEENE!
YES?
EIGHTH-GRADE HOMEROOMS ARE THAT DIRECTION.

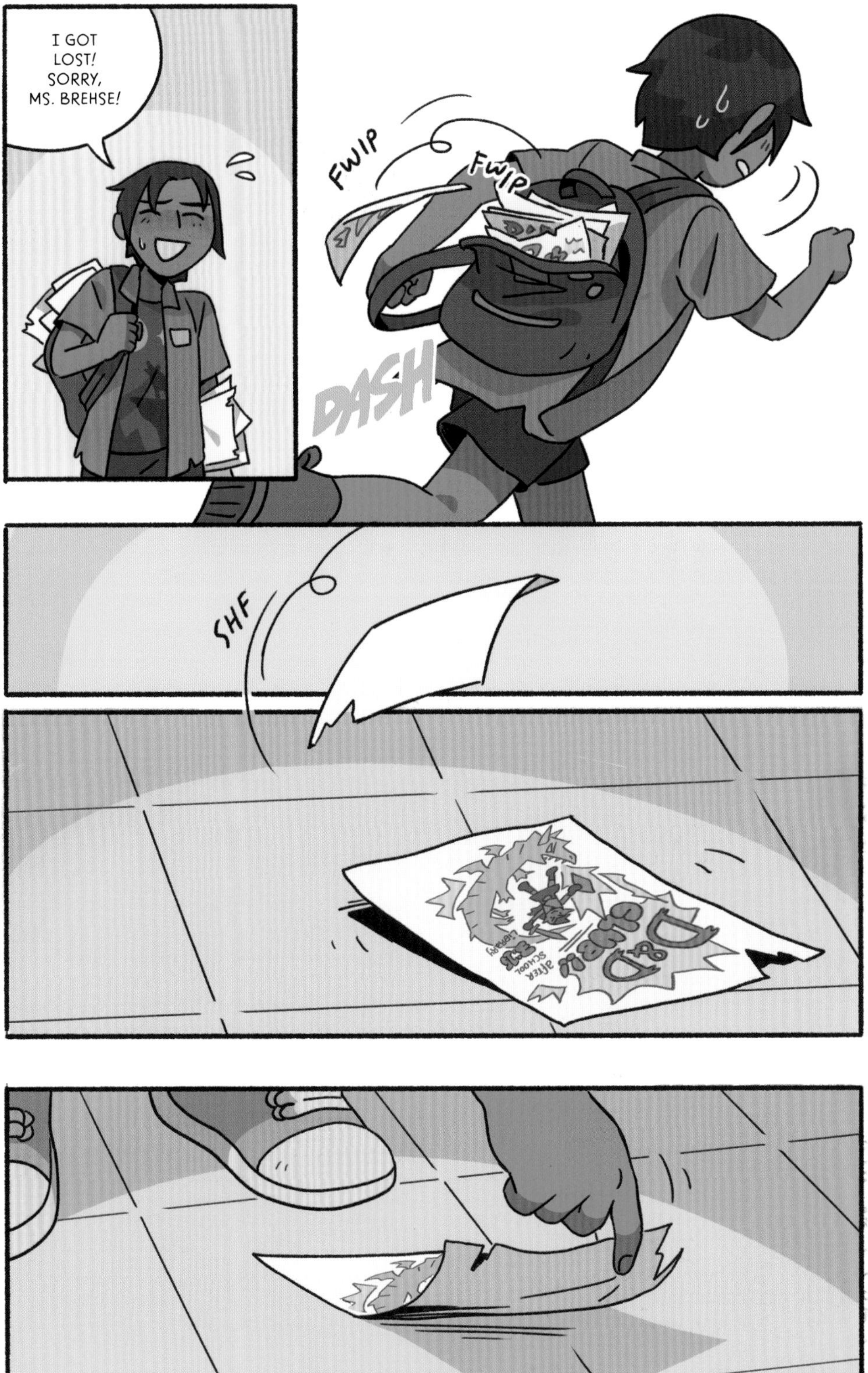
I GOT LOST! SORRY, MS. BREHSE!
FWIP
FWIP
DASH
SHF

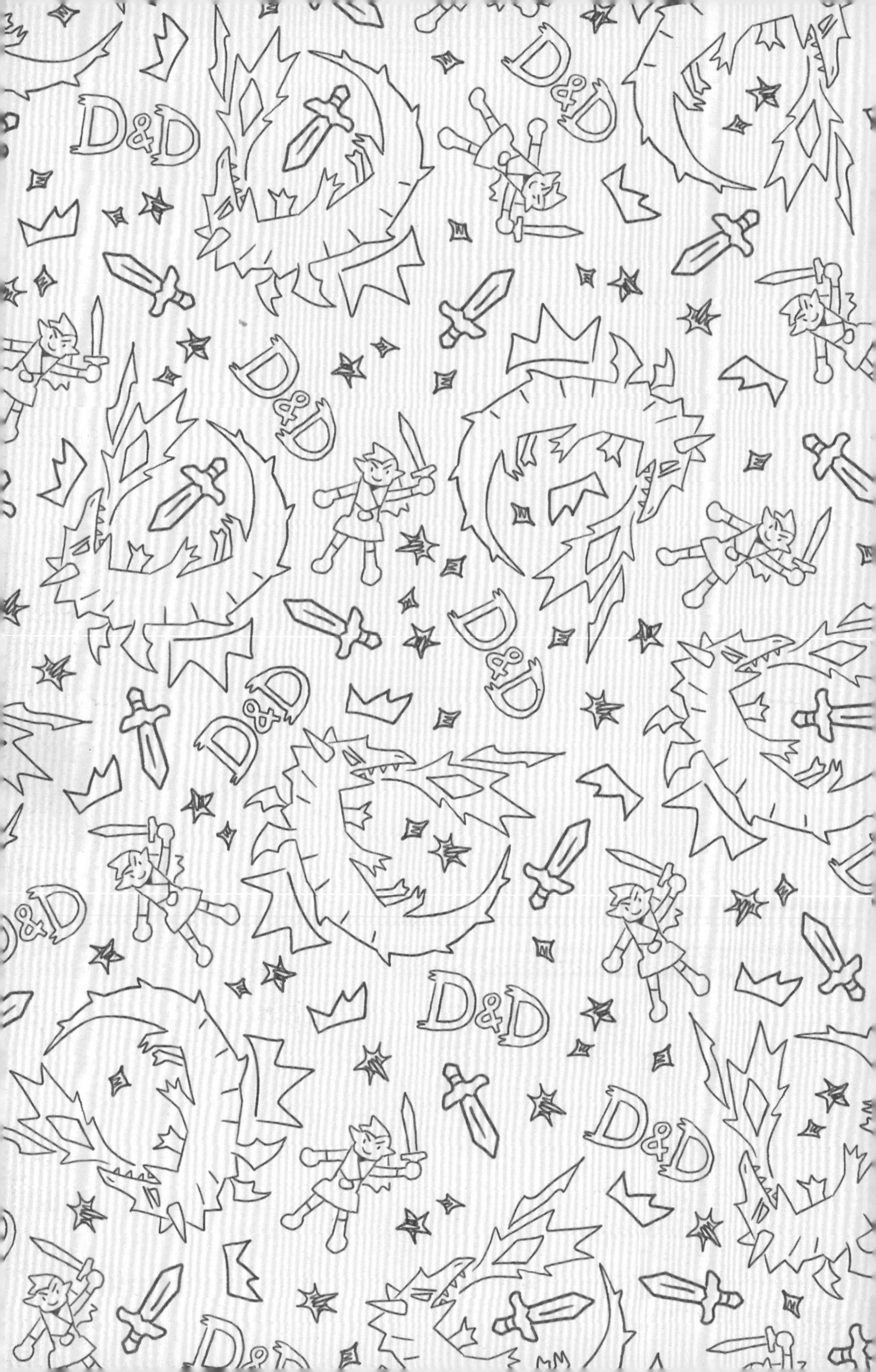
D&D

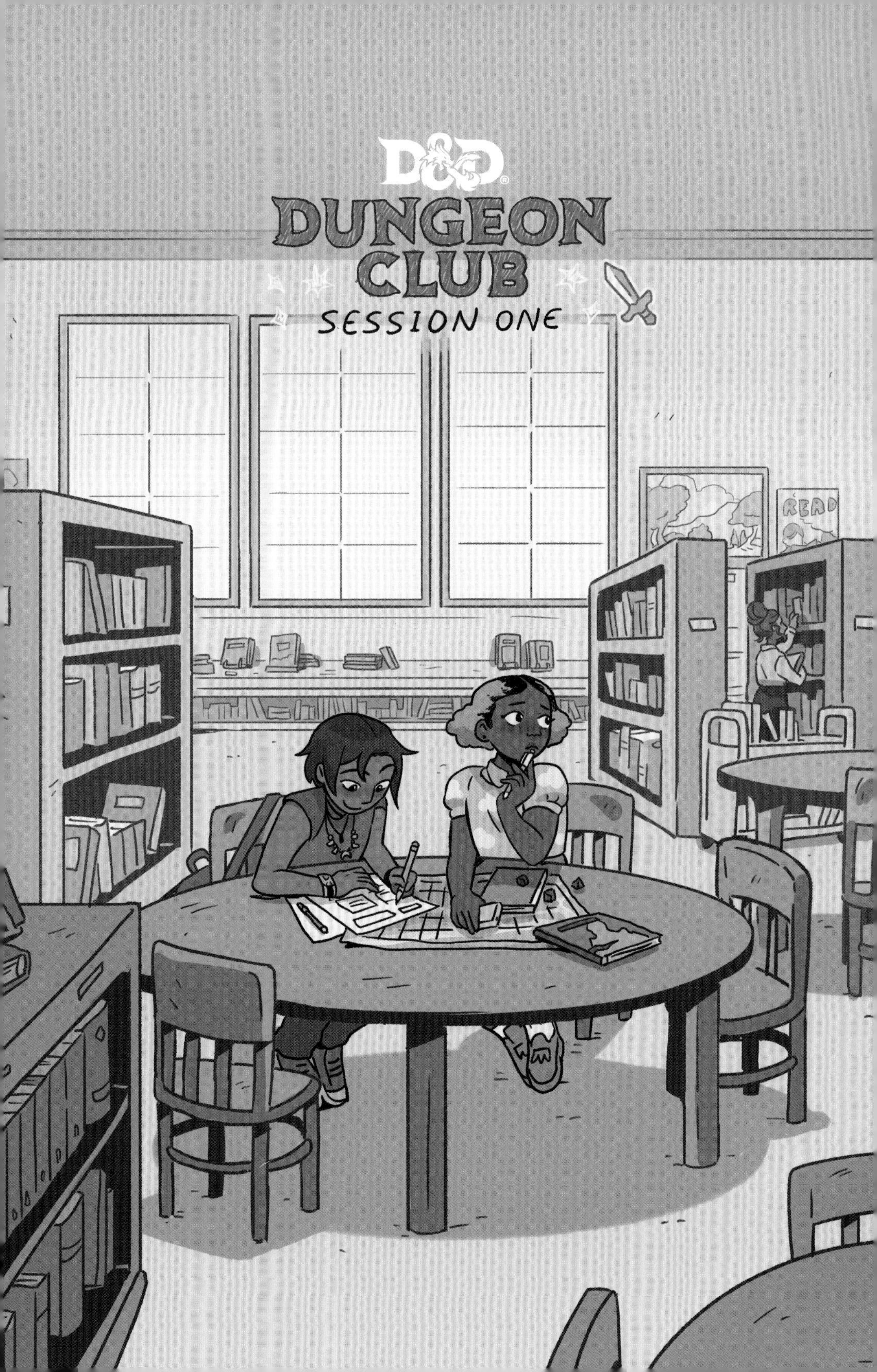
D&D
DUNGEON CLUB
SESSION ONE
READ

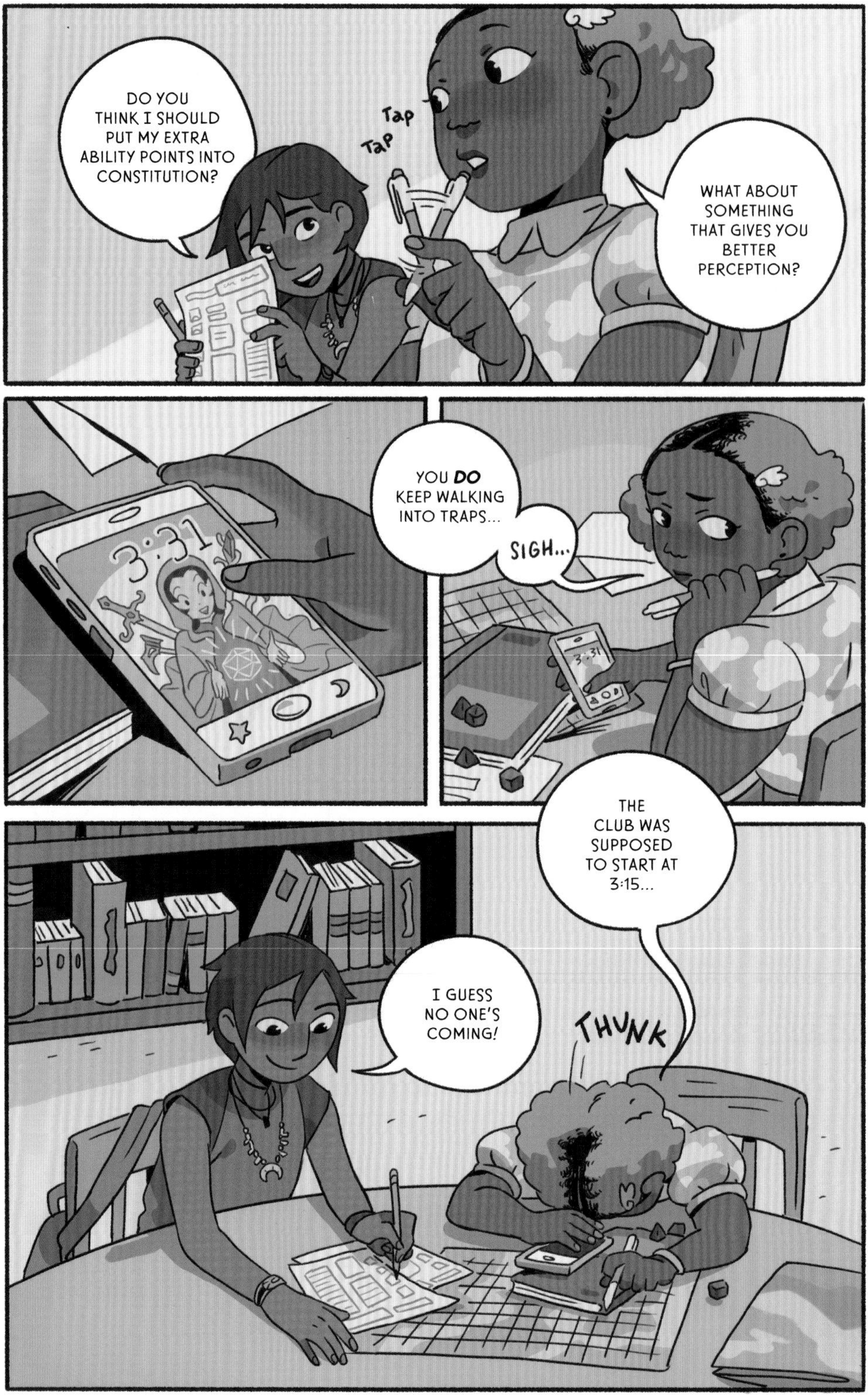
DO YOU THINK I SHOULD PUT MY EXTRA ABILITY POINTS INTO CONSTITUTION?
Tap
Tap
WHAT ABOUT SOMETHING THAT GIVES YOU BETTER PERCEPTION?
3:31
YOU **DO** KEEP WALKING INTO TRAPS...
SIGH...
THE CLUB WAS SUPPOSED TO START AT 3:15...
I GUESS NO ONE'S COMING!
THUNK

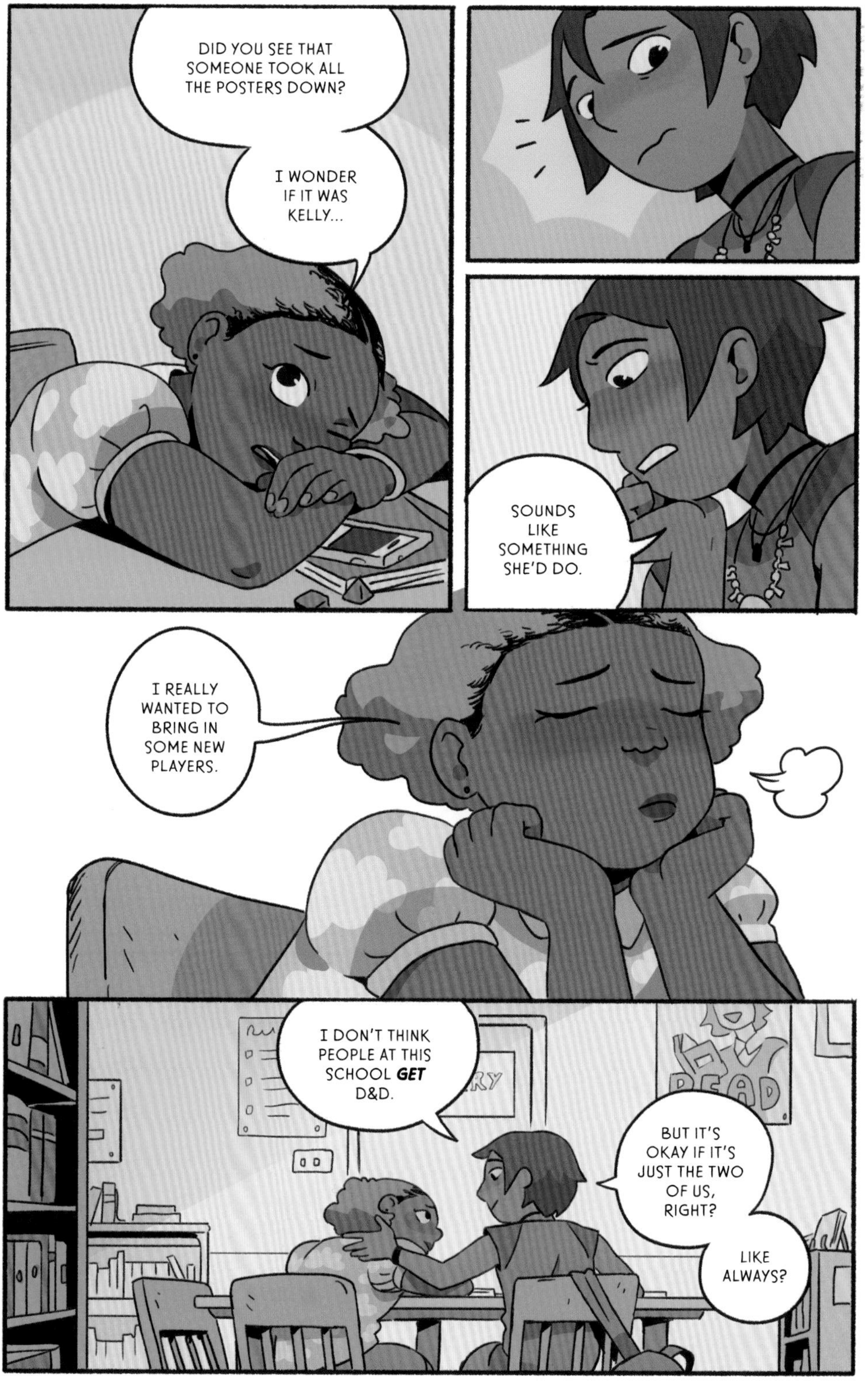
DID YOU SEE THAT SOMEONE TOOK ALL THE POSTERS DOWN?
I WONDER IF IT WAS KELLY...
SOUNDS LIKE SOMETHING SHE'D DO.
I REALLY WANTED TO BRING IN SOME NEW PLAYERS.
I DON'T THINK PEOPLE AT THIS SCHOOL **GET** D&D.
READ
BUT IT'S OKAY IF IT'S JUST THE TWO OF US, RIGHT?
LIKE ALWAYS?

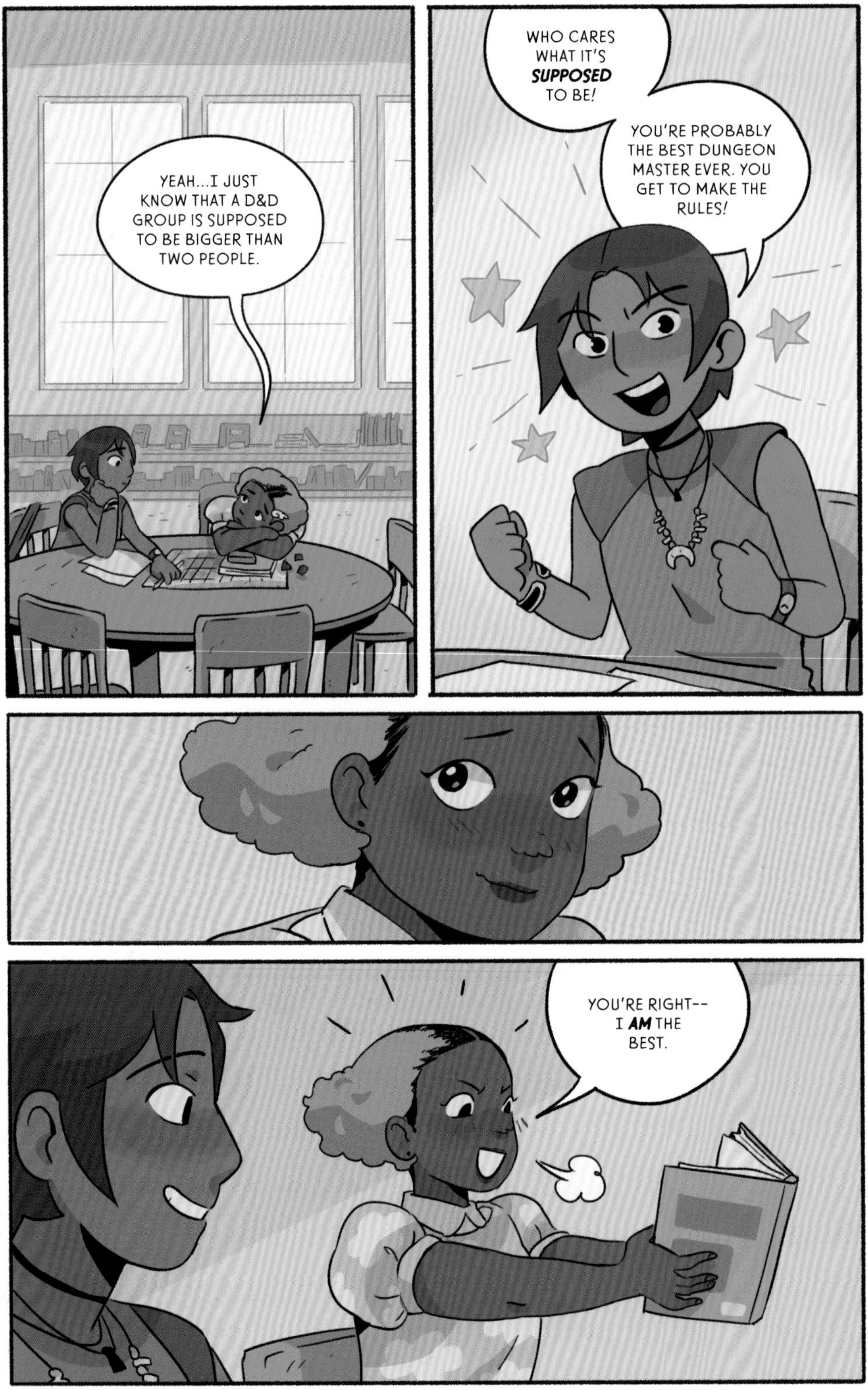

YEAH...I JUST KNOW THAT A D&D GROUP IS SUPPOSED TO BE BIGGER THAN TWO PEOPLE.
WHO CARES WHAT IT'S ***SUPPOSED*** TO BE!
YOU'RE PROBABLY THE BEST DUNGEON MASTER EVER. YOU GET TO MAKE THE RULES!
YOU'RE RIGHT-- I ***AM*** THE BEST.

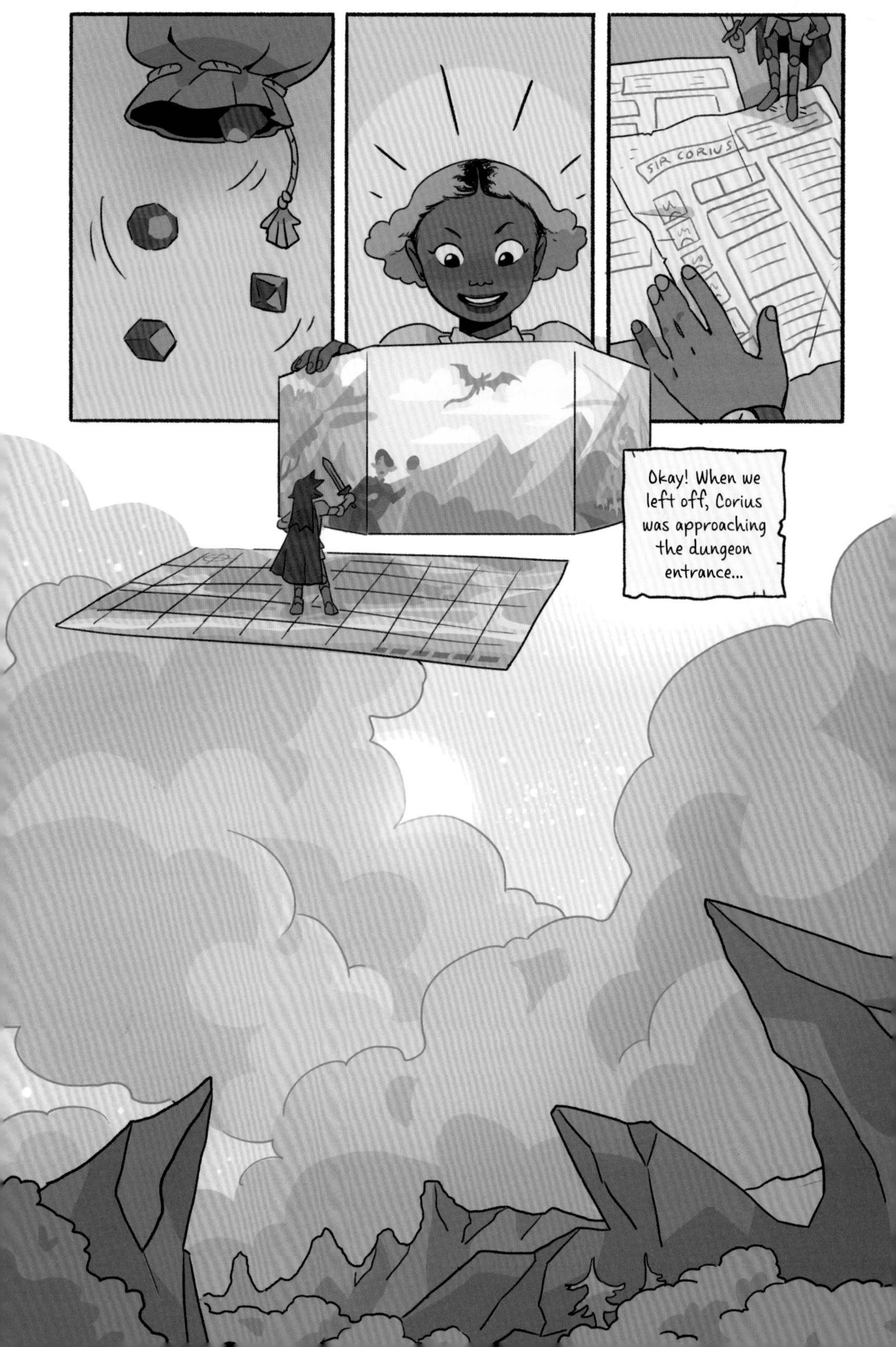
SIR CORIUS
Okay! When we left off, Corius was approaching the dungeon entrance...

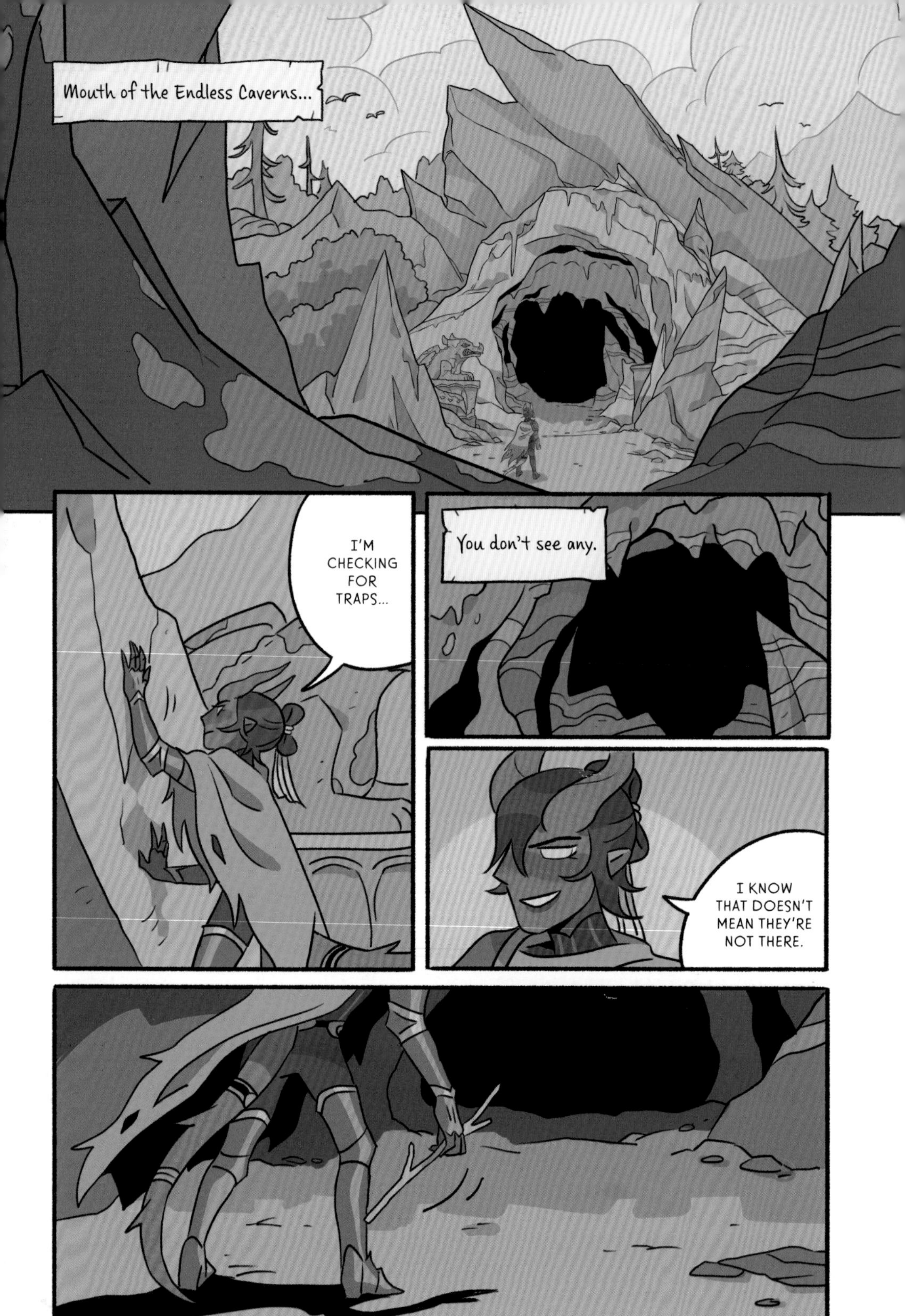
Mouth of the Endless Caverns...
I'M CHECKING FOR TRAPS...
You don't see any.
I KNOW THAT DOESN'T MEAN THEY'RE NOT THERE.

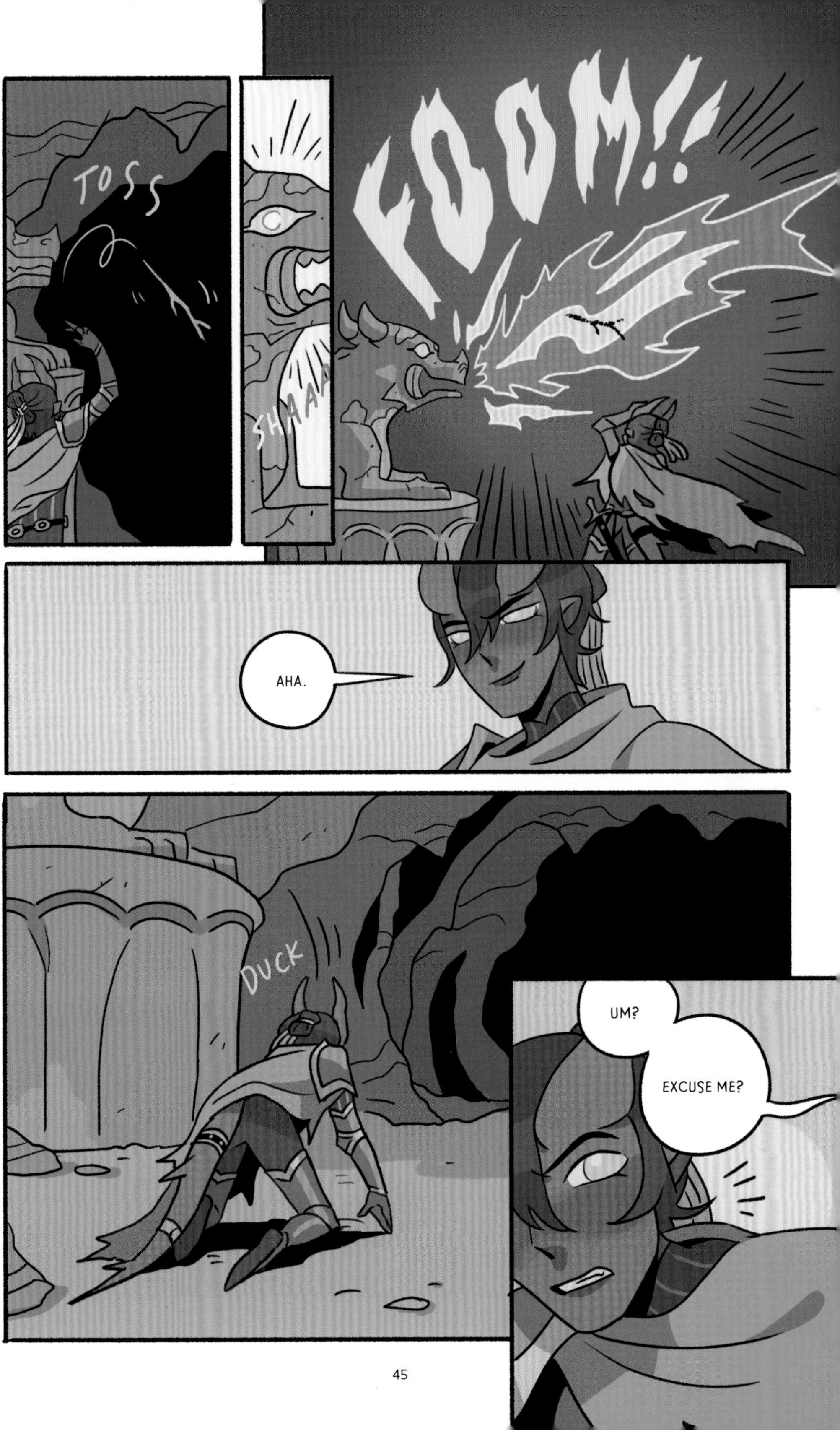
TOSS
SHAAA
FOOM!!
AHA.
DUCK
UM?
EXCUSE ME?

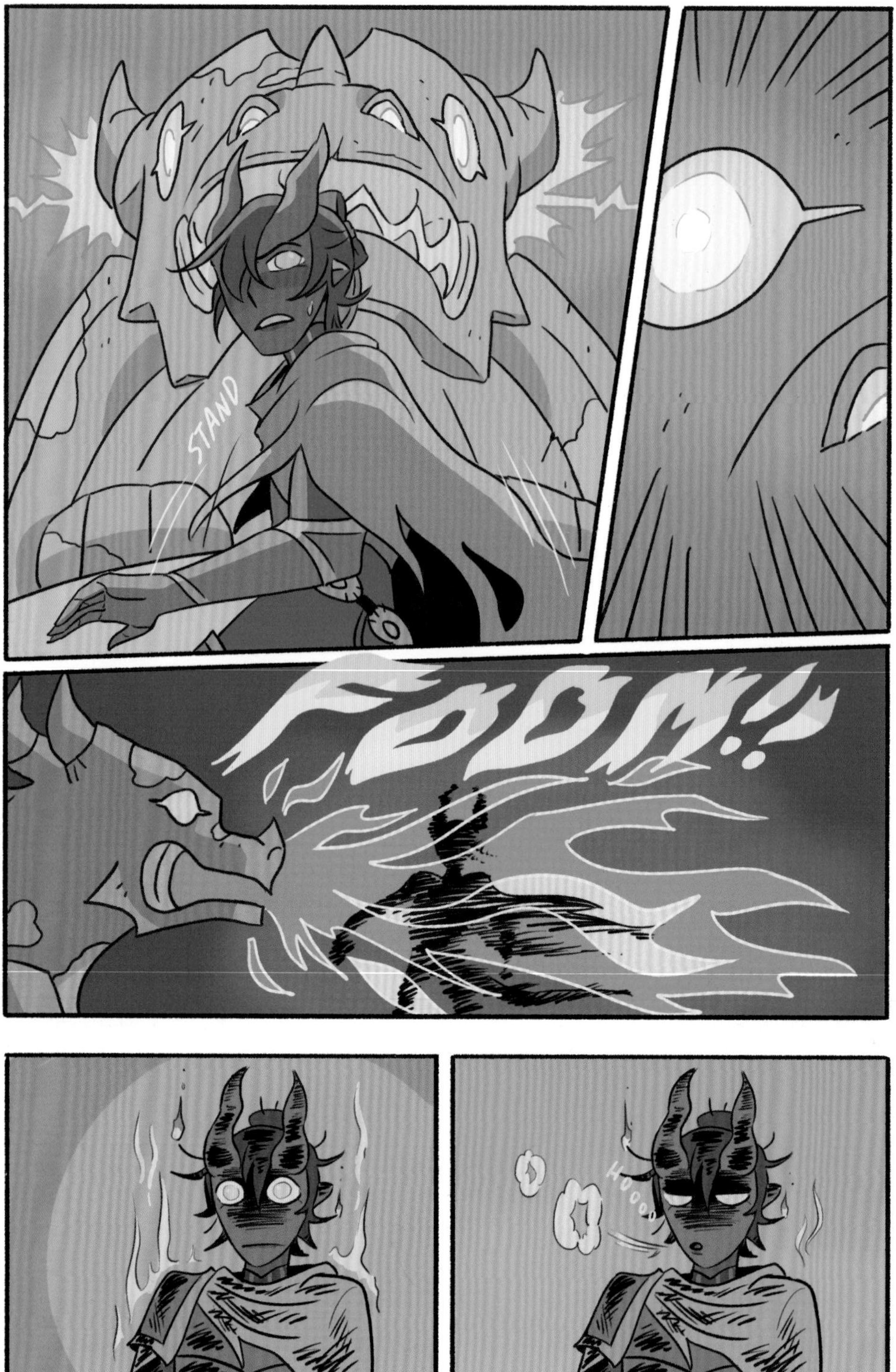
STAND
FOOM!!

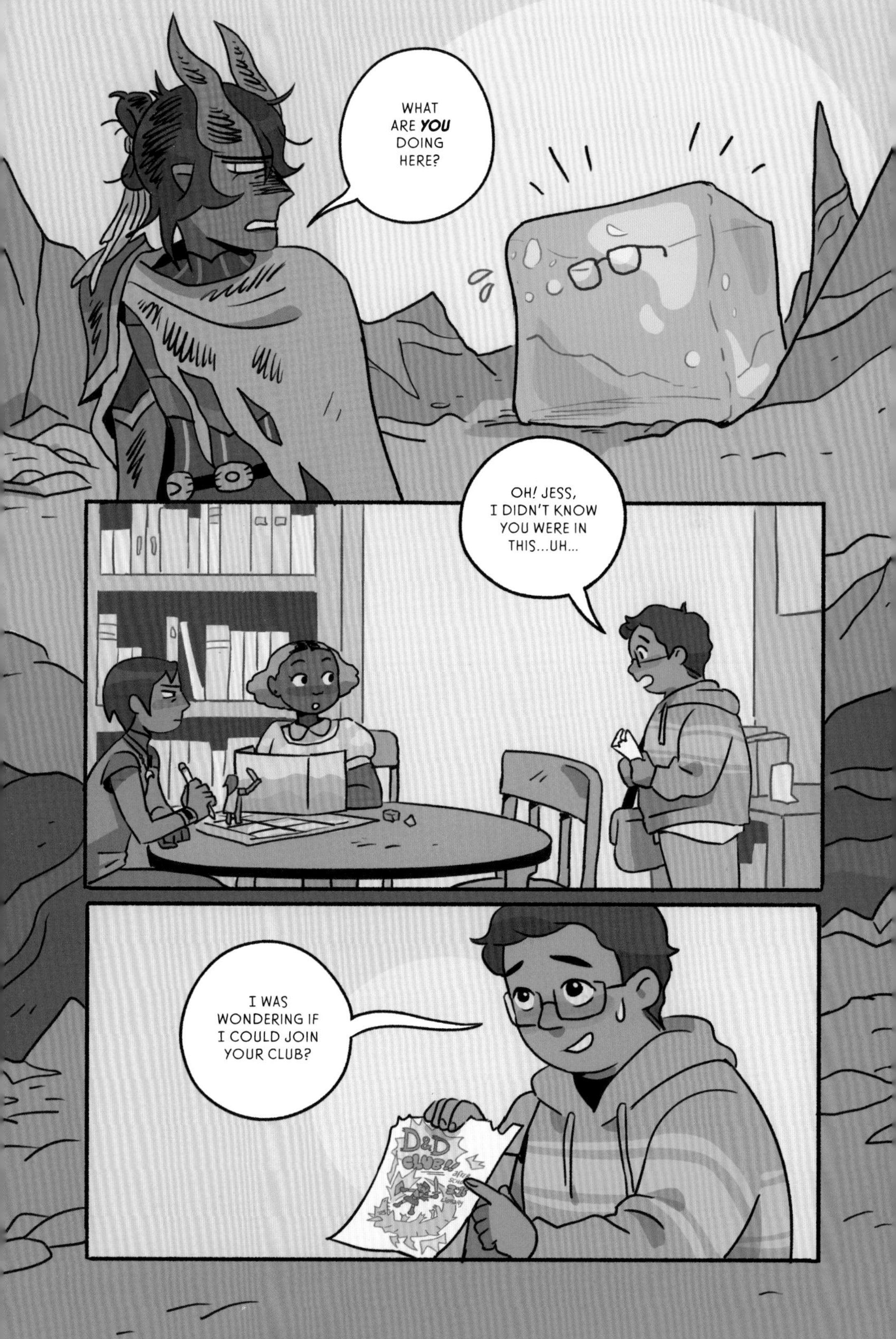
WHAT ARE *YOU* DOING HERE?
OH! JESS, I DIDN'T KNOW YOU WERE IN THIS...UH...
I WAS WONDERING IF I COULD JOIN YOUR CLUB?
D&D CLUB!!

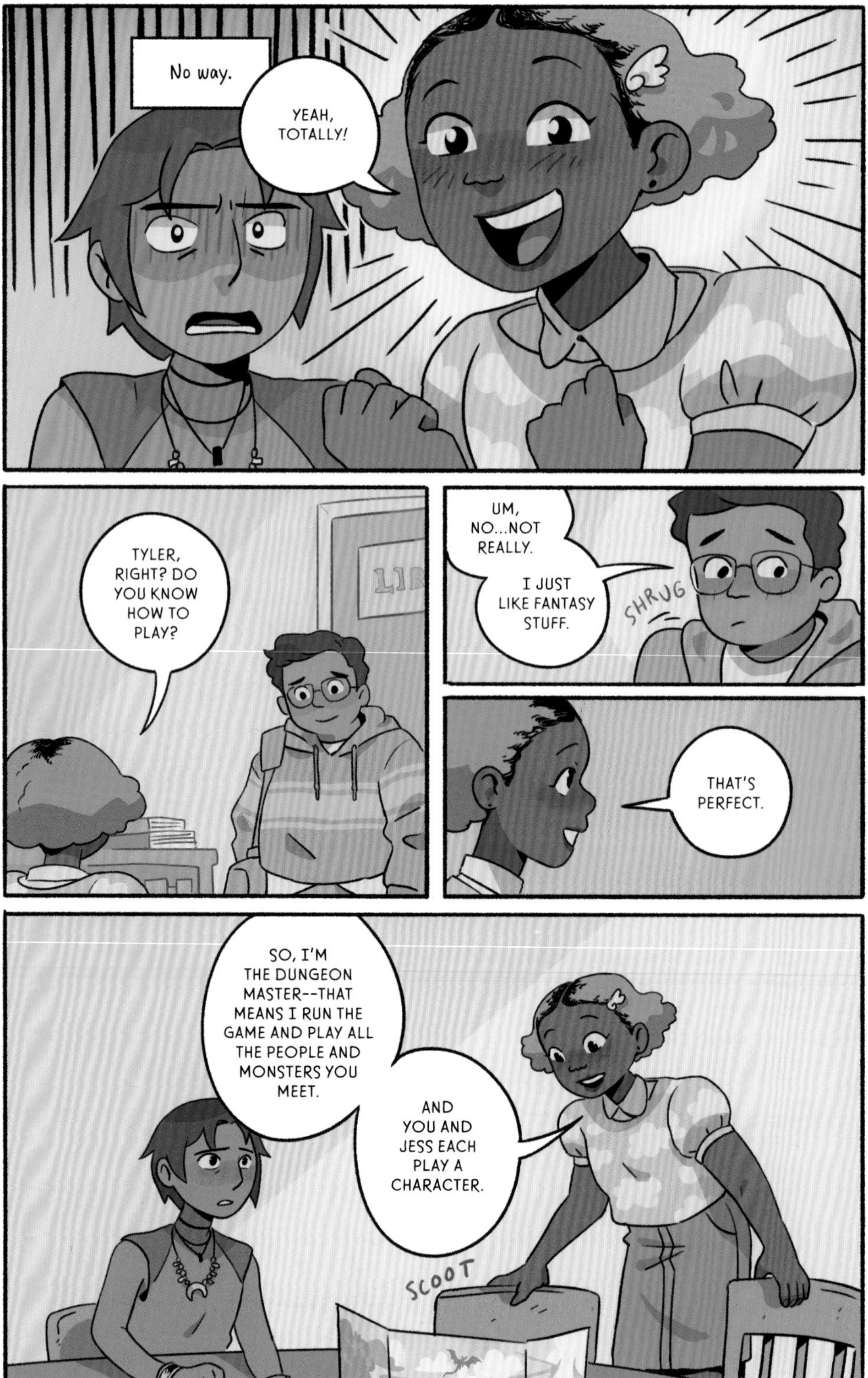
No way.
YEAH, TOTALLY!
TYLER, RIGHT? DO YOU KNOW HOW TO PLAY?
UM, NO...NOT REALLY.
I JUST LIKE FANTASY STUFF.
SHRUG
THAT'S PERFECT.
SO, I'M THE DUNGEON MASTER--THAT MEANS I RUN THE GAME AND PLAY ALL THE PEOPLE AND MONSTERS YOU MEET.
AND YOU AND JESS EACH PLAY A CHARACTER.
SCOOT

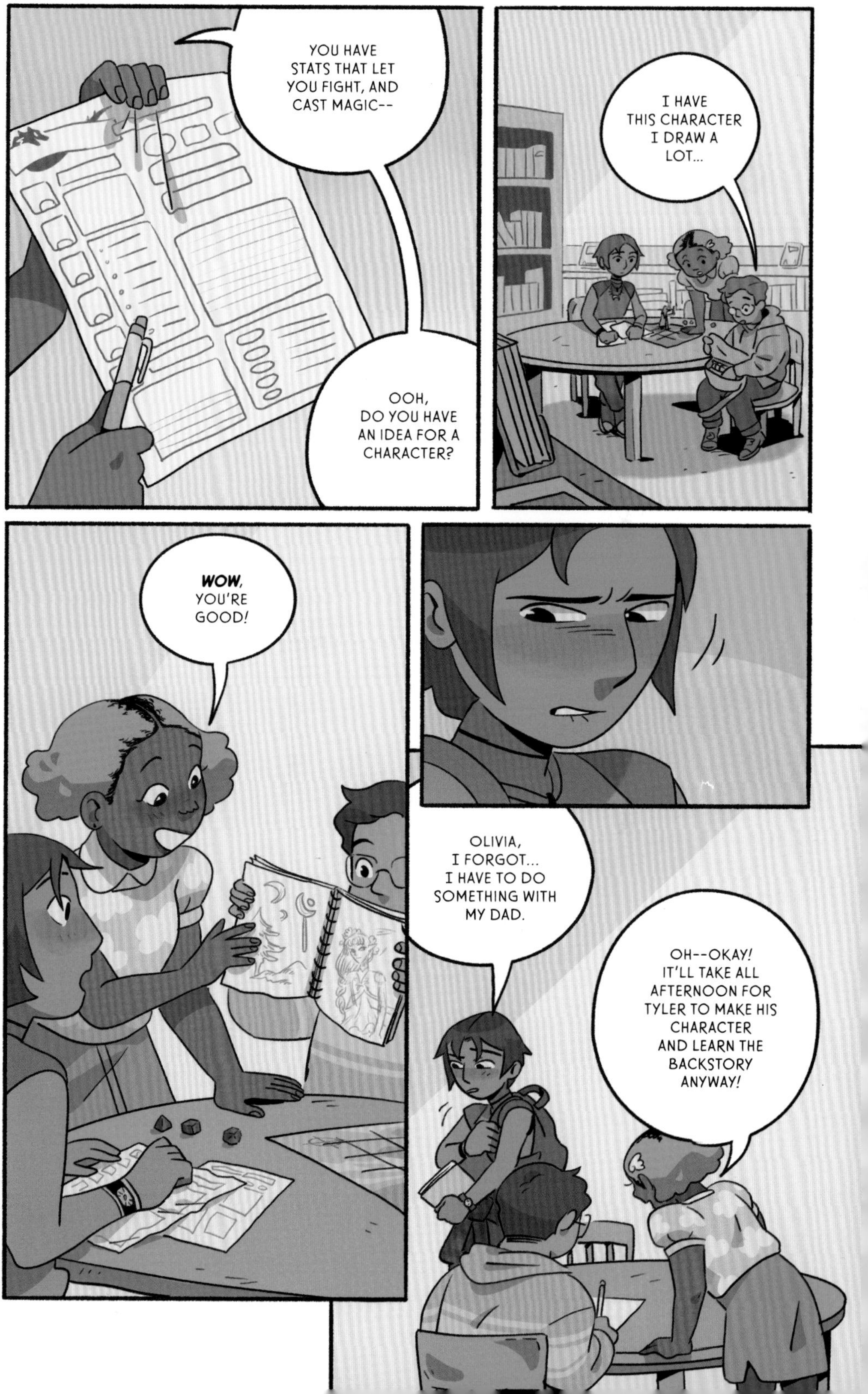
YOU HAVE STATS THAT LET YOU FIGHT, AND CAST MAGIC--
OOH, DO YOU HAVE AN IDEA FOR A CHARACTER?
I HAVE THIS CHARACTER I DRAW A LOT...
WOW, YOU'RE GOOD!
OLIVIA, I FORGOT... I HAVE TO DO SOMETHING WITH MY DAD.
OH--OKAY! IT'LL TAKE ALL AFTERNOON FOR TYLER TO MAKE HIS CHARACTER AND LEARN THE BACKSTORY ANYWAY!

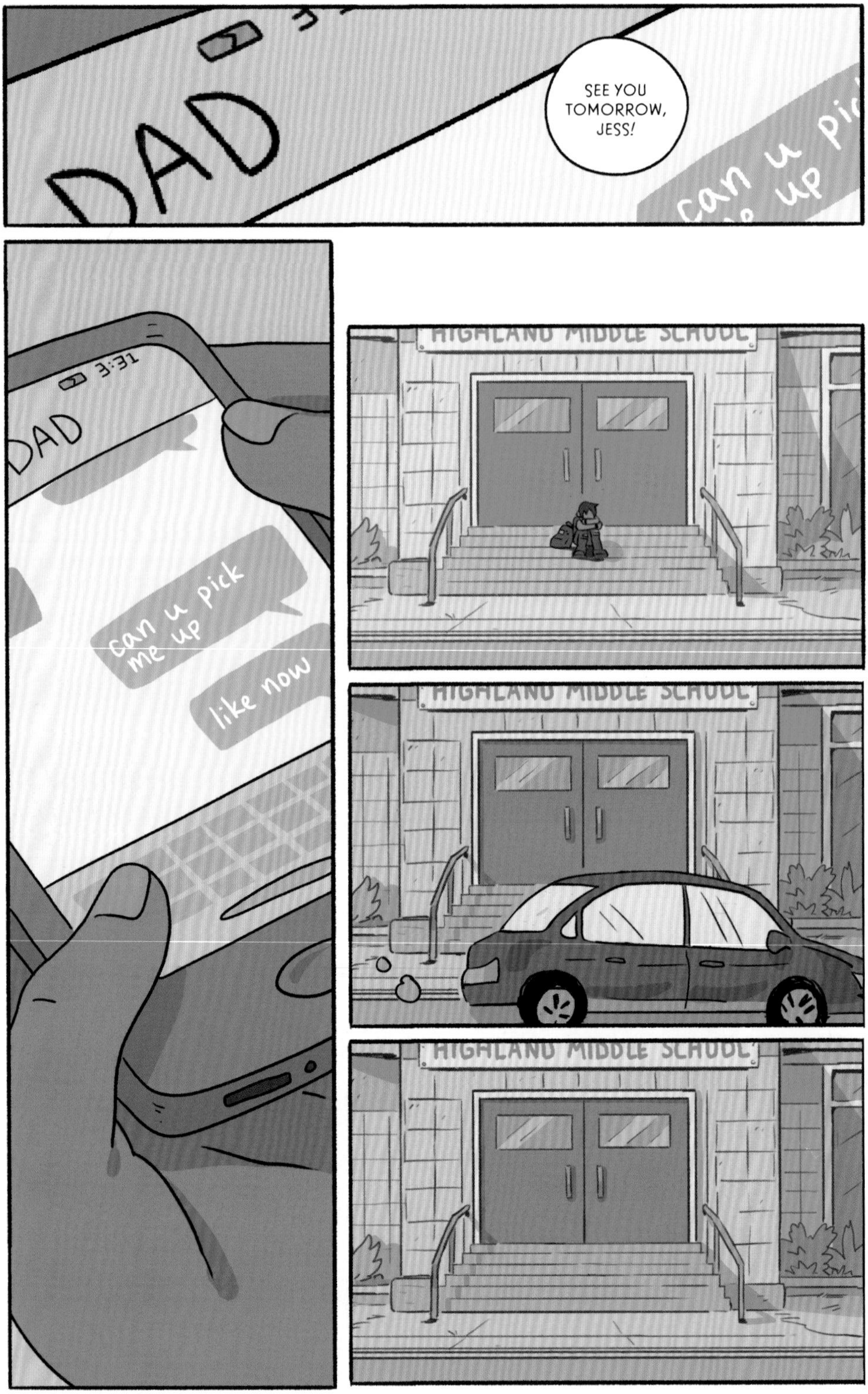
DAD
3:3
SEE YOU TOMORROW, JESS!
can u pick me up
3:31
DAD
can u pick me up
like now
HIGHLAND MIDDLE SCHOOL
HIGHLAND MIDDLE SCHOOL
HIGHLAND MIDDLE SCHOOL

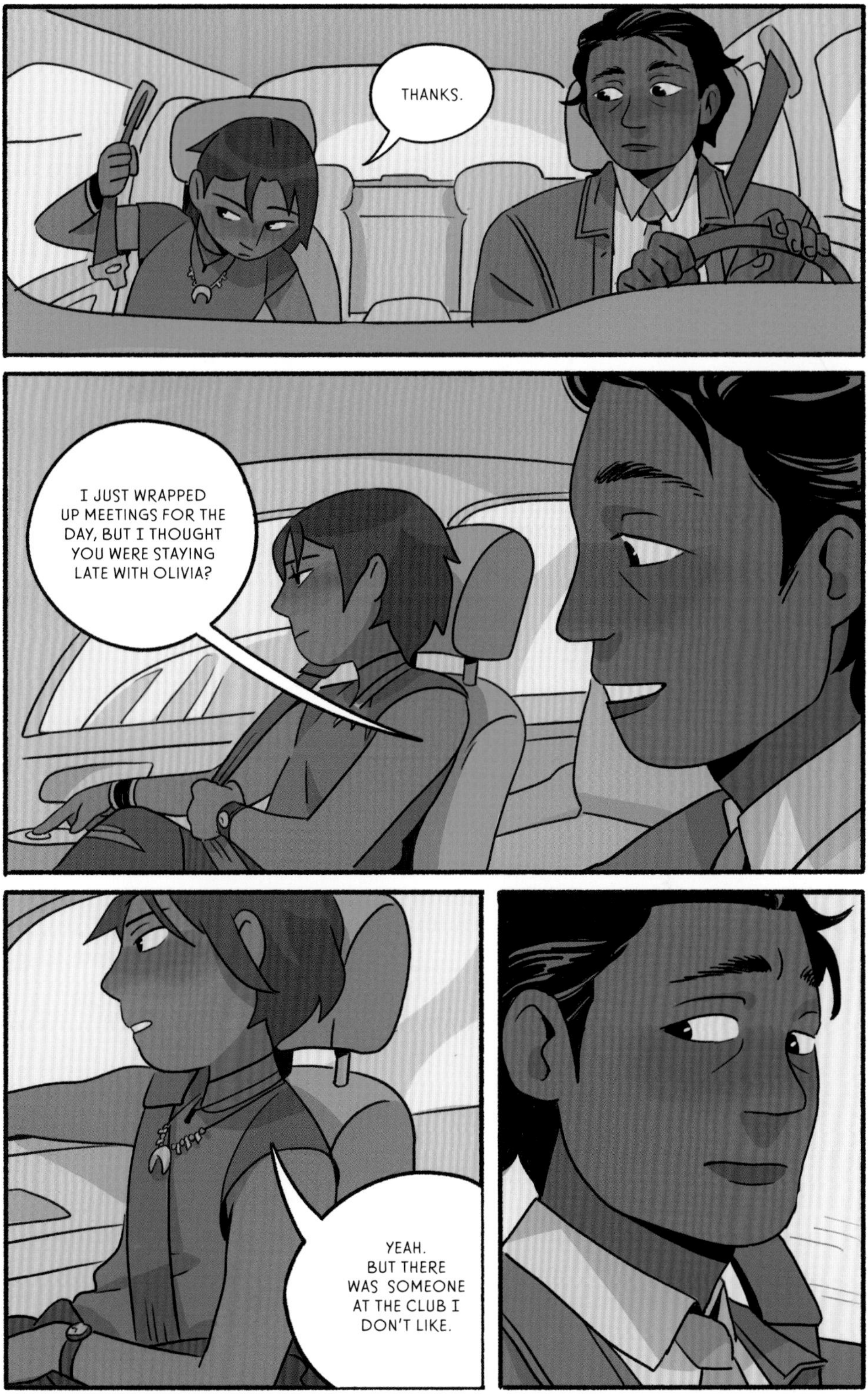
THANKS.
I JUST WRAPPED UP MEETINGS FOR THE DAY, BUT I THOUGHT YOU WERE STAYING LATE WITH OLIVIA?
YEAH. BUT THERE WAS SOMEONE AT THE CLUB I DON'T LIKE.

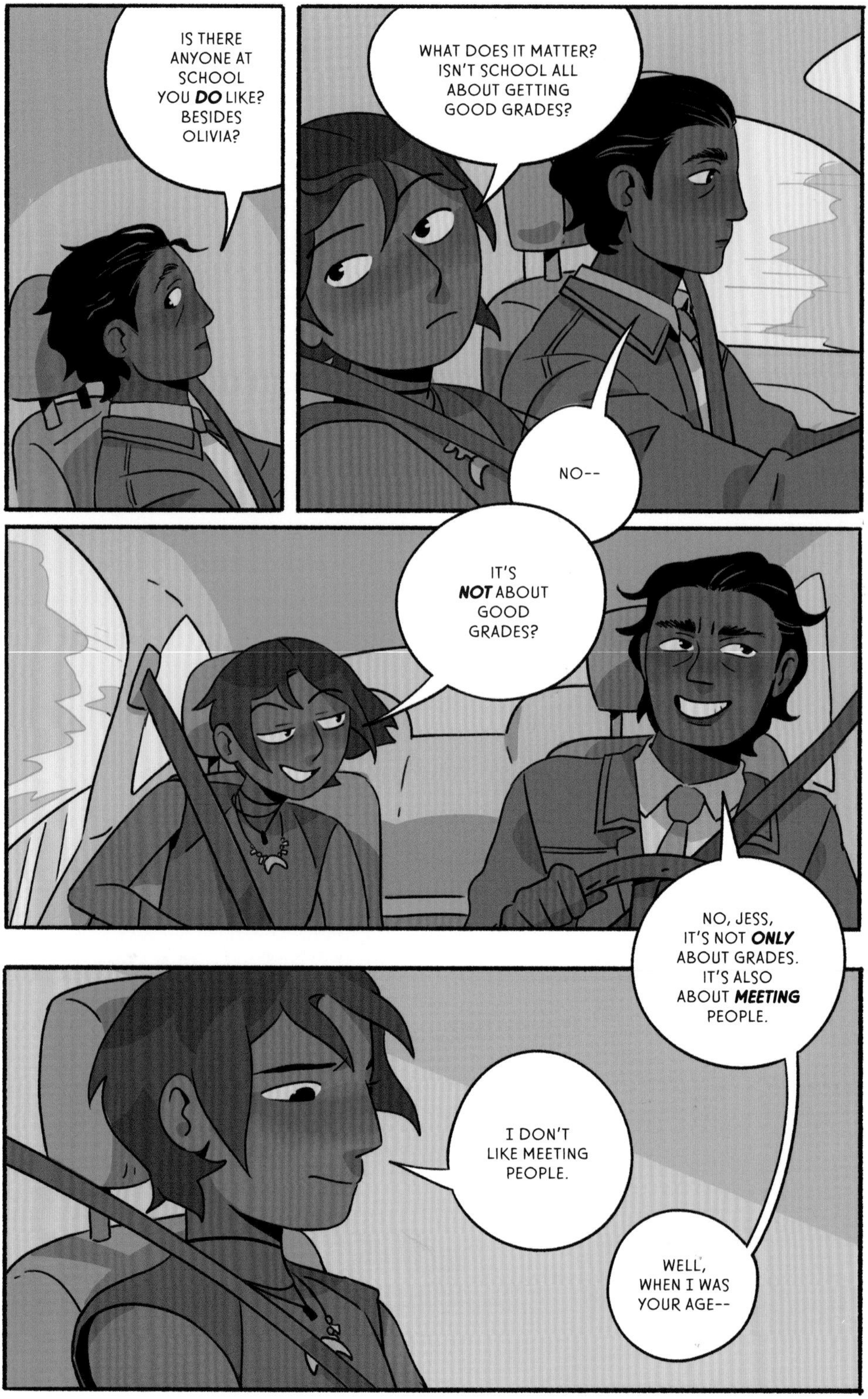
IS THERE ANYONE AT SCHOOL YOU **DO** LIKE? BESIDES OLIVIA?
WHAT DOES IT MATTER? ISN'T SCHOOL ALL ABOUT GETTING GOOD GRADES?
NO--
IT'S **NOT** ABOUT GOOD GRADES?
NO, JESS, IT'S NOT **ONLY** ABOUT GRADES. IT'S ALSO ABOUT **MEETING** PEOPLE.
I DON'T LIKE MEETING PEOPLE.
WELL, WHEN I WAS YOUR AGE--

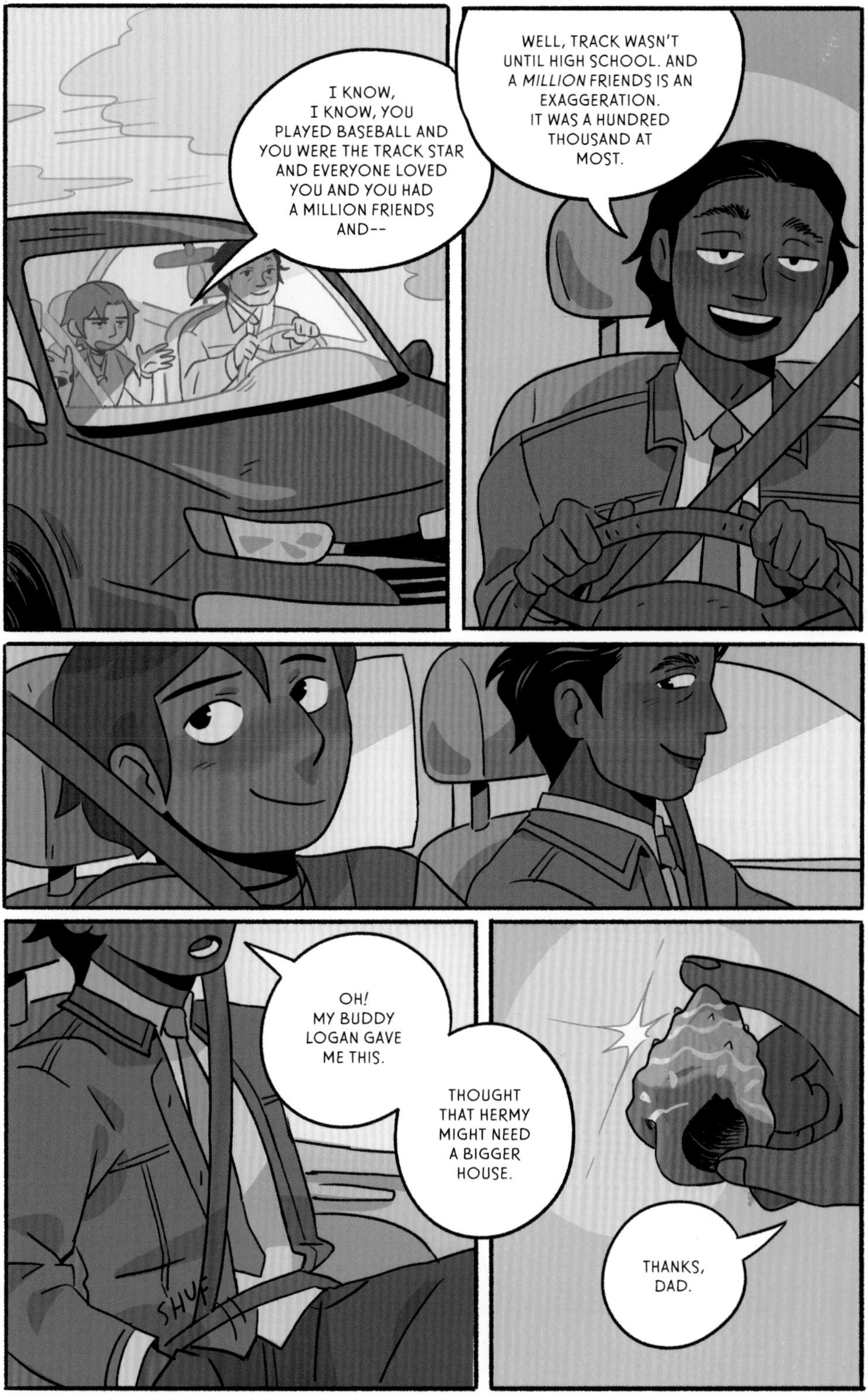
I KNOW, I KNOW, YOU PLAYED BASEBALL AND YOU WERE THE TRACK STAR AND EVERYONE LOVED YOU AND YOU HAD A MILLION FRIENDS AND--
WELL, TRACK WASN'T UNTIL HIGH SCHOOL. AND A *MILLION* FRIENDS IS AN EXAGGERATION. IT WAS A HUNDRED THOUSAND AT MOST.
OH! MY BUDDY LOGAN GAVE ME THIS.
THOUGHT THAT HERMY MIGHT NEED A BIGGER HOUSE.
SHUF
THANKS, DAD.

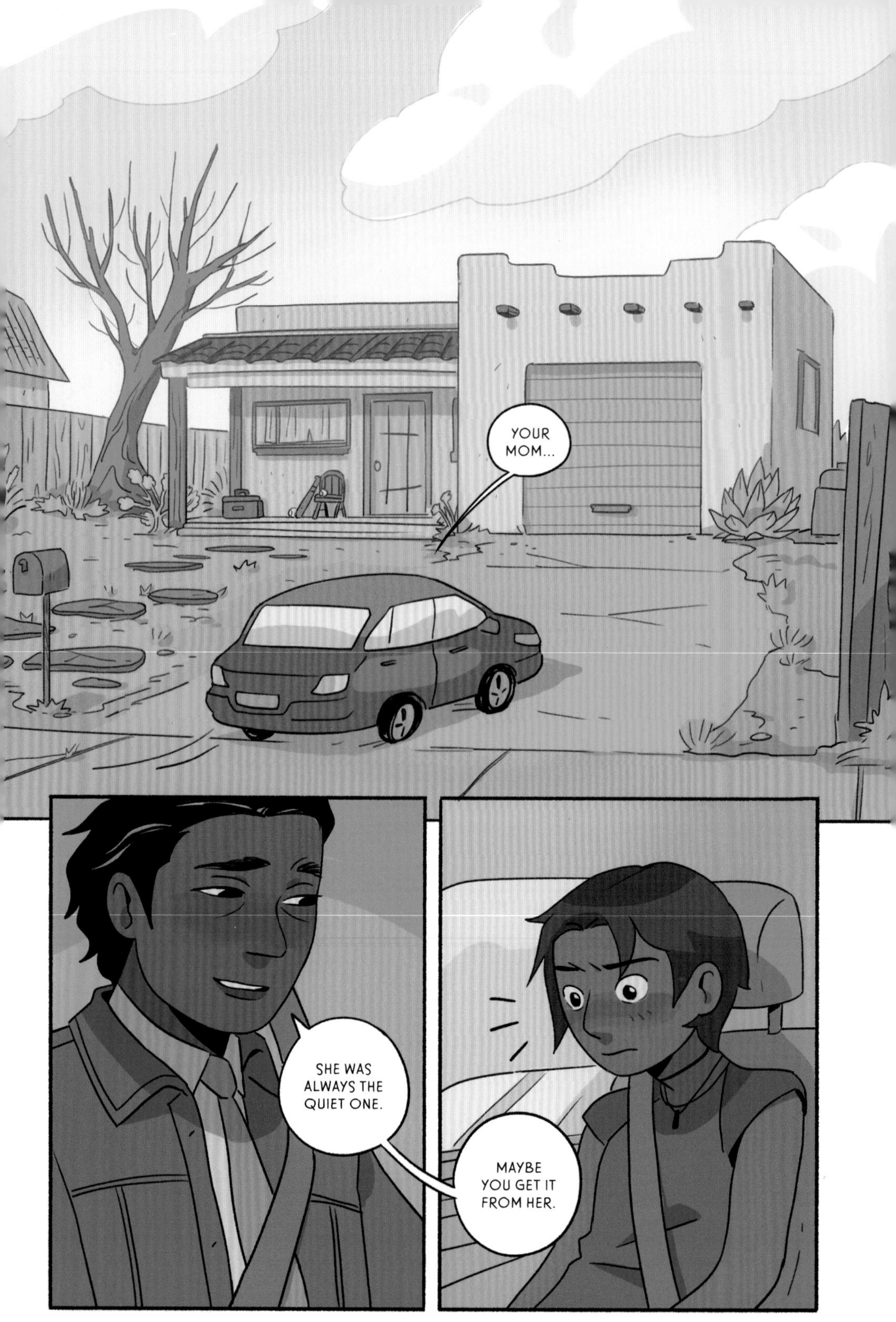
YOUR MOM...
SHE WAS ALWAYS THE QUIET ONE.
MAYBE YOU GET IT FROM HER.

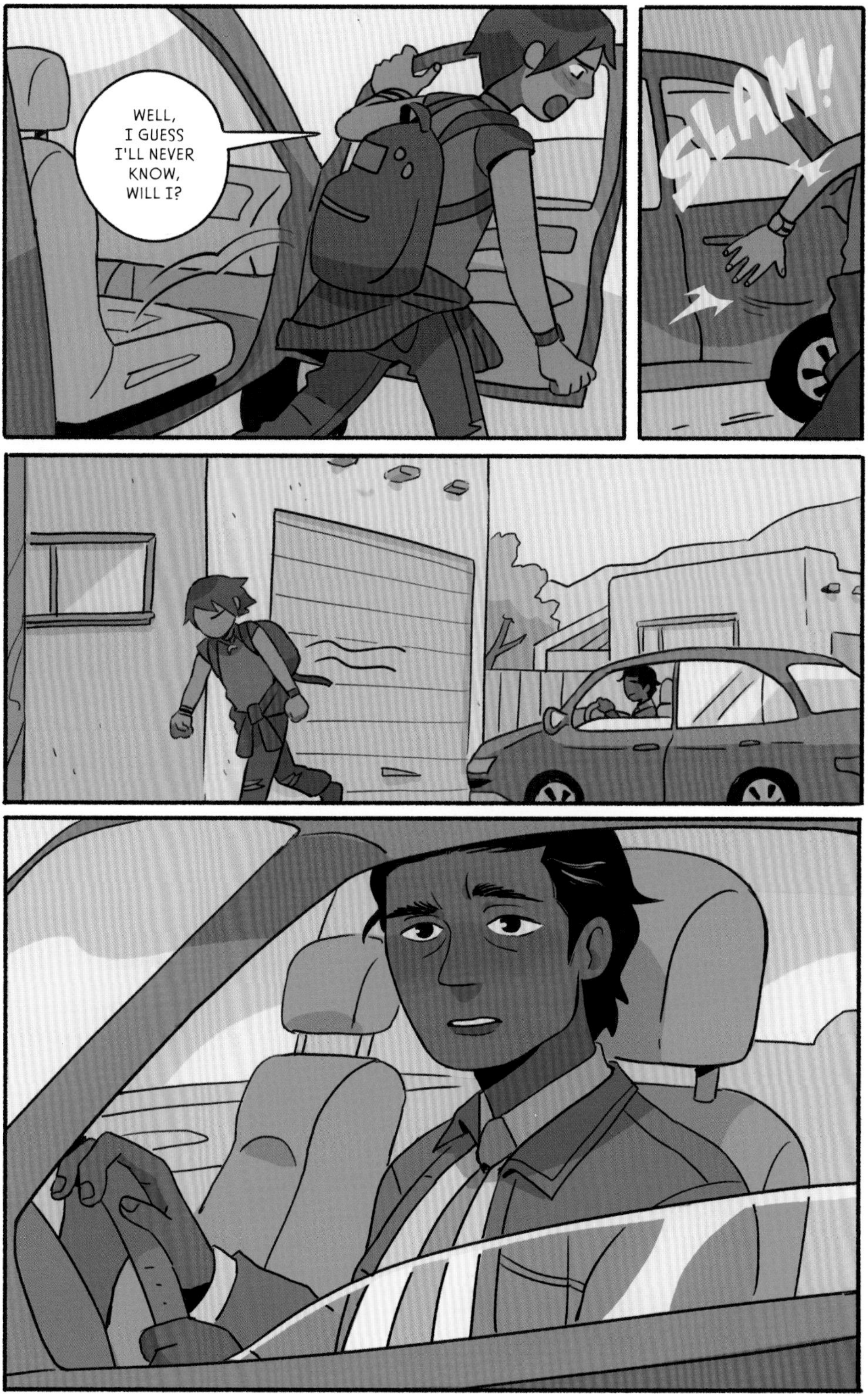
WELL, I GUESS I'LL NEVER KNOW, WILL I?
SLAM!

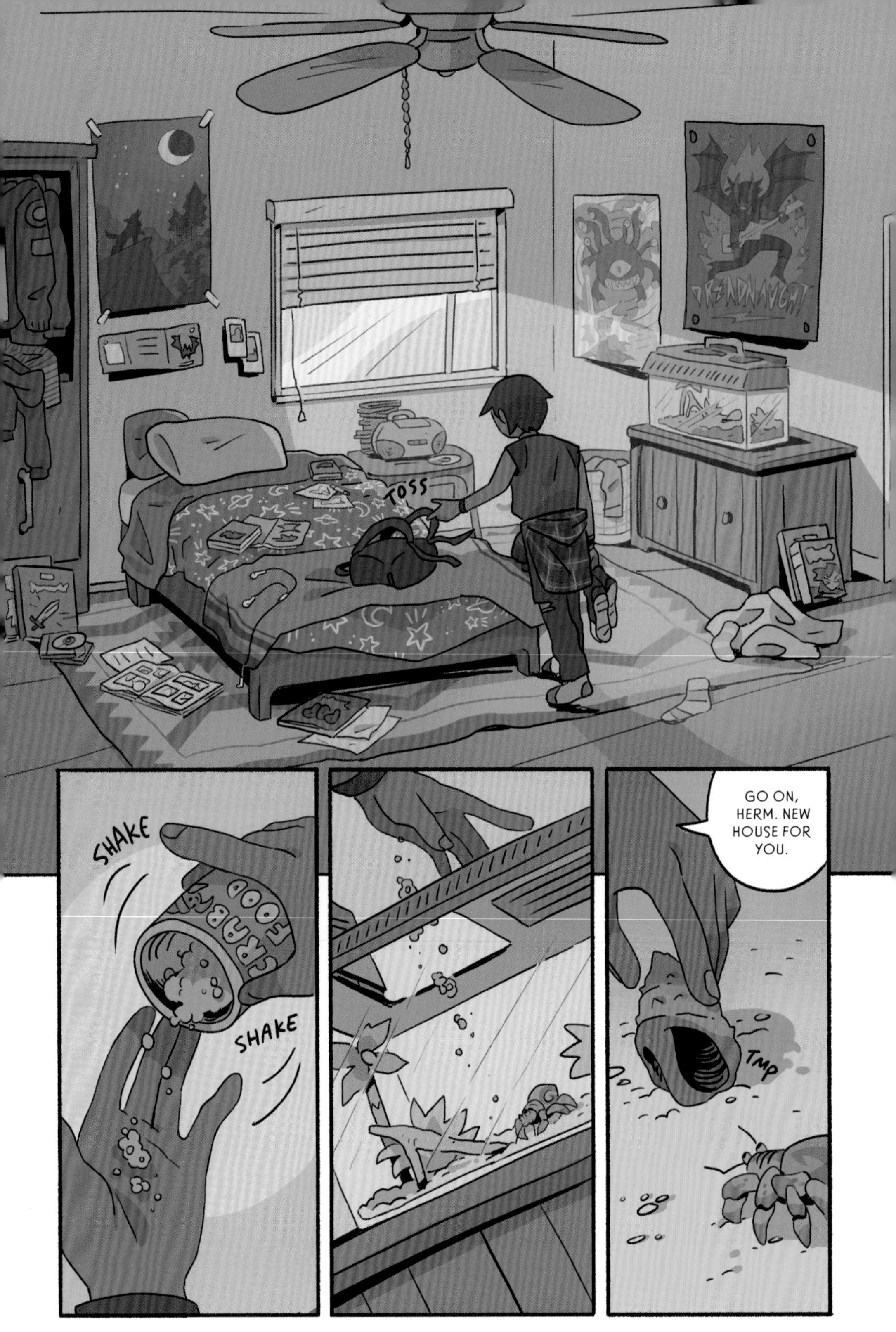
TOSS
SHAKE
SHAKE
GO ON, HERM. NEW HOUSE FOR YOU.
TMP

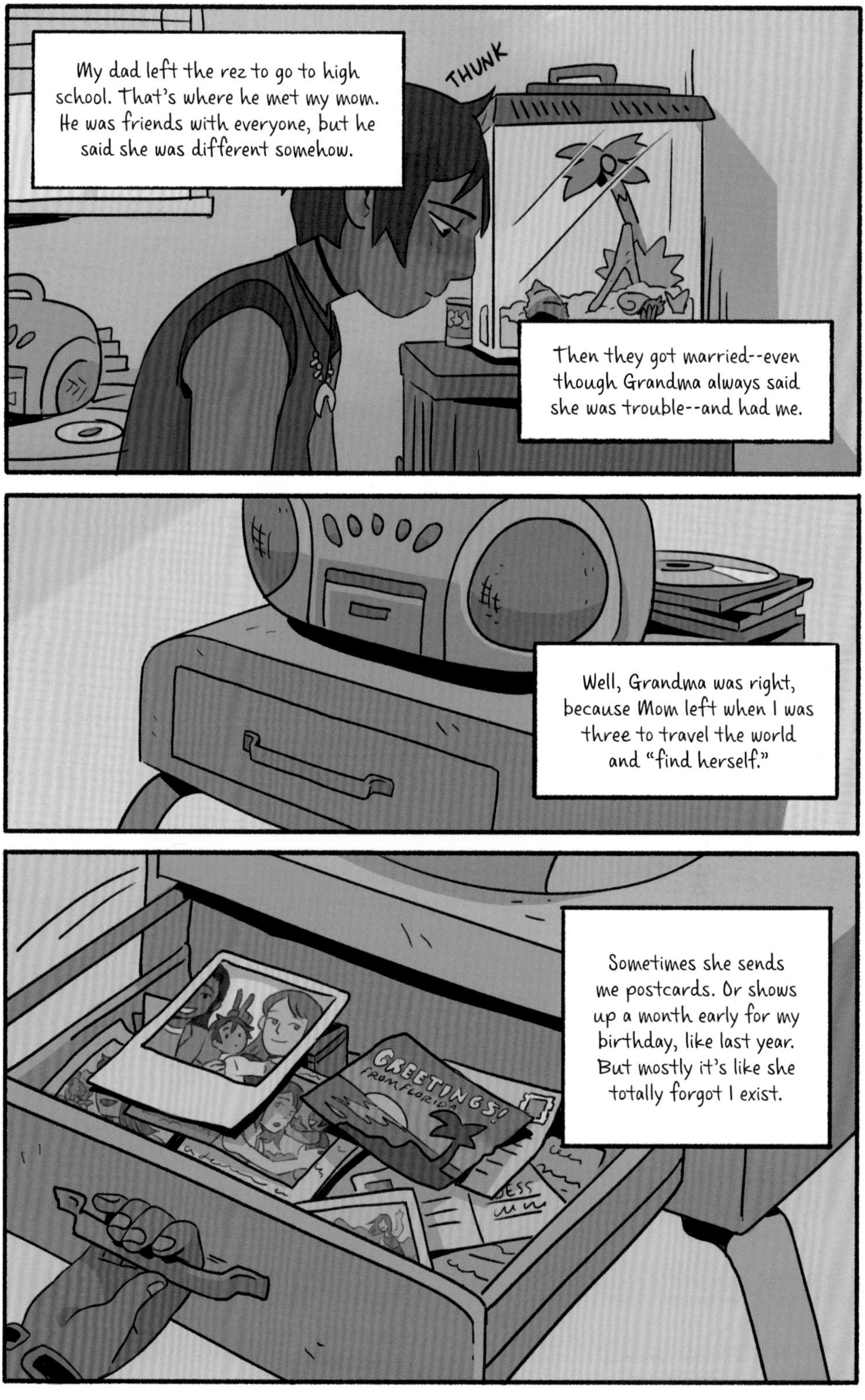
My dad left the rez to go to high school. That's where he met my mom. He was friends with everyone, but he said she was different somehow.
THUNK
Then they got married--even though Grandma always said she was trouble--and had me.
Well, Grandma was right, because Mom left when I was three to travel the world and "find herself."
Sometimes she sends me postcards. Or shows up a month early for my birthday, like last year. But mostly it's like she totally forgot I exist.
GREETINGS!
FROM FLORIDA

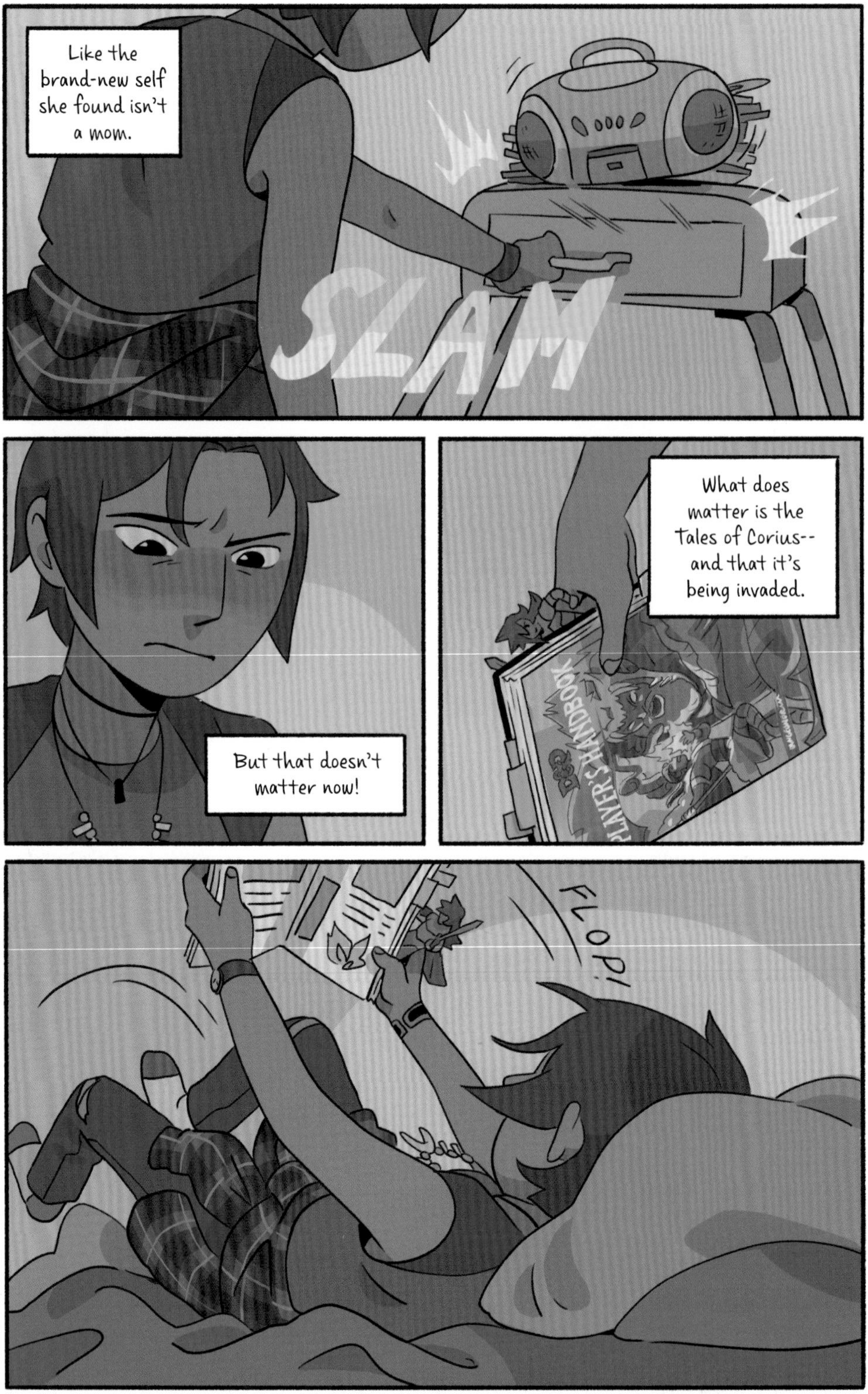
Like the brand-new self she found isn't a mom.
SLAM
But that doesn't matter now!
What does matter is the Tales of Corius-- and that it's being invaded.
PLAYER'S HANDBOOK
FLOP!

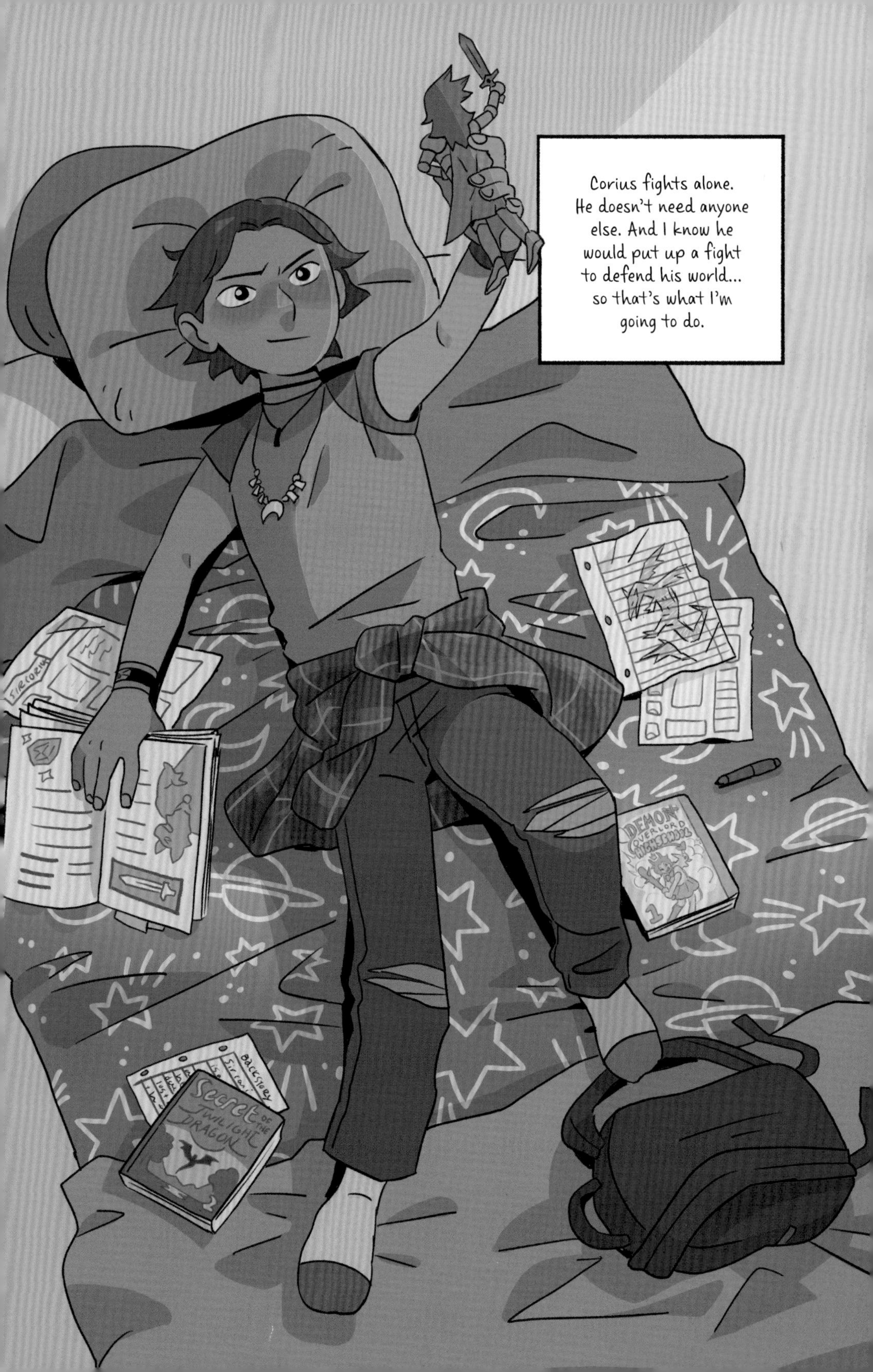
Corius fights alone. He doesn't need anyone else. And I know he would put up a fight to defend his world... so that's what I'm going to do.
DEMON OVERLORD HIGHSCHOOL 1
Secret of the TWILIGHT DRAGON

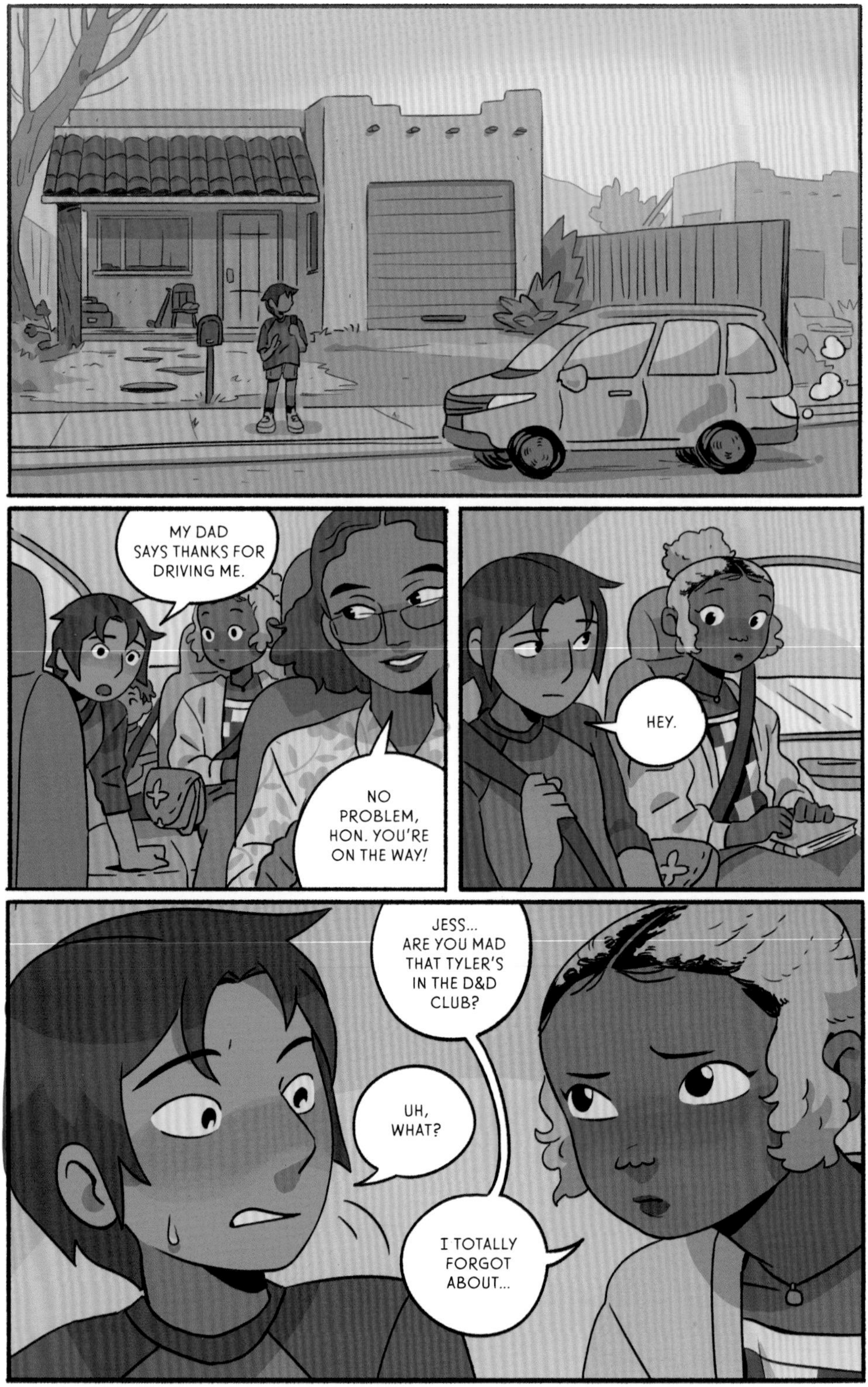
MY DAD SAYS THANKS FOR DRIVING ME.
NO PROBLEM, HON. YOU'RE ON THE WAY!
HEY.
JESS... ARE YOU MAD THAT TYLER'S IN THE D&D CLUB?
UH, WHAT?
I TOTALLY FORGOT ABOUT...

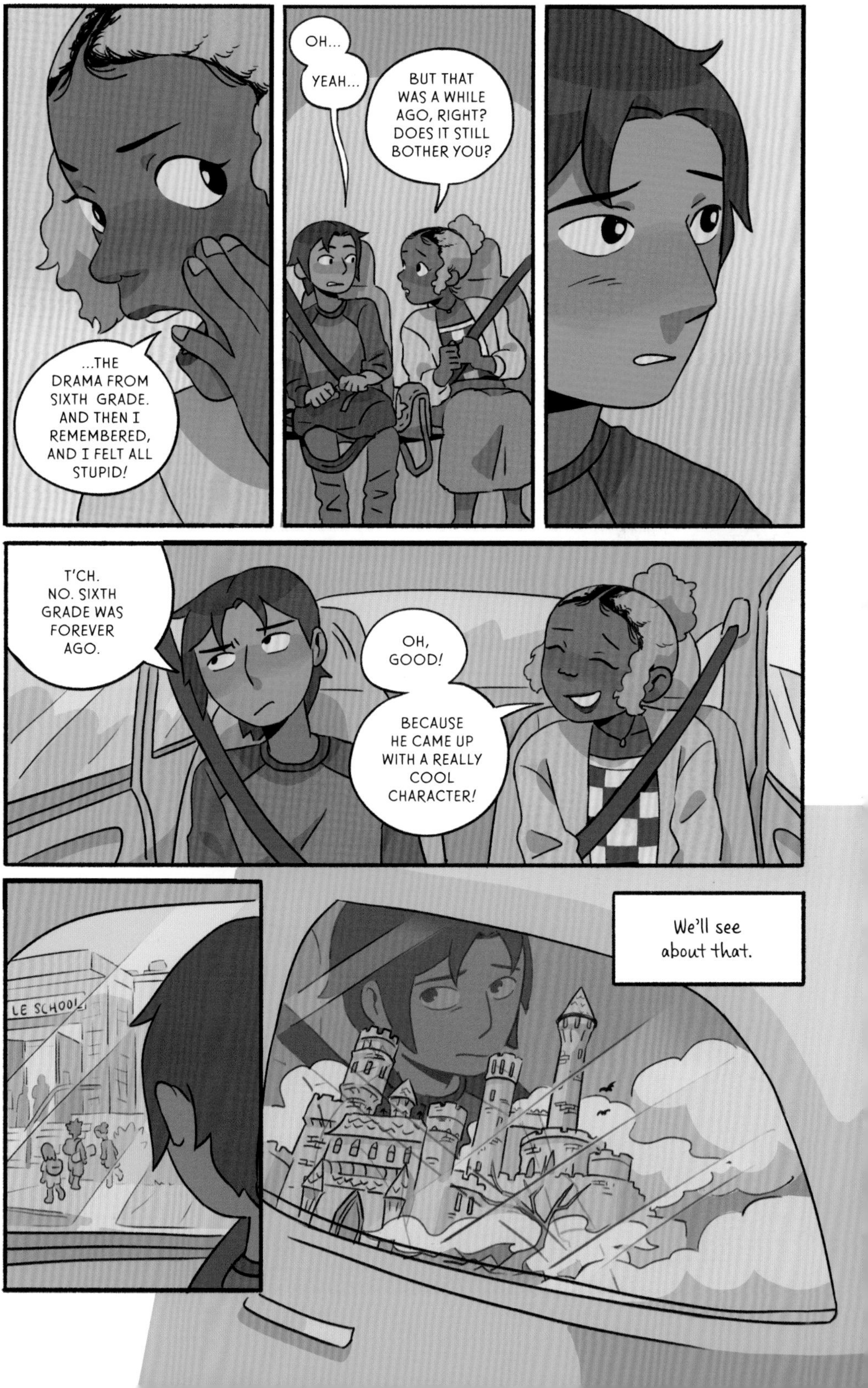
...THE DRAMA FROM SIXTH GRADE. AND THEN I REMEMBERED, AND I FELT ALL STUPID!
OH...
YEAH...
BUT THAT WAS A WHILE AGO, RIGHT? DOES IT STILL BOTHER YOU?
T'CH. NO. SIXTH GRADE WAS FOREVER AGO.
OH, GOOD!
BECAUSE HE CAME UP WITH A REALLY COOL CHARACTER!
LE SCHOOL
We'll see about that.

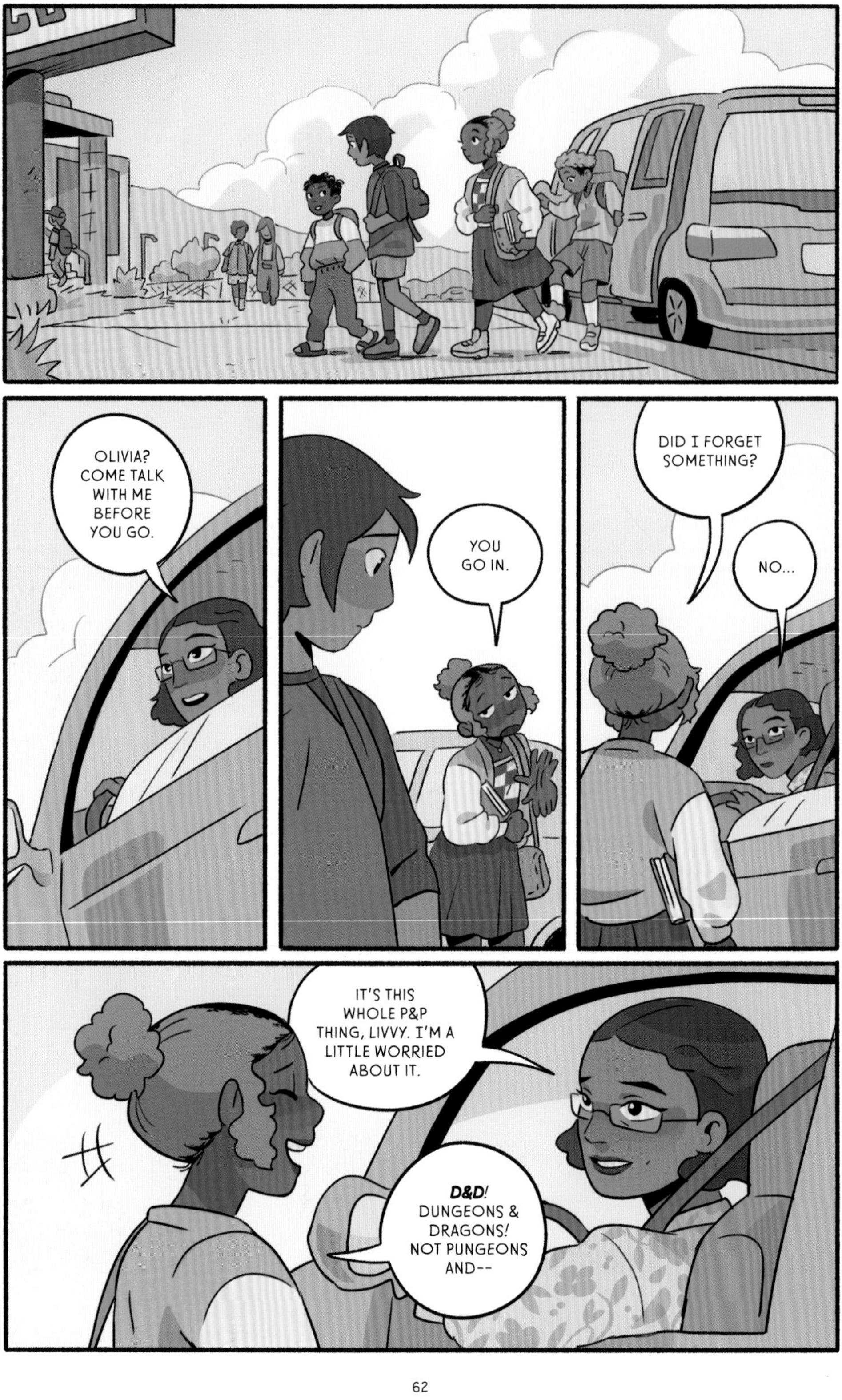
OLIVIA? COME TALK WITH ME BEFORE YOU GO.
YOU GO IN.
DID I FORGET SOMETHING?
NO...
IT'S THIS WHOLE P&P THING, LIVVY. I'M A LITTLE WORRIED ABOUT IT.
D&D! DUNGEONS & DRAGONS! NOT PUNGEONS AND--

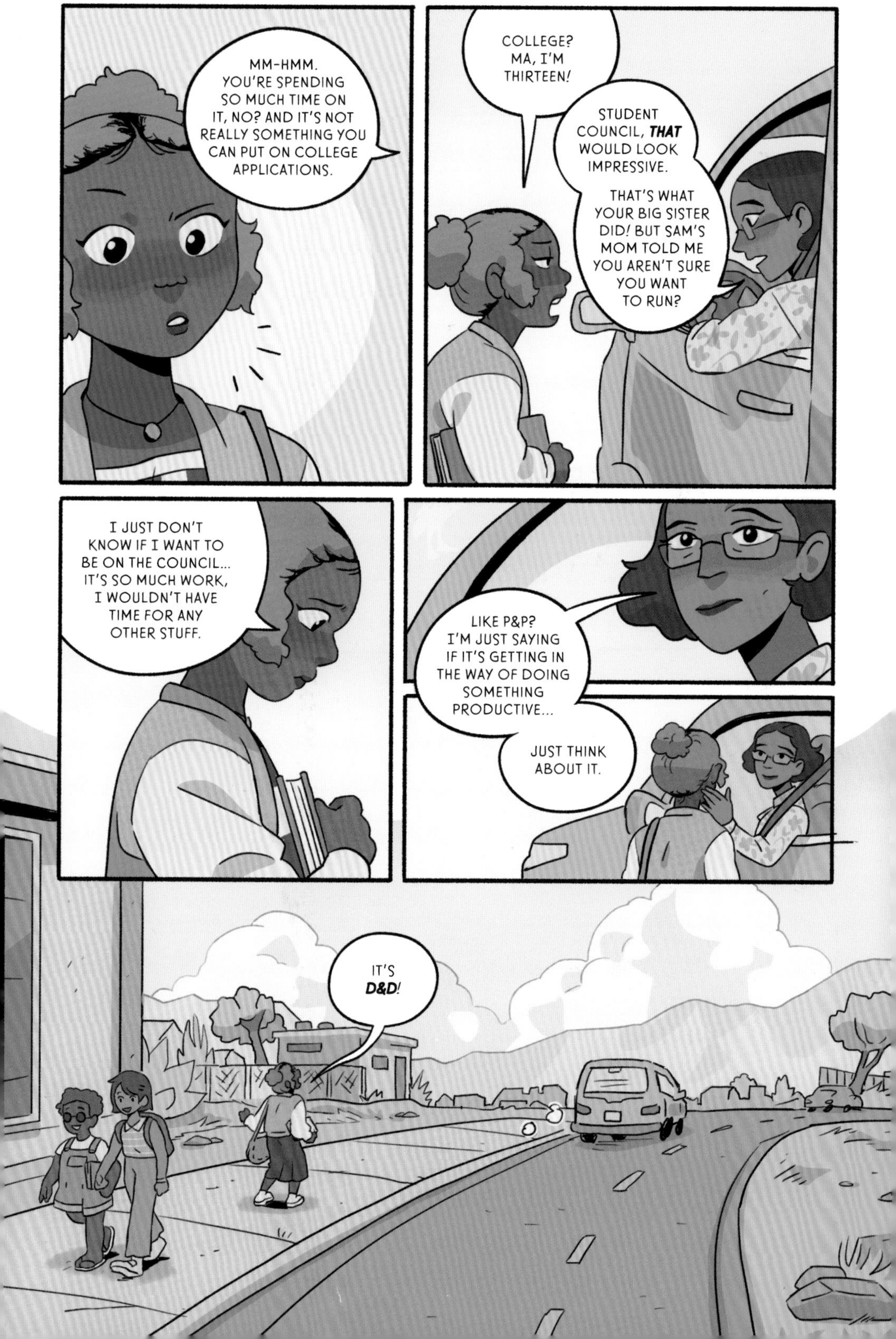
MM-HMM. YOU'RE SPENDING SO MUCH TIME ON IT, NO? AND IT'S NOT REALLY SOMETHING YOU CAN PUT ON COLLEGE APPLICATIONS.
COLLEGE? MA, I'M THIRTEEN!
STUDENT COUNCIL, **THAT** WOULD LOOK IMPRESSIVE.
THAT'S WHAT YOUR BIG SISTER DID! BUT SAM'S MOM TOLD ME YOU AREN'T SURE YOU WANT TO RUN?
I JUST DON'T KNOW IF I WANT TO BE ON THE COUNCIL... IT'S SO MUCH WORK, I WOULDN'T HAVE TIME FOR ANY OTHER STUFF.
LIKE P&P? I'M JUST SAYING IF IT'S GETTING IN THE WAY OF DOING SOMETHING PRODUCTIVE...
JUST THINK ABOUT IT.
IT'S ***D&D!***

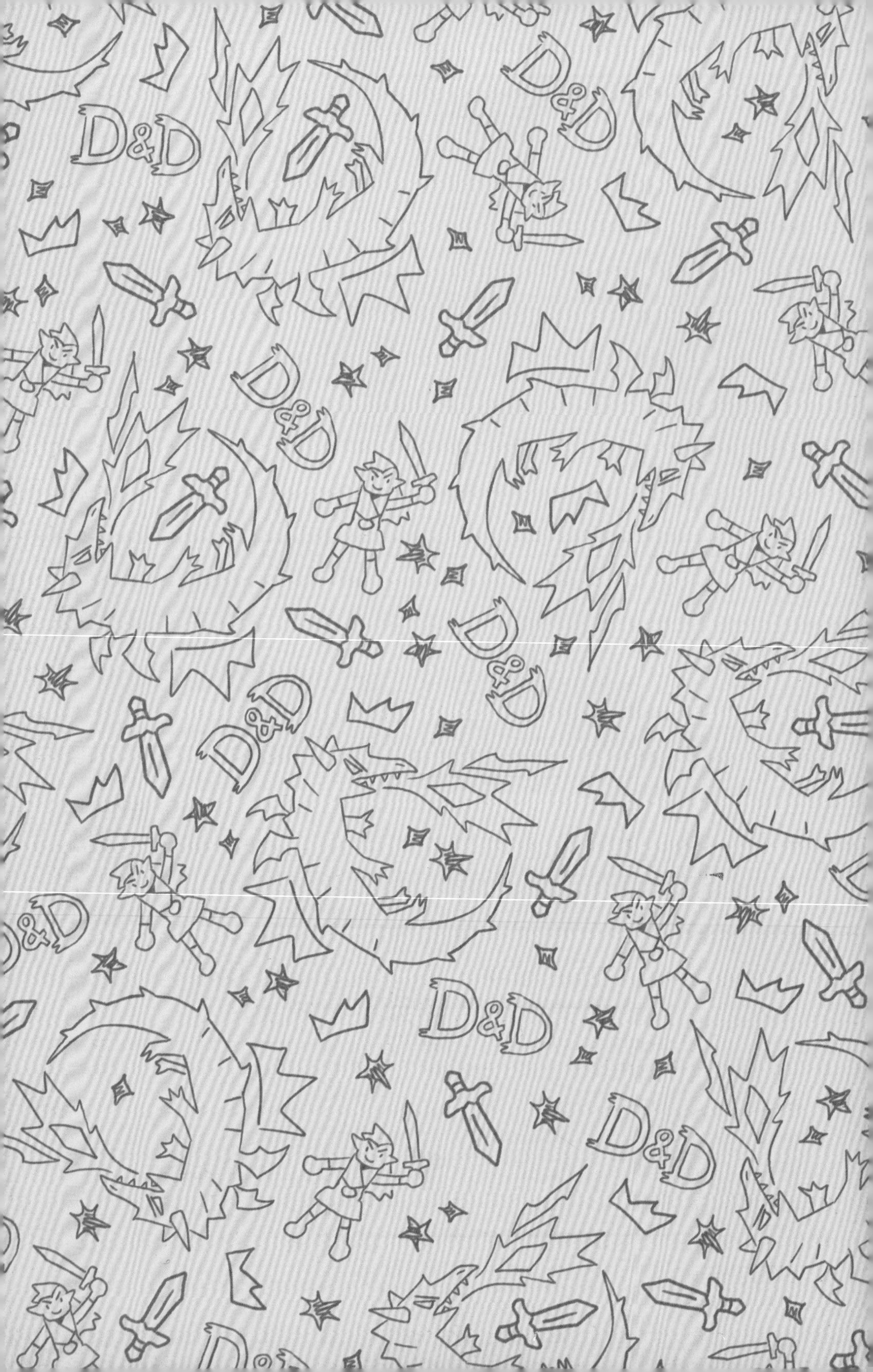
D&D

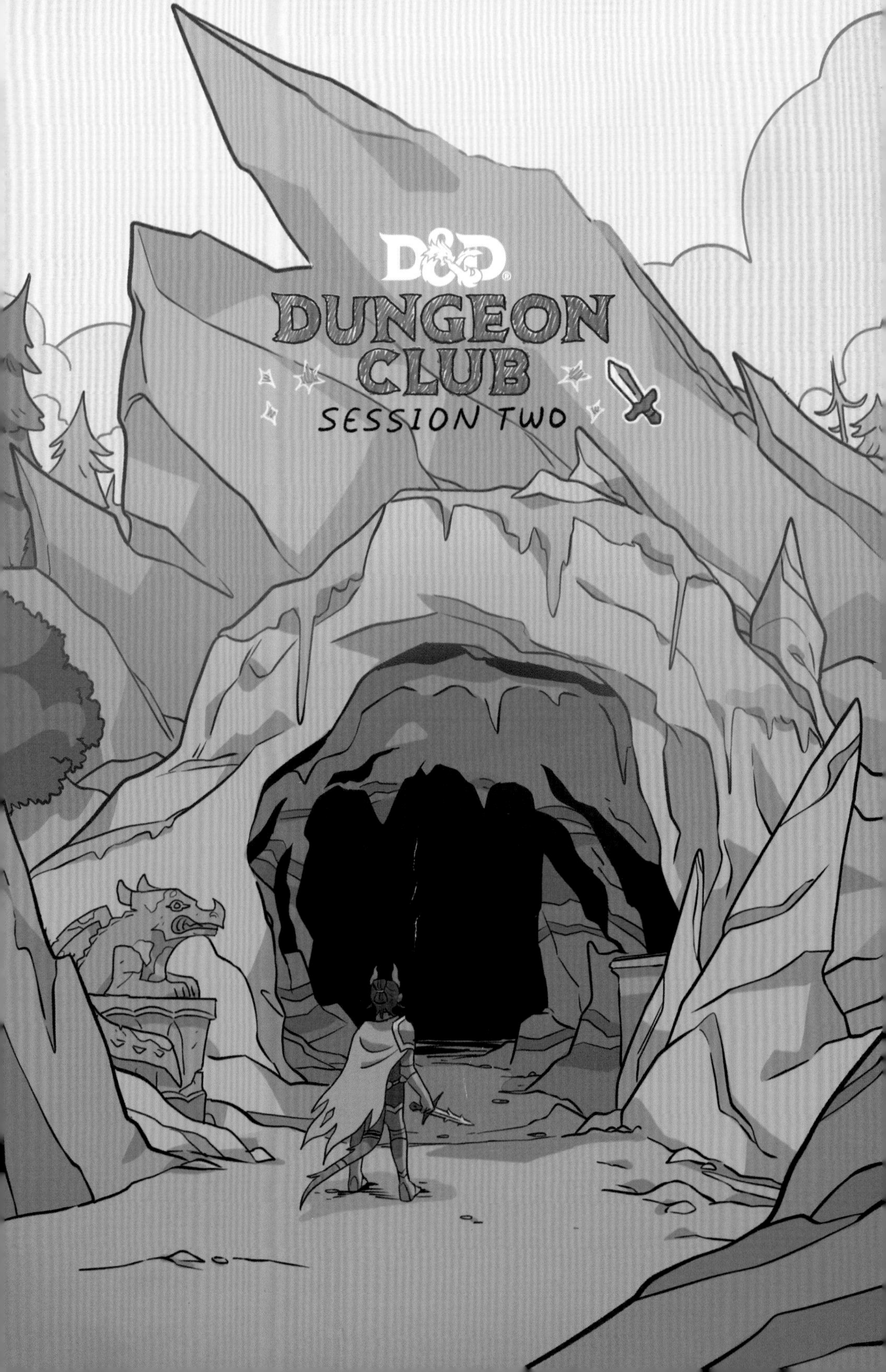
DUNGEON CLUB
SESSION TWO

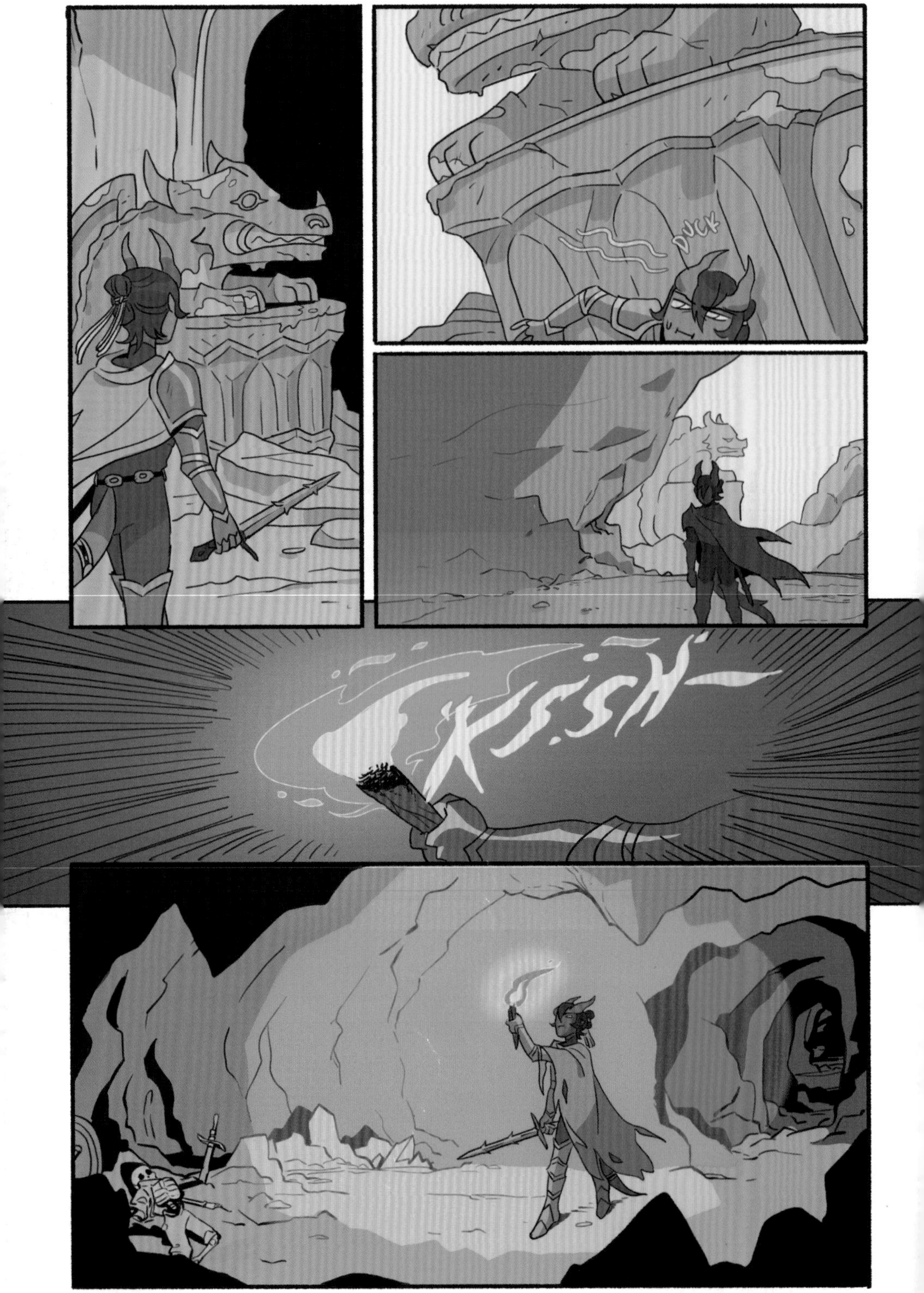
DUCK
KSSH

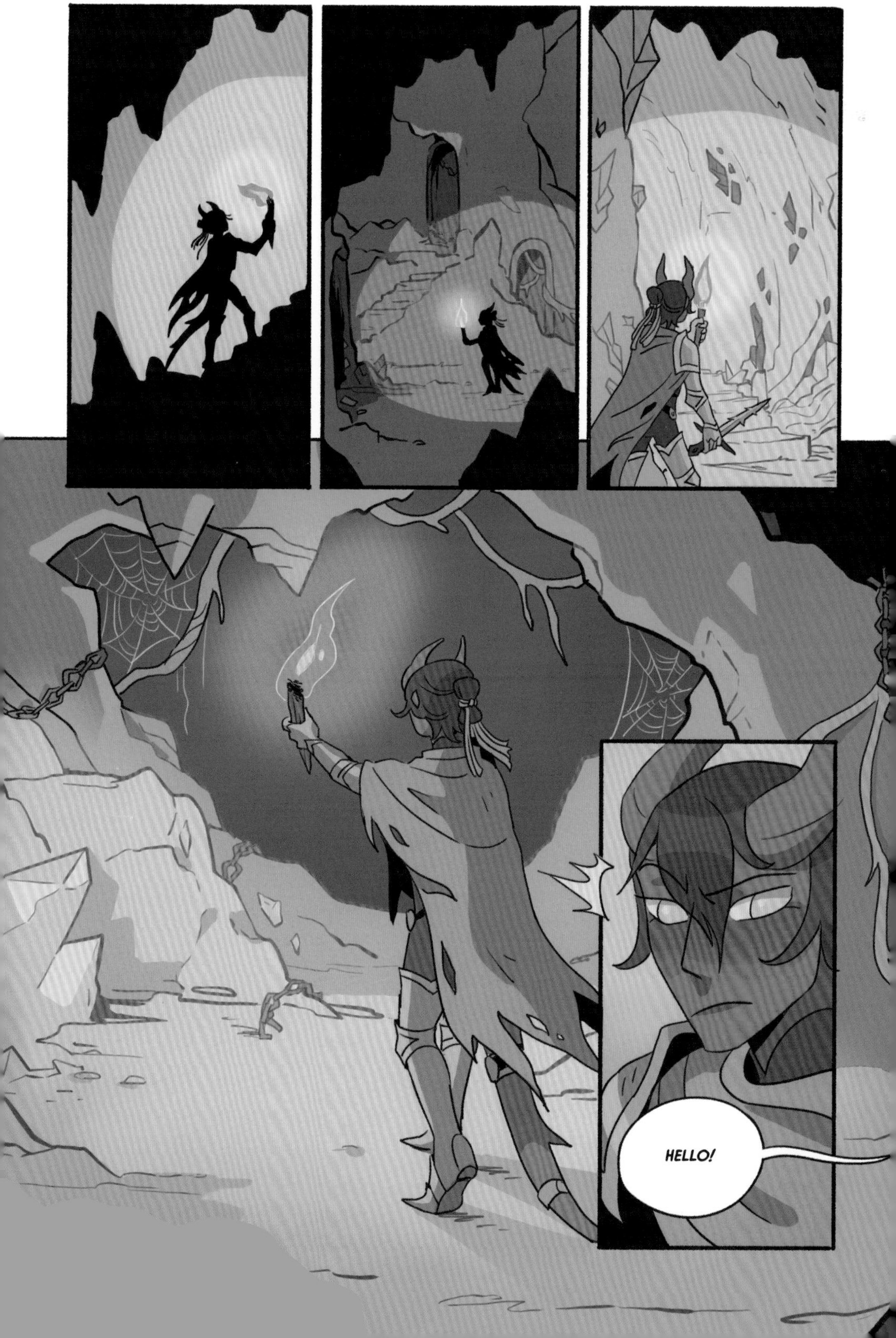
HELLO!

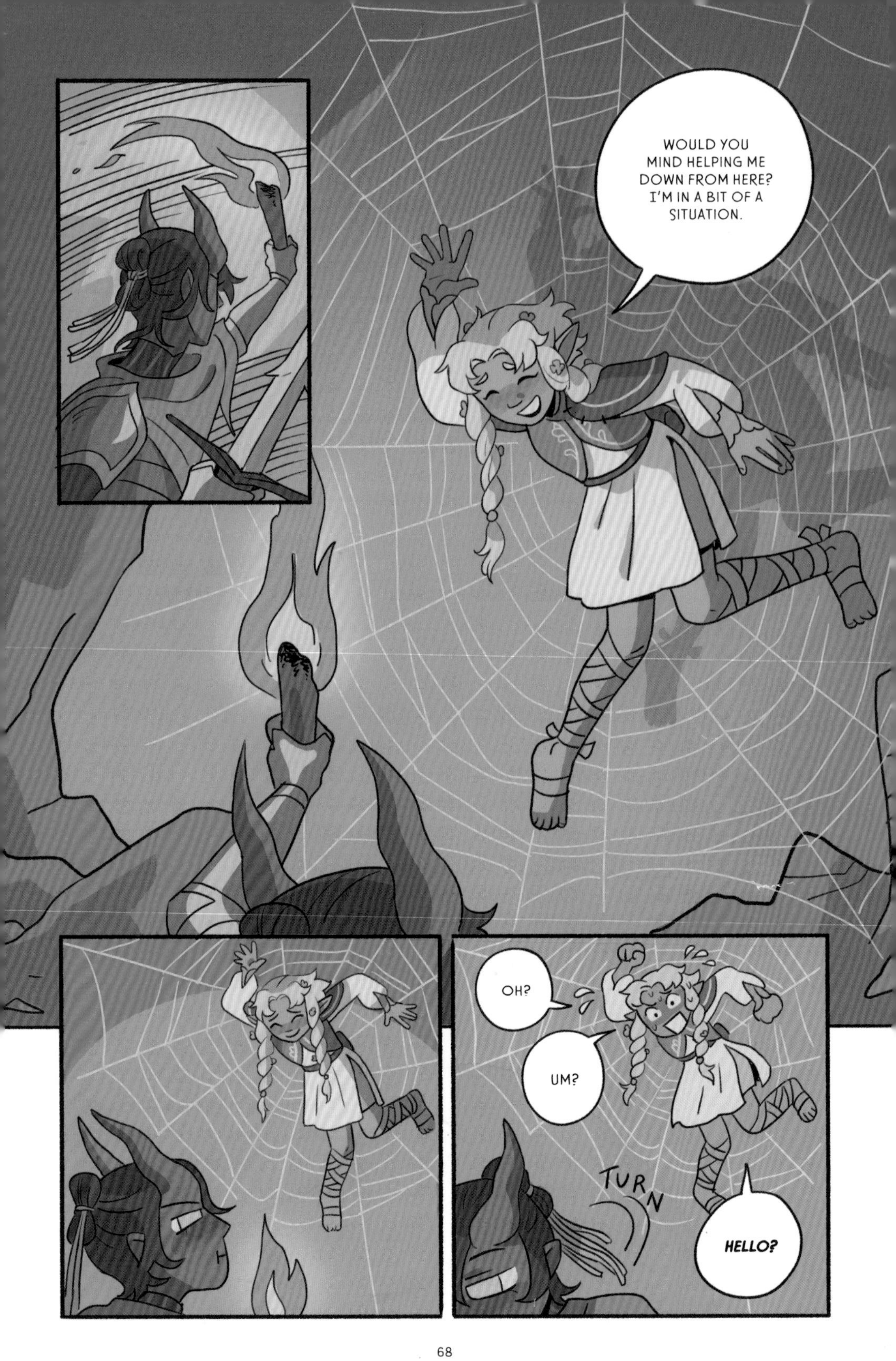
WOULD YOU MIND HELPING ME DOWN FROM HERE? I'M IN A BIT OF A SITUATION.
OH?
UM?
TURN
HELLO?

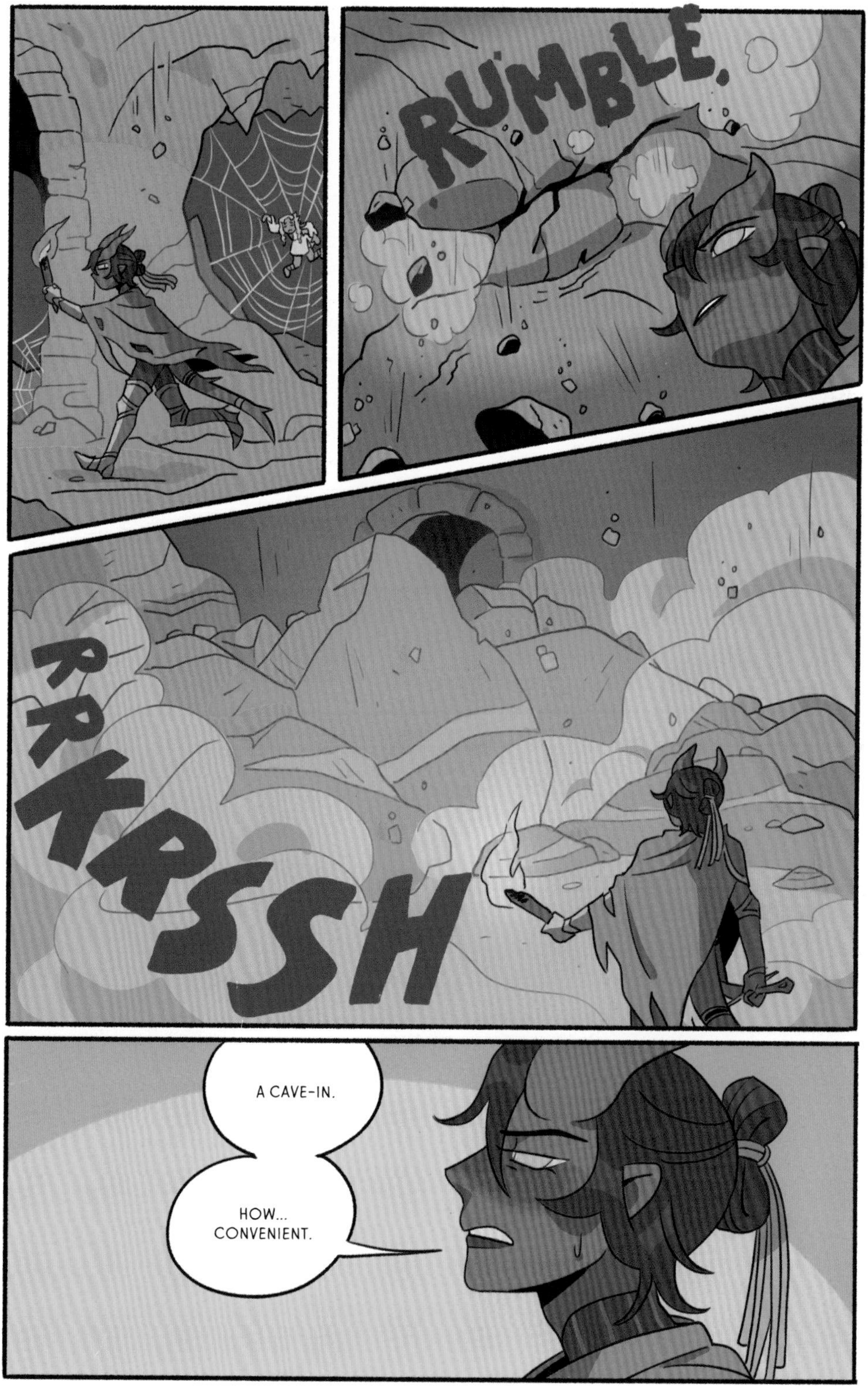
RUMBLE.
RRKRSSH
A CAVE-IN.
HOW... CONVENIENT.

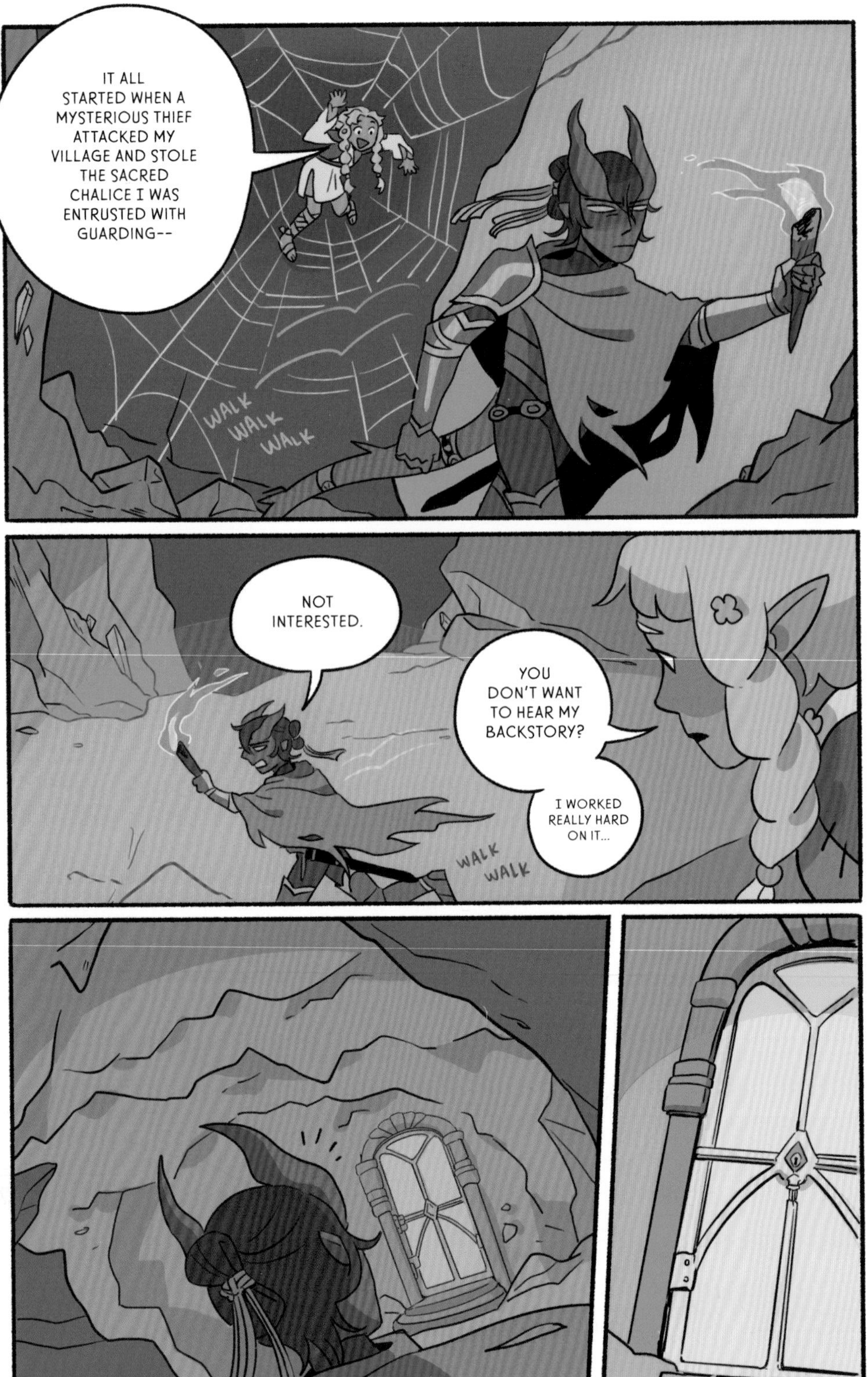

IT ALL STARTED WHEN A MYSTERIOUS THIEF ATTACKED MY VILLAGE AND STOLE THE SACRED CHALICE I WAS ENTRUSTED WITH GUARDING--
WALK WALK WALK
NOT INTERESTED.
YOU DON'T WANT TO HEAR MY BACKSTORY?
I WORKED REALLY HARD ON IT...
WALK WALK

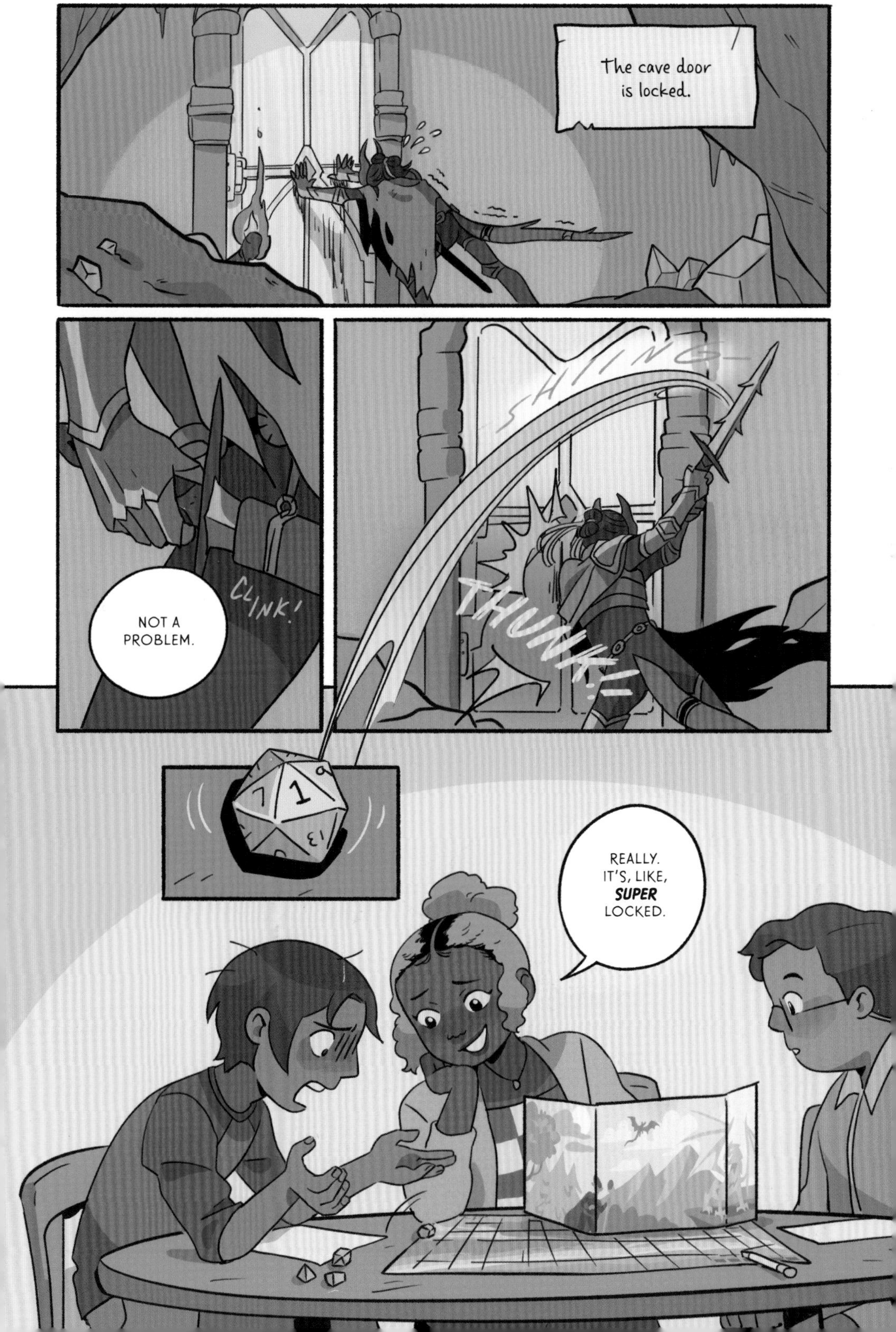

The cave door is locked.
CLINK!
NOT A PROBLEM.
SHIING—
THUNK!!!
REALLY. IT'S, LIKE, **SUPER** LOCKED.

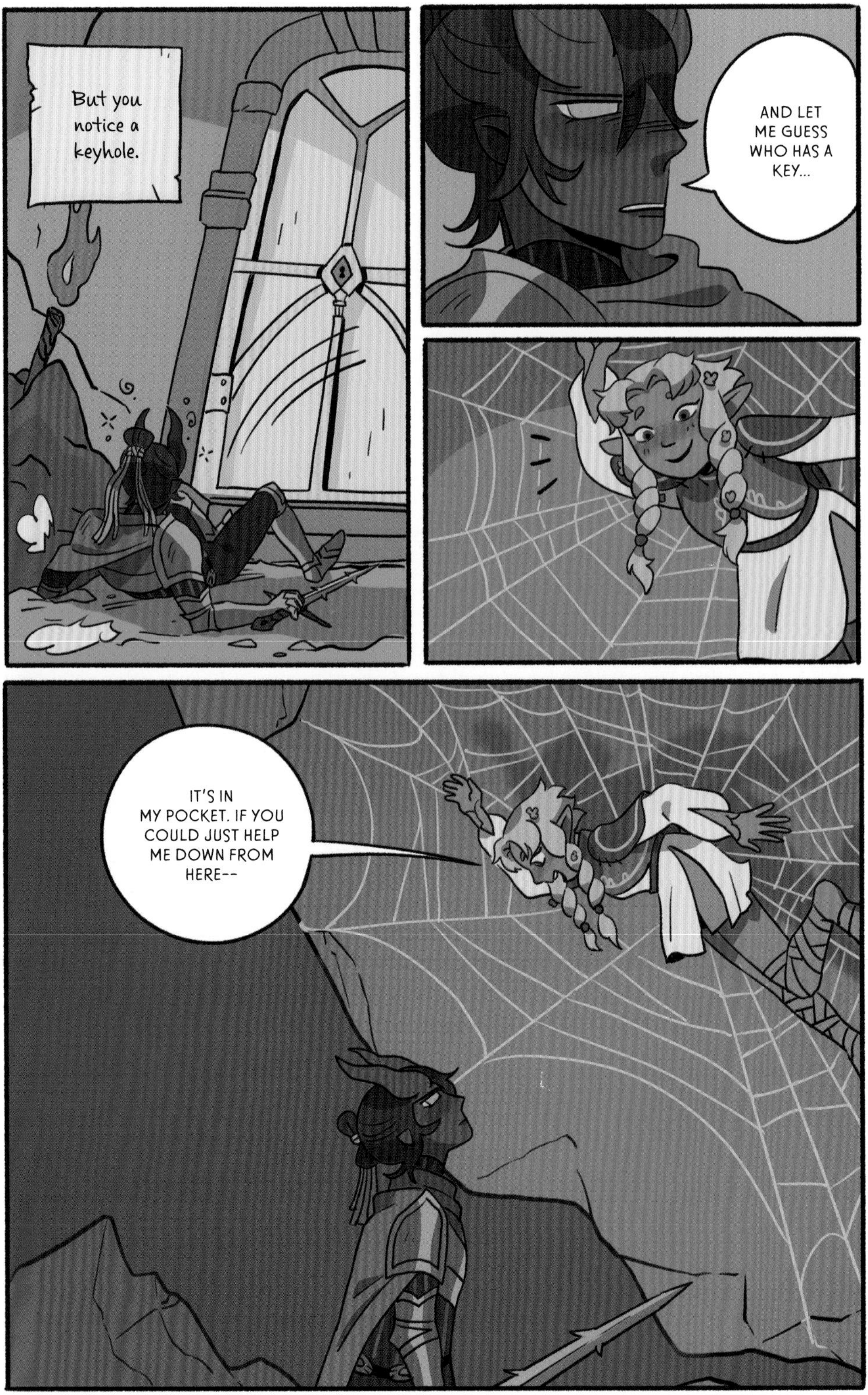
But you notice a keyhole.
AND LET ME GUESS WHO HAS A KEY...
IT'S IN MY POCKET. IF YOU COULD JUST HELP ME DOWN FROM HERE--

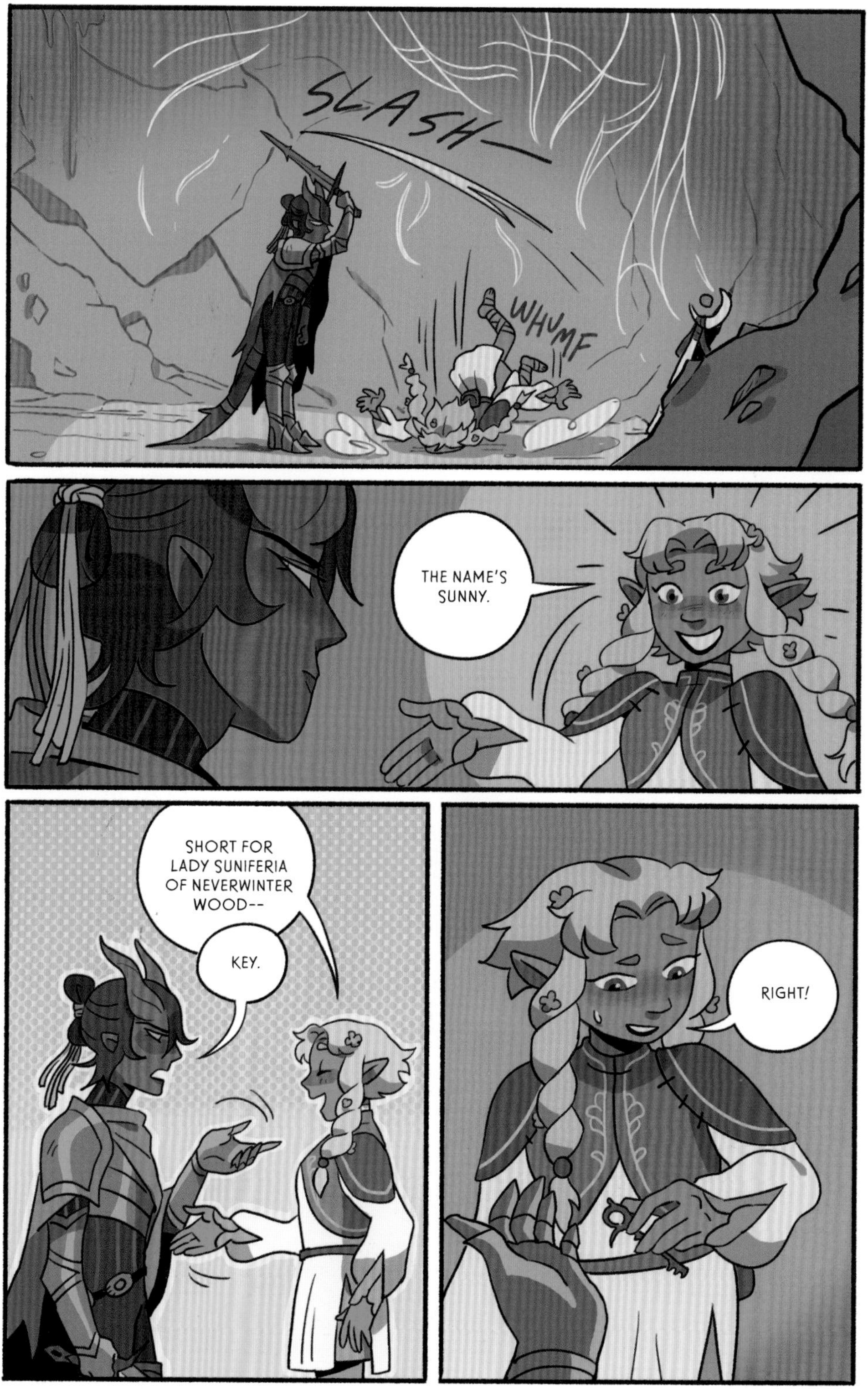
SLASH—
WHUMF
THE NAME'S SUNNY.
SHORT FOR LADY SUNIFERIA OF NEVERWINTER WOOD--
KEY.
RIGHT!

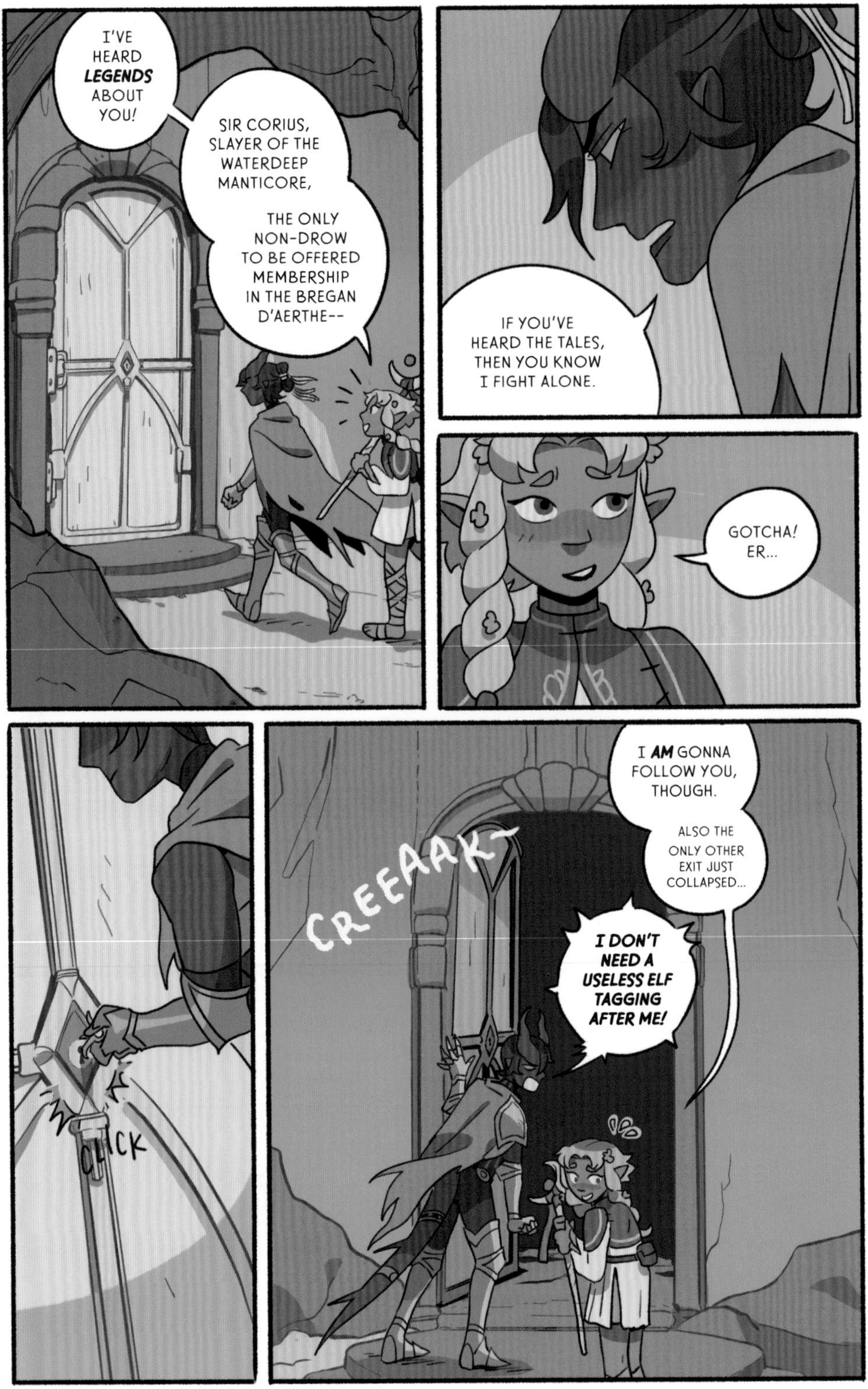
I'VE HEARD **LEGENDS** ABOUT YOU!
SIR CORIUS, SLAYER OF THE WATERDEEP MANTICORE,
THE ONLY NON-DROW TO BE OFFERED MEMBERSHIP IN THE BREGAN D'AERTHE--
IF YOU'VE HEARD THE TALES, THEN YOU KNOW I FIGHT ALONE.
GOTCHA! ER...
CLICK
CREEAAK-
I **AM** GONNA FOLLOW YOU, THOUGH.
ALSO THE ONLY OTHER EXIT JUST COLLAPSED...
I DON'T NEED A USELESS ELF TAGGING AFTER ME!

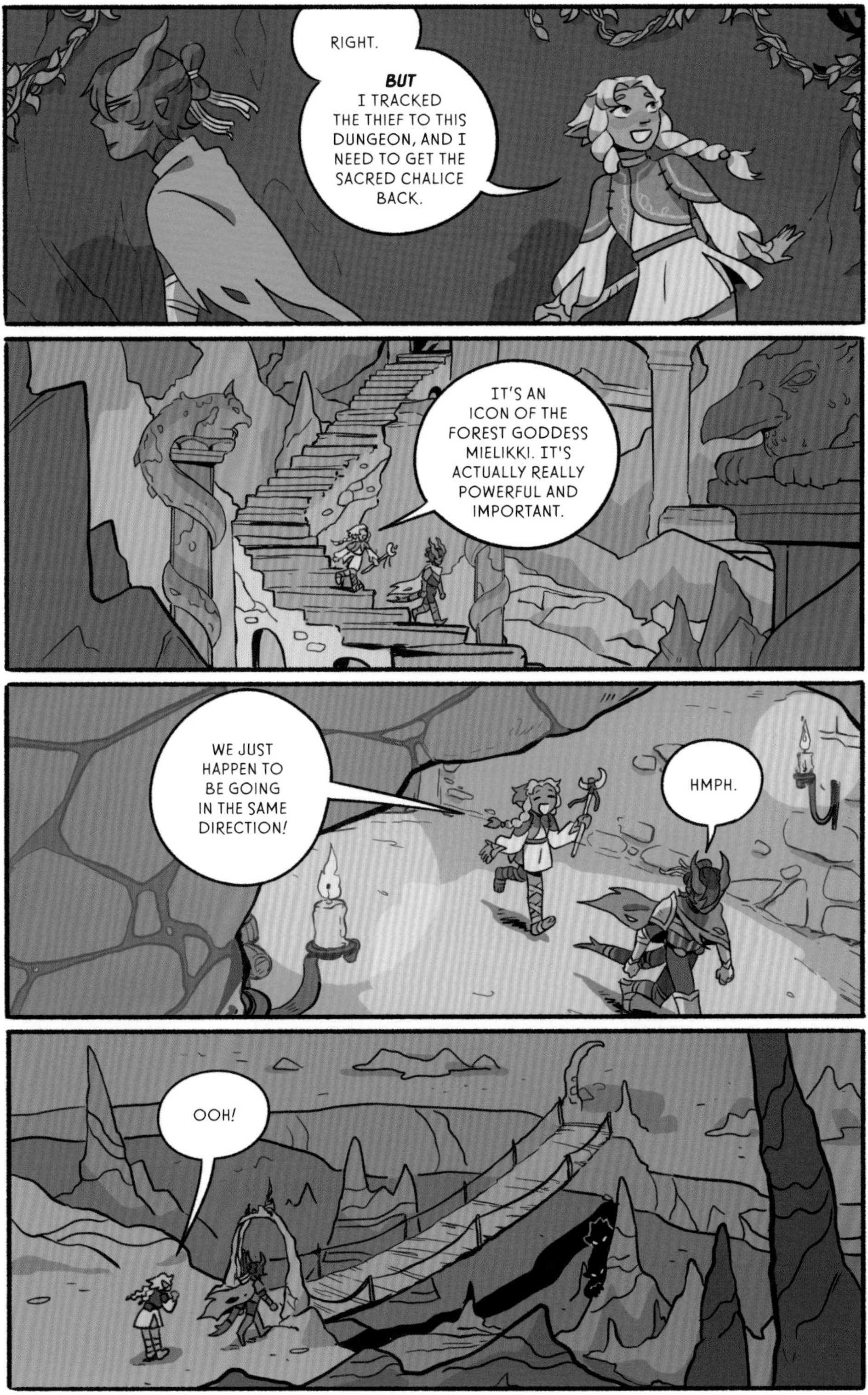
RIGHT.
BUT I TRACKED THE THIEF TO THIS DUNGEON, AND I NEED TO GET THE SACRED CHALICE BACK.
IT'S AN ICON OF THE FOREST GODDESS MIELIKKI. IT'S ACTUALLY REALLY POWERFUL AND IMPORTANT.
WE JUST HAPPEN TO BE GOING IN THE SAME DIRECTION!
HMPH.
OOH!

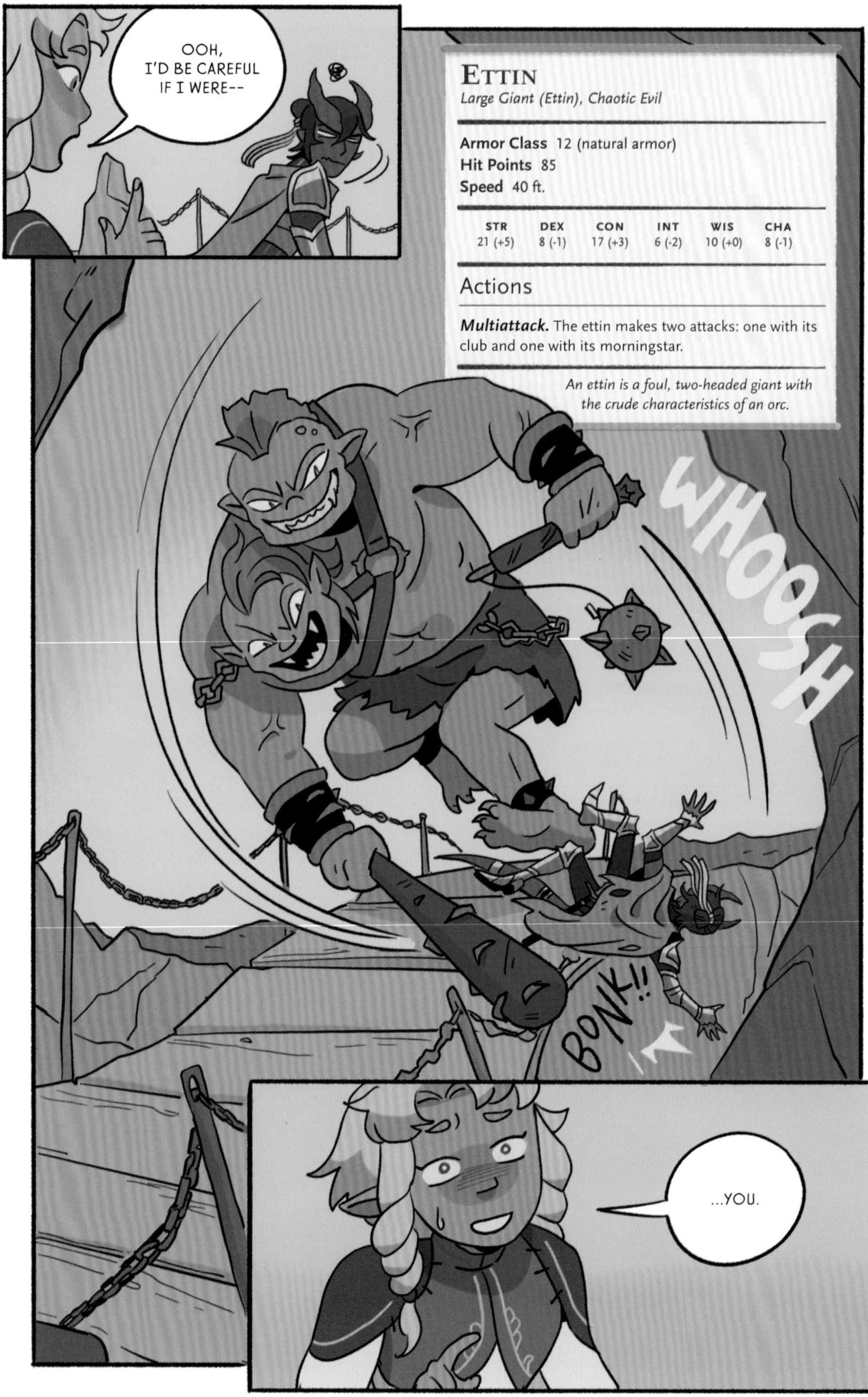
OOH, I'D BE CAREFUL IF I WERE--
ETTIN
Large Giant (Ettin), Chaotic Evil
Armor Class 12 (natural armor)
Hit Points 85
Speed 40 ft.
STR 21 (+5) DEX 8 (-1) CON 17 (+3) INT 6 (-2) WIS 10 (+0) CHA 8 (-1)
Actions
Multiattack. The ettin makes two attacks: one with its club and one with its morningstar.
An ettin is a foul, two-headed giant with the crude characteristics of an orc.
WHOOSH
BONK!!
...YOU.

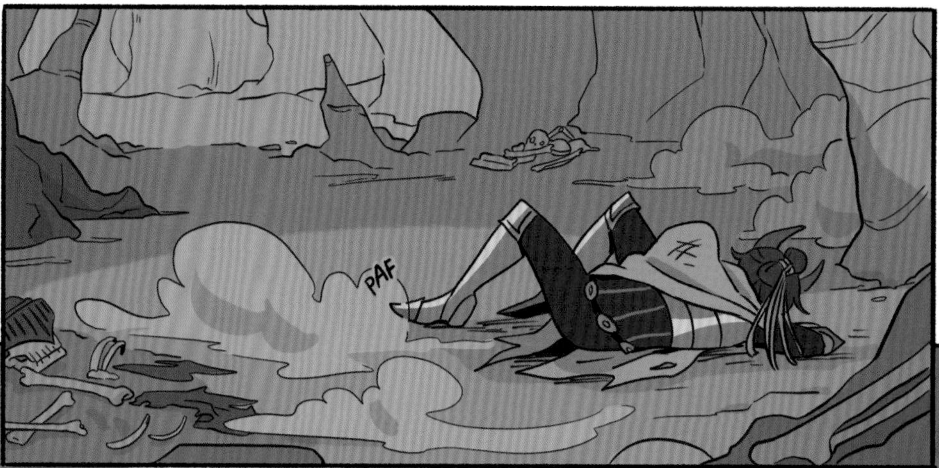
PAF

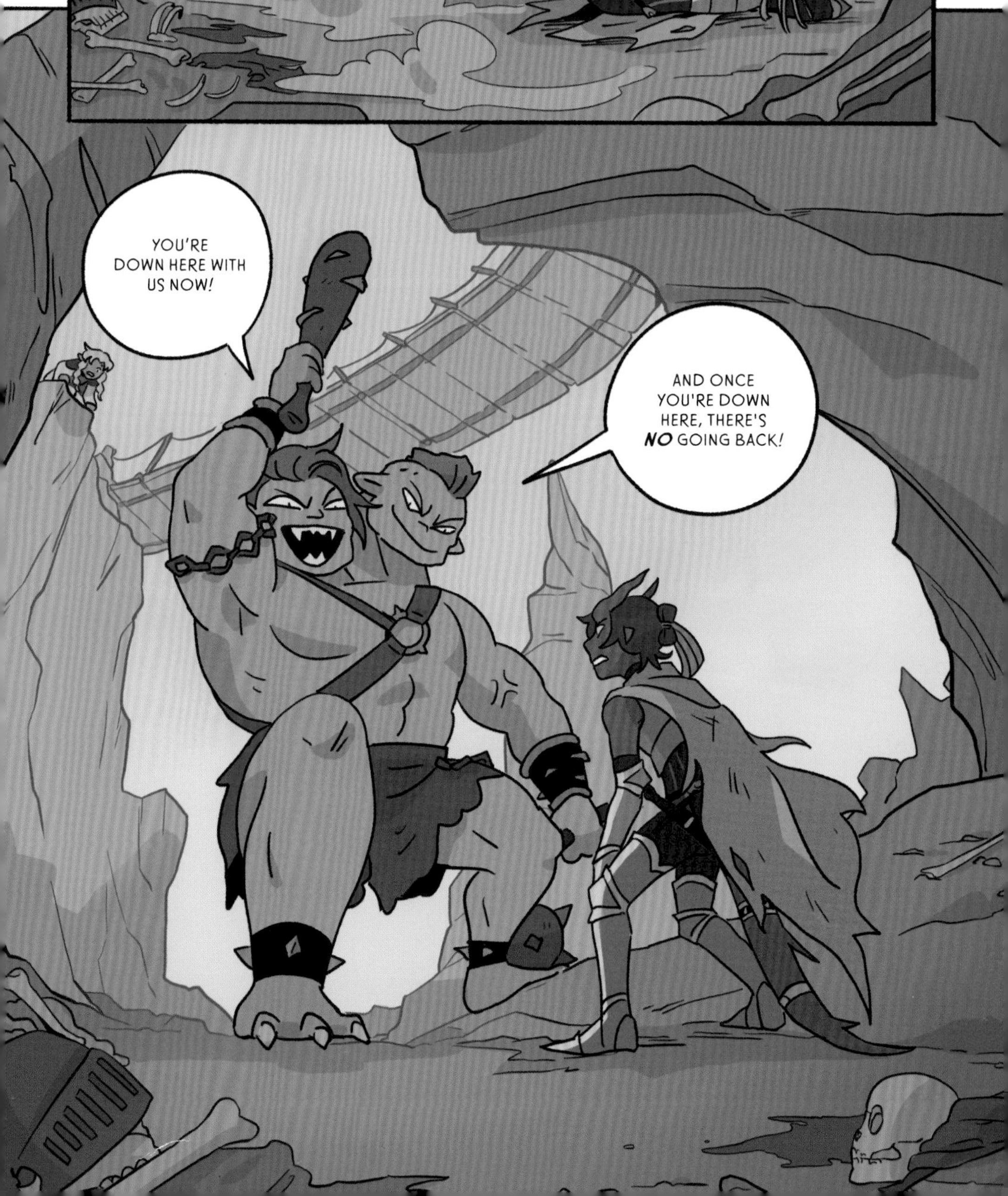
YOU'RE DOWN HERE WITH US NOW!
AND ONCE YOU'RE DOWN HERE, THERE'S **NO** GOING BACK!

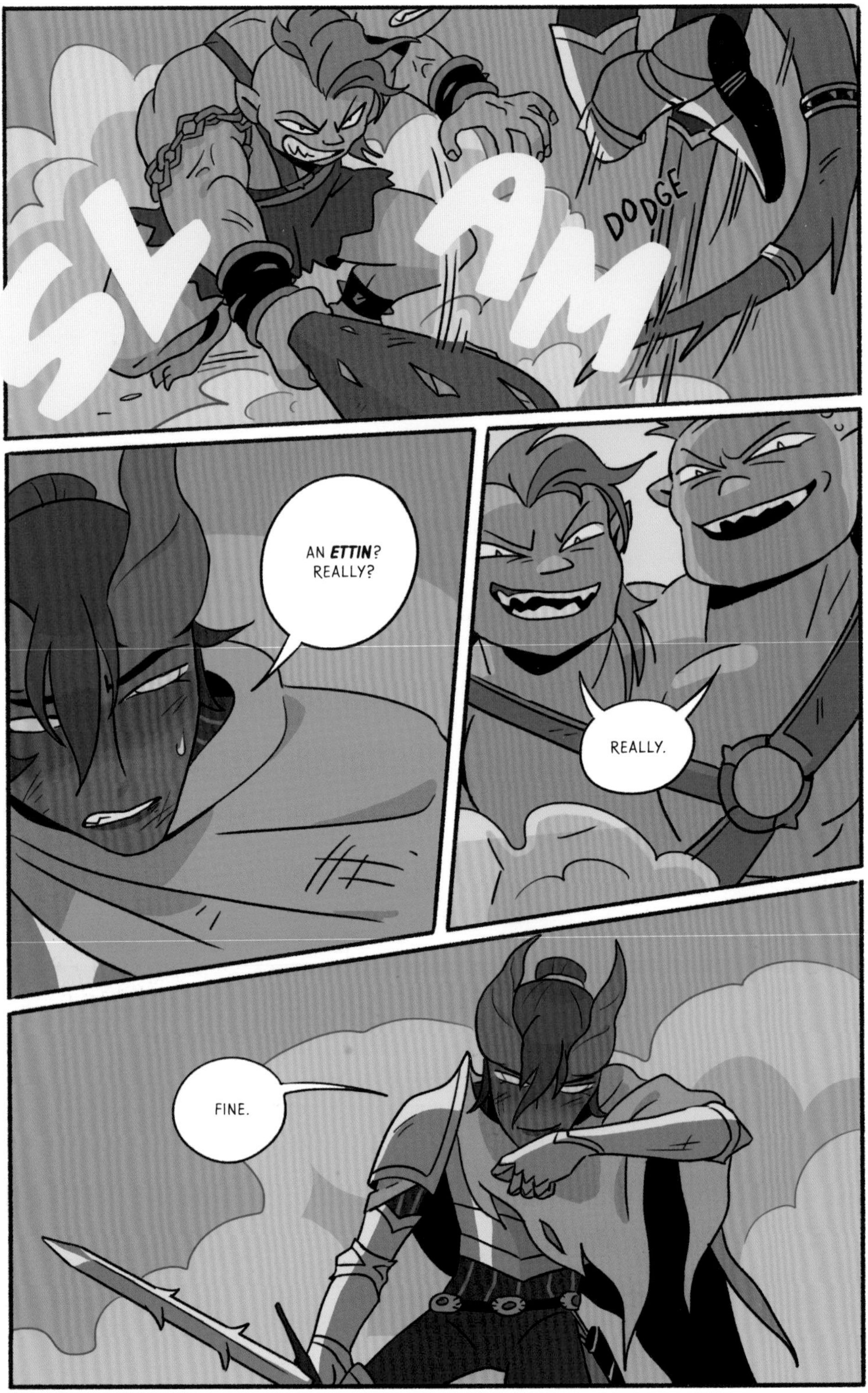
SLAM
DODGE
AN ETTIN? REALLY?
REALLY.
FINE.

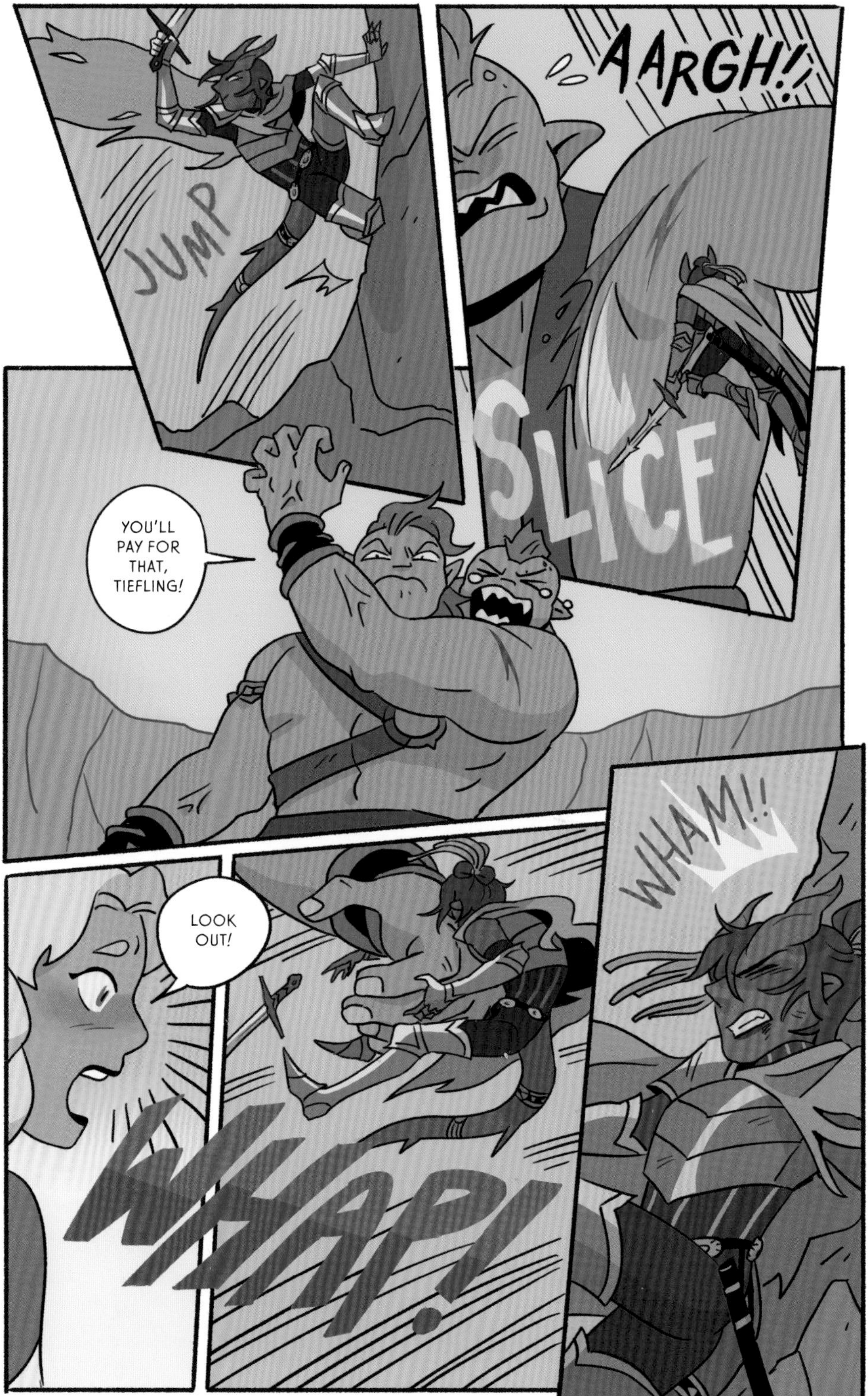
JUMP
AARGH!!
SLICE
YOU'LL PAY FOR THAT, TIEFLING!
LOOK OUT!
WAP!
WHAM!!

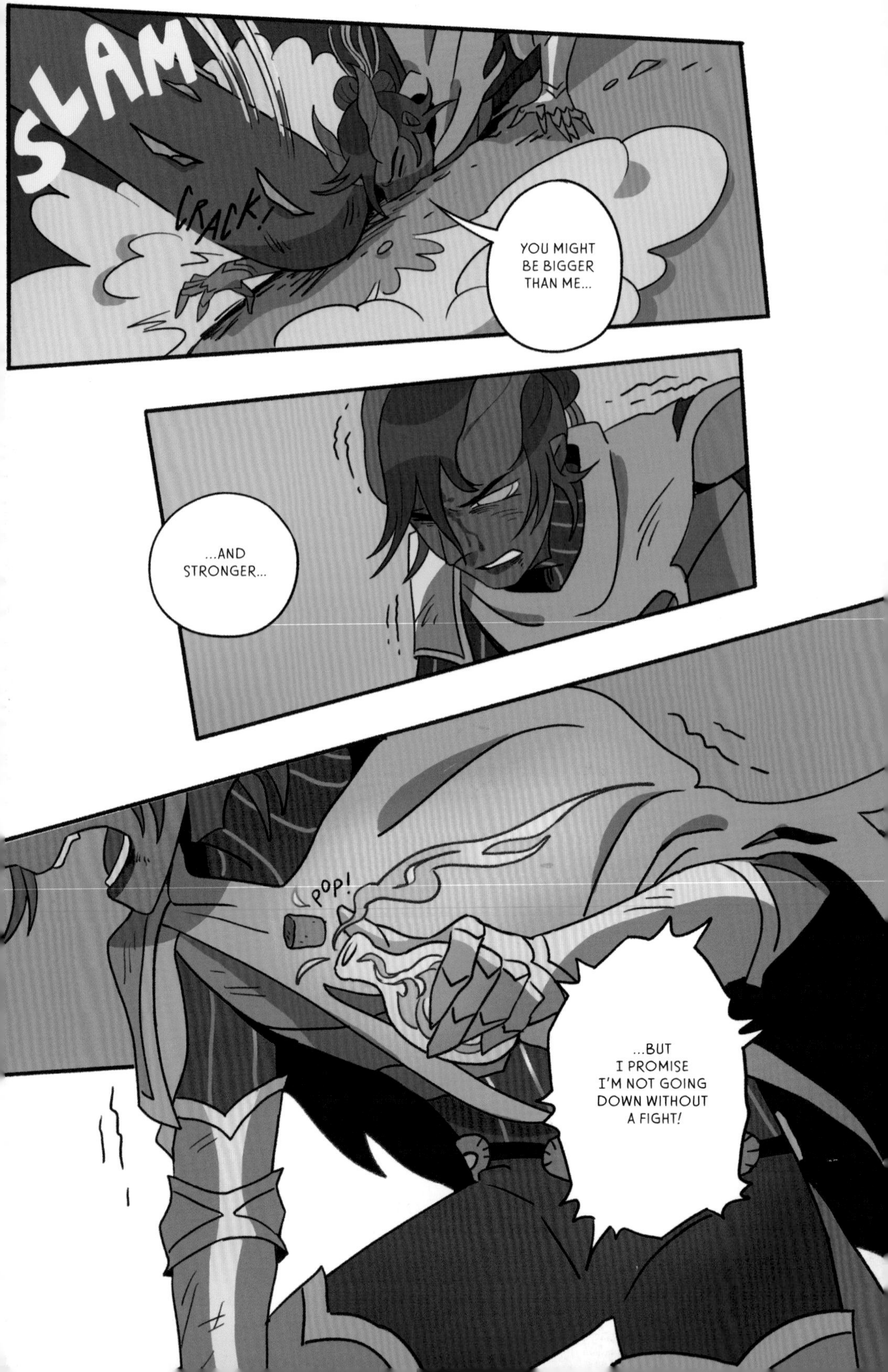
SLAM!!!
CRACK!
YOU MIGHT BE BIGGER THAN ME...
...AND STRONGER...
POP!
...BUT I PROMISE I'M NOT GOING DOWN WITHOUT A FIGHT!

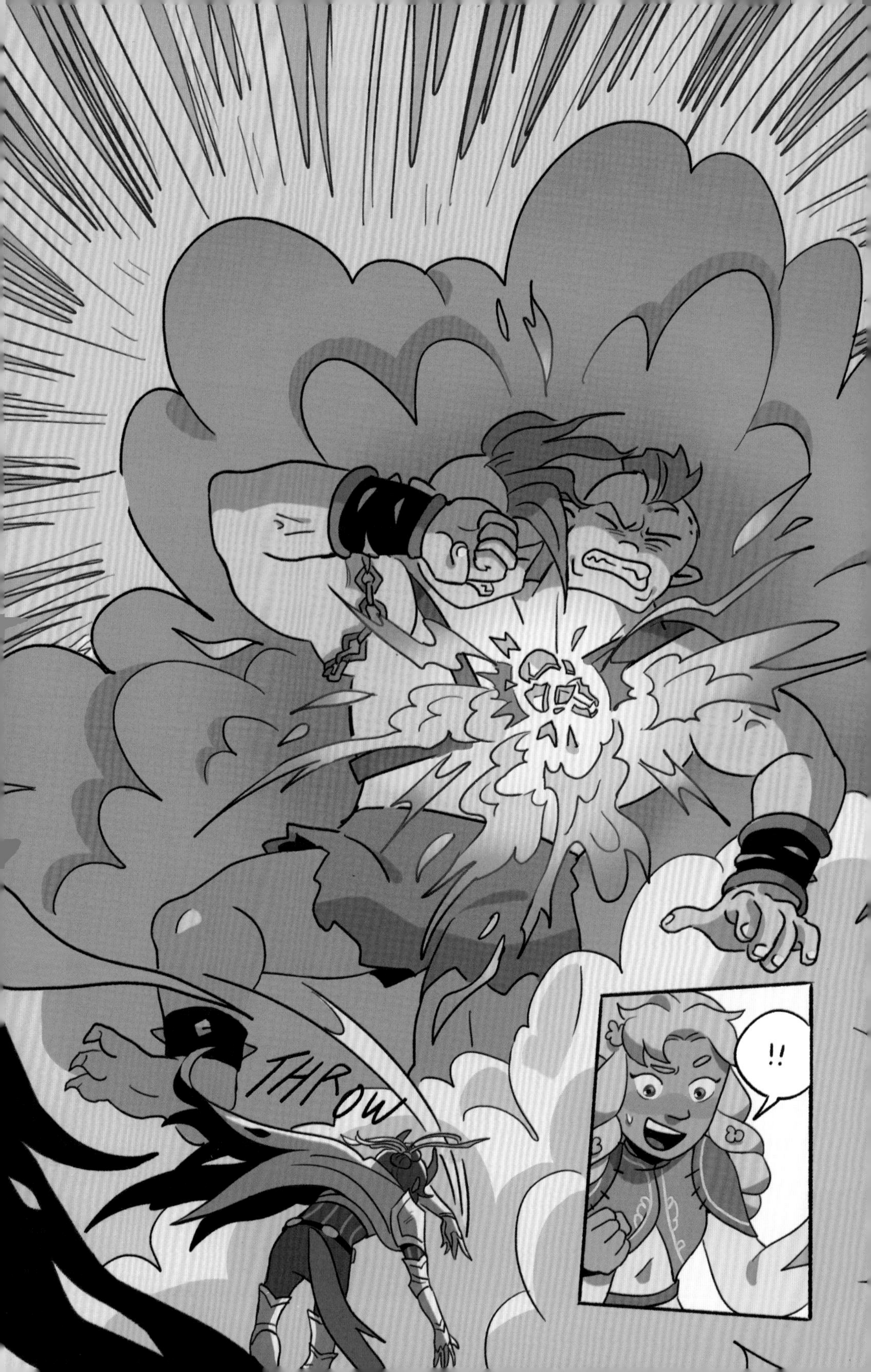
THROW
!!

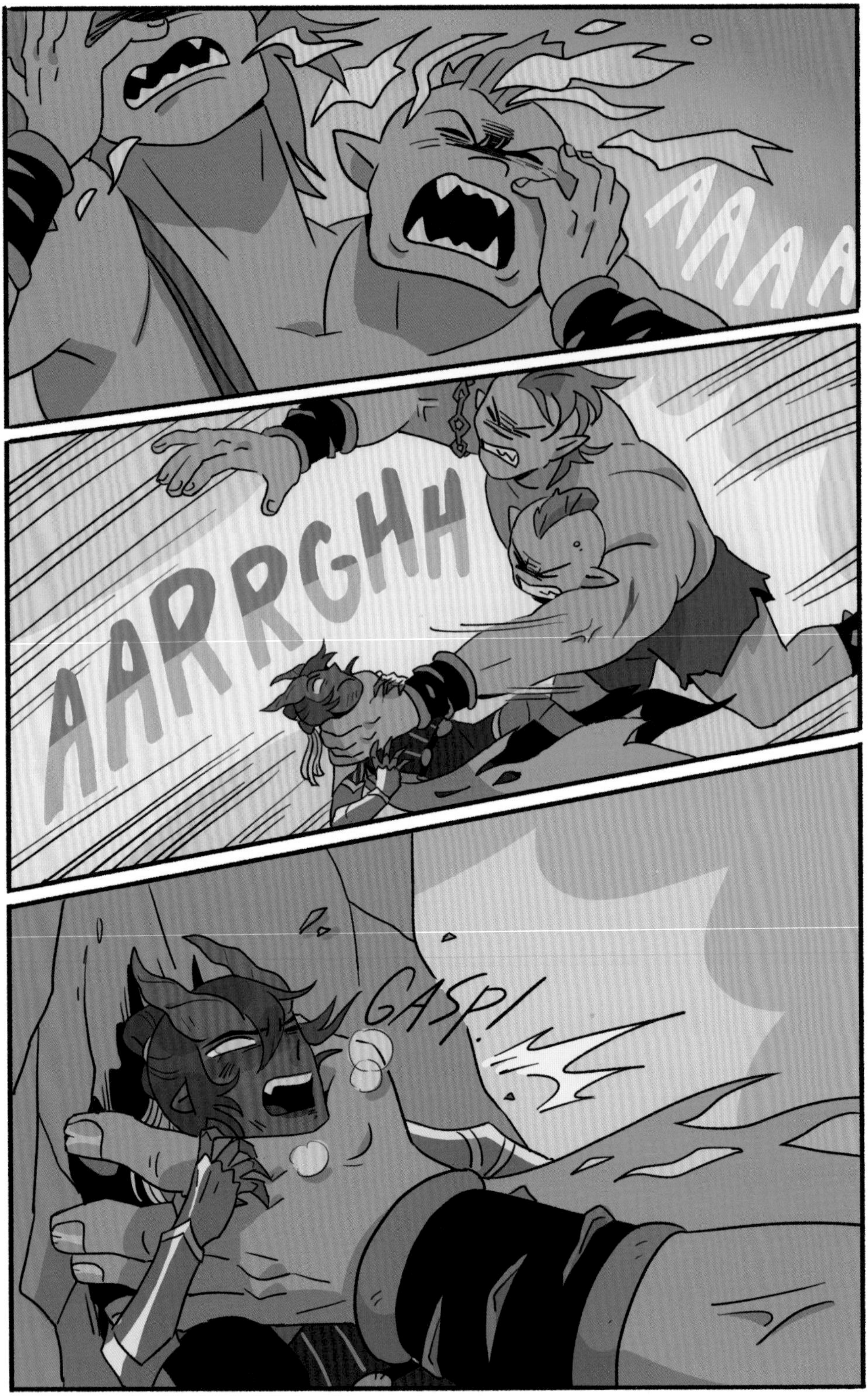
AAAAA
AARRGHH
GASP!

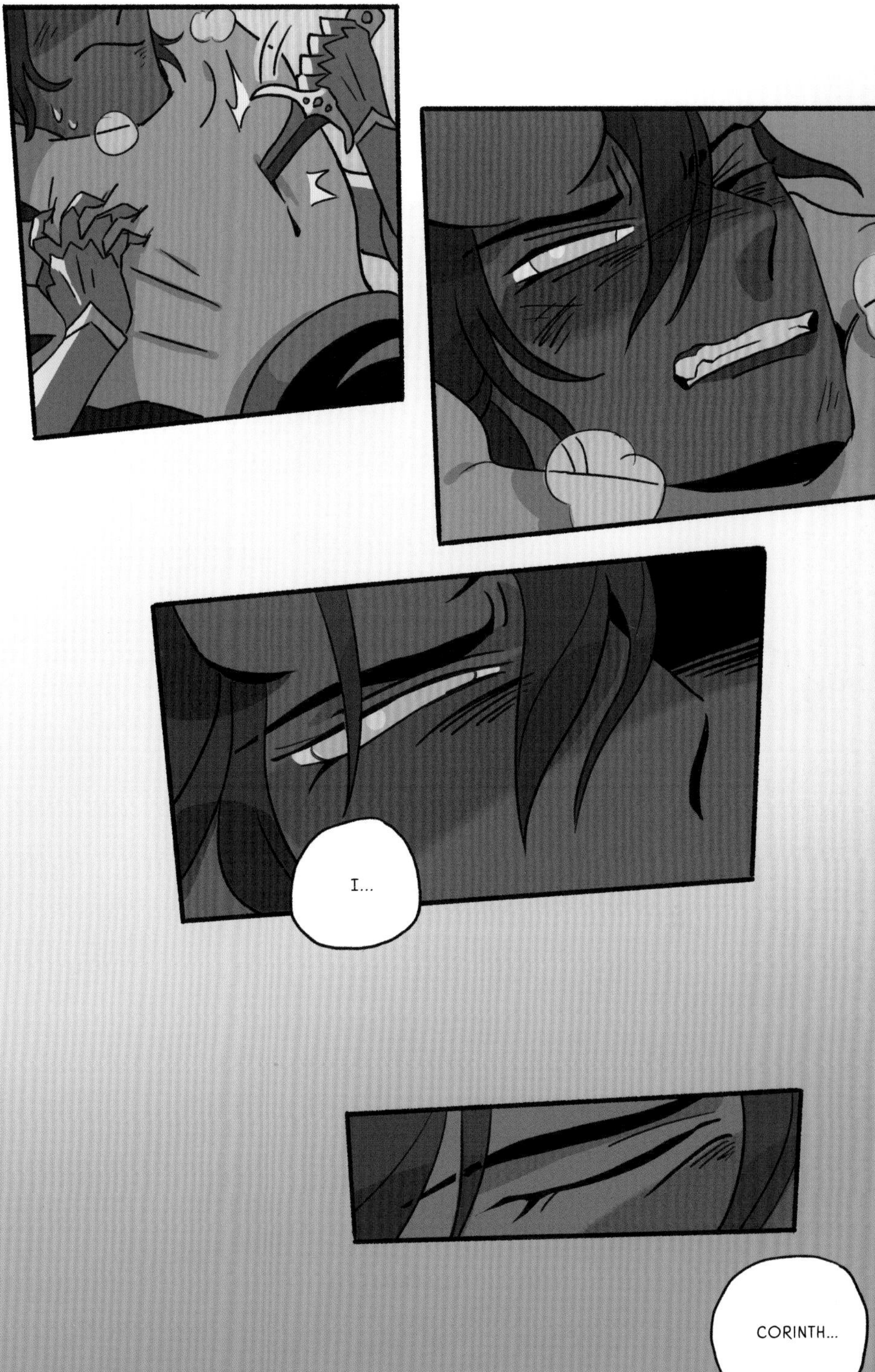
I...
CORINTH...

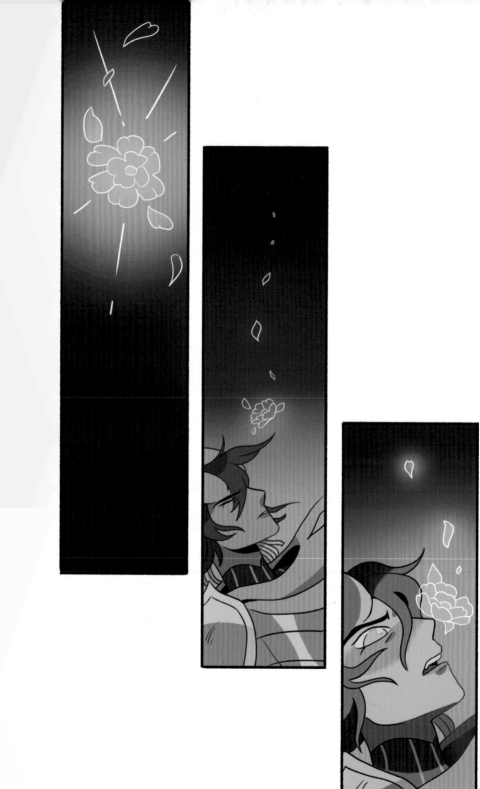

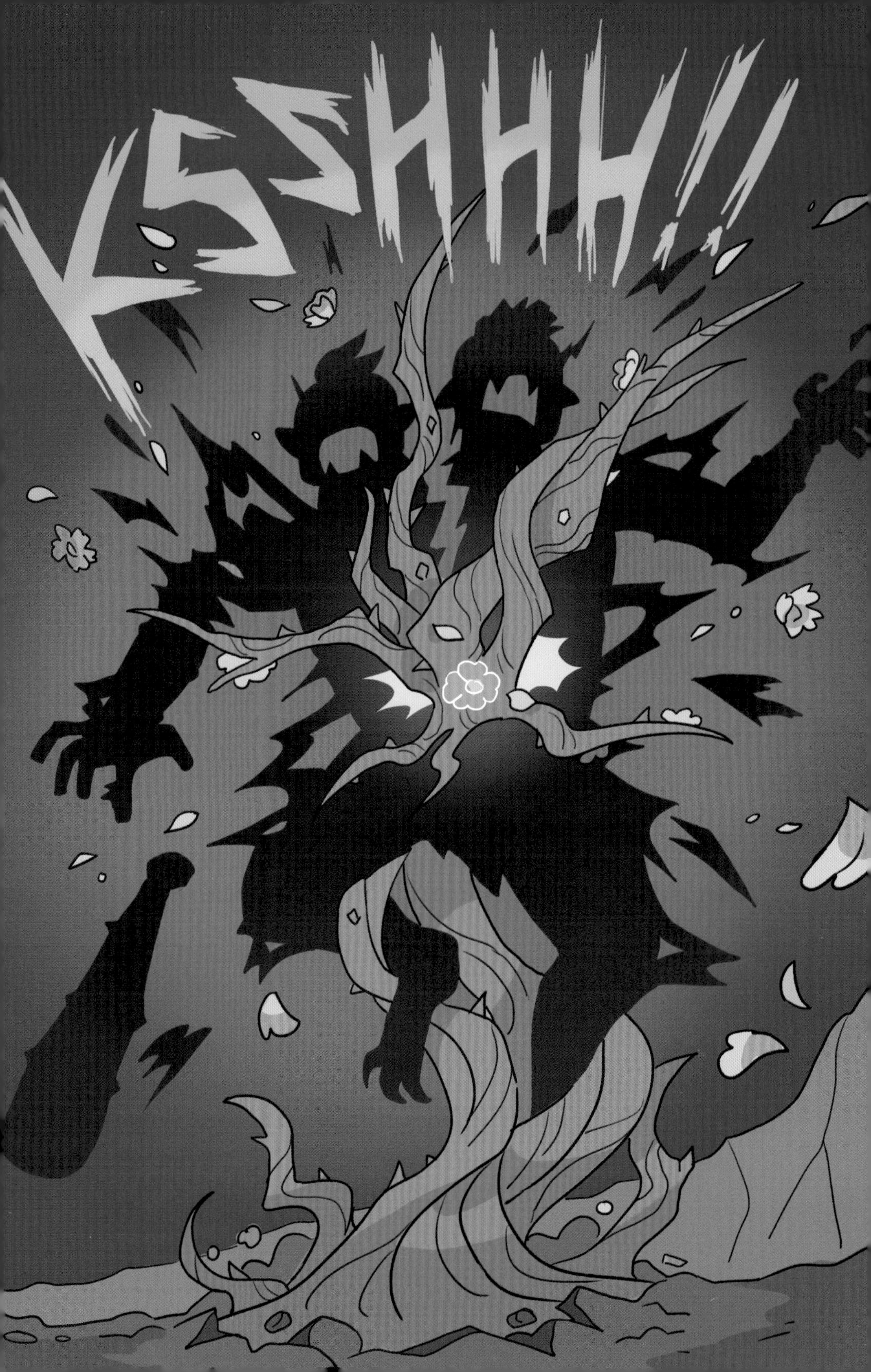
KSSHHH!!

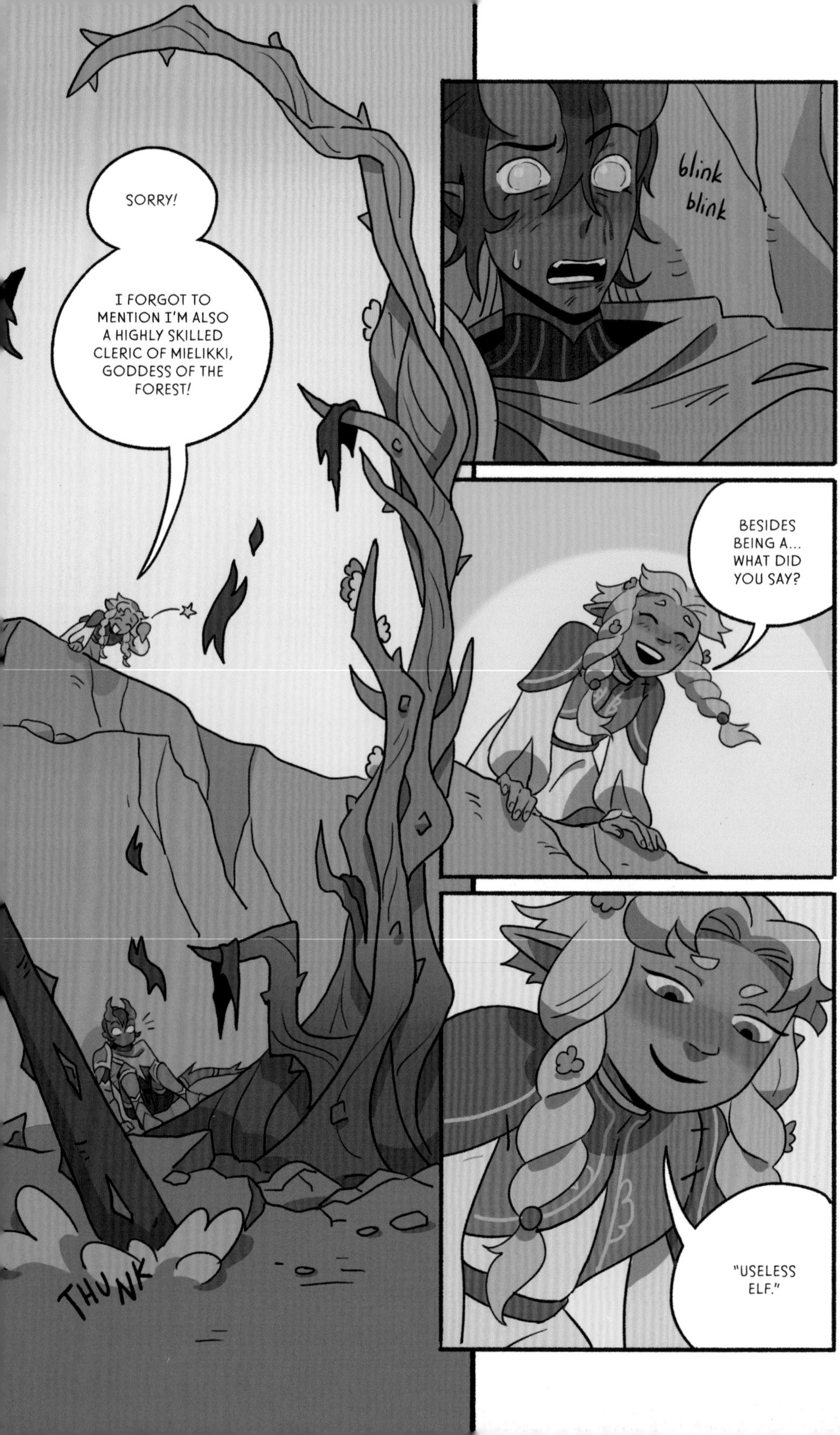
SORRY!
I FORGOT TO MENTION I'M ALSO A HIGHLY SKILLED CLERIC OF MIELIKKI, GODDESS OF THE FOREST!
THUNK
blink blink
BESIDES BEING A... WHAT DID YOU SAY?
"USELESS ELF."

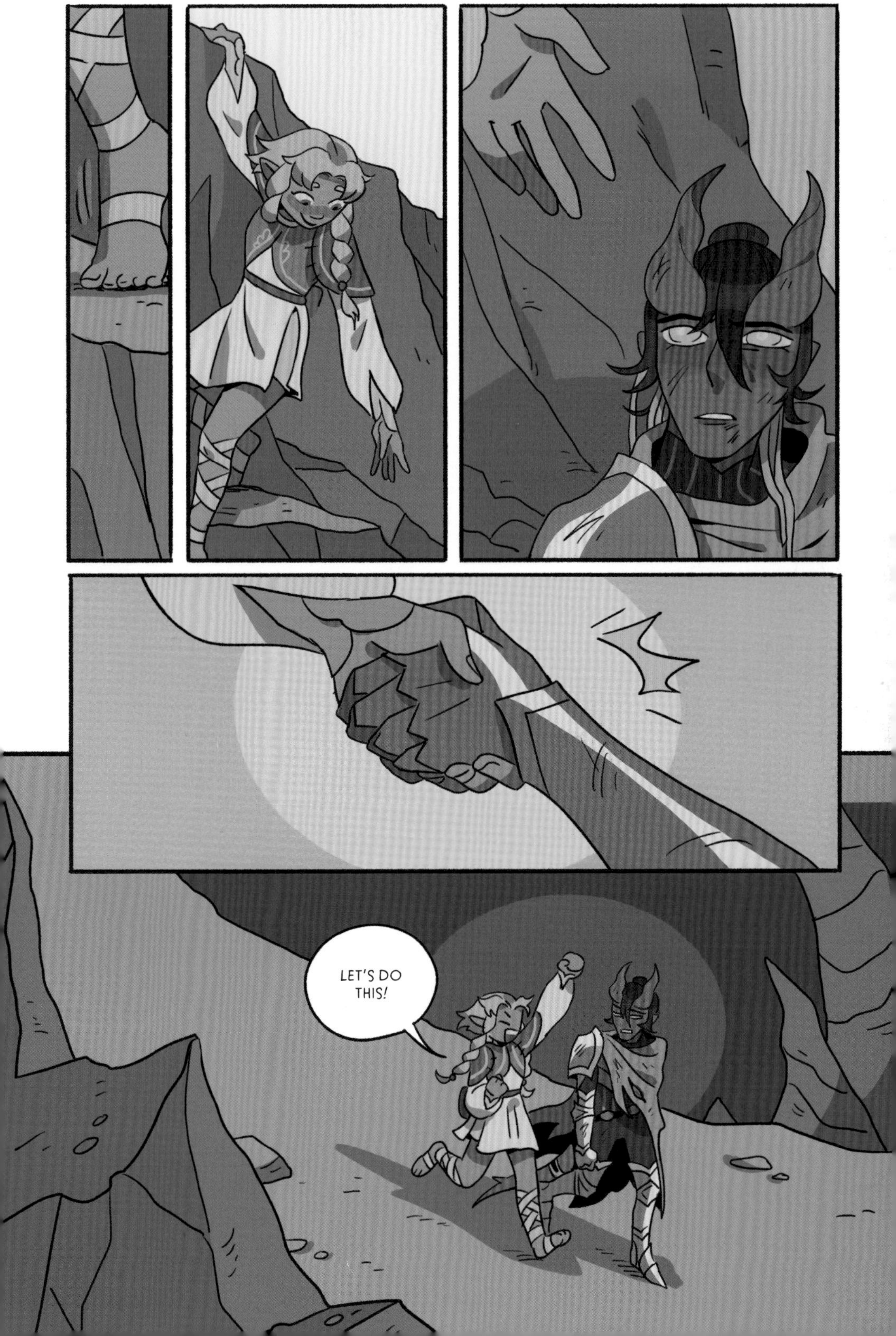
LET'S DO THIS!

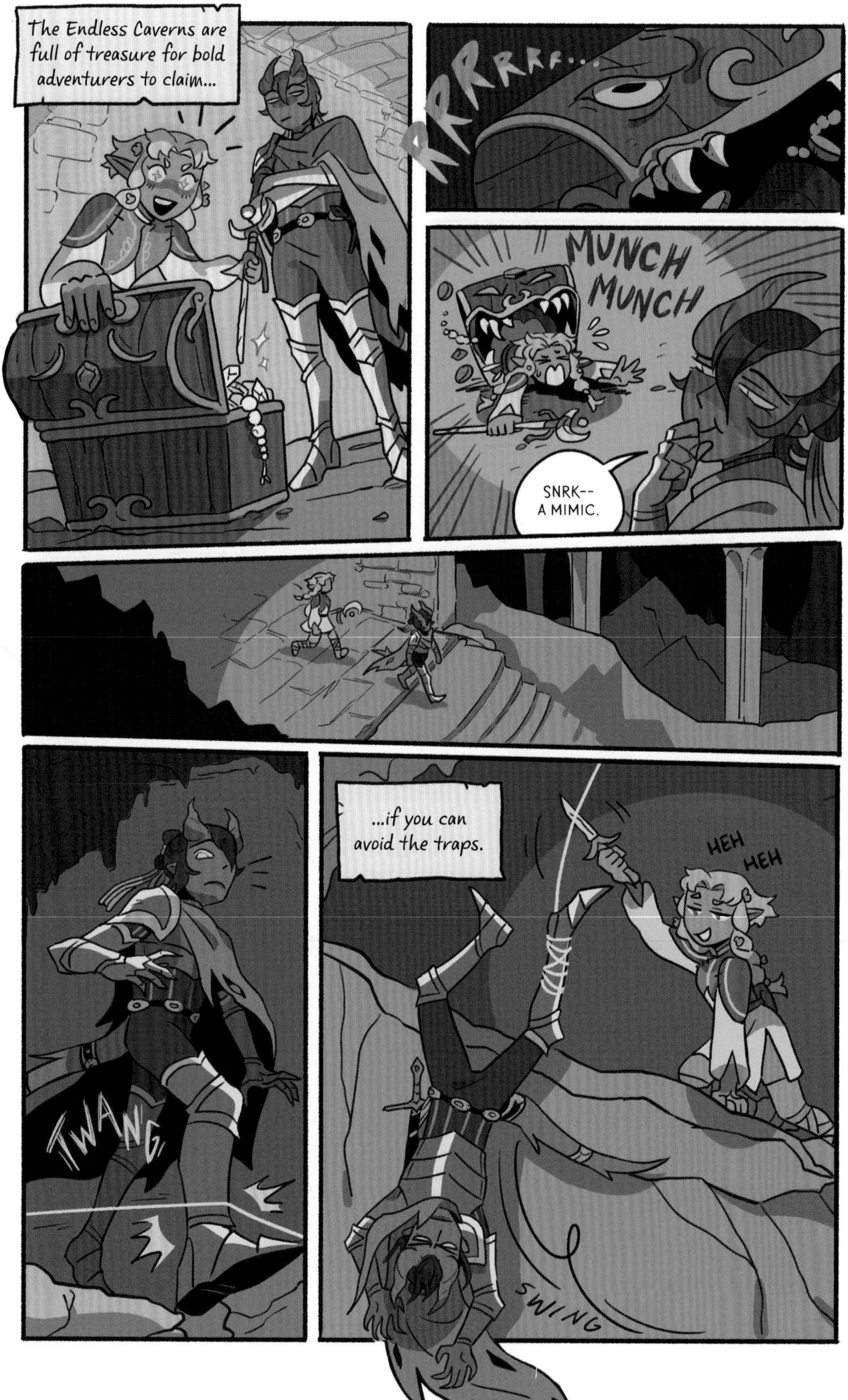

The Endless Caverns are full of treasure for bold adventurers to claim...
PRRRRF...
MUNCH
MUNCH
SNRK-- A MIMIC.
TWANG
...if you can avoid the traps.
HEH HEH
SWING

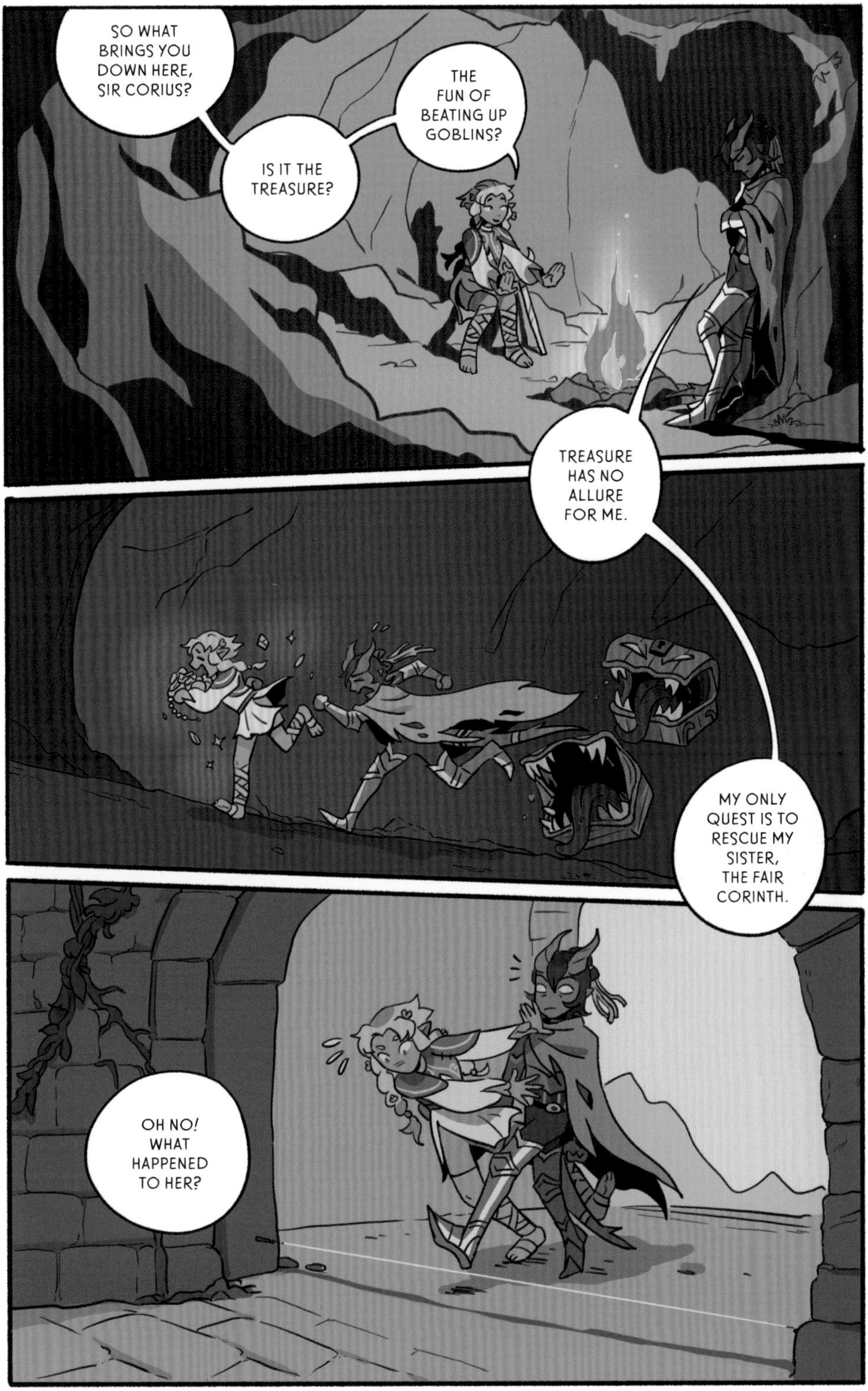
SO WHAT BRINGS YOU DOWN HERE, SIR CORIUS?
IS IT THE TREASURE?
THE FUN OF BEATING UP GOBLINS?
TREASURE HAS NO ALLURE FOR ME.
MY ONLY QUEST IS TO RESCUE MY SISTER, THE FAIR CORINTH.
OH NO! WHAT HAPPENED TO HER?

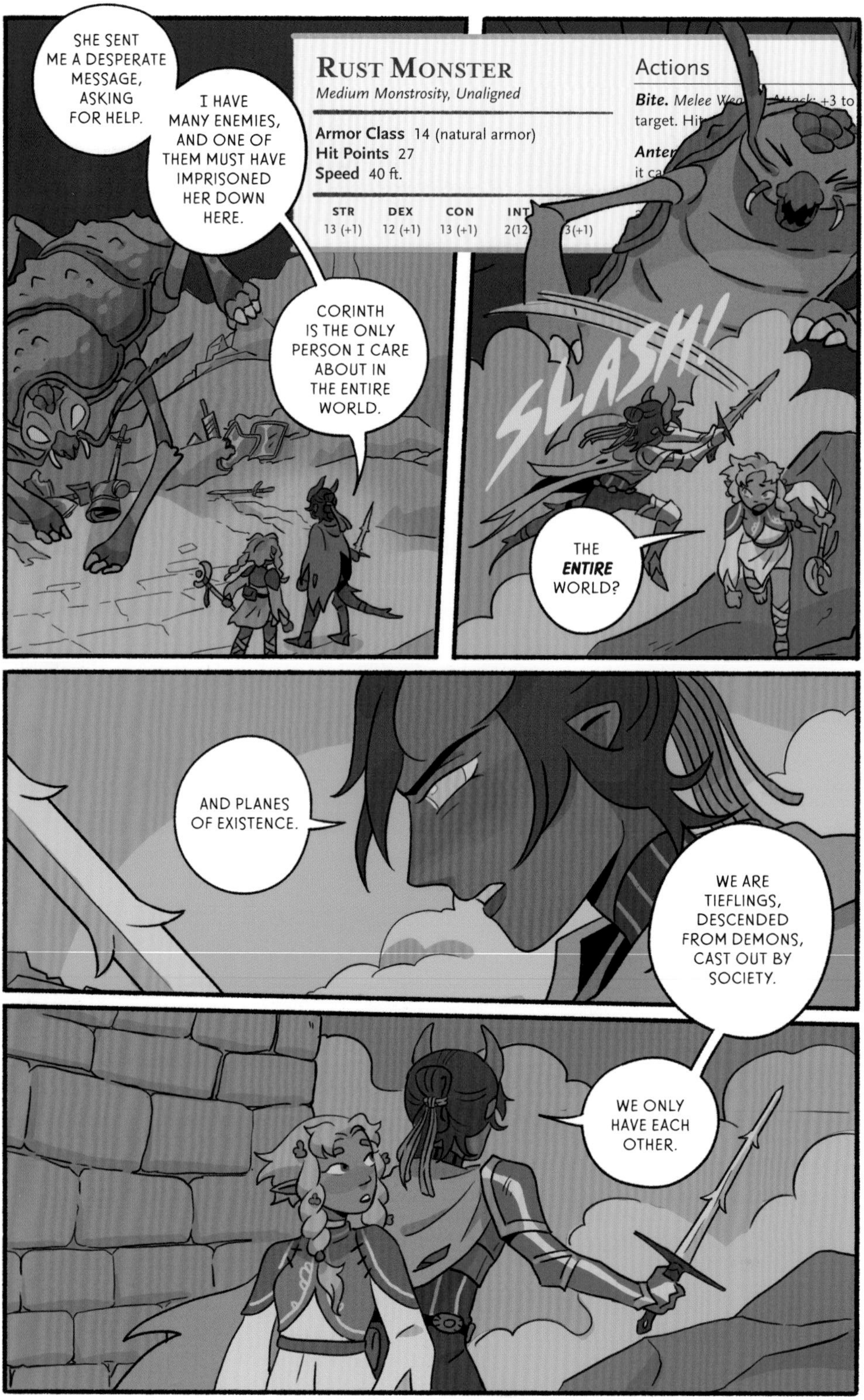
SHE SENT ME A DESPERATE MESSAGE, ASKING FOR HELP.
I HAVE MANY ENEMIES, AND ONE OF THEM MUST HAVE IMPRISONED HER DOWN HERE.
CORINTH IS THE ONLY PERSON I CARE ABOUT IN THE ENTIRE WORLD.
RUST MONSTER
Medium Monstrosity, Unaligned
Armor Class 14 (natural armor)
Hit Points 27
Speed 40 ft.
STR 13 (+1)
DEX 12 (+1)
CON 13 (+1)
Actions
SLASH!
THE *ENTIRE* WORLD?
AND PLANES OF EXISTENCE.
WE ARE TIEFLINGS, DESCENDED FROM DEMONS, CAST OUT BY SOCIETY.
WE ONLY HAVE EACH OTHER.

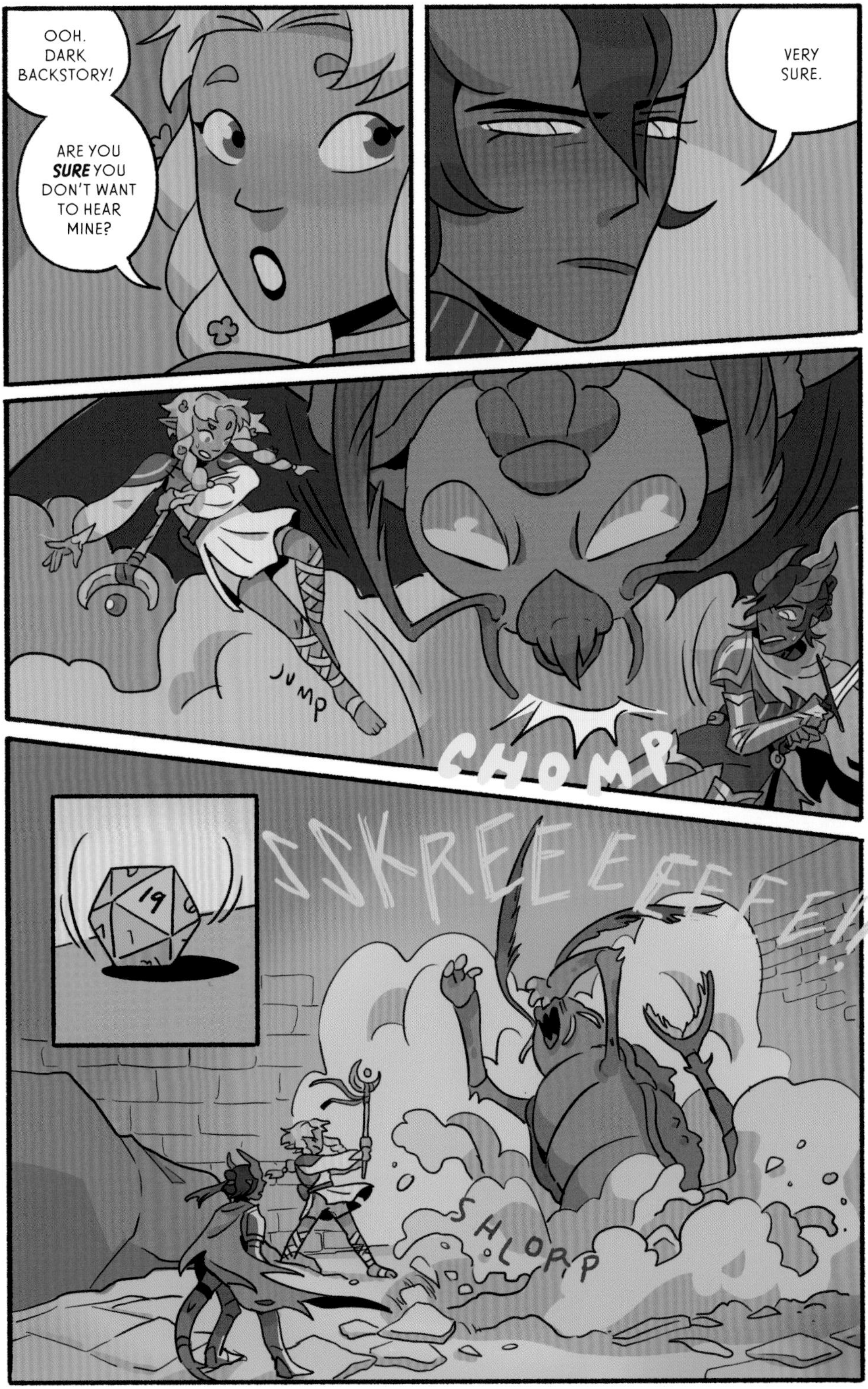
OOH. DARK BACKSTORY!
ARE YOU **SURE** YOU DON'T WANT TO HEAR MINE?
VERY SURE.
JUMP
CHOMP
19
SSKREEEEEEEE!!
SHLORP

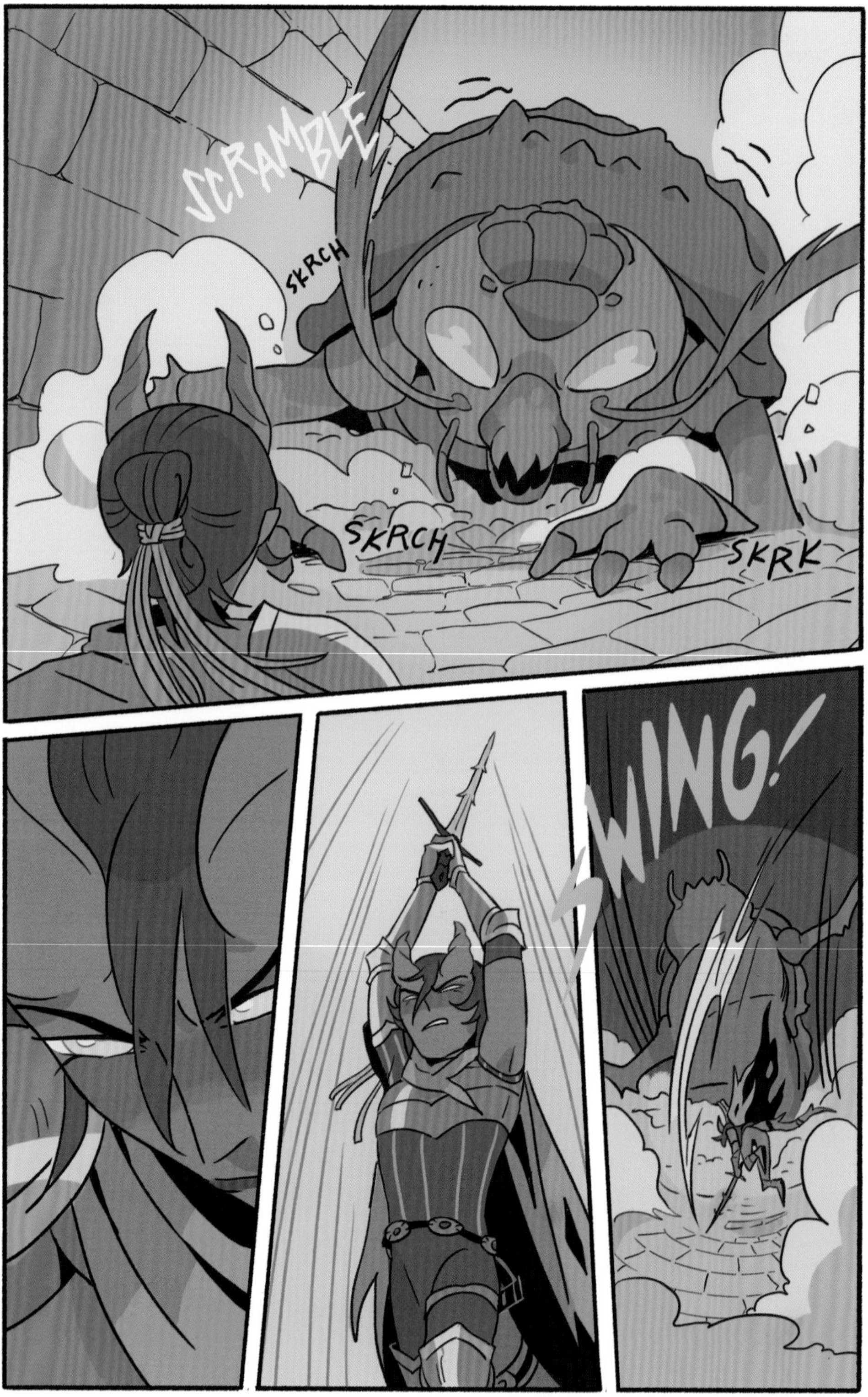
SCRAMBLE
SKRCH
SKRCH
SKRK
SWING!

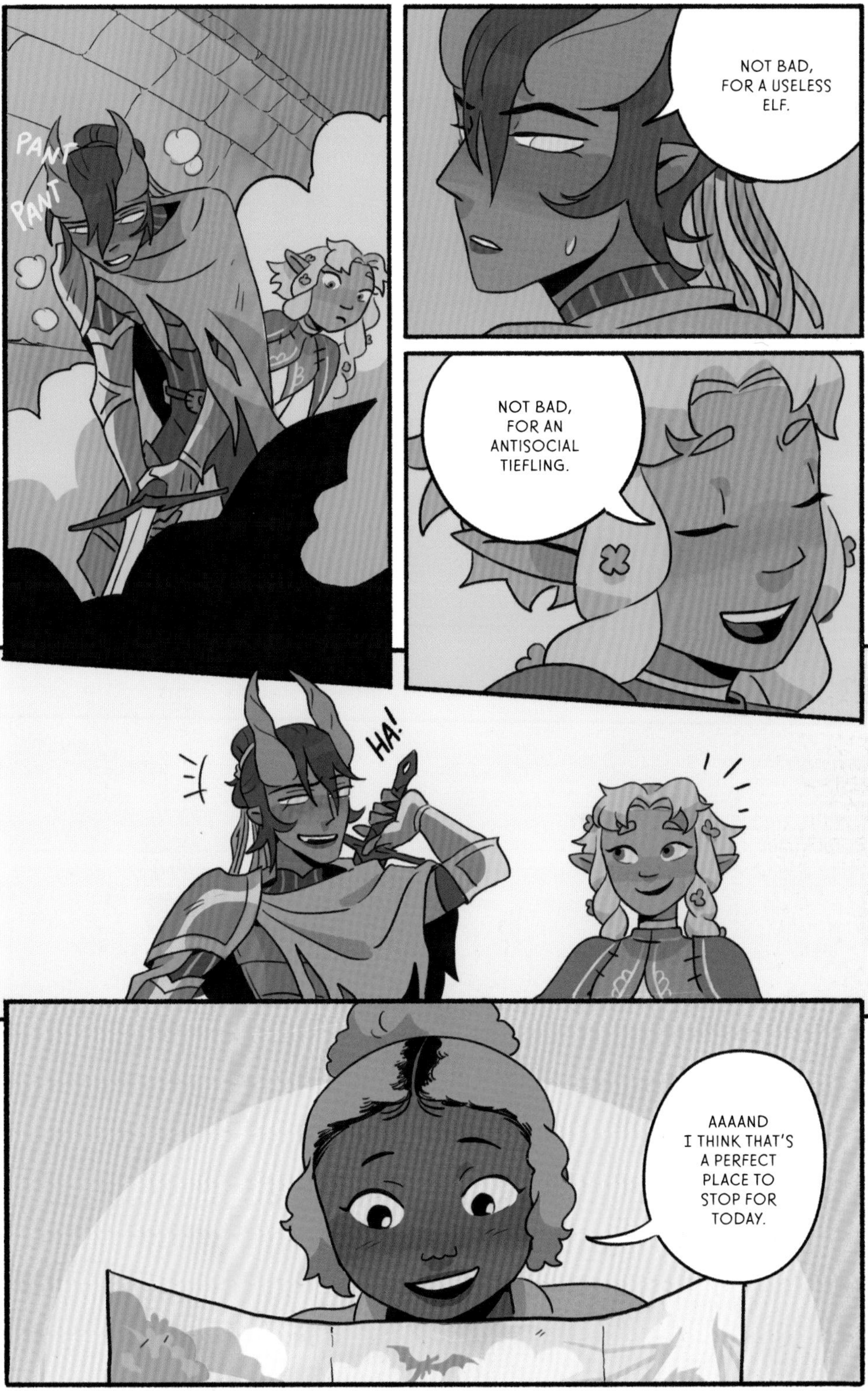

PANT
PANT
NOT BAD, FOR A USELESS ELF.
NOT BAD, FOR AN ANTISOCIAL TIEFLING.
HA!
AAAAND I THINK THAT'S A PERFECT PLACE TO STOP FOR TODAY.

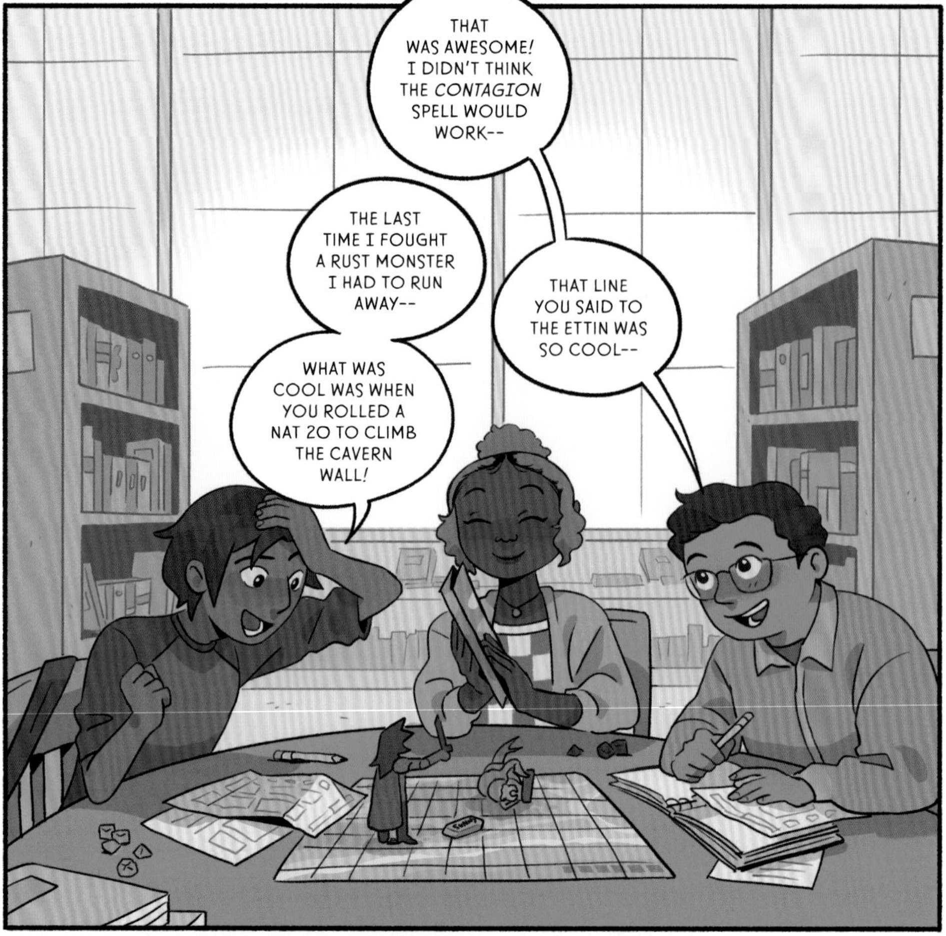
THAT WAS AWESOME! I DIDN'T THINK THE *CONTAGION* SPELL WOULD WORK--
THE LAST TIME I FOUGHT A RUST MONSTER I HAD TO RUN AWAY--
THAT LINE YOU SAID TO THE ETTIN WAS SO COOL--
WHAT WAS COOL WAS WHEN YOU ROLLED A NAT 20 TO CLIMB THE CAVERN WALL!

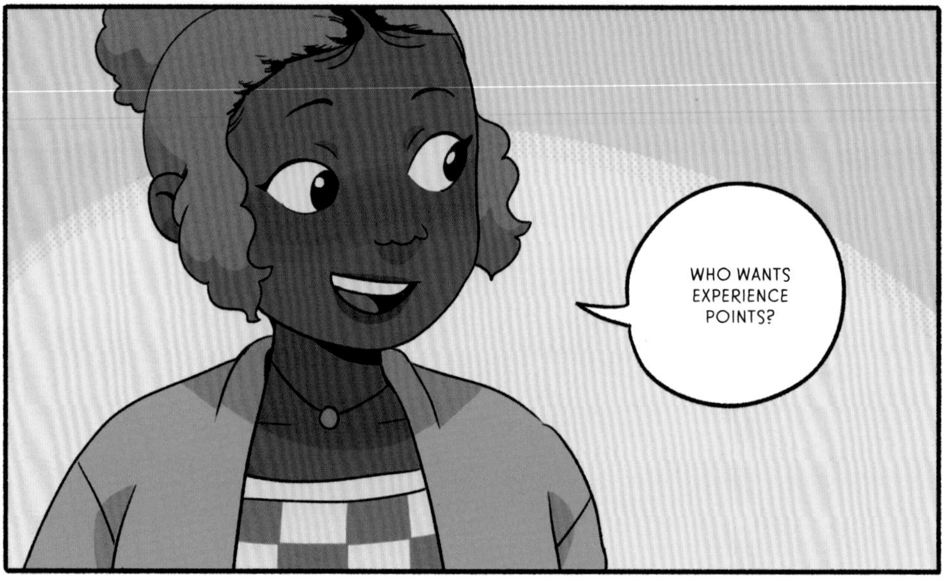
WHO WANTS EXPERIENCE POINTS?

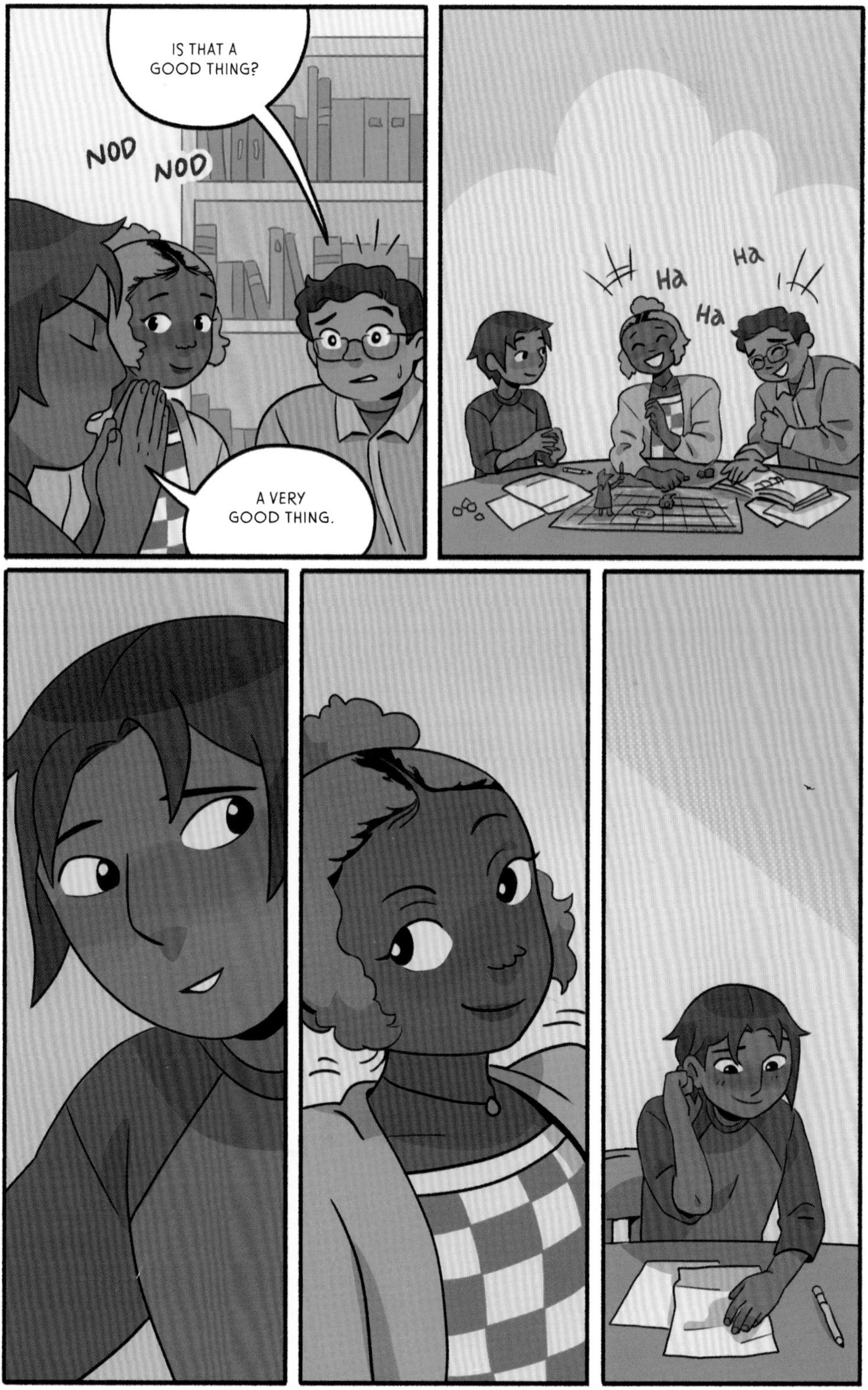
IS THAT A GOOD THING?
NOD
NOD
A VERY GOOD THING.
Ha
Ha
Ha

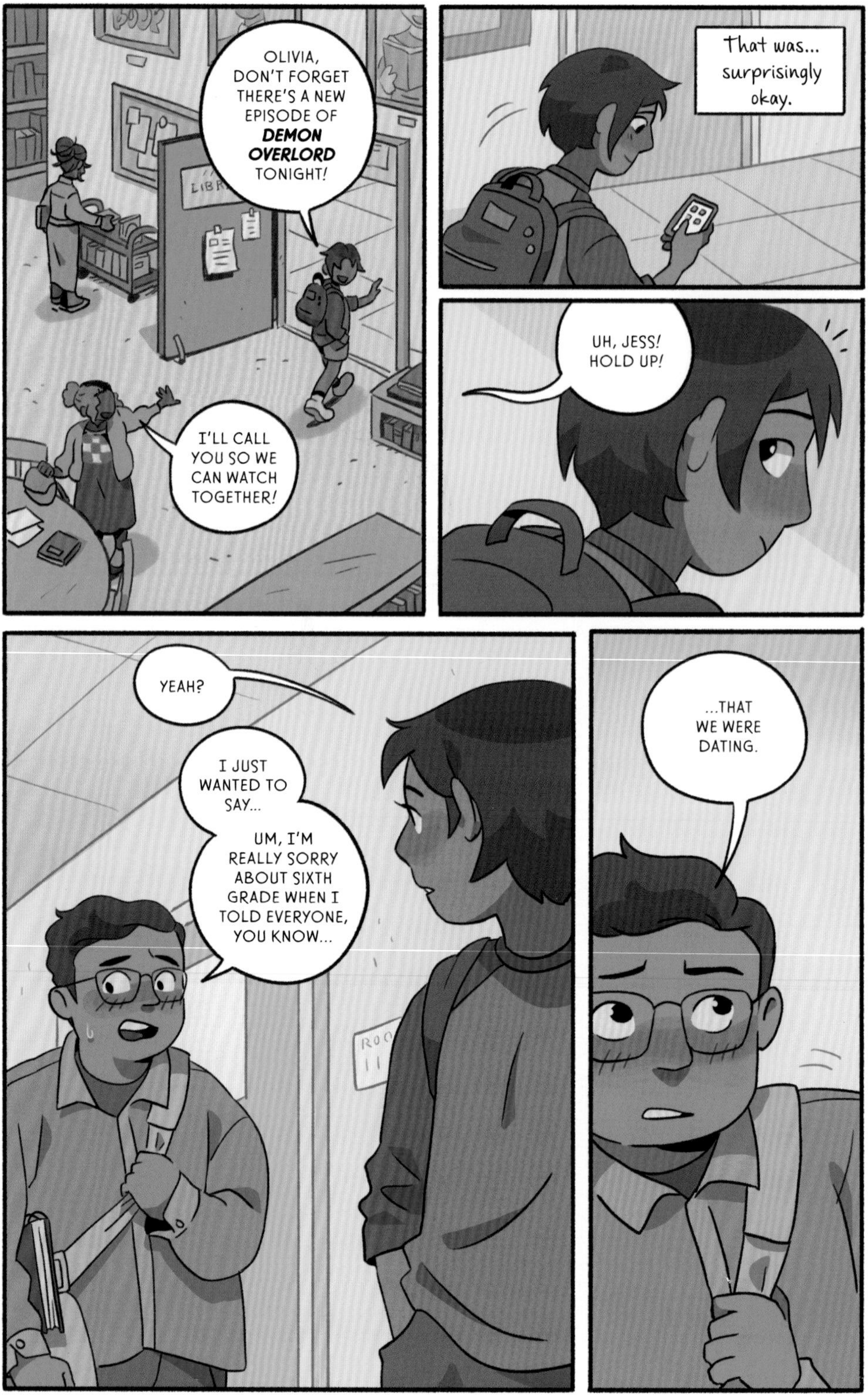
OLIVIA, DON'T FORGET THERE'S A NEW EPISODE OF **DEMON OVERLORD** TONIGHT!
I'LL CALL YOU SO WE CAN WATCH TOGETHER!
That was... surprisingly okay.
UH, JESS! HOLD UP!
YEAH?
I JUST WANTED TO SAY...
UM, I'M REALLY SORRY ABOUT SIXTH GRADE WHEN I TOLD EVERYONE, YOU KNOW...
...THAT WE WERE DATING.

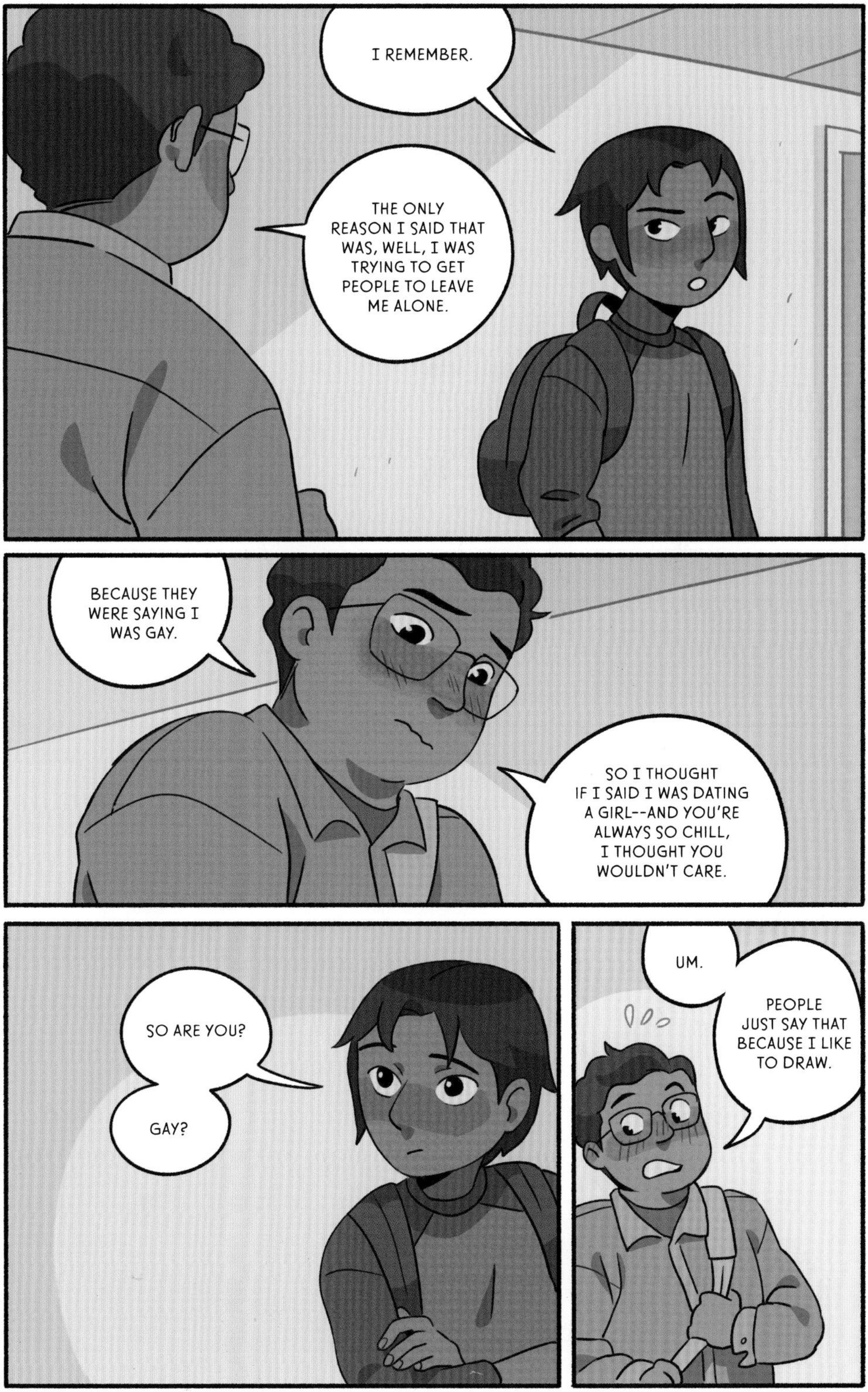
I REMEMBER.
THE ONLY REASON I SAID THAT WAS, WELL, I WAS TRYING TO GET PEOPLE TO LEAVE ME ALONE.
BECAUSE THEY WERE SAYING I WAS GAY.
SO I THOUGHT IF I SAID I WAS DATING A GIRL--AND YOU'RE ALWAYS SO CHILL, I THOUGHT YOU WOULDN'T CARE.
SO ARE YOU?
GAY?
UM.
PEOPLE JUST SAY THAT BECAUSE I LIKE TO DRAW.

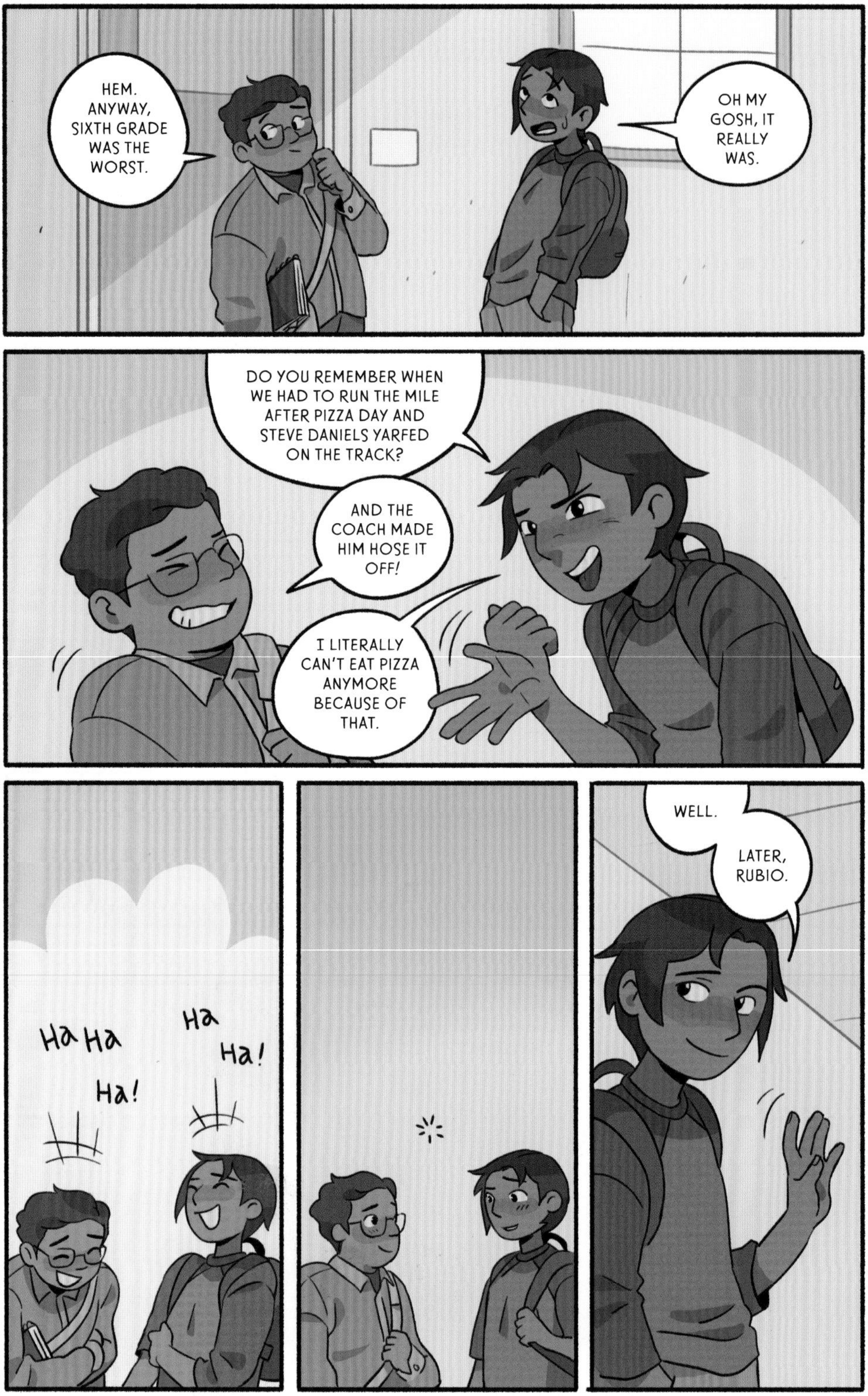
HEM. ANYWAY, SIXTH GRADE WAS THE WORST.
OH MY GOSH, IT REALLY WAS.
DO YOU REMEMBER WHEN WE HAD TO RUN THE MILE AFTER PIZZA DAY AND STEVE DANIELS YARFED ON THE TRACK?
AND THE COACH MADE HIM HOSE IT OFF!
I LITERALLY CAN'T EAT PIZZA ANYMORE BECAUSE OF THAT.
Ha Ha
Ha!
Ha
Ha!
WELL.
LATER, RUBIO.

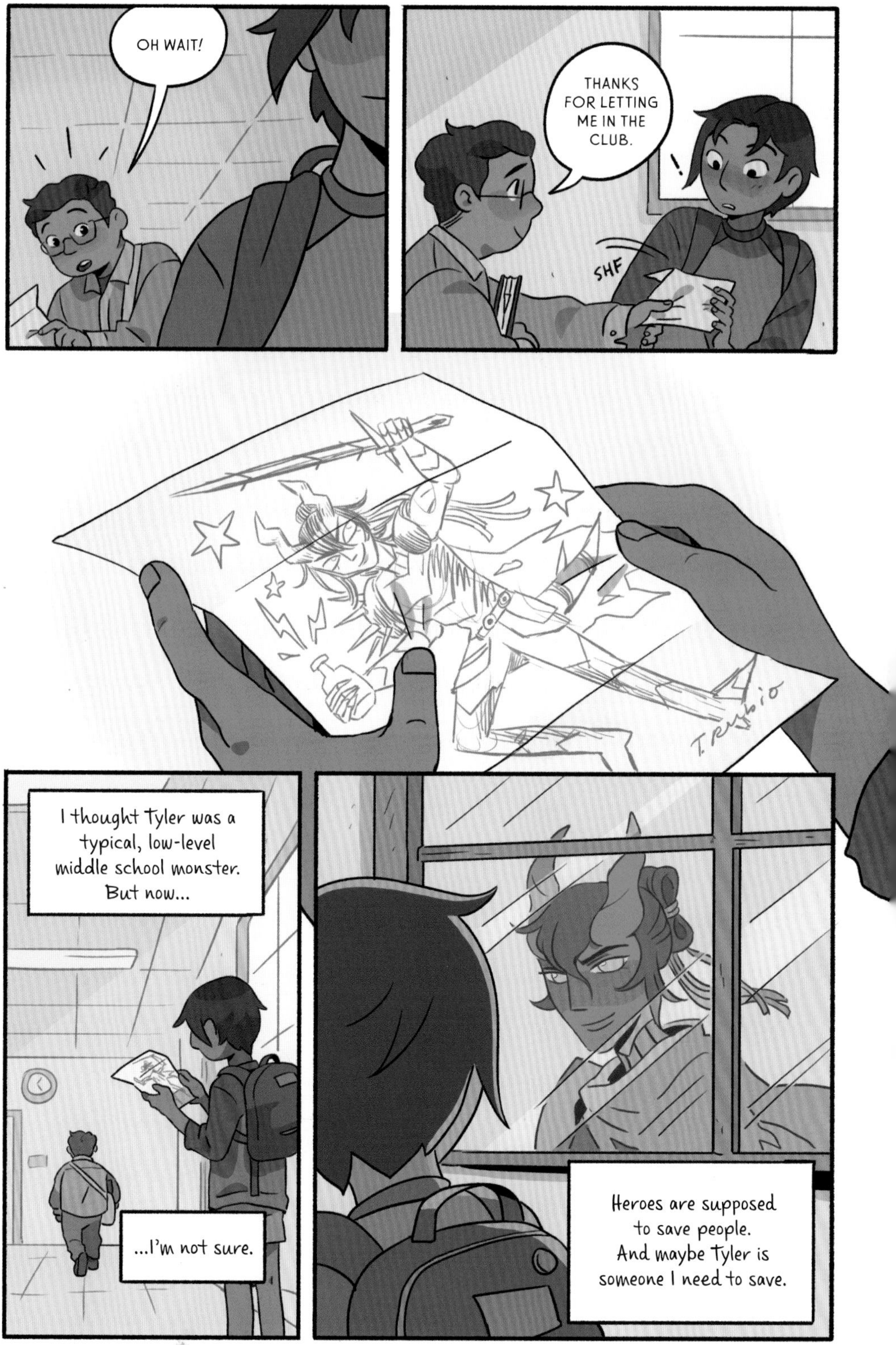
OH WAIT!
THANKS FOR LETTING ME IN THE CLUB.
!
SHF
I thought Tyler was a typical, low-level middle school monster. But now...
...I'm not sure.
Heroes are supposed to save people. And maybe Tyler is someone I need to save.

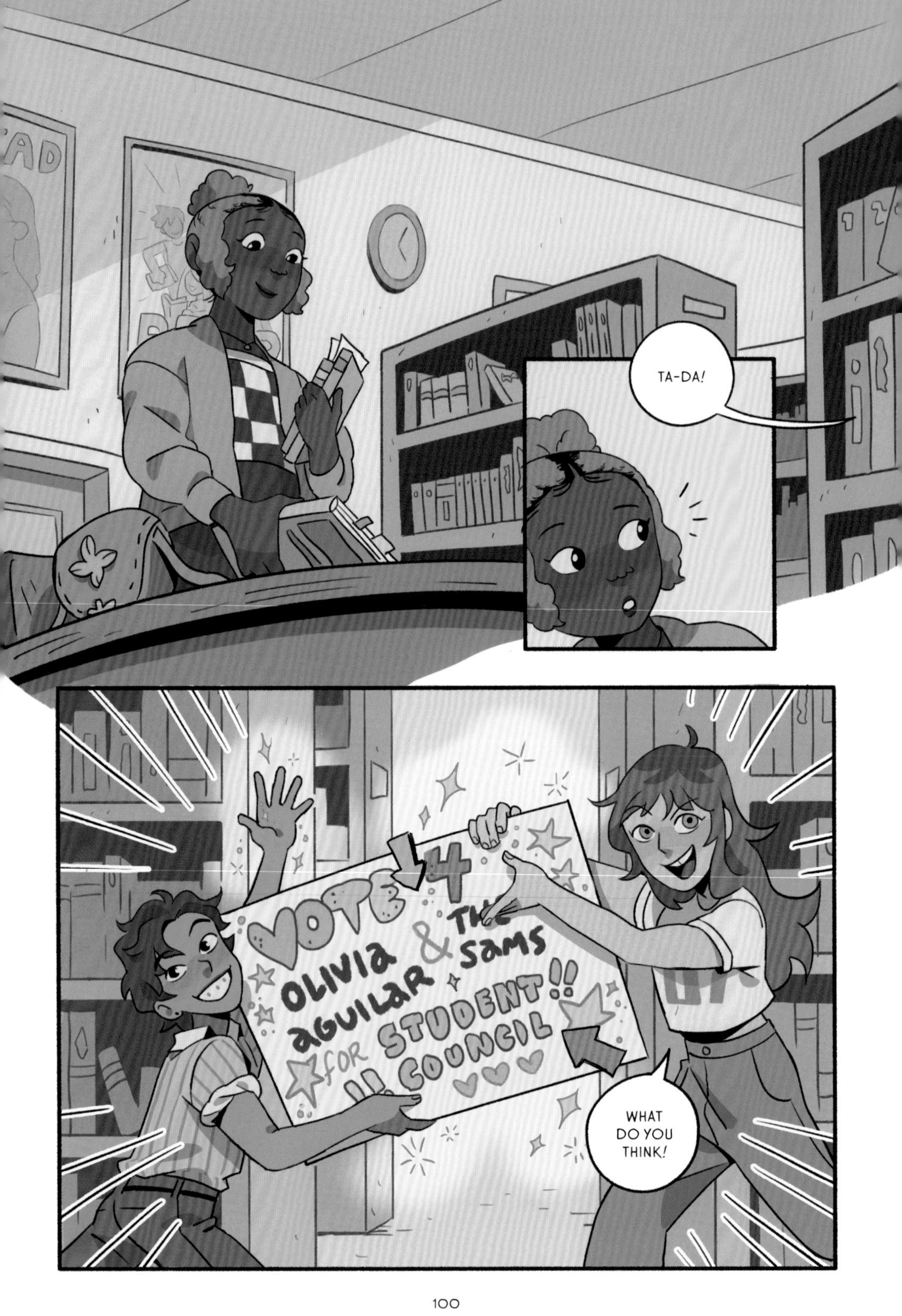

TA-DA!
VOTE 4
OLIVIA AGUILAR & THE SAMS
FOR STUDENT COUNCIL!!
WHAT DO YOU THINK!

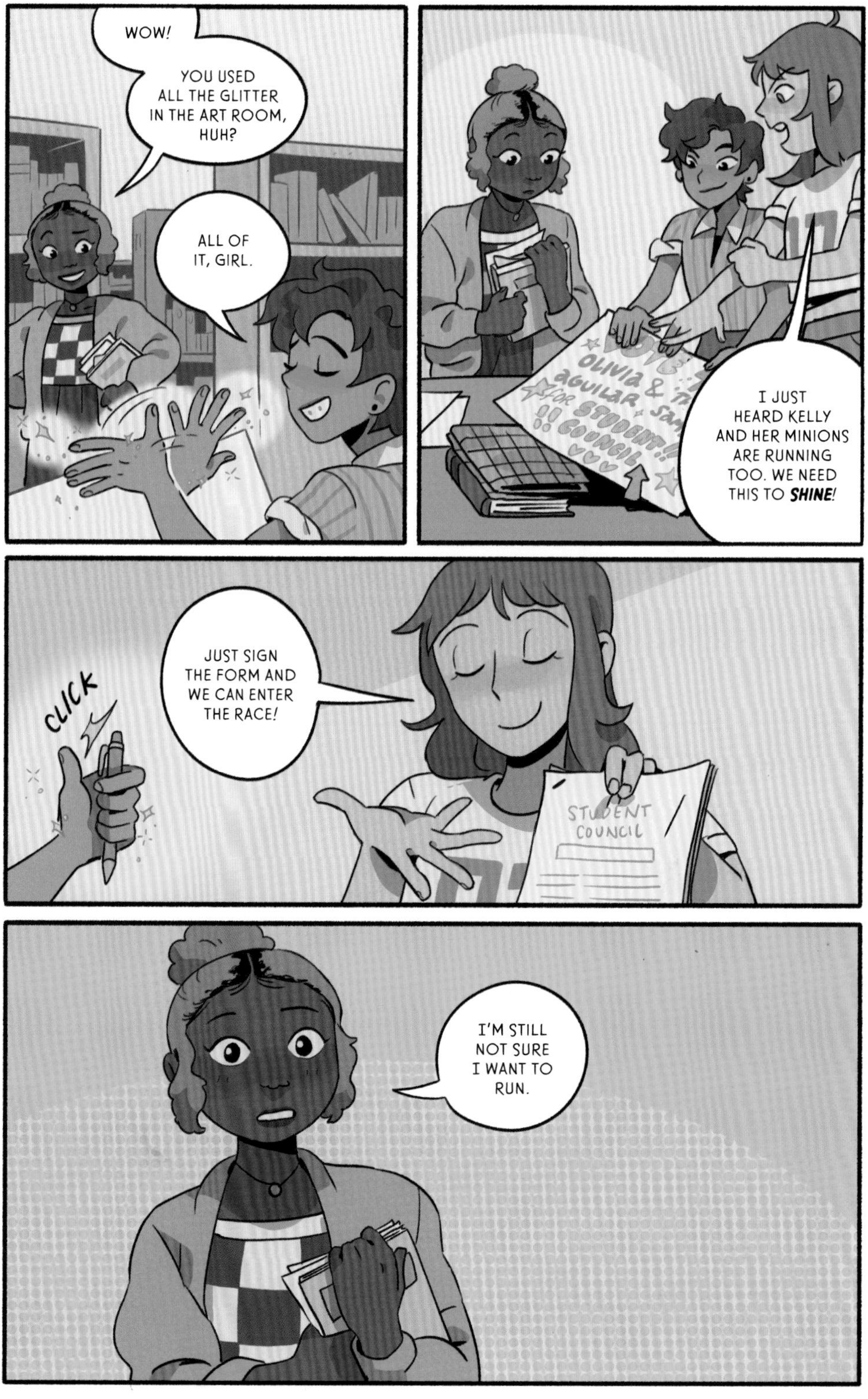
WOW!
YOU USED ALL THE GLITTER IN THE ART ROOM, HUH?
ALL OF IT, GIRL.
OLIVIA &
AGUILAR
FOR STUDENT
COUNCIL
I JUST HEARD KELLY AND HER MINIONS ARE RUNNING TOO. WE NEED THIS TO **SHINE**!
CLICK
JUST SIGN THE FORM AND WE CAN ENTER THE RACE!
STUDENT COUNCIL
I'M STILL NOT SURE I WANT TO RUN.

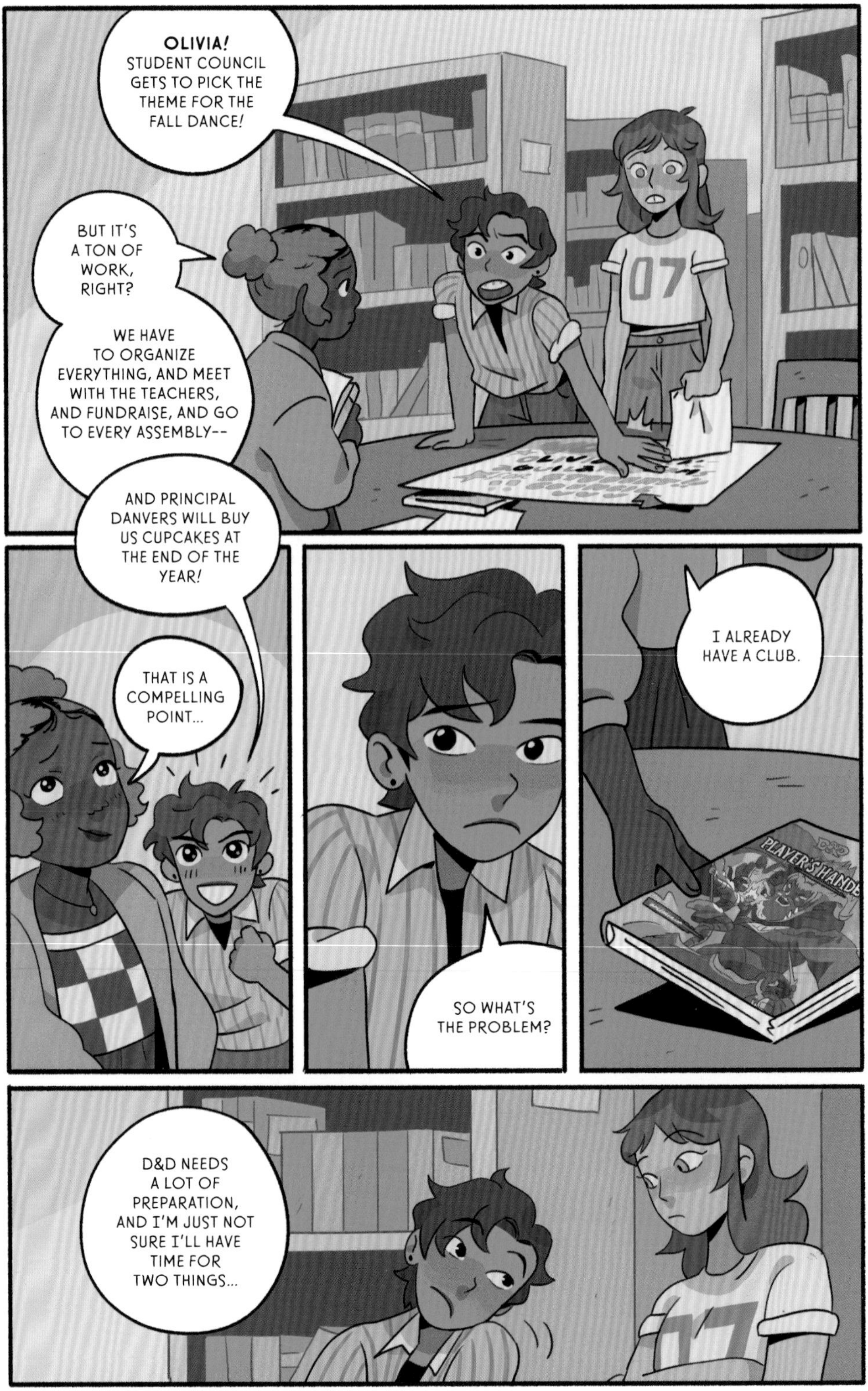
OLIVIA! STUDENT COUNCIL GETS TO PICK THE THEME FOR THE FALL DANCE!
BUT IT'S A TON OF WORK, RIGHT?
WE HAVE TO ORGANIZE EVERYTHING, AND MEET WITH THE TEACHERS, AND FUNDRAISE, AND GO TO EVERY ASSEMBLY--
AND PRINCIPAL DANVERS WILL BUY US CUPCAKES AT THE END OF THE YEAR!
THAT IS A COMPELLING POINT...
SO WHAT'S THE PROBLEM?
I ALREADY HAVE A CLUB.
PLAYER'S HANDB
D&D NEEDS A LOT OF PREPARATION, AND I'M JUST NOT SURE I'LL HAVE TIME FOR TWO THINGS...

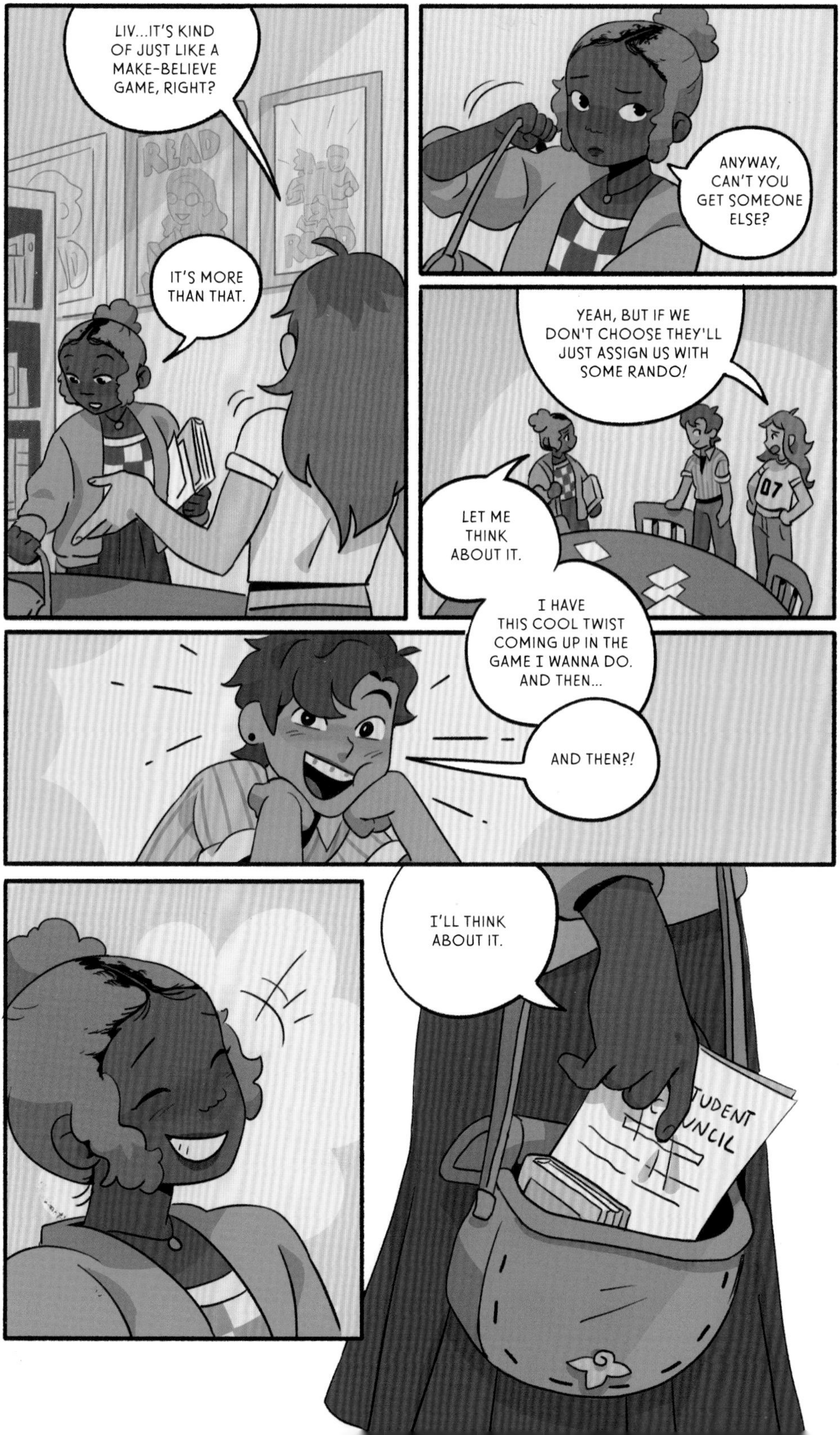
LIV...IT'S KIND OF JUST LIKE A MAKE-BELIEVE GAME, RIGHT?
IT'S MORE THAN THAT.
ANYWAY, CAN'T YOU GET SOMEONE ELSE?
YEAH, BUT IF WE DON'T CHOOSE THEY'LL JUST ASSIGN US WITH SOME RANDO!
LET ME THINK ABOUT IT.
I HAVE THIS COOL TWIST COMING UP IN THE GAME I WANNA DO. AND THEN...
AND THEN?!
I'LL THINK ABOUT IT.

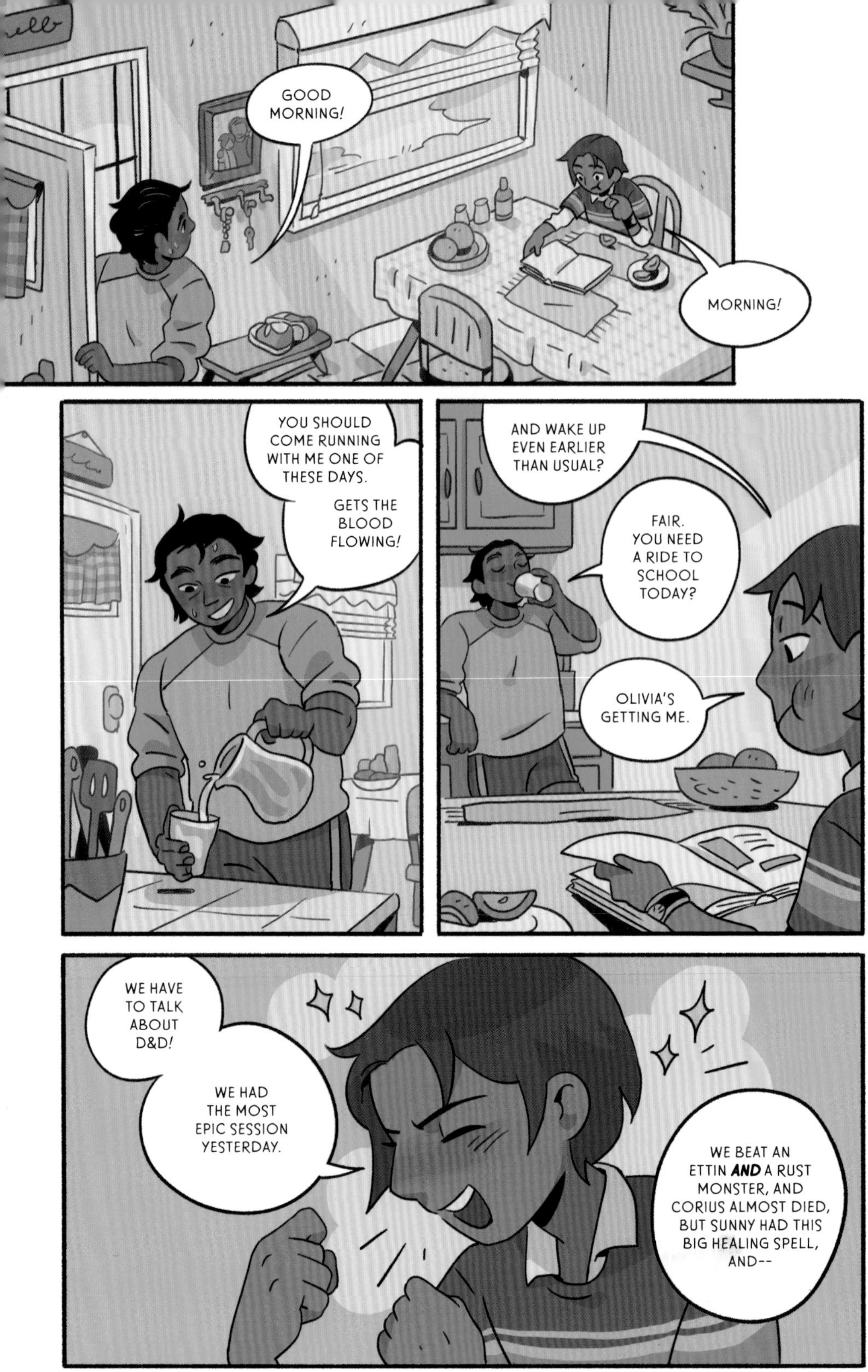
GOOD MORNING!
MORNING!
YOU SHOULD COME RUNNING WITH ME ONE OF THESE DAYS.
GETS THE BLOOD FLOWING!
AND WAKE UP EVEN EARLIER THAN USUAL?
FAIR. YOU NEED A RIDE TO SCHOOL TODAY?
OLIVIA'S GETTING ME.
WE HAVE TO TALK ABOUT D&D!
WE HAD THE MOST EPIC SESSION YESTERDAY.
WE BEAT AN ETTIN ***AND*** A RUST MONSTER, AND CORIUS ALMOST DIED, BUT SUNNY HAD THIS BIG HEALING SPELL, AND--

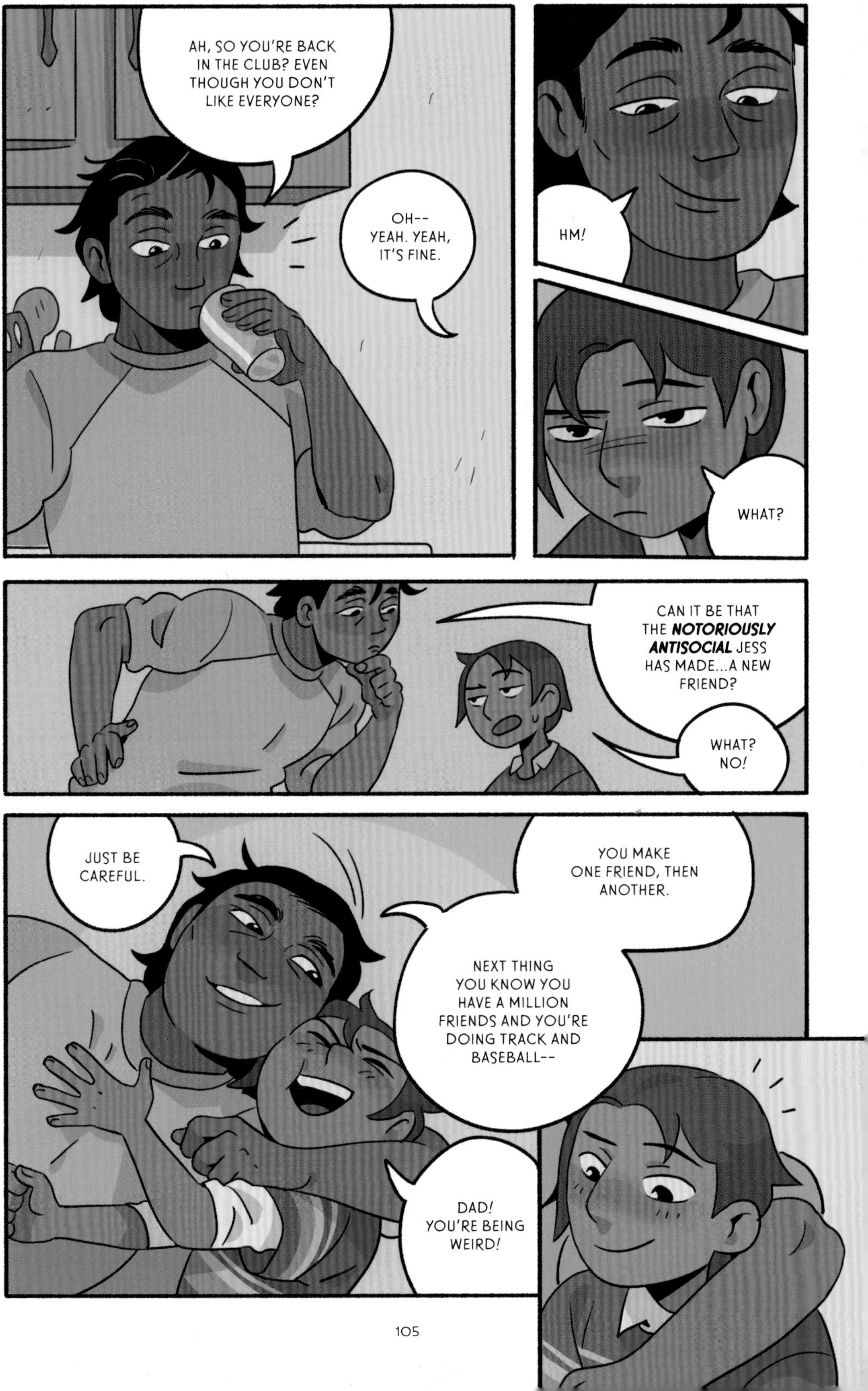
AH, SO YOU'RE BACK IN THE CLUB? EVEN THOUGH YOU DON'T LIKE EVERYONE?
OH-- YEAH. YEAH, IT'S FINE.
HM!
WHAT?
CAN IT BE THAT THE **NOTORIOUSLY ANTISOCIAL** JESS HAS MADE...A NEW FRIEND?
WHAT? NO!
JUST BE CAREFUL.
YOU MAKE ONE FRIEND, THEN ANOTHER.
NEXT THING YOU KNOW YOU HAVE A MILLION FRIENDS AND YOU'RE DOING TRACK AND BASEBALL--
DAD! YOU'RE BEING WEIRD!

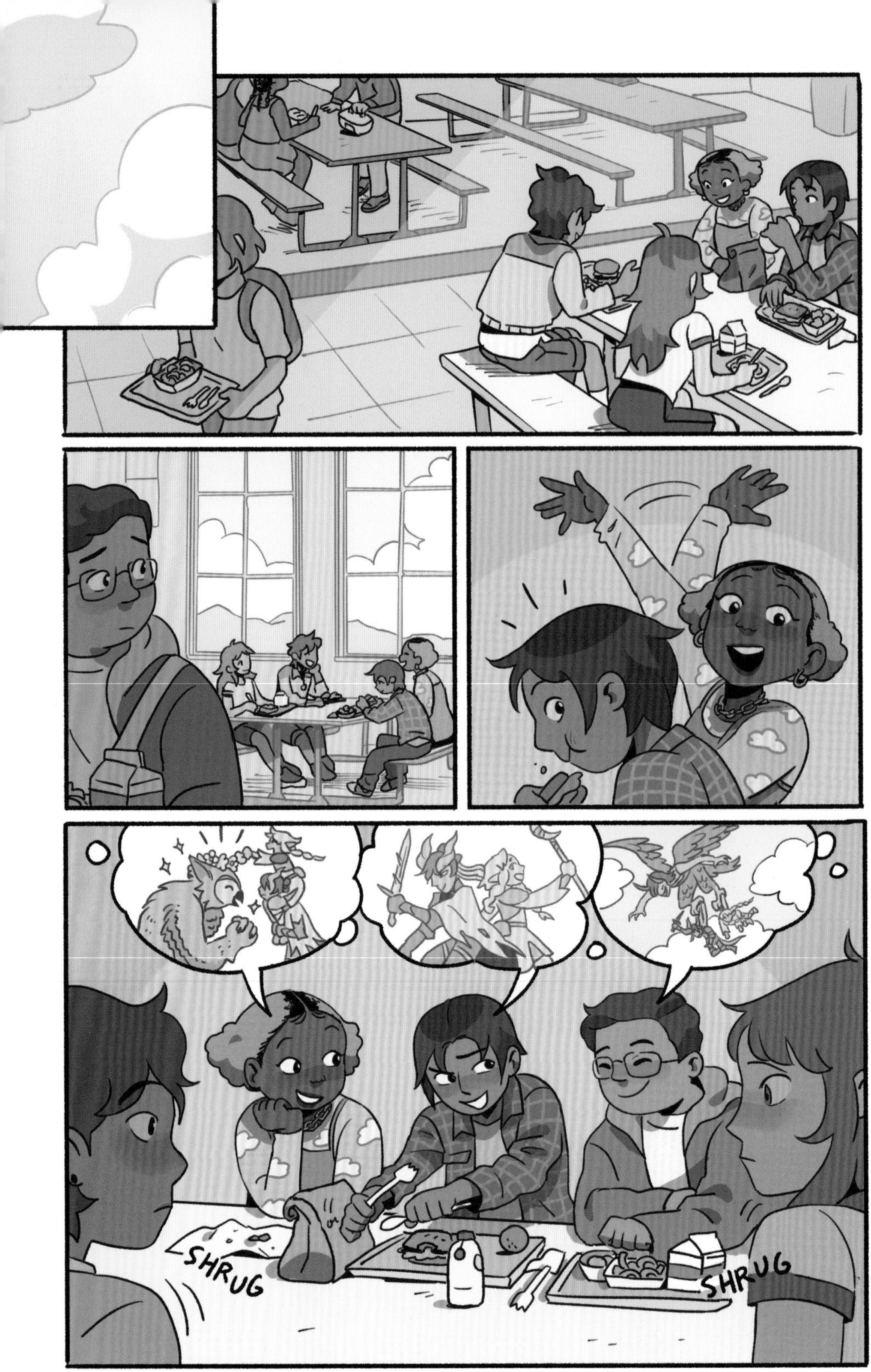
SHRUG
SHRUG

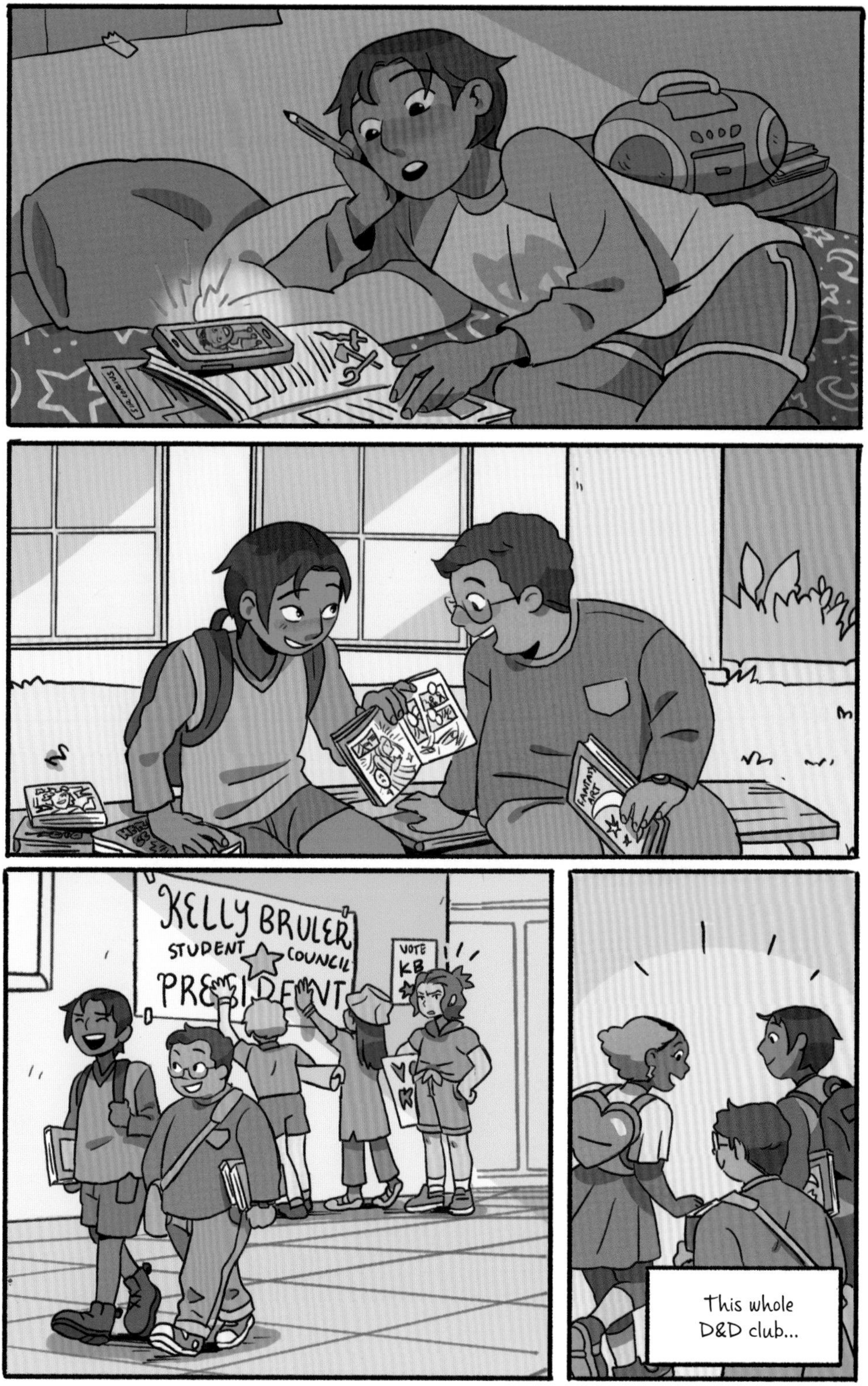
KELLY BRULER
STUDENT COUNCIL
PRESIDENT
VOTE KB
This whole D&D club...

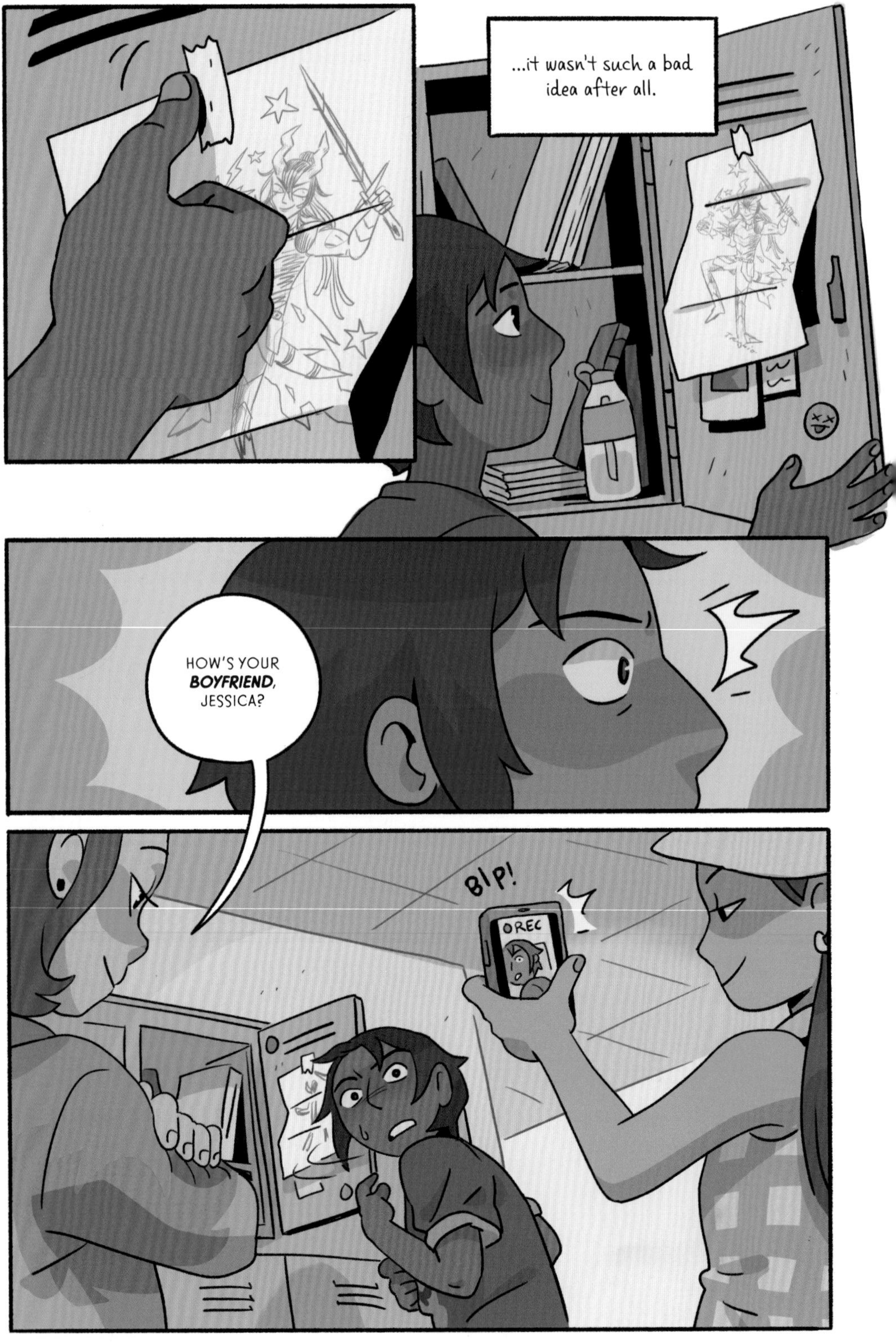
...it wasn't such a bad idea after all.
HOW'S YOUR **BOYFRIEND**, JESSICA?
BIP!
REC

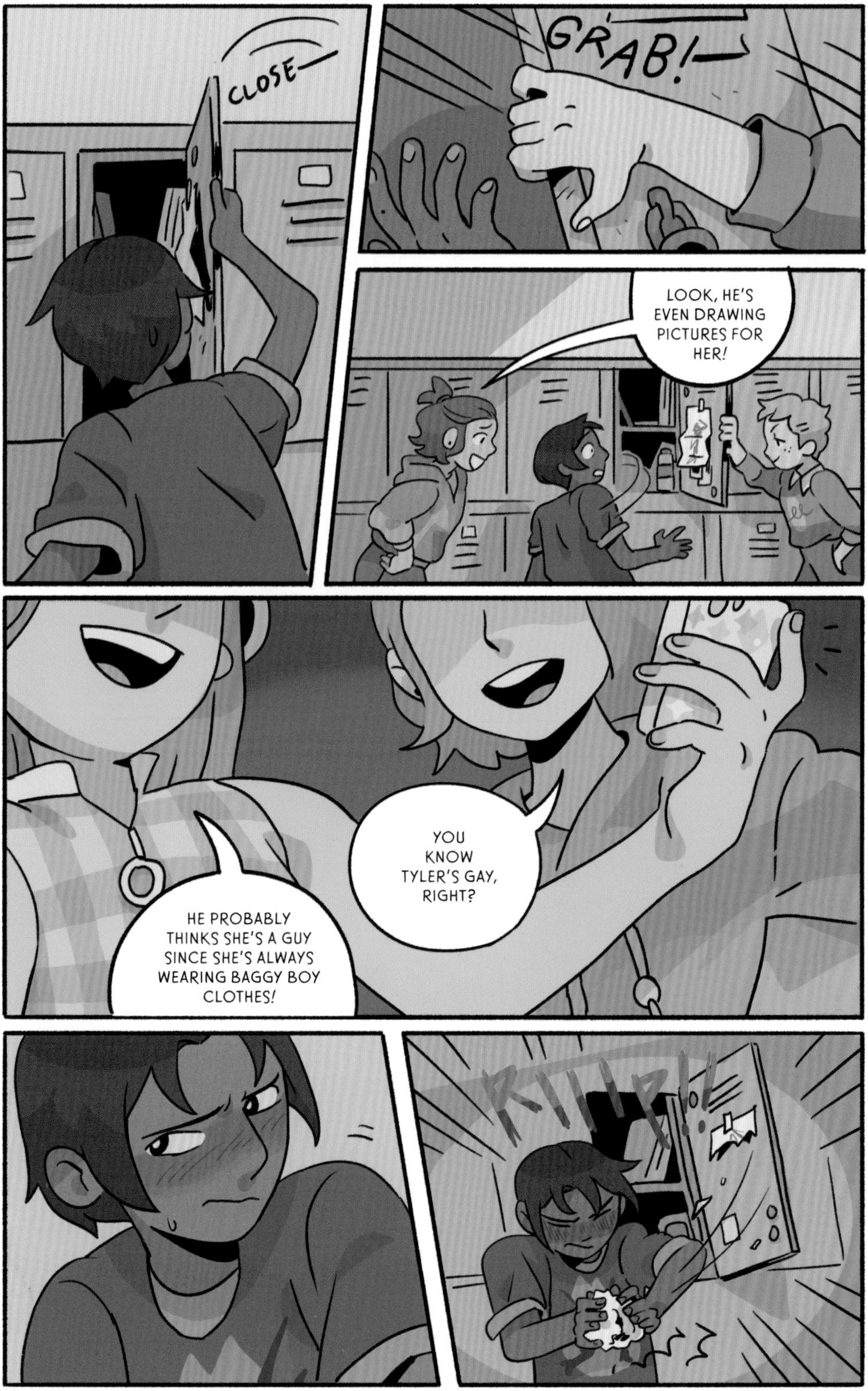
CLOSE
GRAB!
LOOK, HE'S EVEN DRAWING PICTURES FOR HER!
YOU KNOW TYLER'S GAY, RIGHT?
HE PROBABLY THINKS SHE'S A GUY SINCE SHE'S ALWAYS WEARING BAGGY BOY CLOTHES!
RIIIIP!!

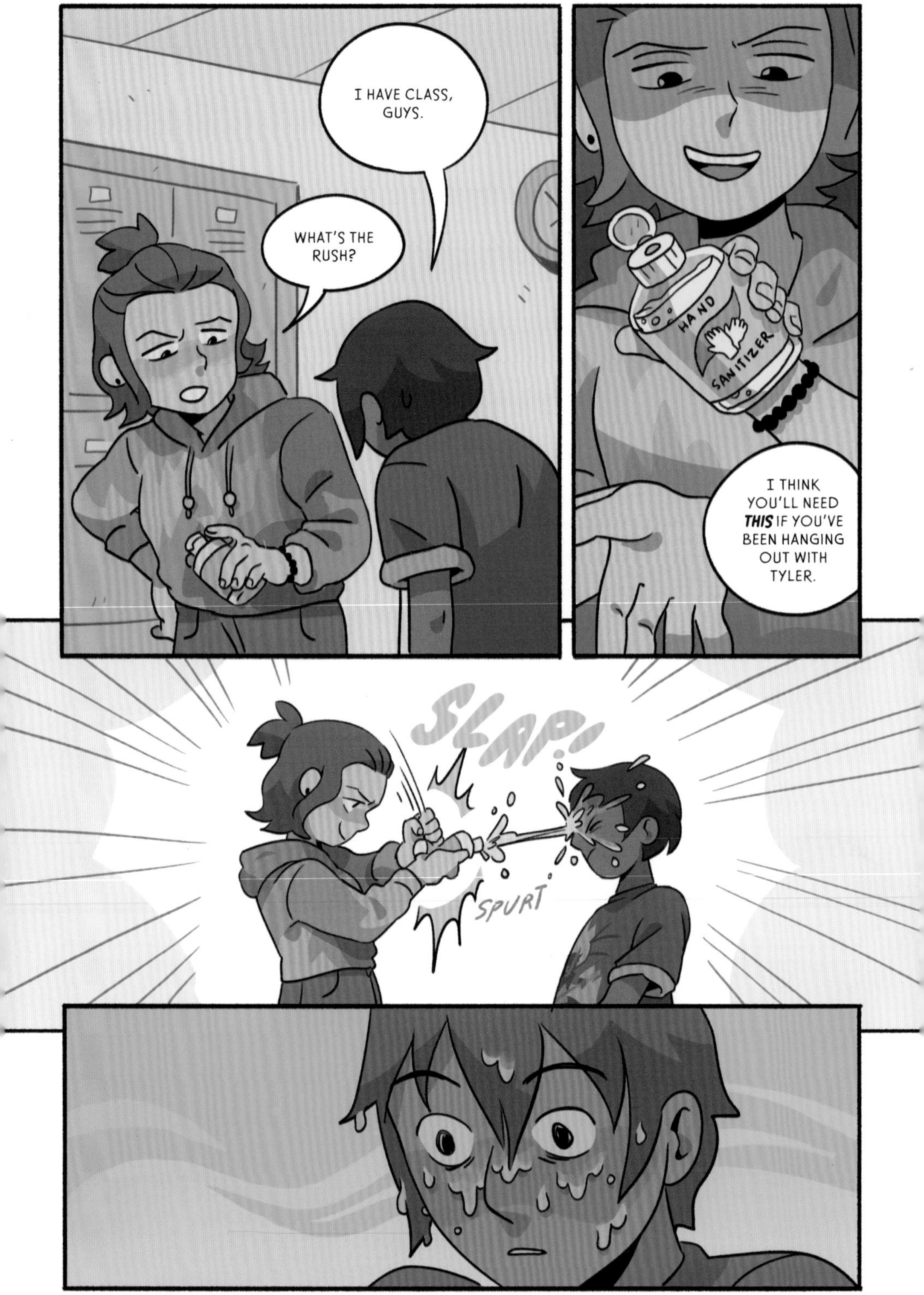
I HAVE CLASS, GUYS.
WHAT'S THE RUSH?
HAND SANITIZER
I THINK YOU'LL NEED **THIS** IF YOU'VE BEEN HANGING OUT WITH TYLER.
SLAP!
SPURT

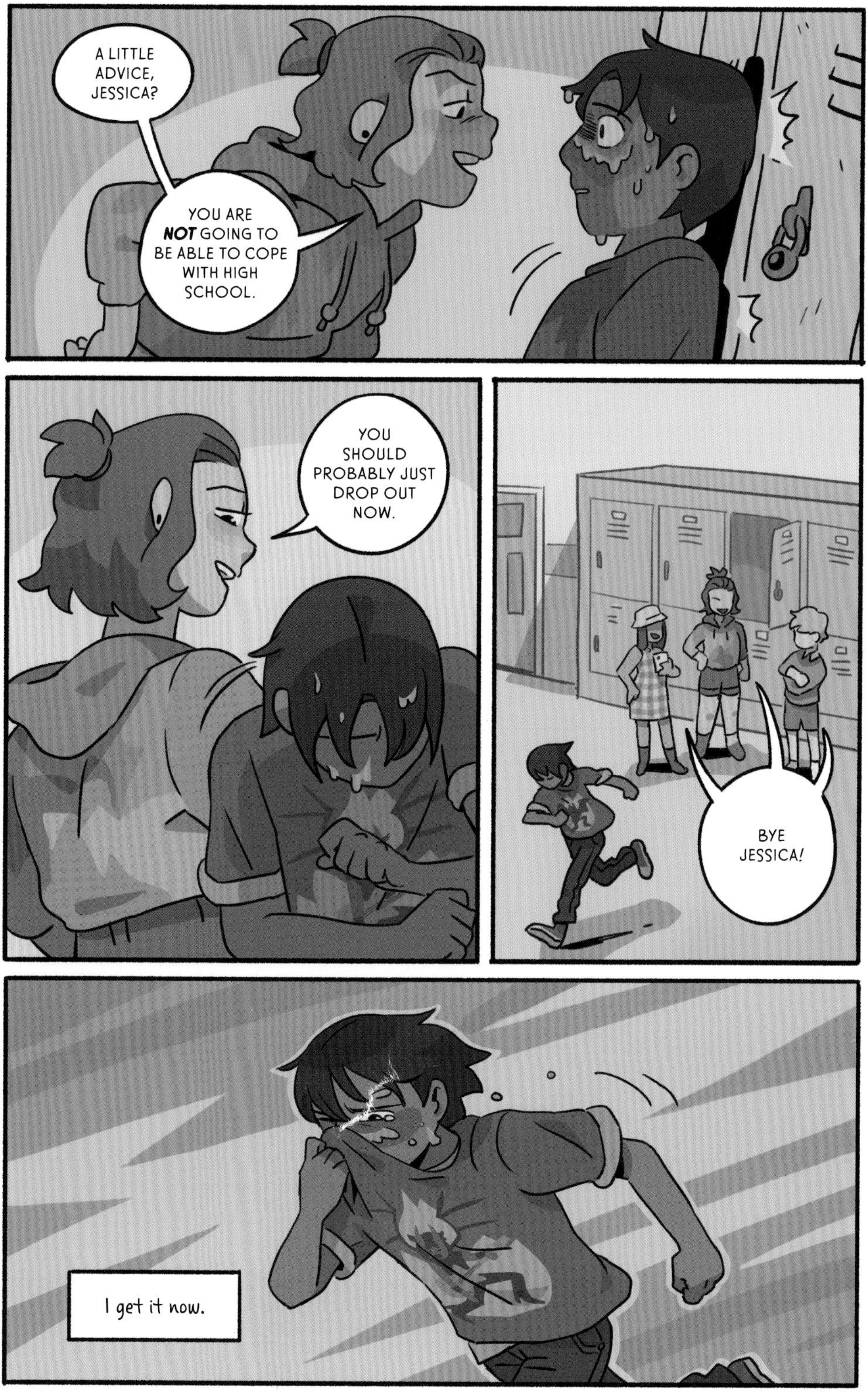

A LITTLE ADVICE, JESSICA?
YOU ARE **NOT** GOING TO BE ABLE TO COPE WITH HIGH SCHOOL.
YOU SHOULD PROBABLY JUST DROP OUT NOW.
BYE JESSICA!
I get it now.

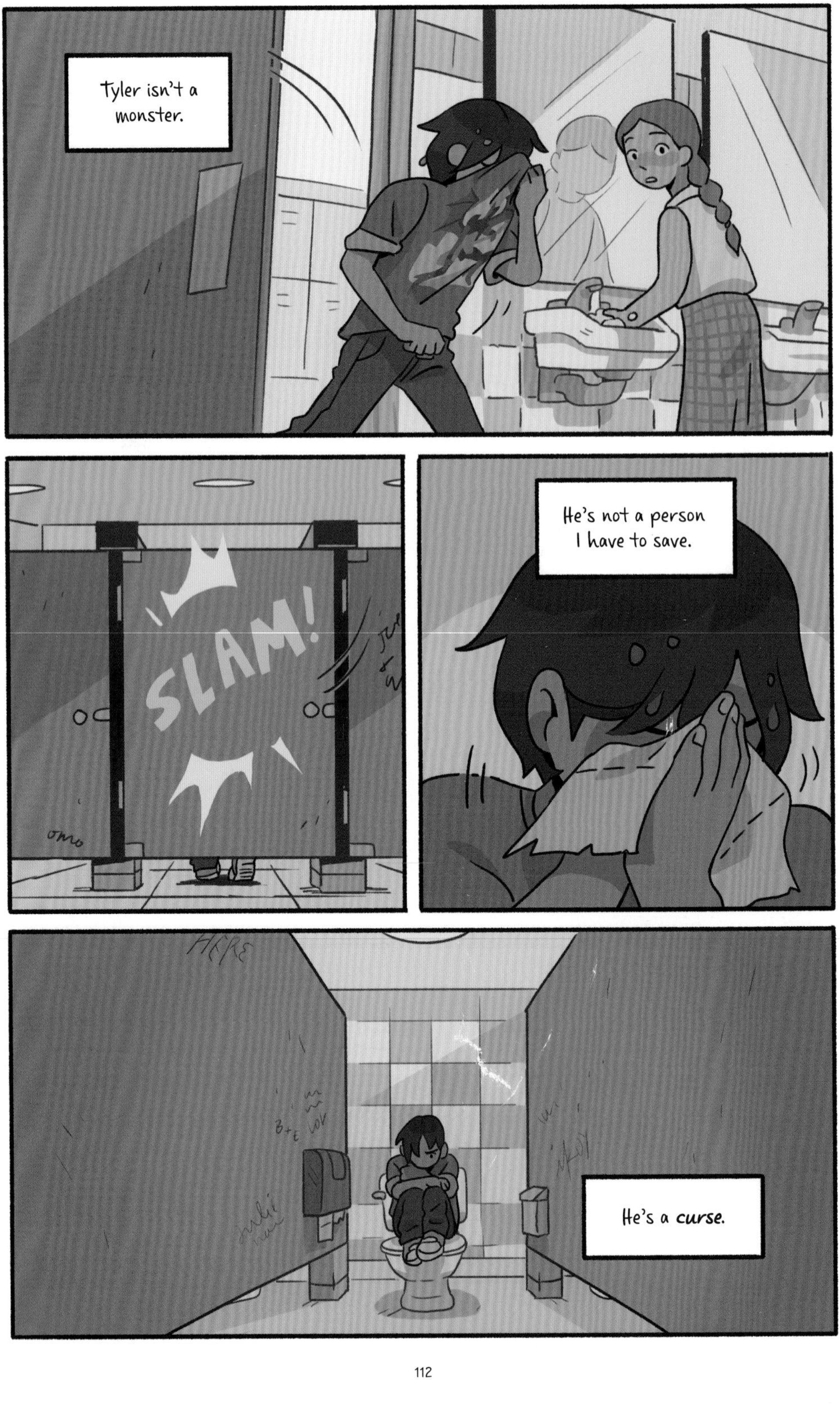
Tyler isn't a monster.
SLAM!
He's not a person I have to save.
He's a **curse**.

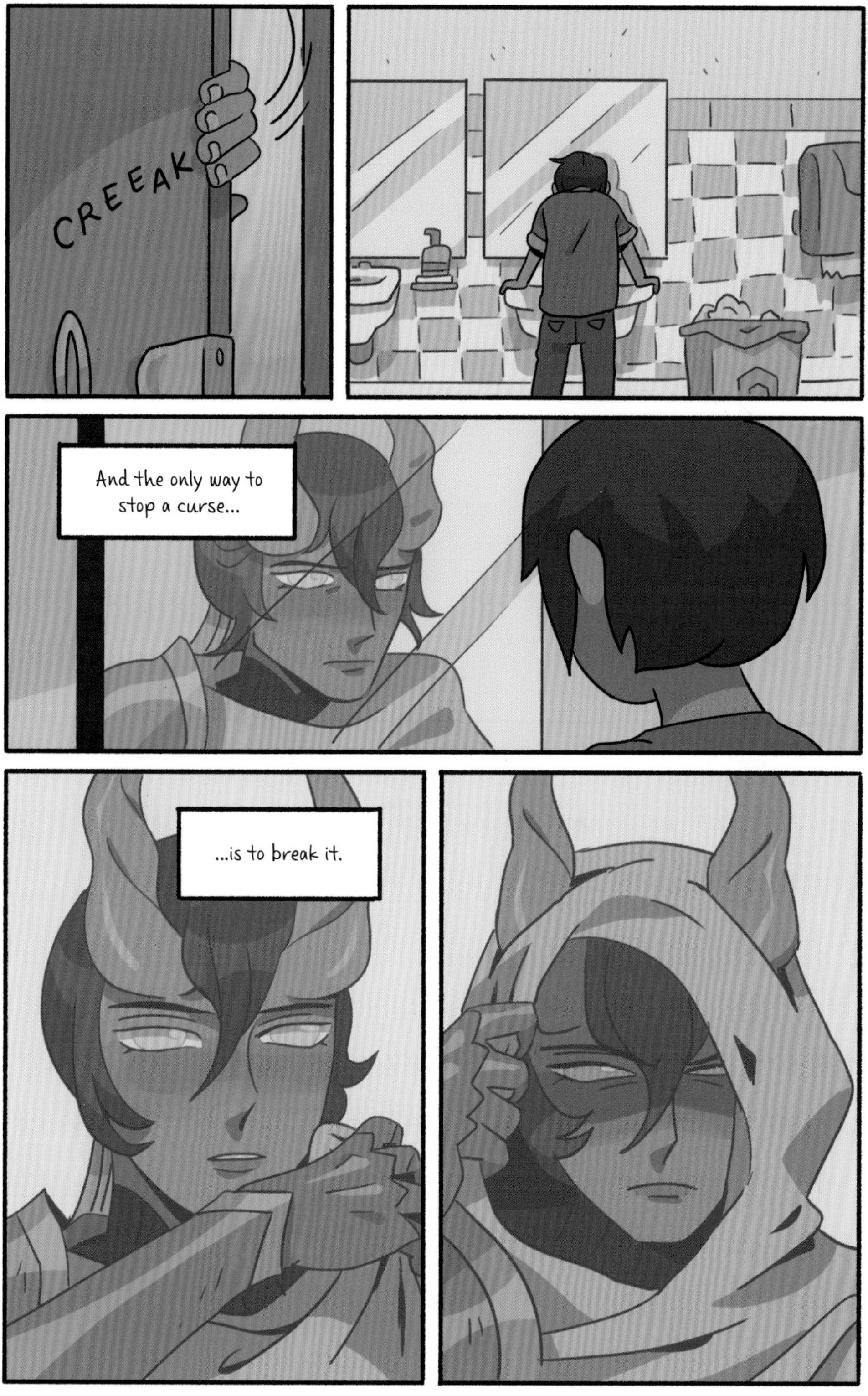
CREEAK
And the only way to stop a curse...
...is to break it.

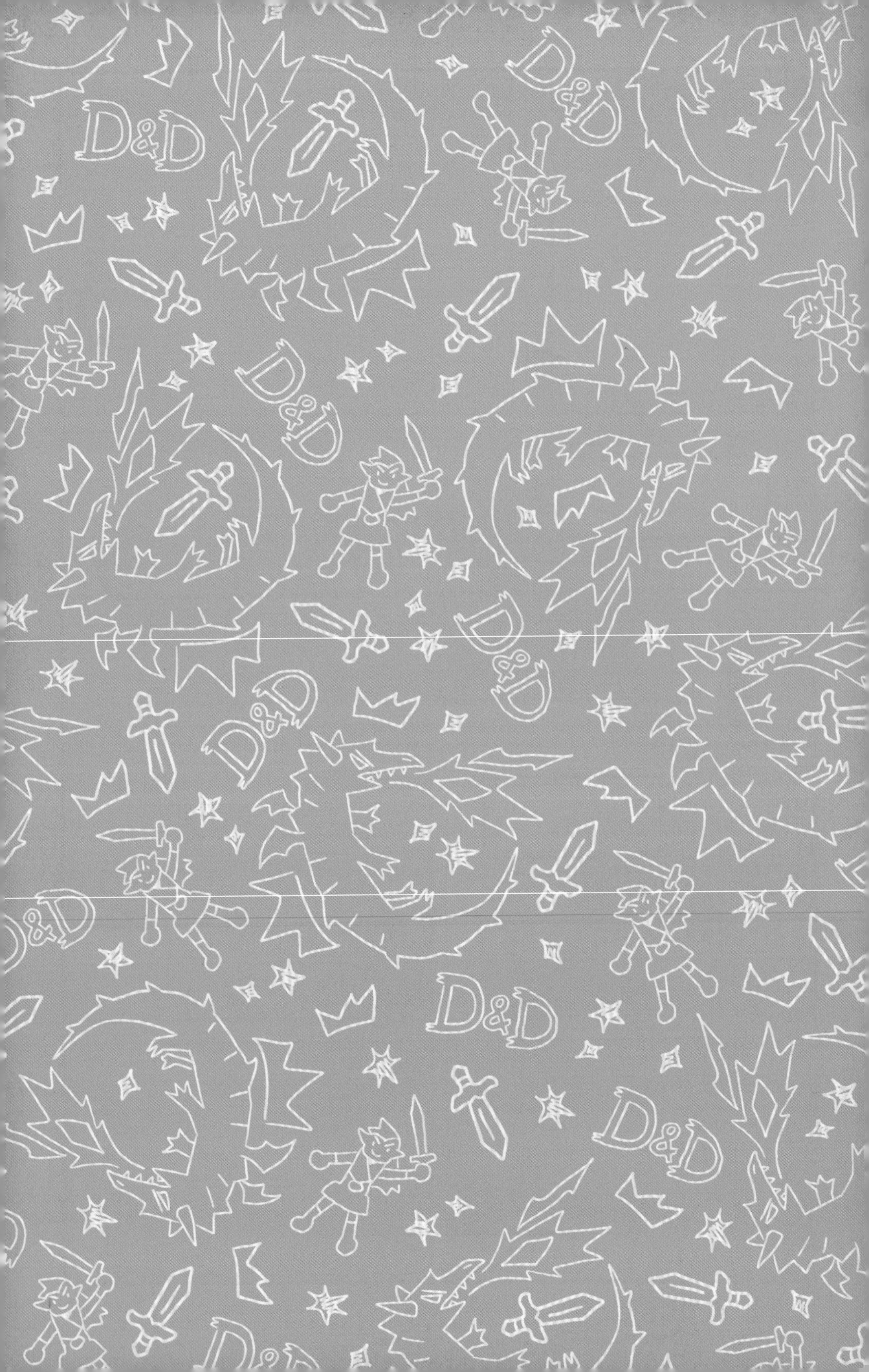
D&D

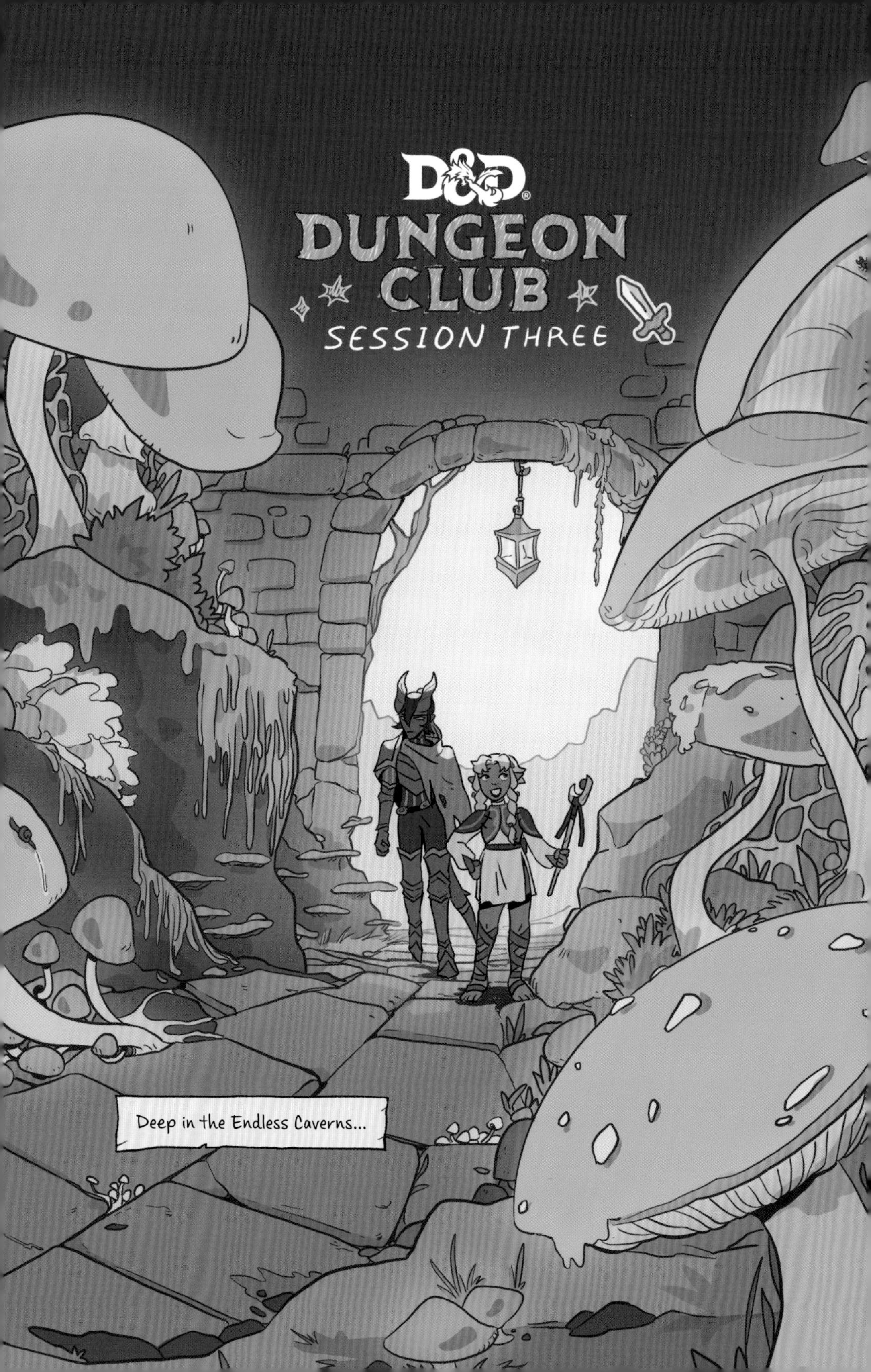
D&D
DUNGEON CLUB
SESSION THREE
Deep in the Endless Caverns...

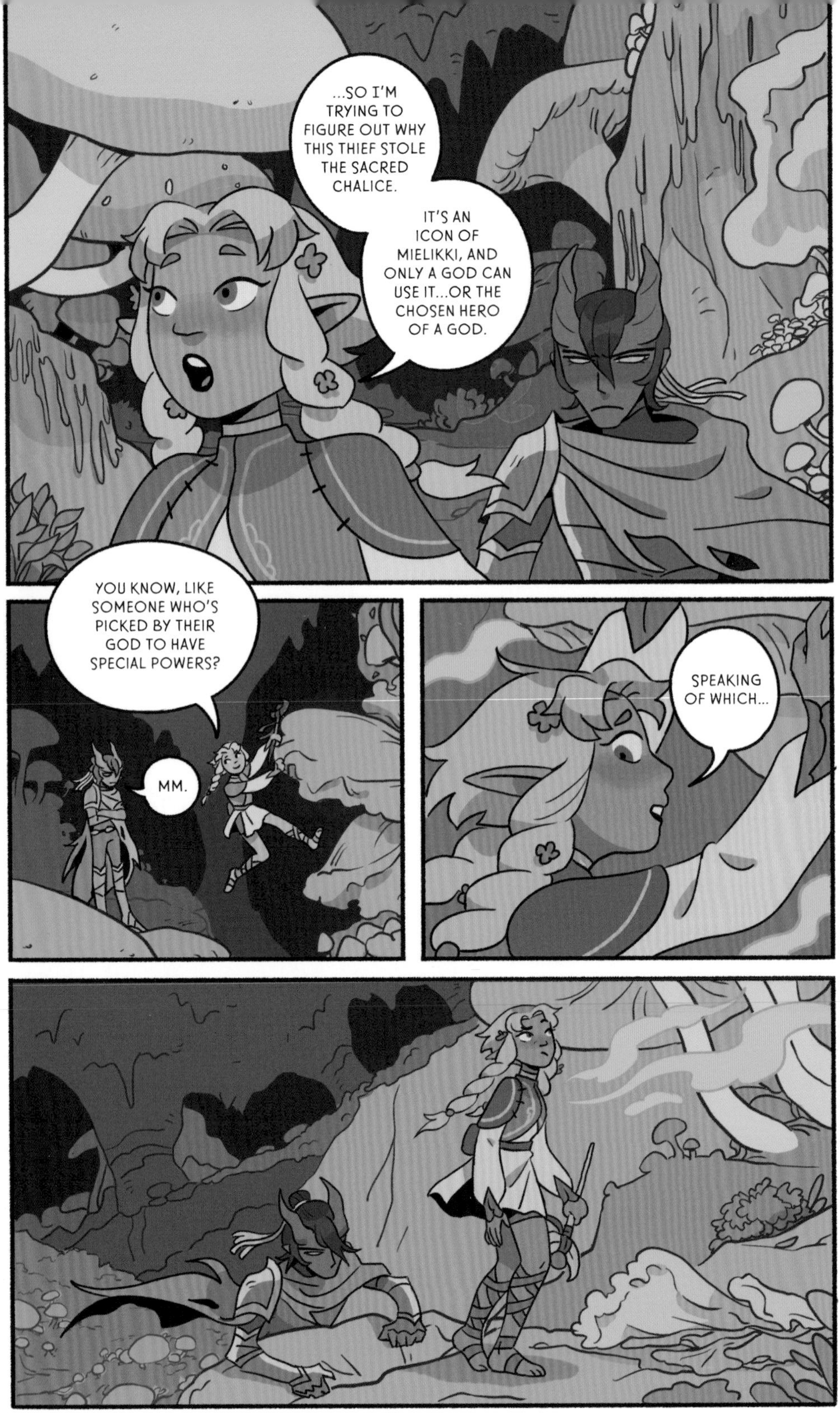
...SO I'M TRYING TO FIGURE OUT WHY THIS THIEF STOLE THE SACRED CHALICE.
IT'S AN ICON OF MIELIKKI, AND ONLY A GOD CAN USE IT...OR THE CHOSEN HERO OF A GOD.
YOU KNOW, LIKE SOMEONE WHO'S PICKED BY THEIR GOD TO HAVE SPECIAL POWERS?
MM.
SPEAKING OF WHICH...

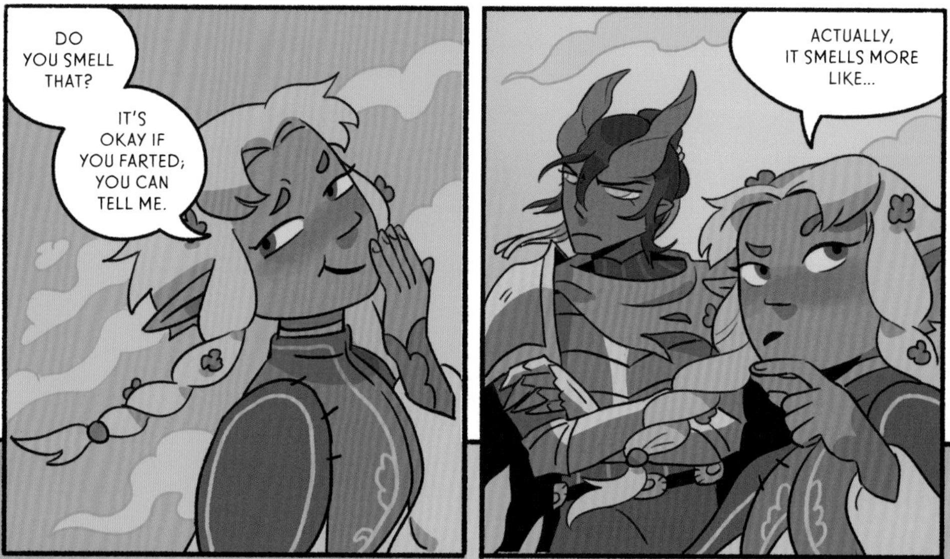
DO YOU SMELL THAT?
IT'S OKAY IF YOU FARTED; YOU CAN TELL ME.
ACTUALLY, IT SMELLS MORE LIKE...

BULLYWUG

Medium Humanoid (Bullywug), Neutral Evil

Armor Class 15 (hide armor, shield)
Hit Points 11
Speed 20 ft, swim 40 ft.

STR	DEX	CON	INT	WIS	CHA
12 (+1)	12 (+1)	12 (+1)	7 (-2)	10 (+0)	7(-2)

Actions

Standing Leap. The bullywug's long jump is up to 20 feet and its high jump is up to 10 feet, with or without a running start.

Multiattack. The bullywug makes two melee attacks: one with its bite and one with its melee weapon.

Life as a bullywug is nasty, brutish, and wet. These frog-headed amphibious humanoids must stay constantly moist, dwelling in rainy forests, marshes, and damp caves. Always hungry and thoroughly evil, bullywugs overwhelm opponents with superior numbers.

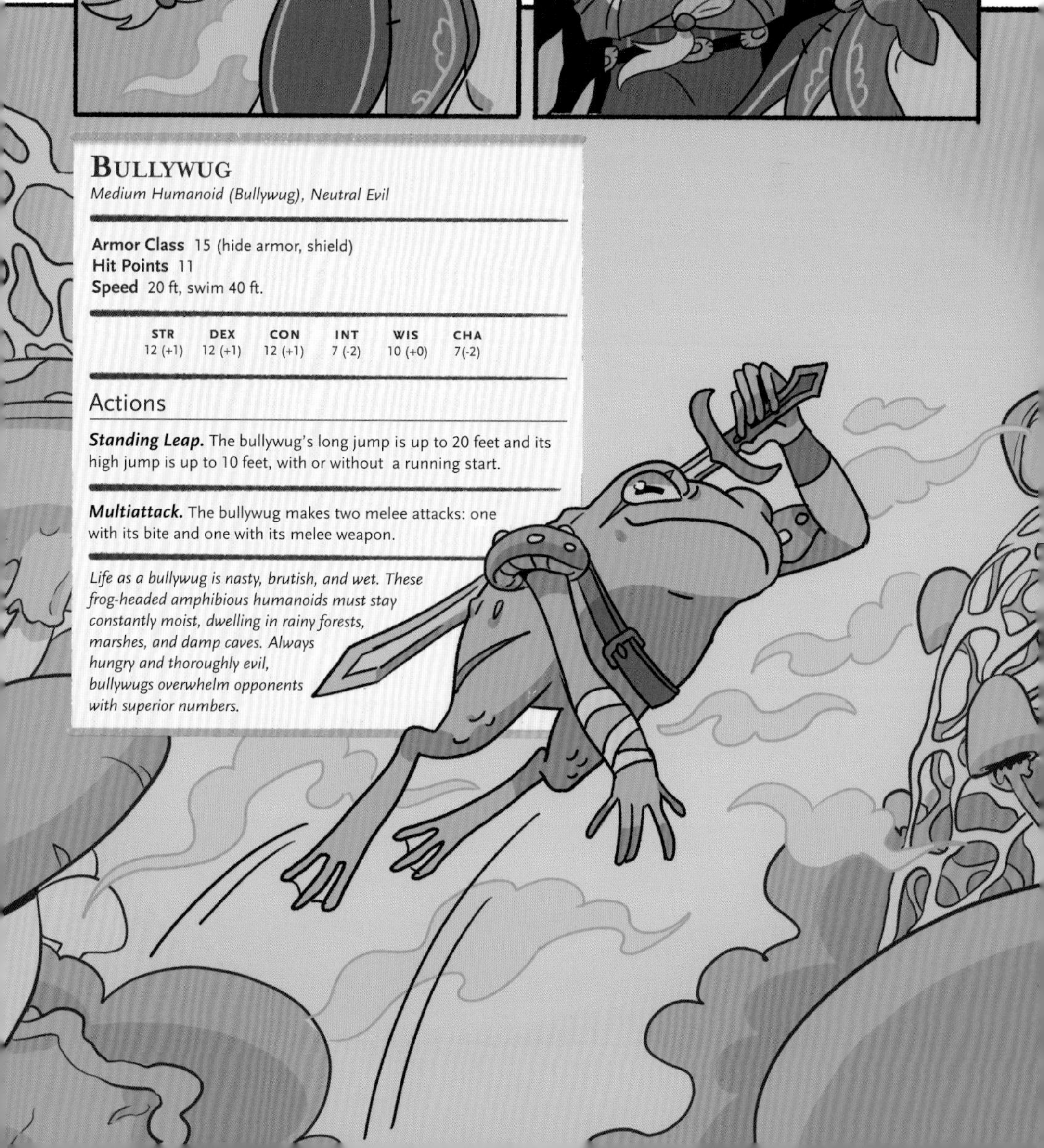

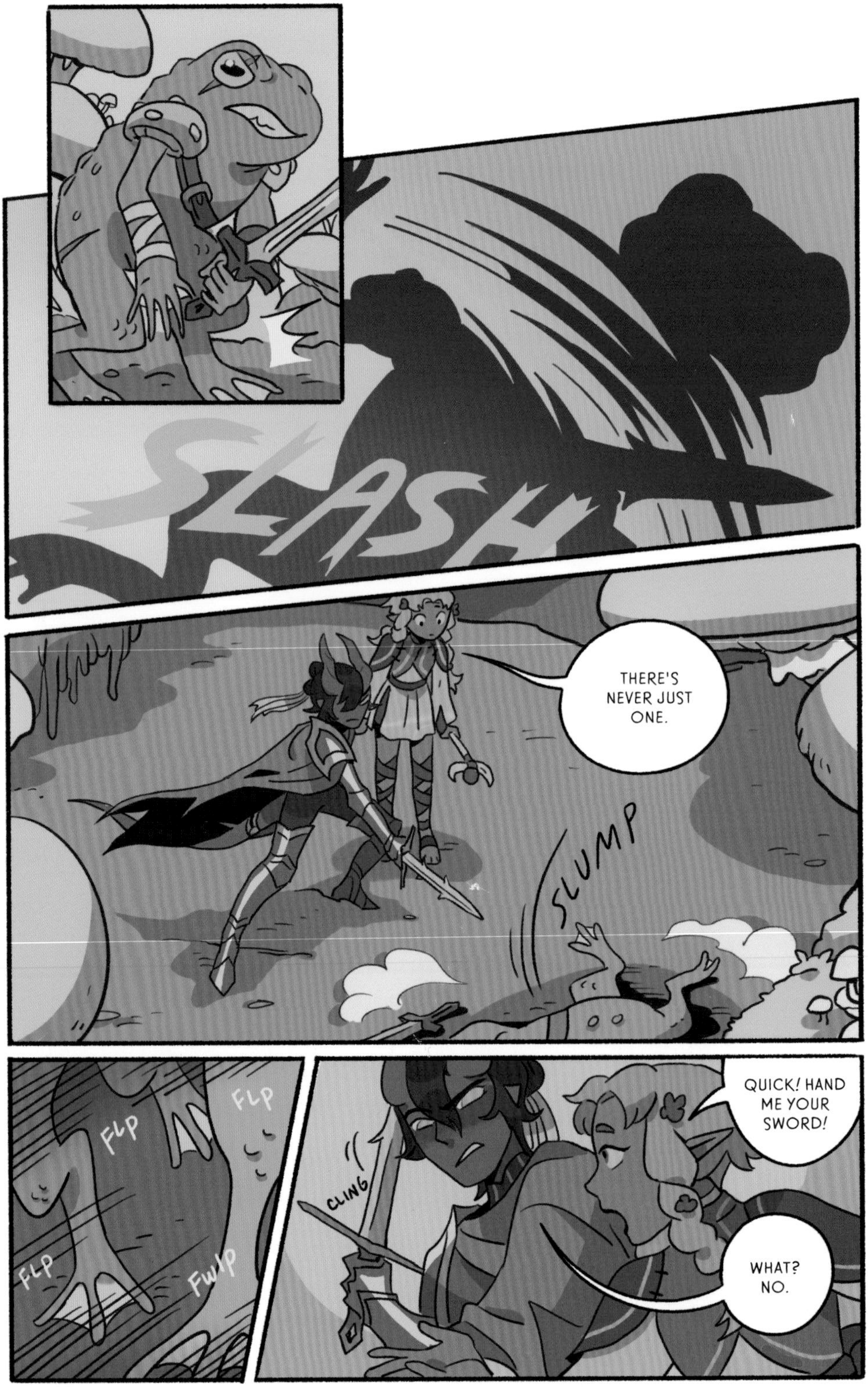
SLASH
THERE'S NEVER JUST ONE.
SLUMP
FLP
FLP
FLP
FWIP
CLING
QUICK! HAND ME YOUR SWORD!
WHAT? NO.

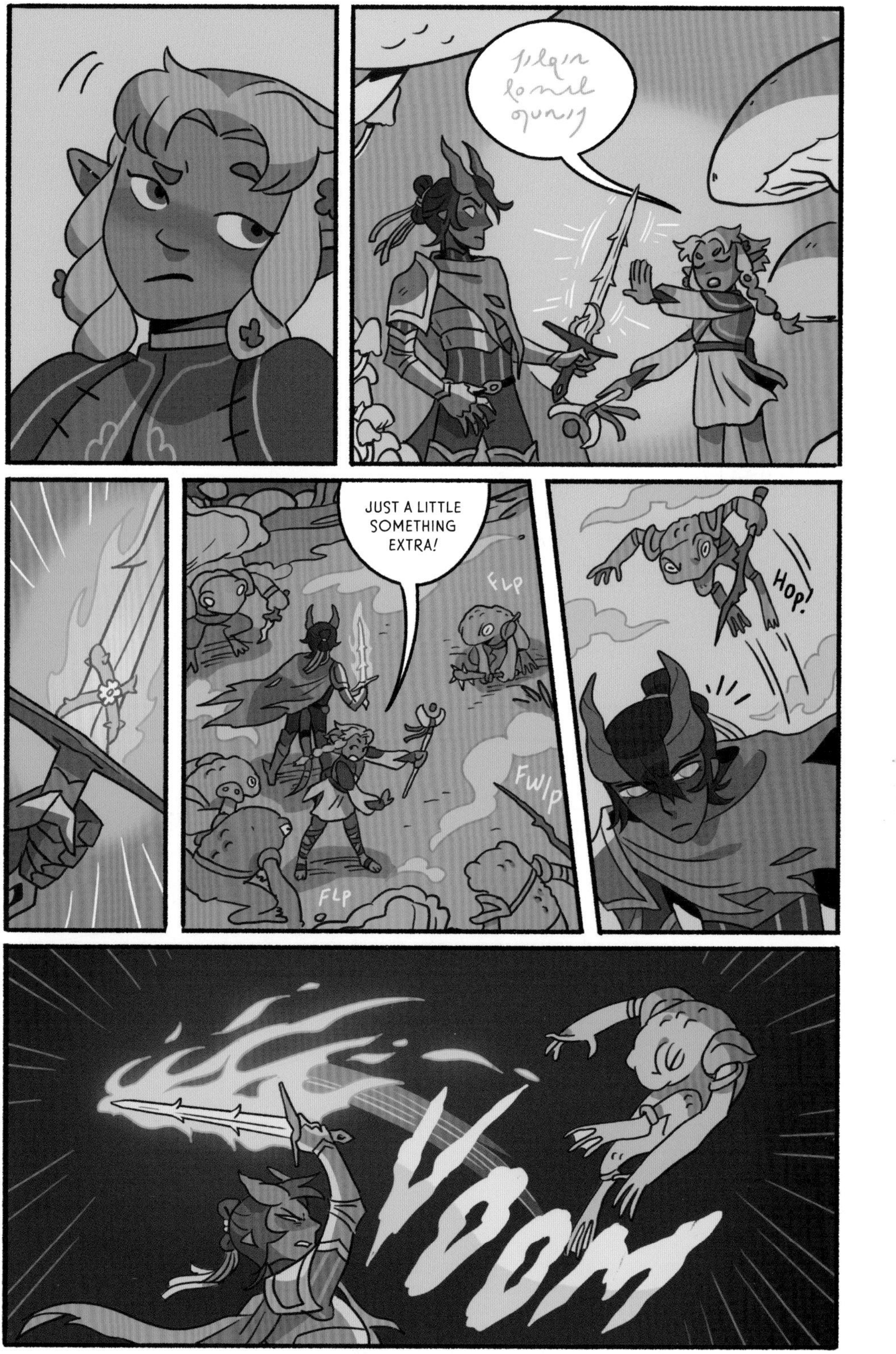
JUST A LITTLE SOMETHING EXTRA!
FLP
FWIP
FLP
HOP!
VOOM

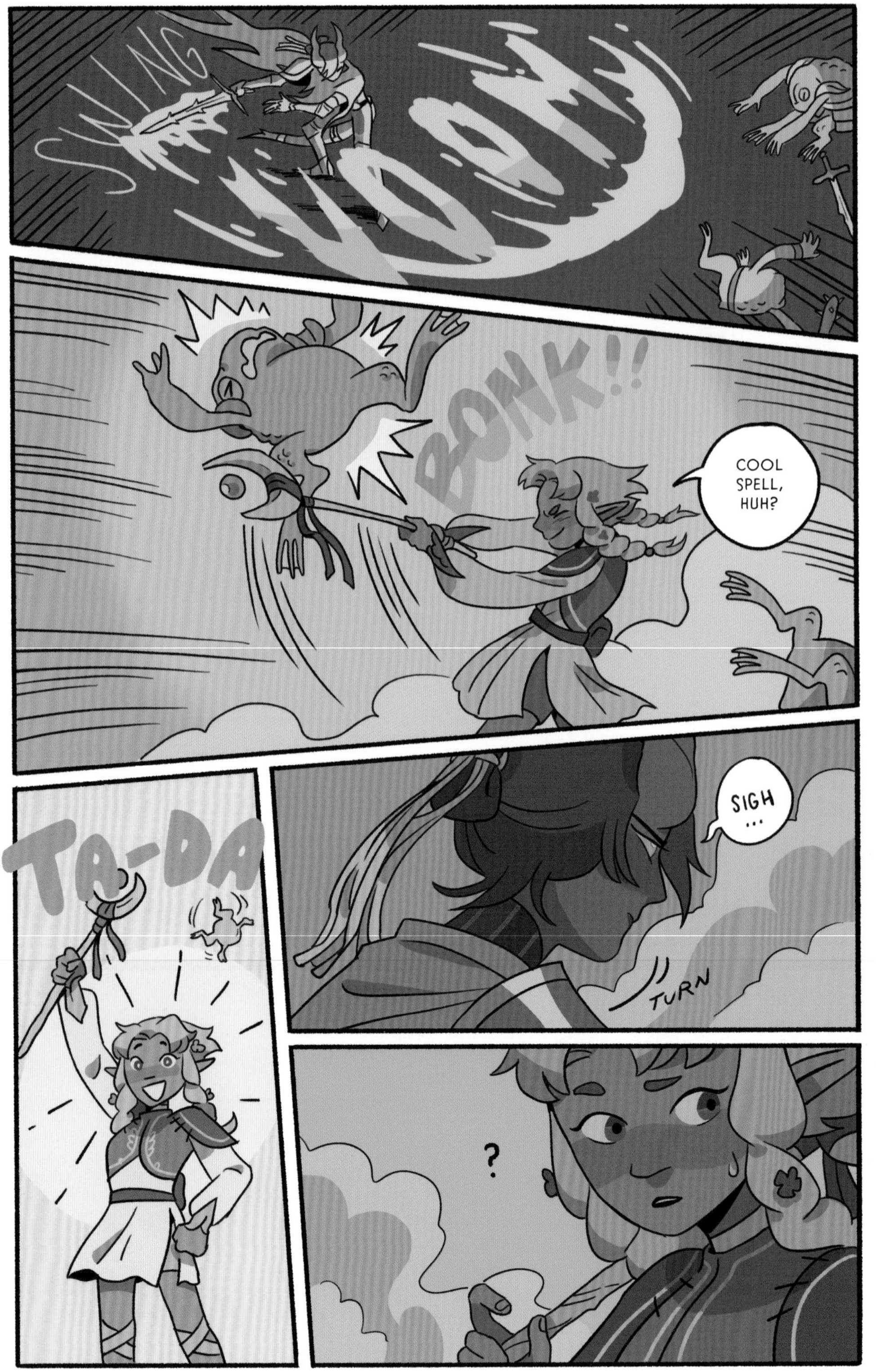
SWING
FWOOM!
BONK!!
COOL SPELL, HUH?
TA-DA
SIGH ...
TURN
?

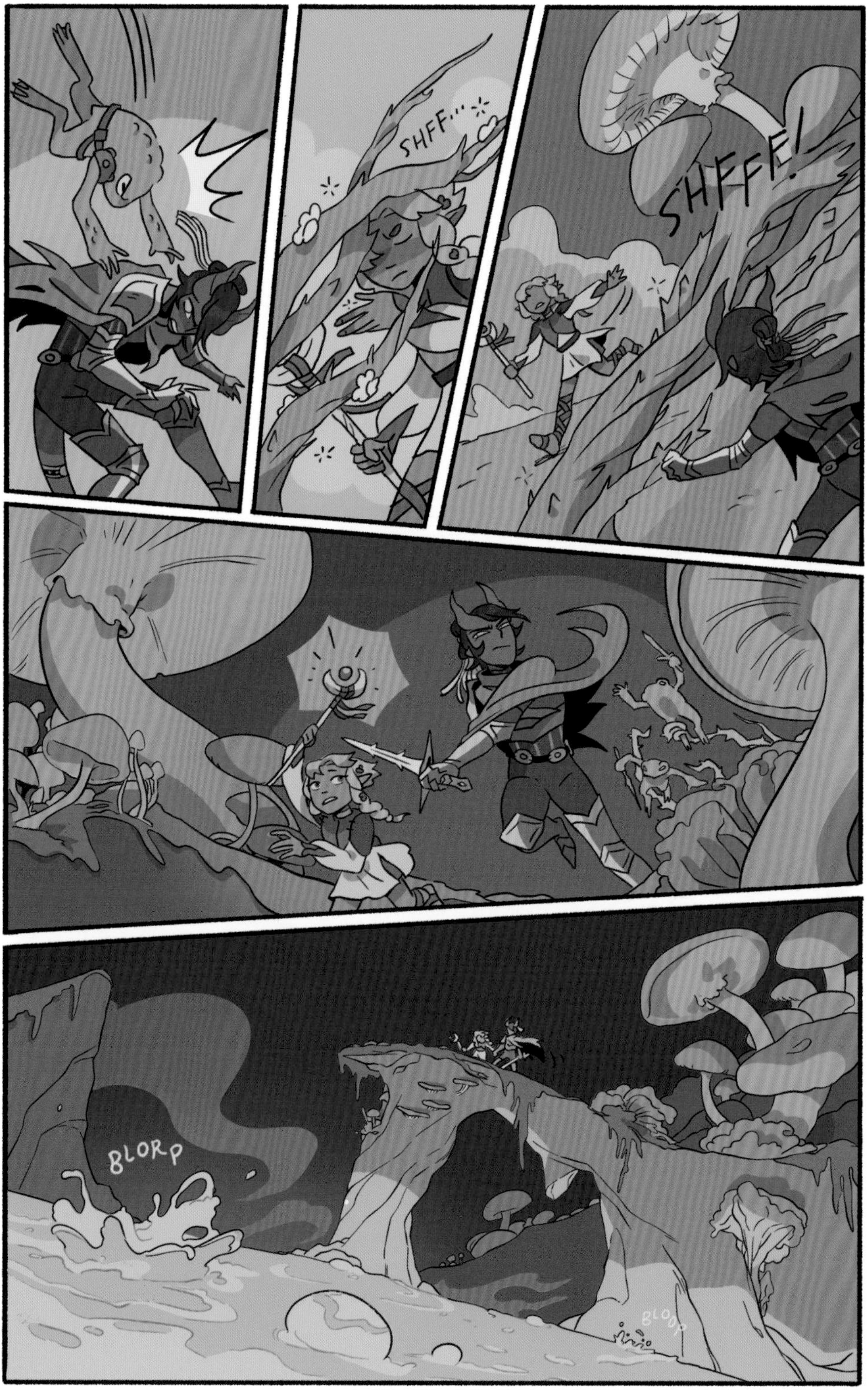
SHFF...
SHFFF!
BLORP
BLOOP

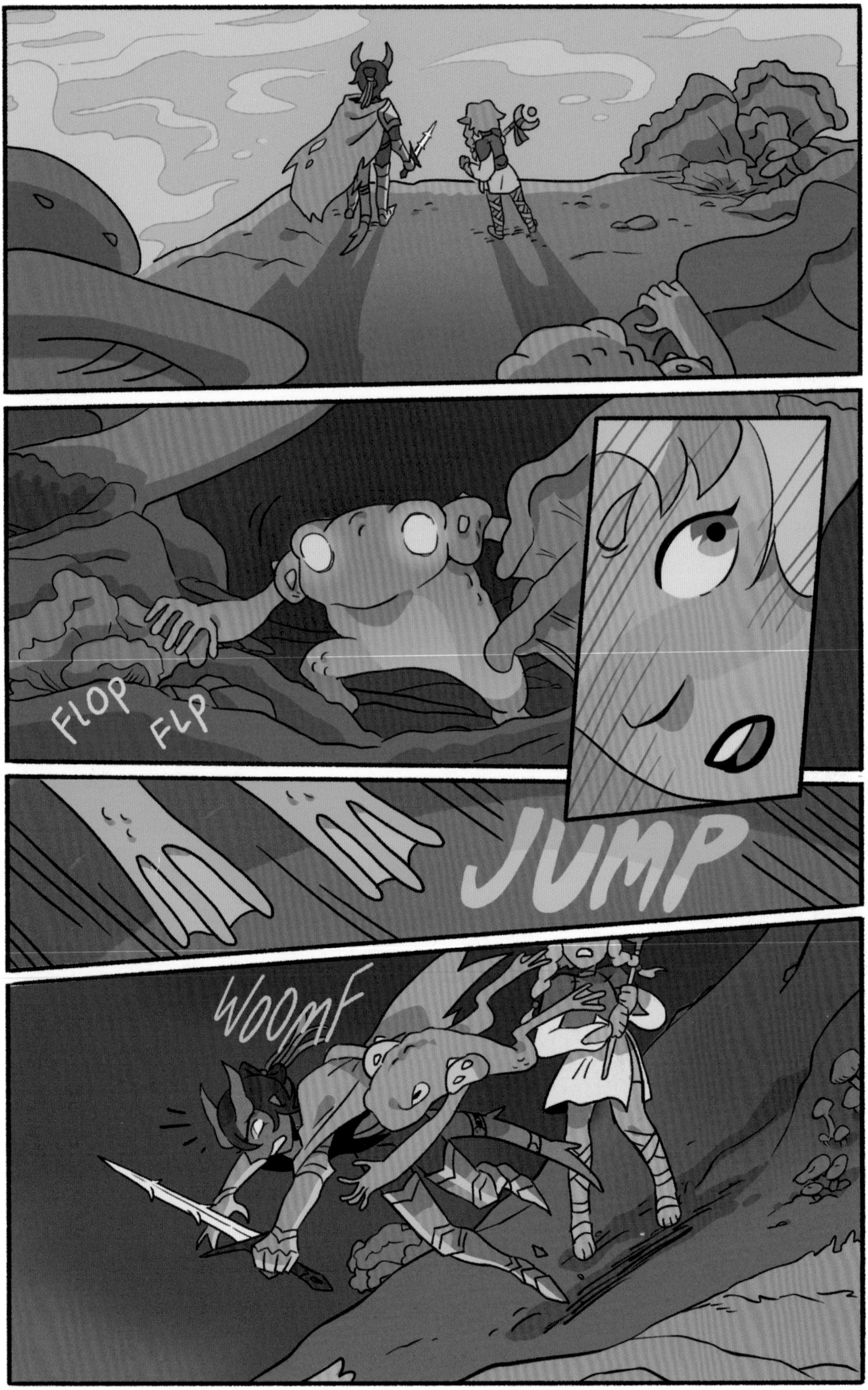
FLOP
FLP
JUMP
WOOMF

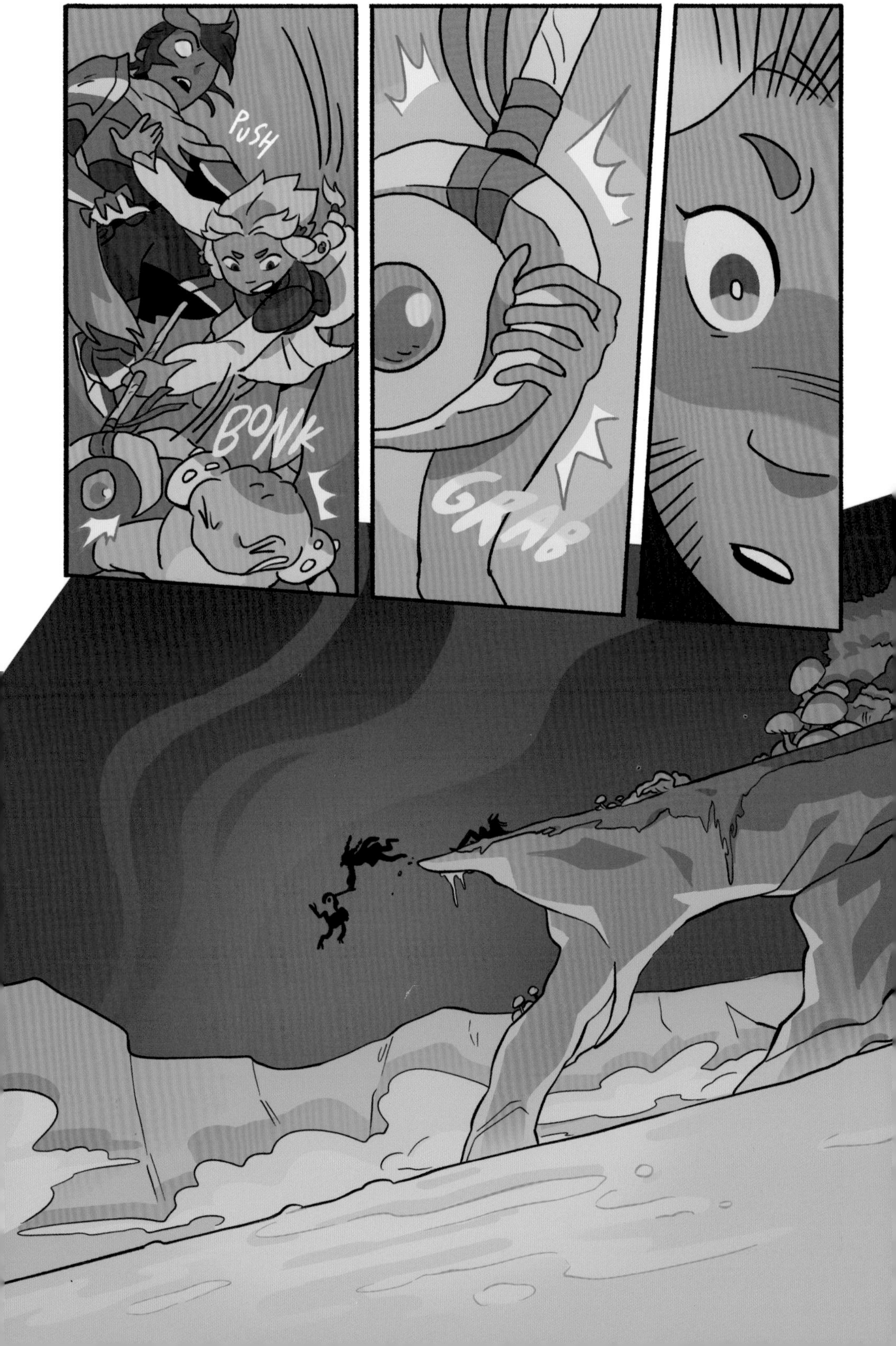
PUSH
BONK
GRAB

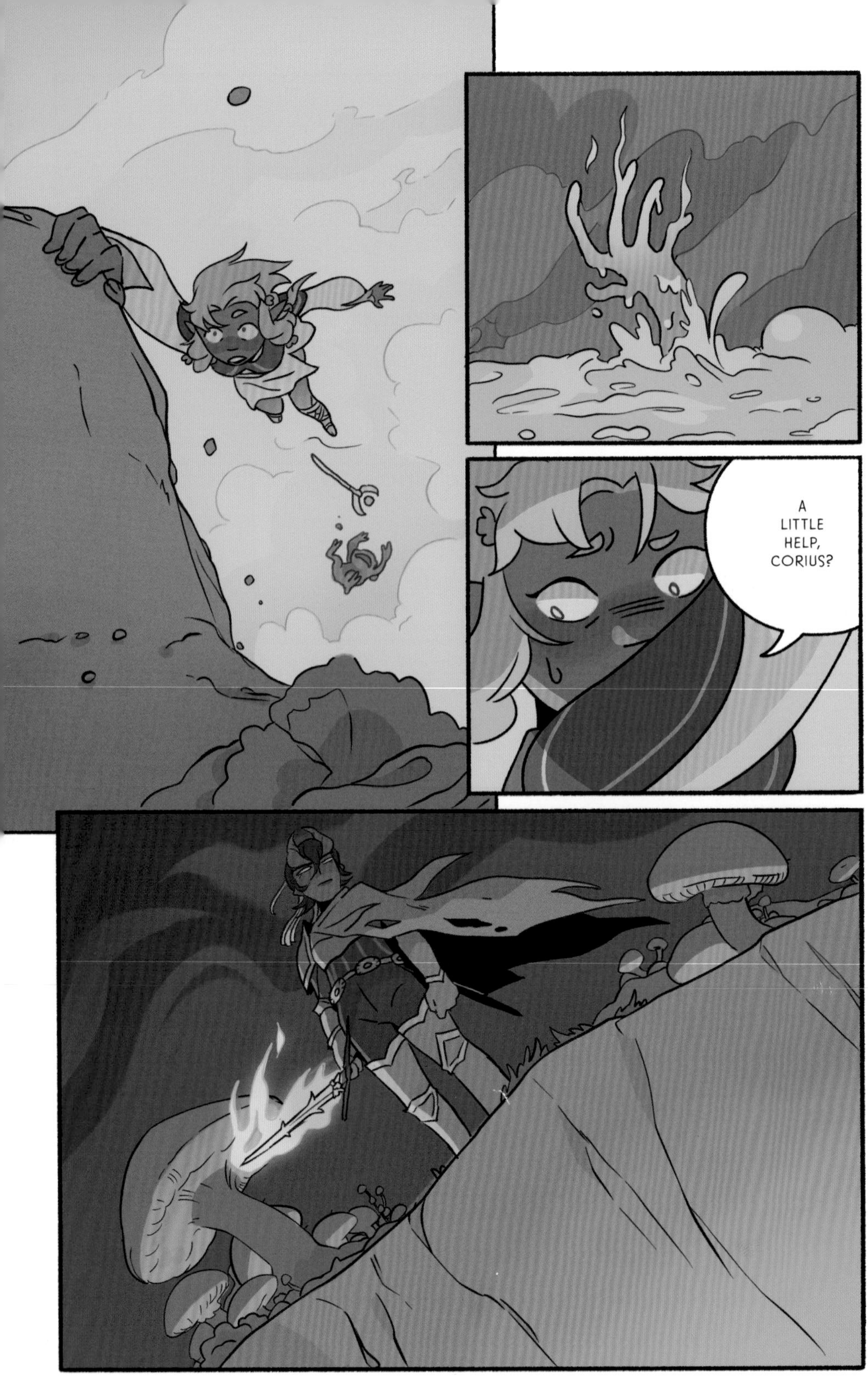
A LITTLE HELP, CORIUS?

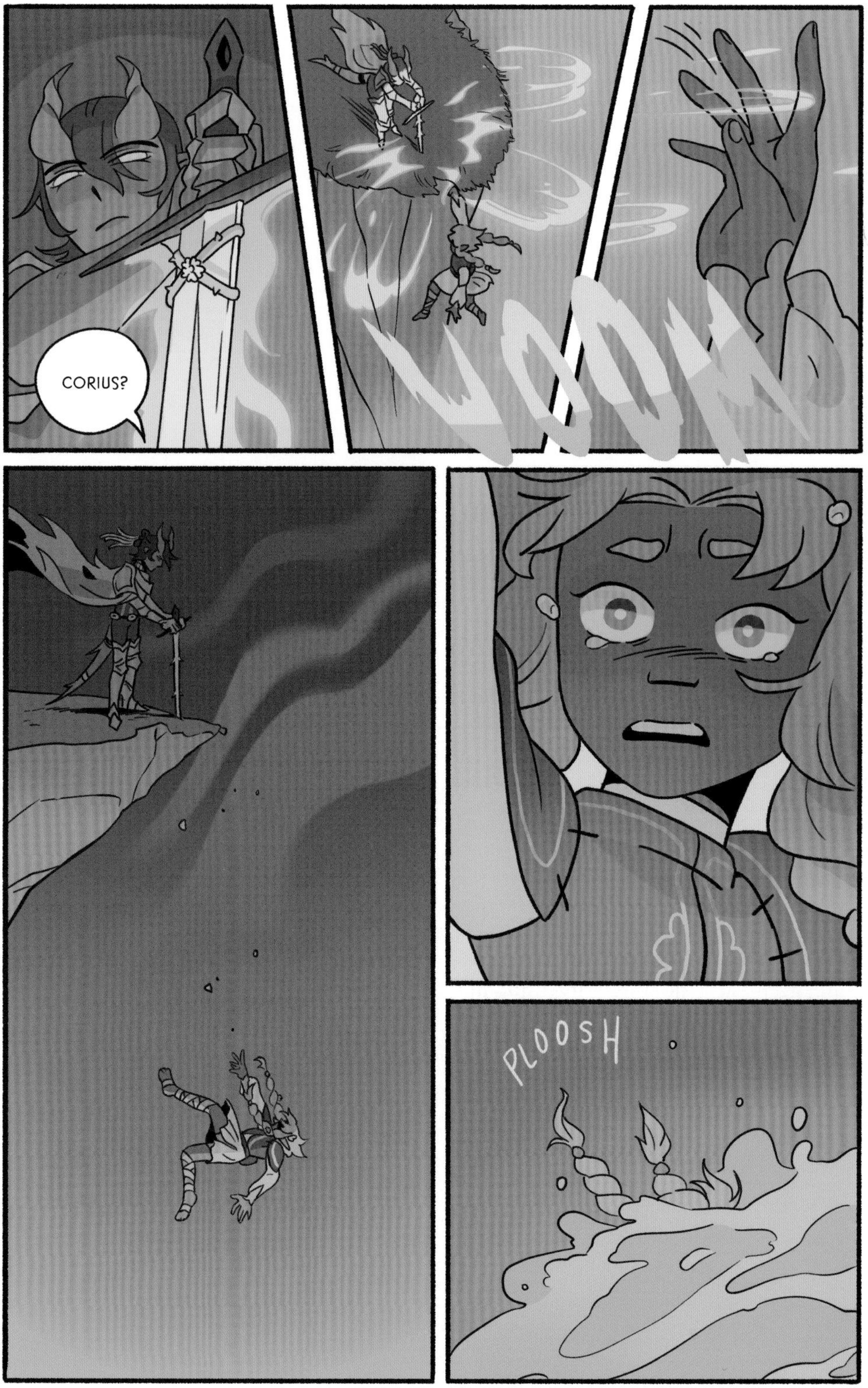
CORIUS?
VOOM
PLOOSH

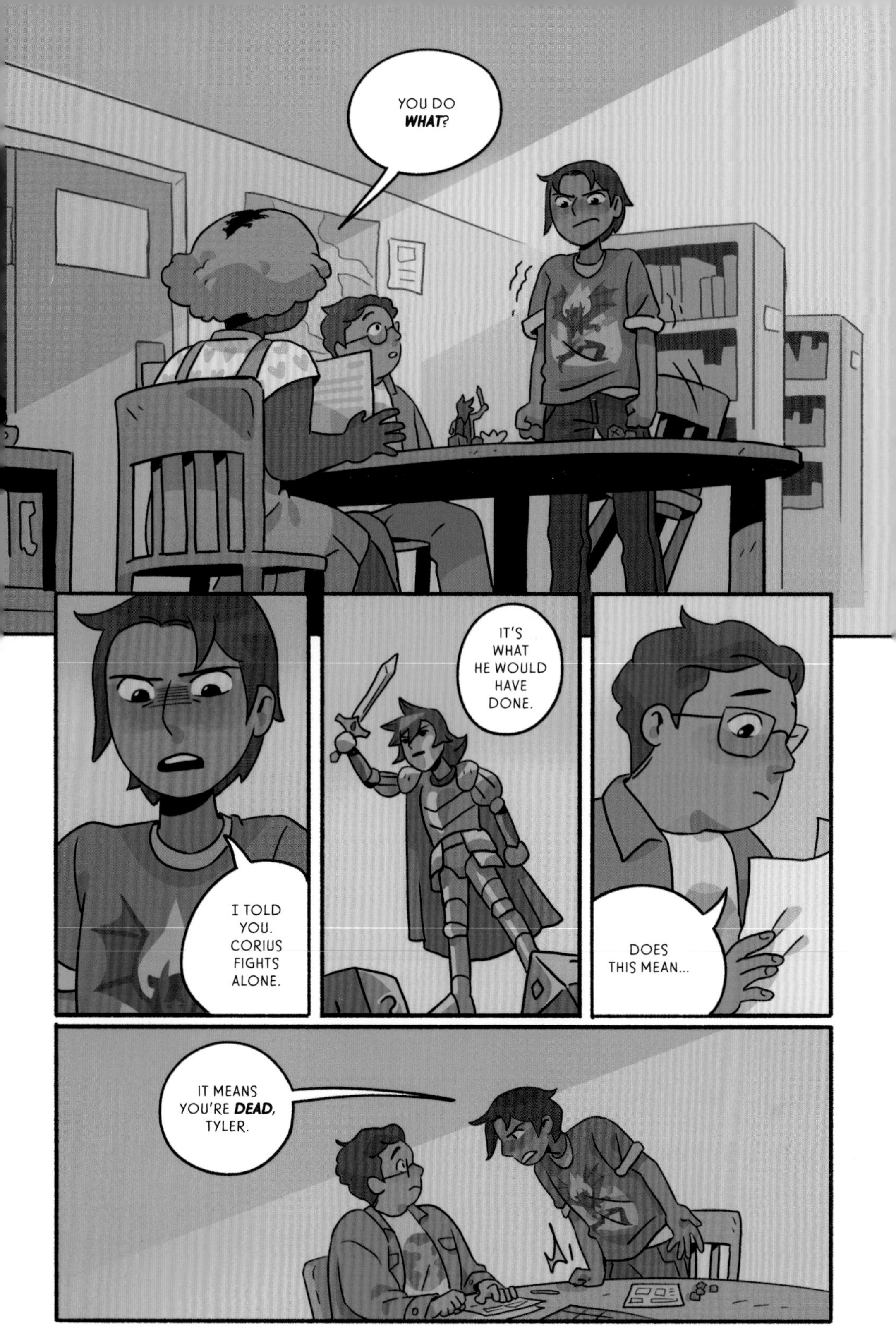
YOU DO **WHAT**?
I TOLD YOU. CORIUS FIGHTS ALONE.
IT'S WHAT HE WOULD HAVE DONE.
DOES THIS MEAN...
IT MEANS YOU'RE **DEAD**, TYLER.

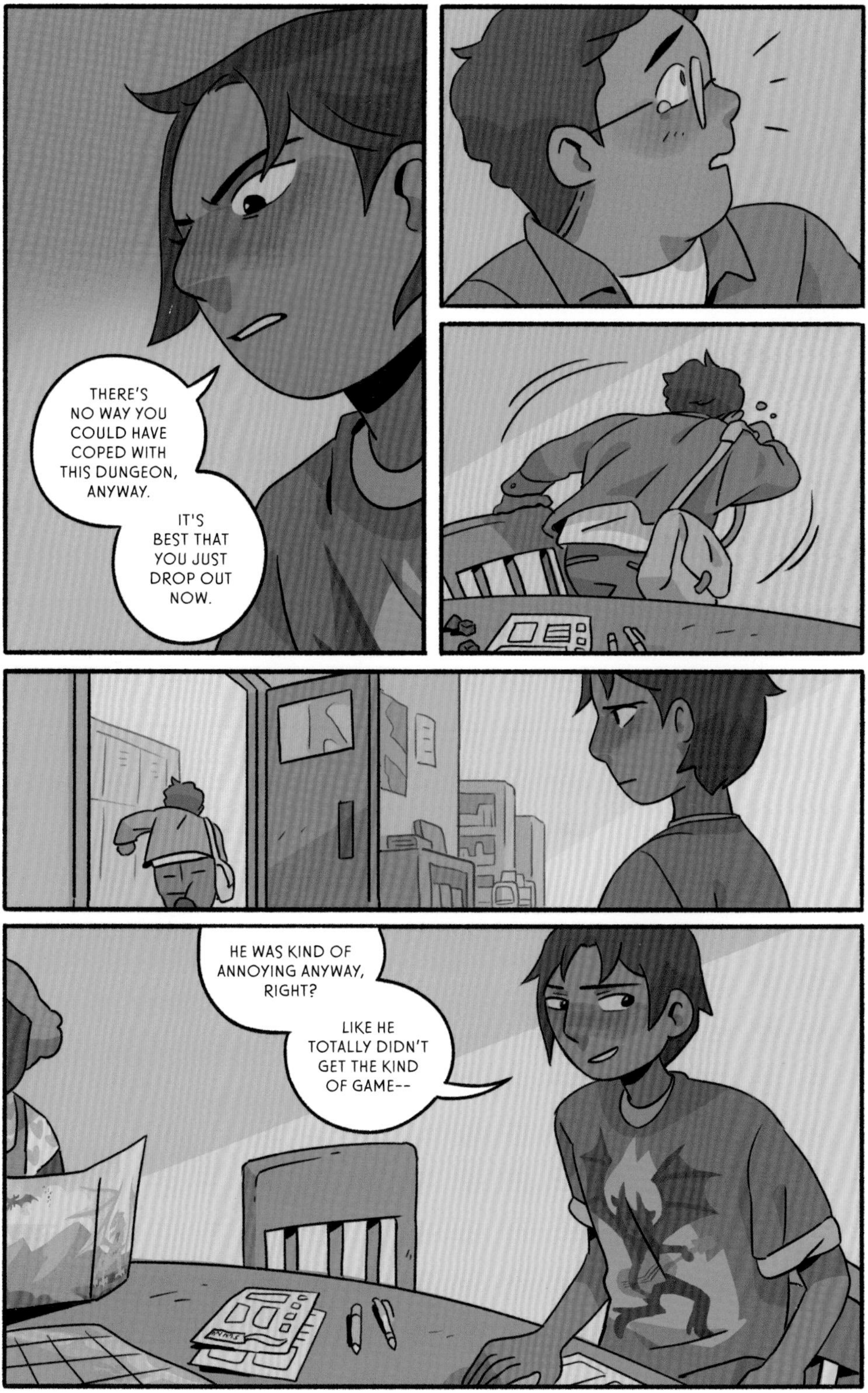
THERE'S NO WAY YOU COULD HAVE COPED WITH THIS DUNGEON, ANYWAY.
IT'S BEST THAT YOU JUST DROP OUT NOW.
HE WAS KIND OF ANNOYING ANYWAY, RIGHT?
LIKE HE TOTALLY DIDN'T GET THE KIND OF GAME--

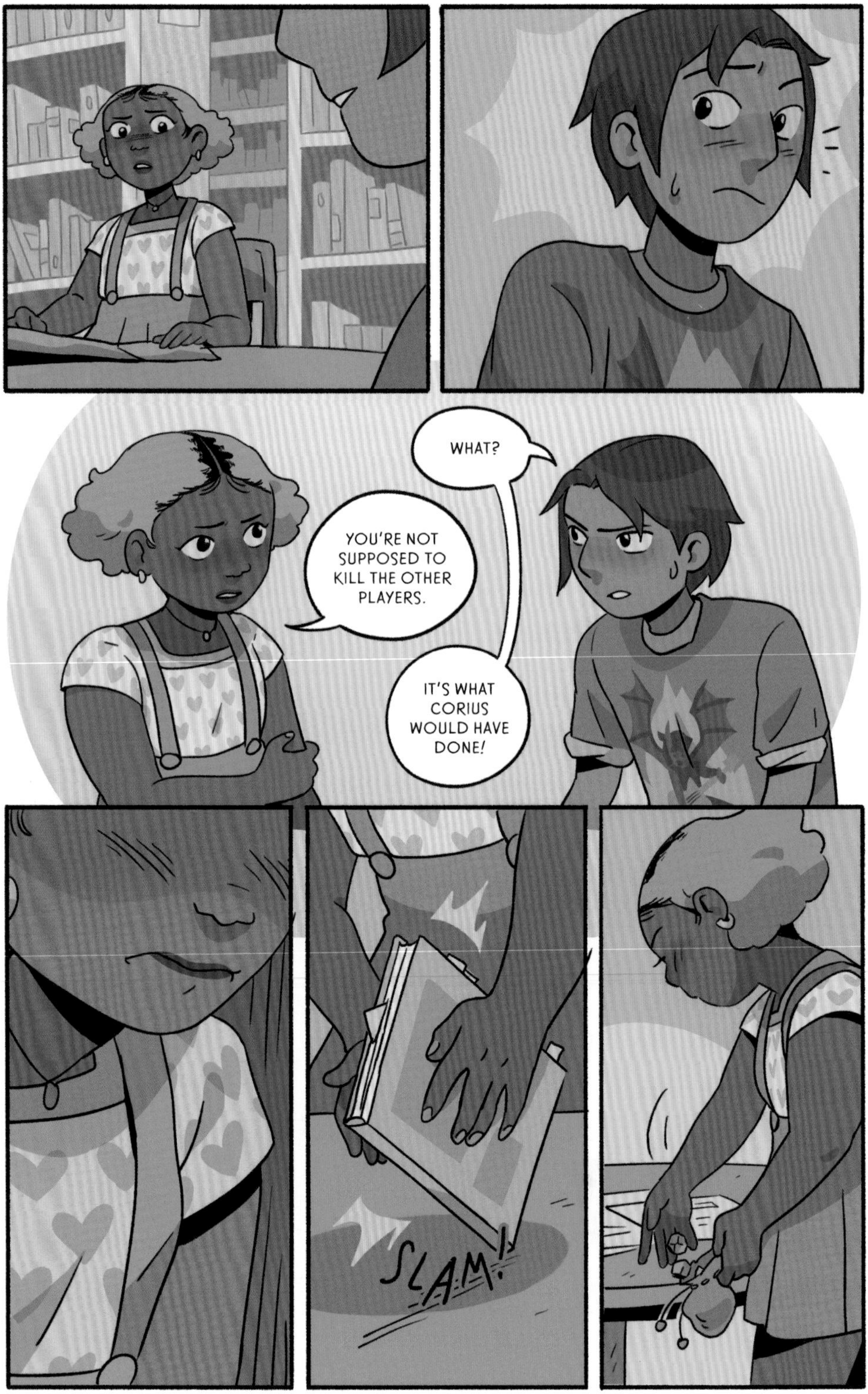
YOU'RE NOT SUPPOSED TO KILL THE OTHER PLAYERS.
WHAT?
IT'S WHAT CORIUS WOULD HAVE DONE!
SLAM!

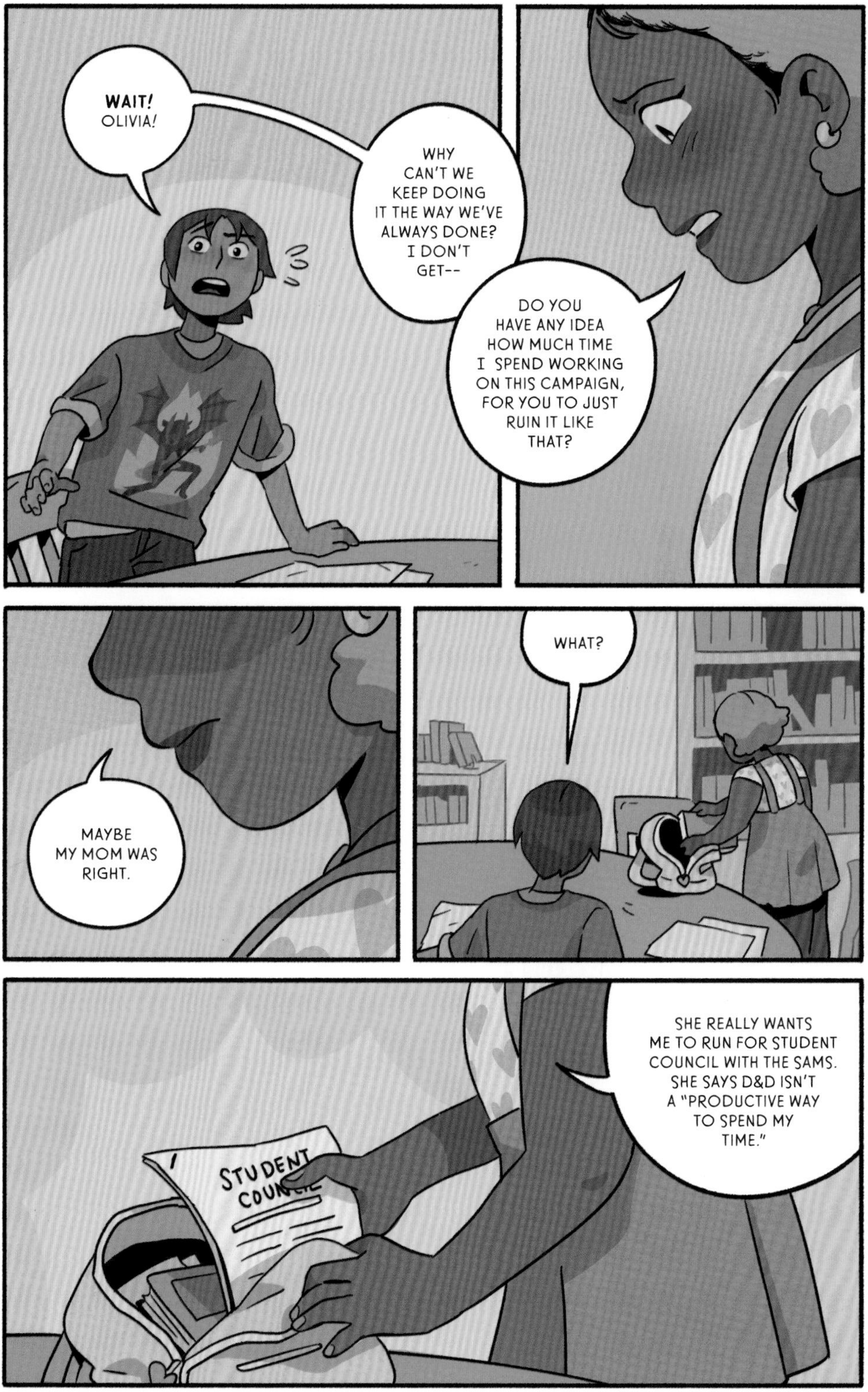
WAIT! OLIVIA!
WHY CAN'T WE KEEP DOING IT THE WAY WE'VE ALWAYS DONE? I DON'T GET--
DO YOU HAVE ANY IDEA HOW MUCH TIME I SPEND WORKING ON THIS CAMPAIGN, FOR YOU TO JUST RUIN IT LIKE THAT?
MAYBE MY MOM WAS RIGHT.
WHAT?
SHE REALLY WANTS ME TO RUN FOR STUDENT COUNCIL WITH THE SAMS. SHE SAYS D&D ISN'T A "PRODUCTIVE WAY TO SPEND MY TIME."
STUDENT

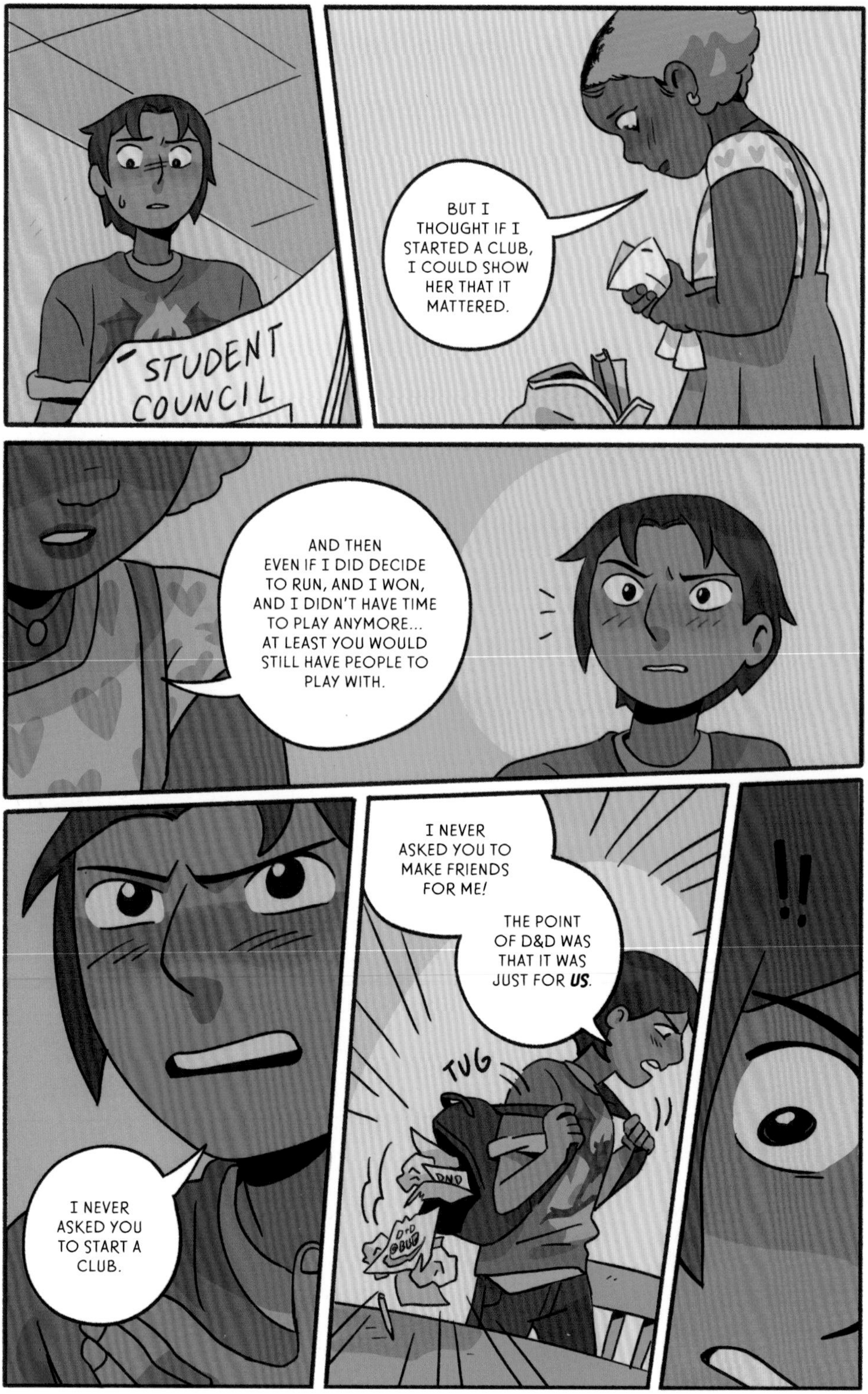
STUDENT COUNCIL
BUT I THOUGHT IF I STARTED A CLUB, I COULD SHOW HER THAT IT MATTERED.
AND THEN EVEN IF I DID DECIDE TO RUN, AND I WON, AND I DIDN'T HAVE TIME TO PLAY ANYMORE... AT LEAST YOU WOULD STILL HAVE PEOPLE TO PLAY WITH.
I NEVER ASKED YOU TO START A CLUB.
I NEVER ASKED YOU TO MAKE FRIENDS FOR ME!
THE POINT OF D&D WAS THAT IT WAS JUST FOR **US**.
TUG
!!

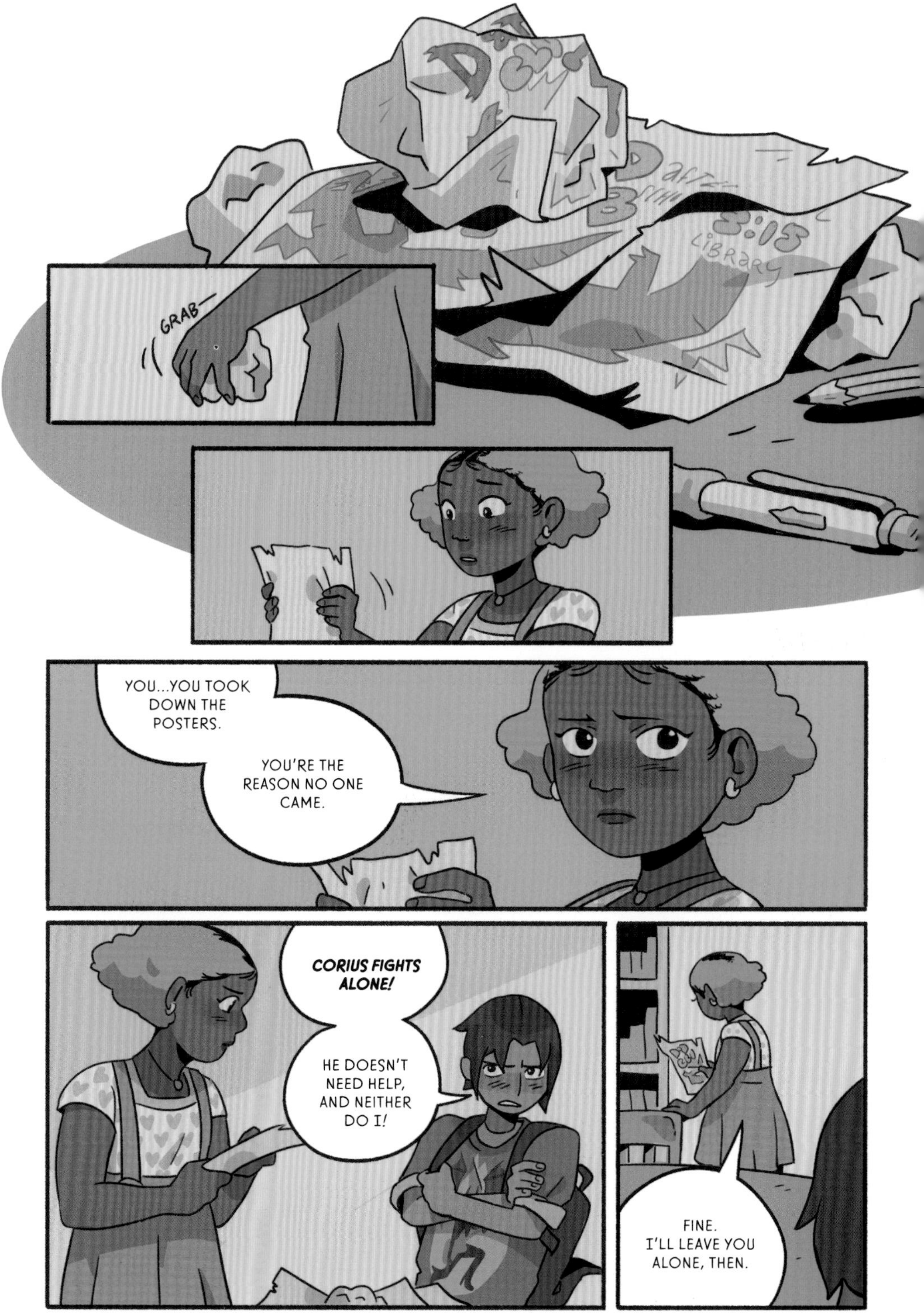
DAFT
3:15
LIBRARY
GRAB—
YOU...YOU TOOK DOWN THE POSTERS.
YOU'RE THE REASON NO ONE CAME.
CORIUS FIGHTS ALONE!
HE DOESN'T NEED HELP, AND NEITHER DO I!
FINE. I'LL LEAVE YOU ALONE, THEN.

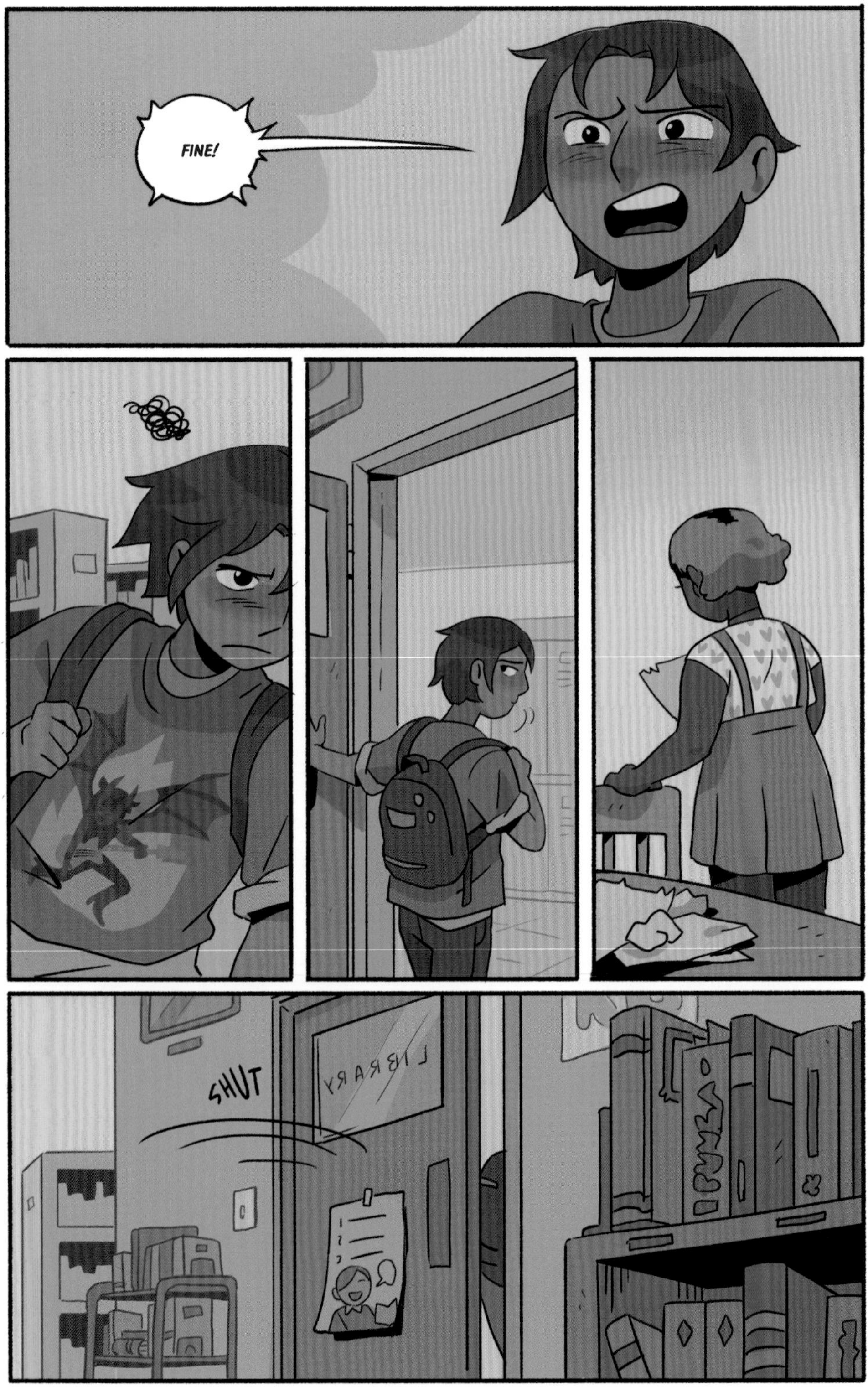
FINE!
SHUT

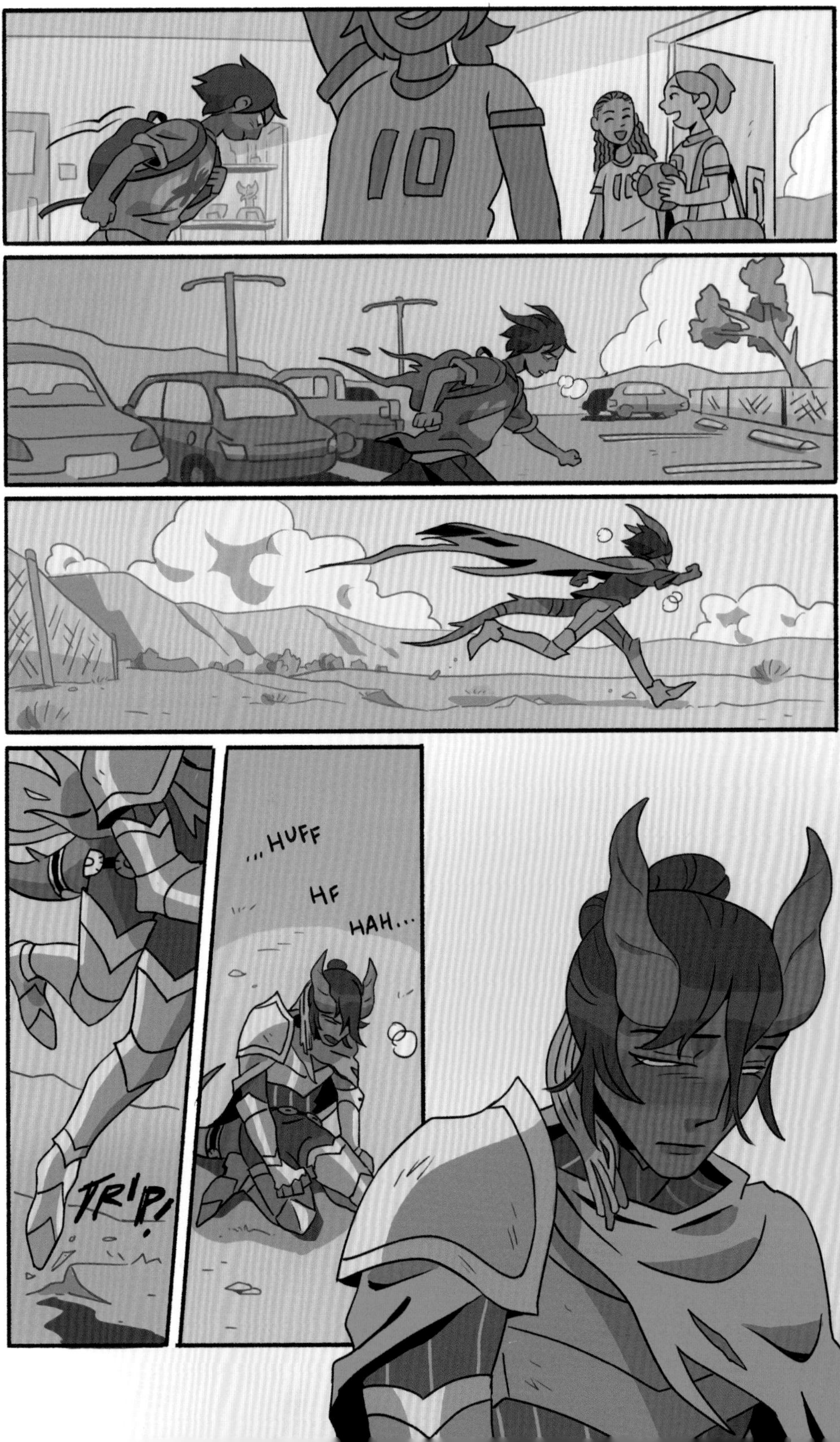

10
...HUFF
HF
HAH...
TRIP!

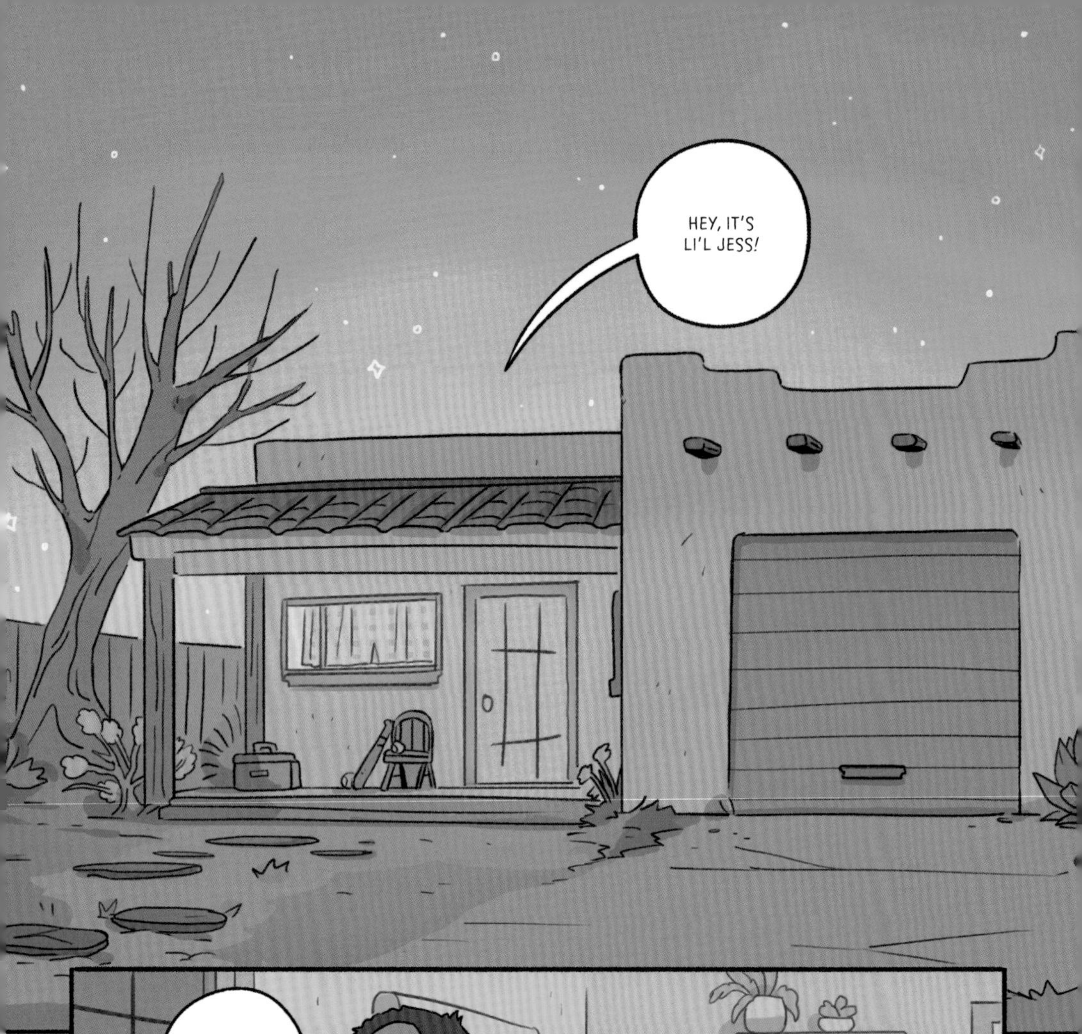
HEY, IT'S
LI'L JESS!

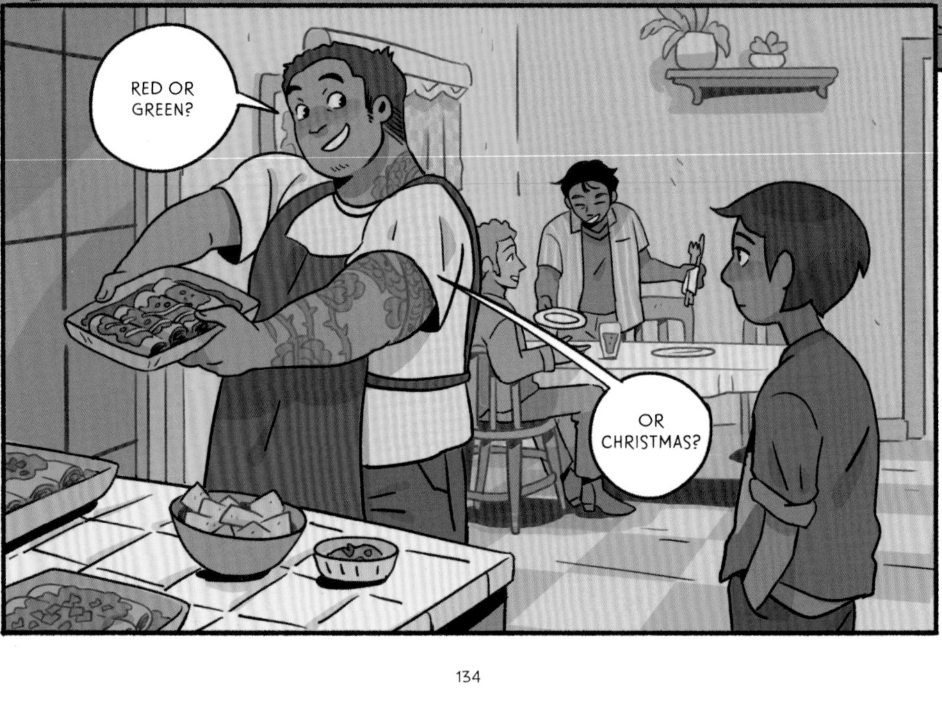
RED OR
GREEN?
OR
CHRISTMAS?

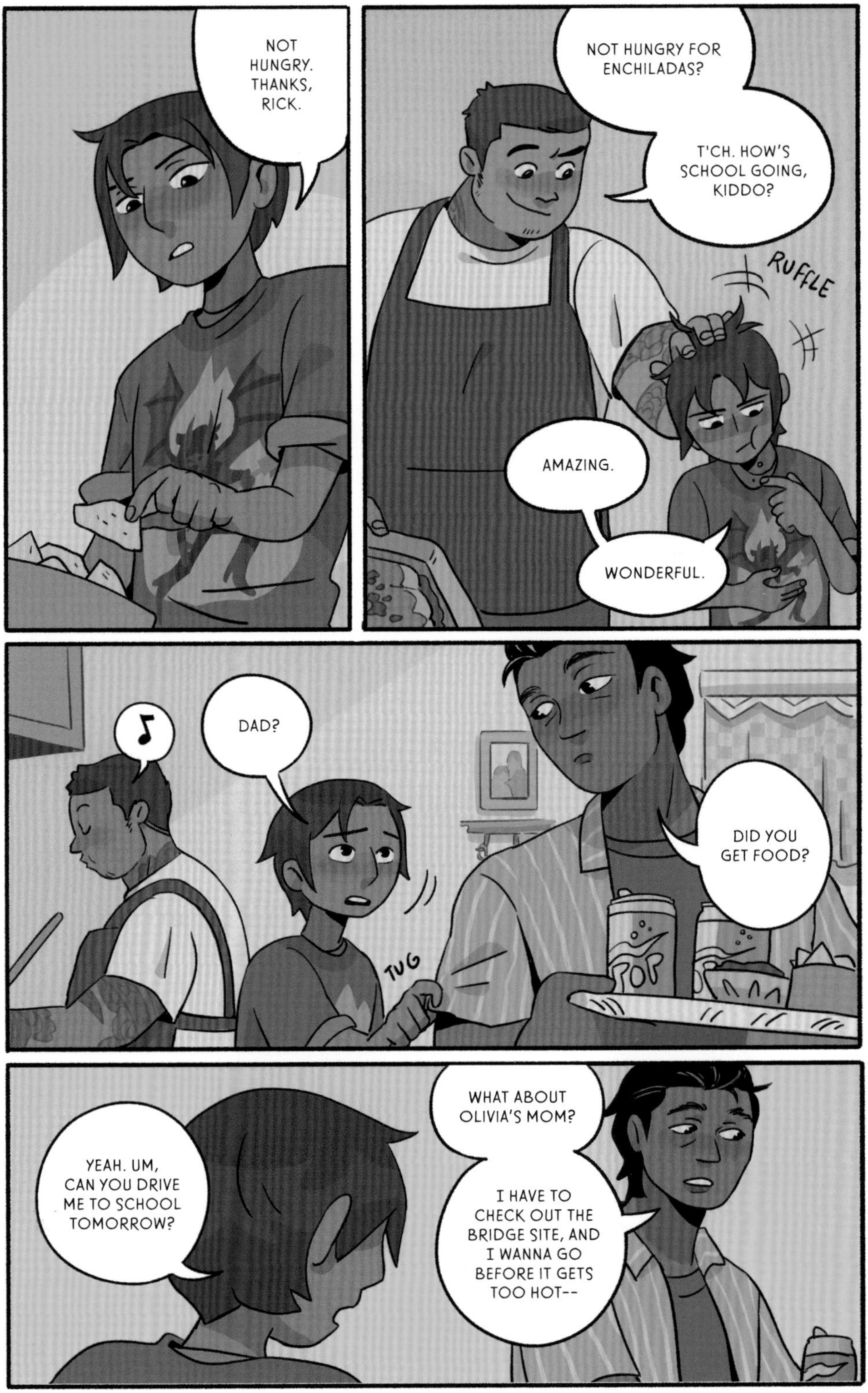
NOT HUNGRY. THANKS, RICK.
NOT HUNGRY FOR ENCHILADAS?
T'CH. HOW'S SCHOOL GOING, KIDDO?
RUFFLE
AMAZING.
WONDERFUL.
DAD?
DID YOU GET FOOD?
TUG
POP
YEAH. UM, CAN YOU DRIVE ME TO SCHOOL TOMORROW?
WHAT ABOUT OLIVIA'S MOM?
I HAVE TO CHECK OUT THE BRIDGE SITE, AND I WANNA GO BEFORE IT GETS TOO HOT--

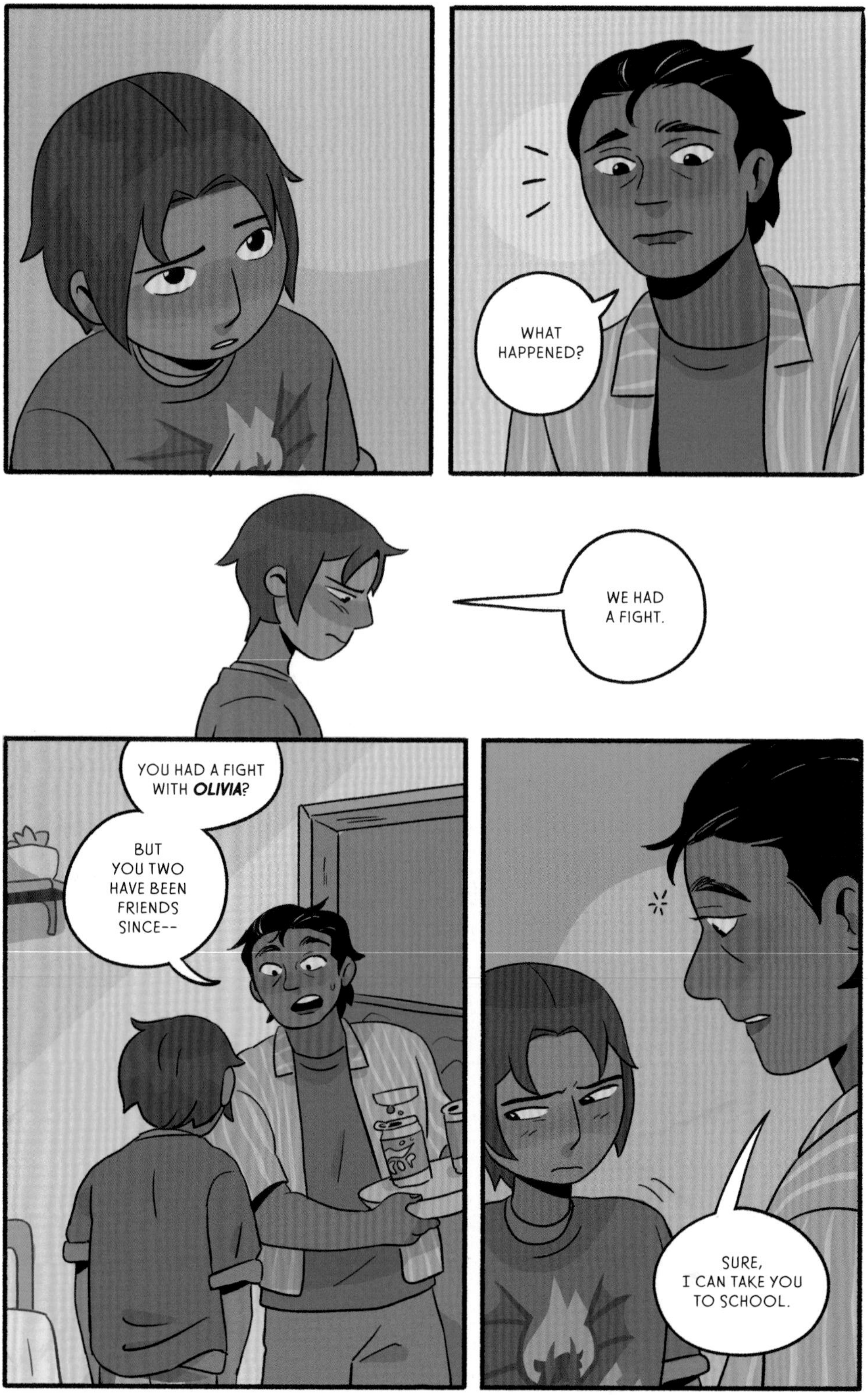
WHAT HAPPENED?
WE HAD A FIGHT.
YOU HAD A FIGHT WITH **OLIVIA**?
BUT YOU TWO HAVE BEEN FRIENDS SINCE--
SURE, I CAN TAKE YOU TO SCHOOL.

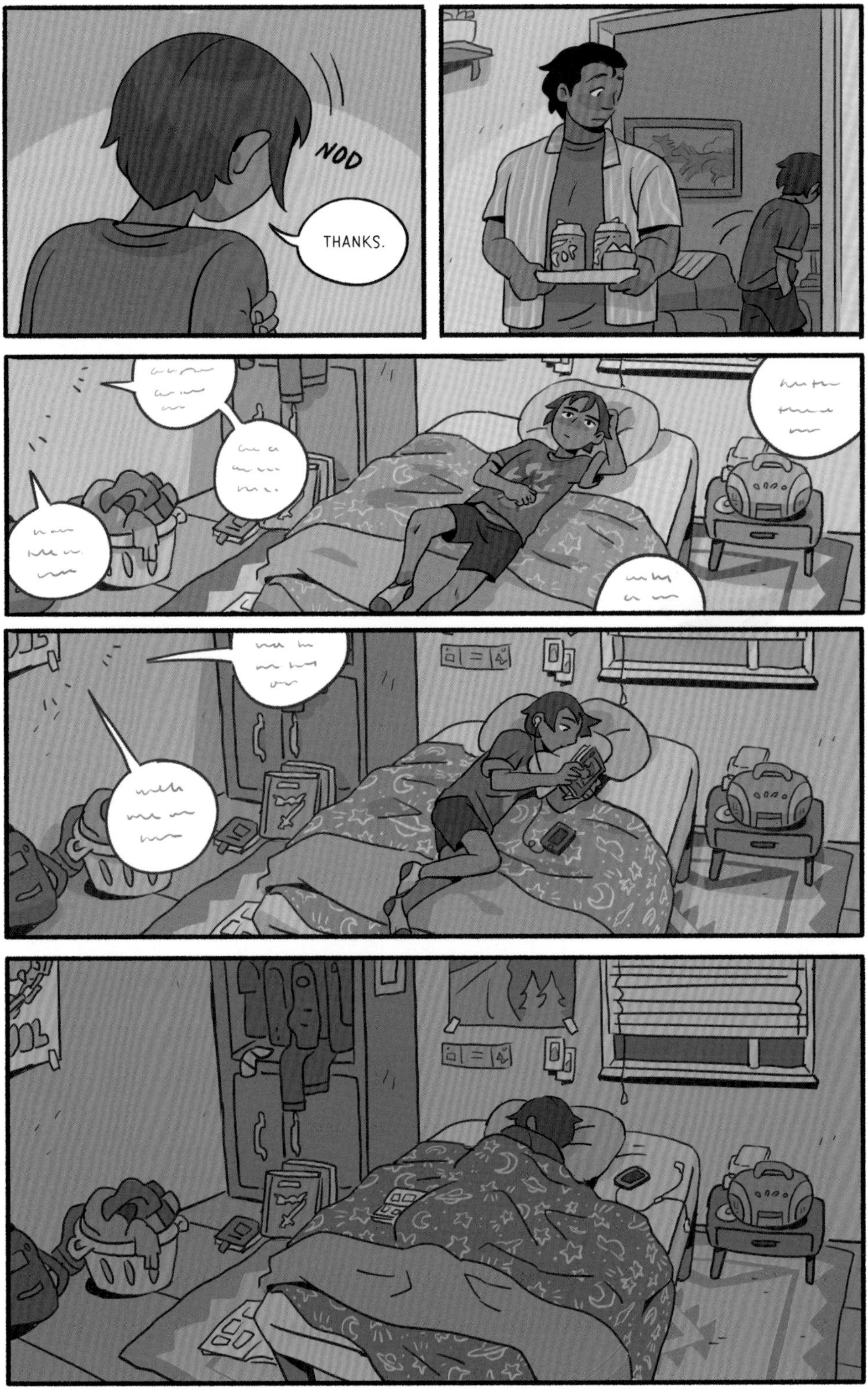
NOD
THANKS.

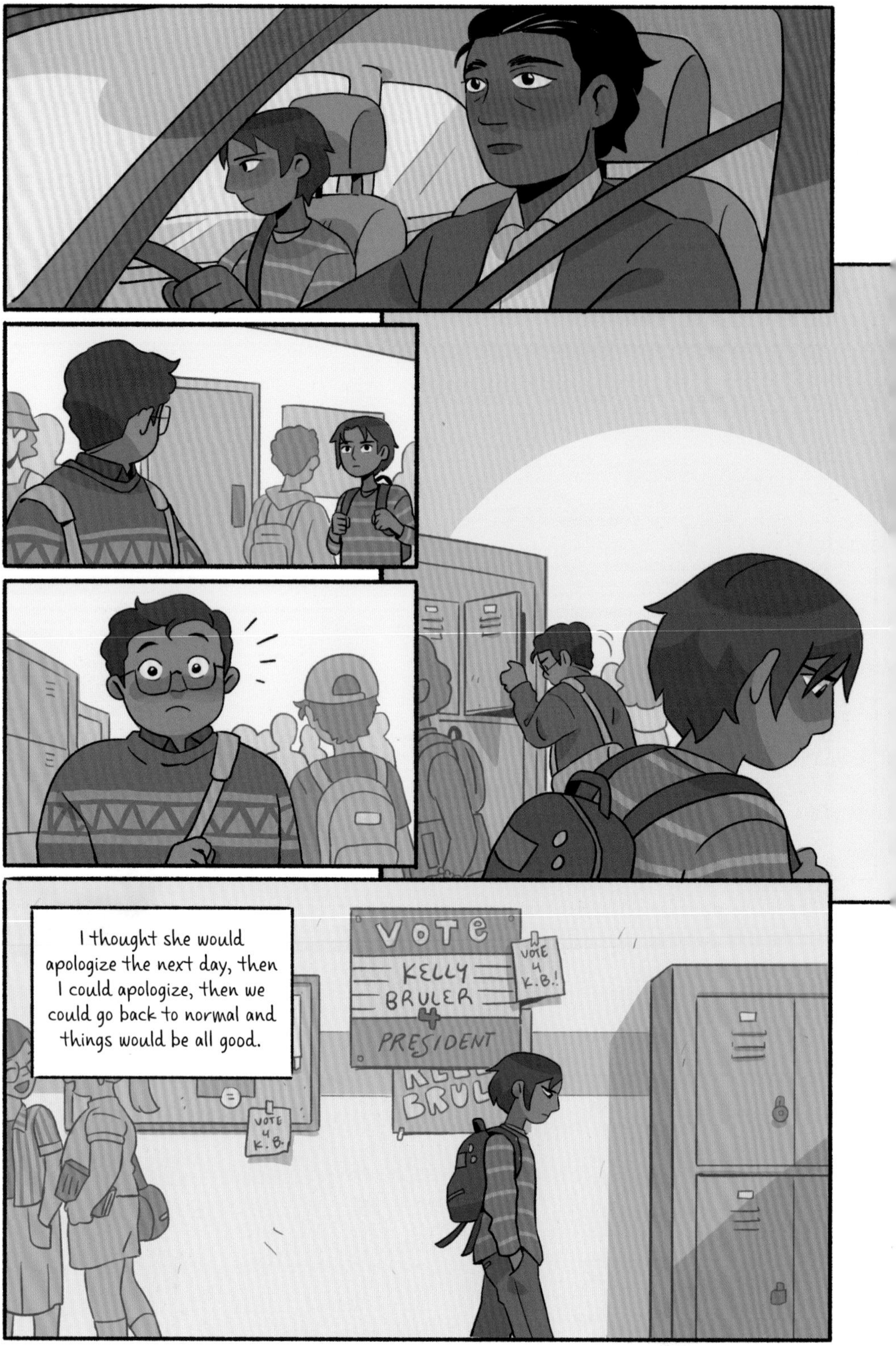
VOTE
KELLY
BRULER
4
PRESIDENT
VOTE
4
K.B.!
I thought she would apologize the next day, then I could apologize, then we could go back to normal and things would be all good.
VOTE
4
K.B.

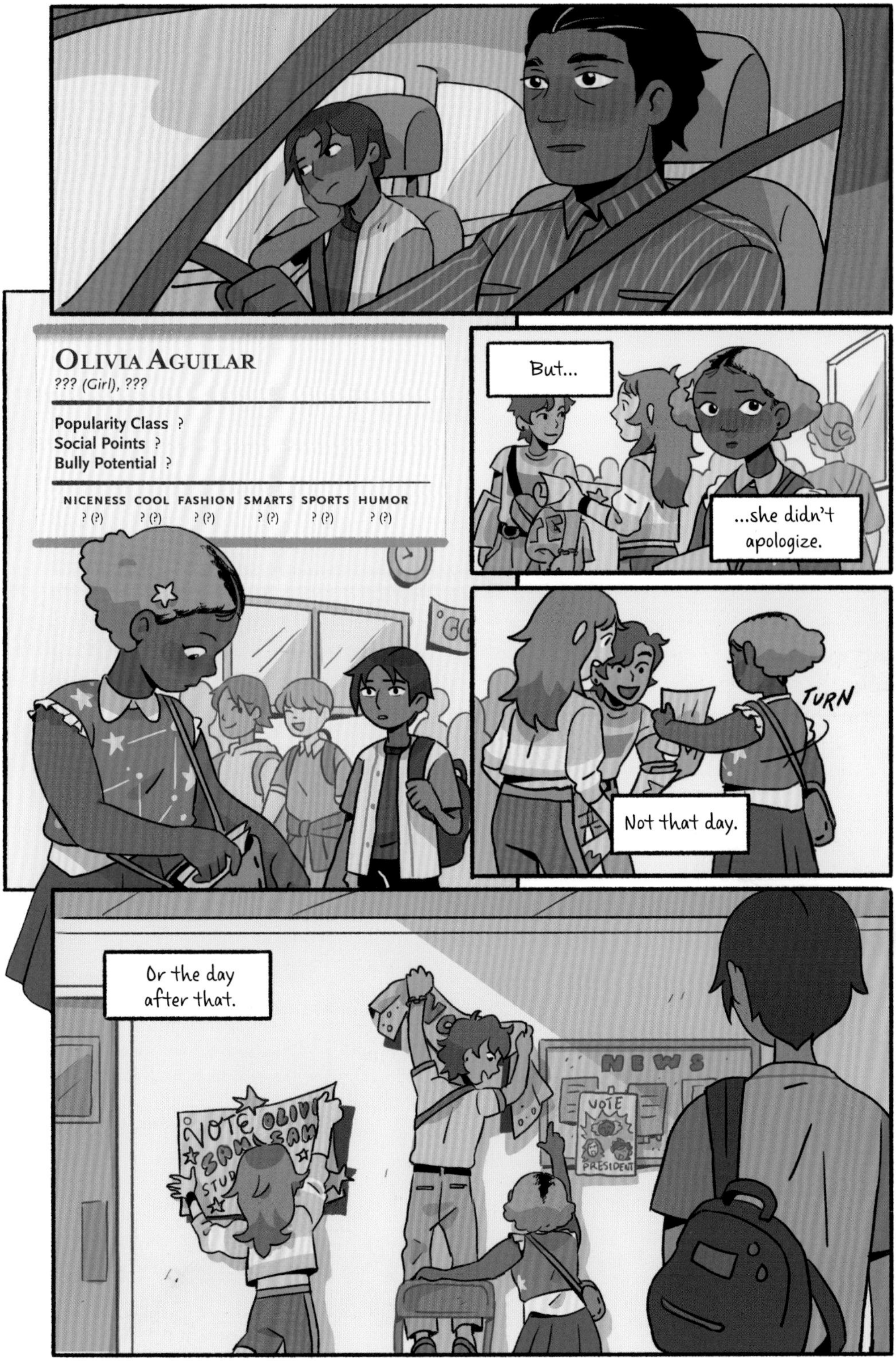
OLIVIA AGUILAR
??? (Girl), ???
Popularity Class ?
Social Points ?
Bully Potential ?
NICENESS ? (?) COOL ? (?) FASHION ? (?) SMARTS ? (?) SPORTS ? (?) HUMOR ? (?)
But...
...she didn't apologize.
TURN
Not that day.
Or the day after that.
NEWS
VOTE
PRESIDENT

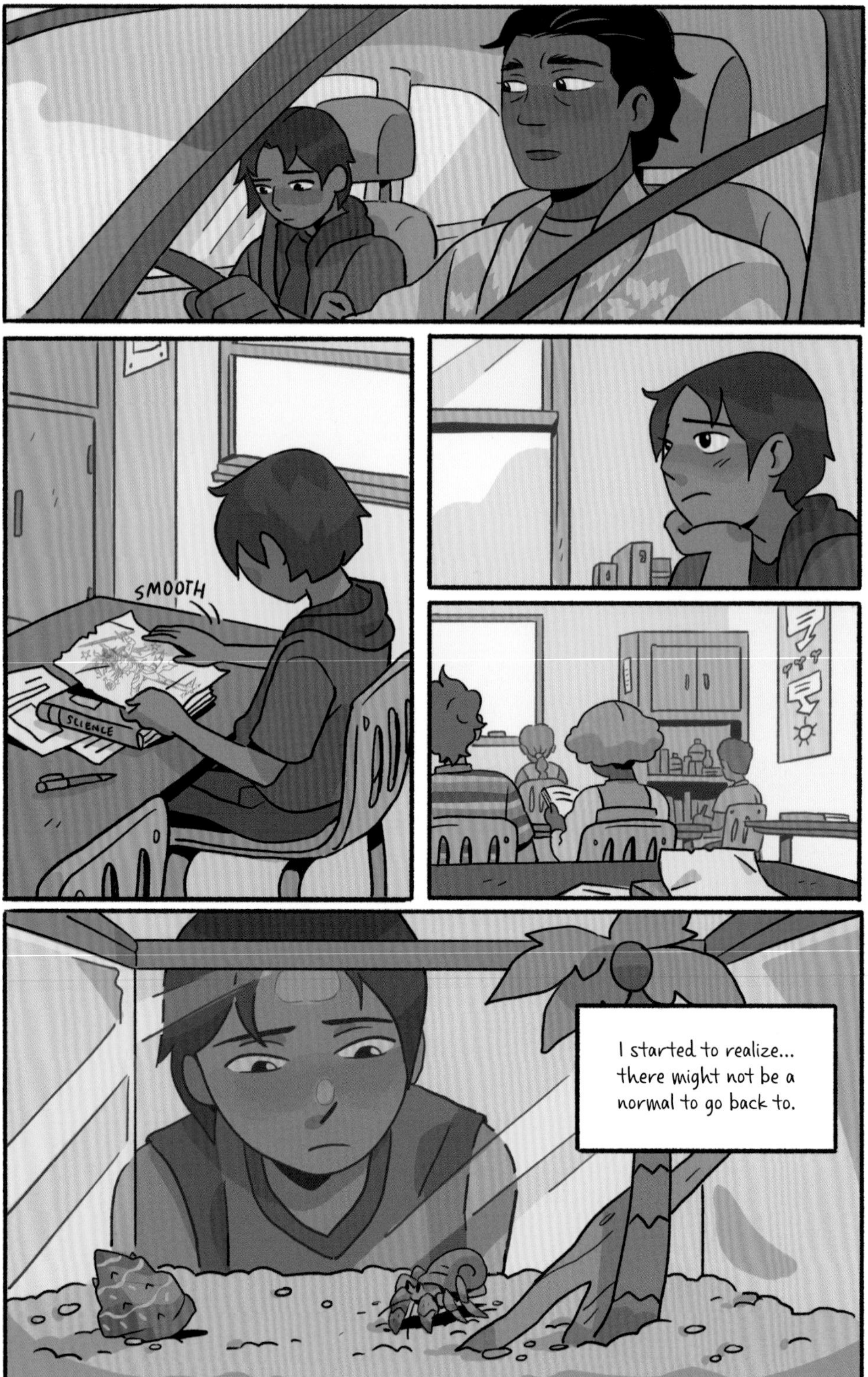
SMOOTH
SCIENCE
I started to realize... there might not be a normal to go back to.

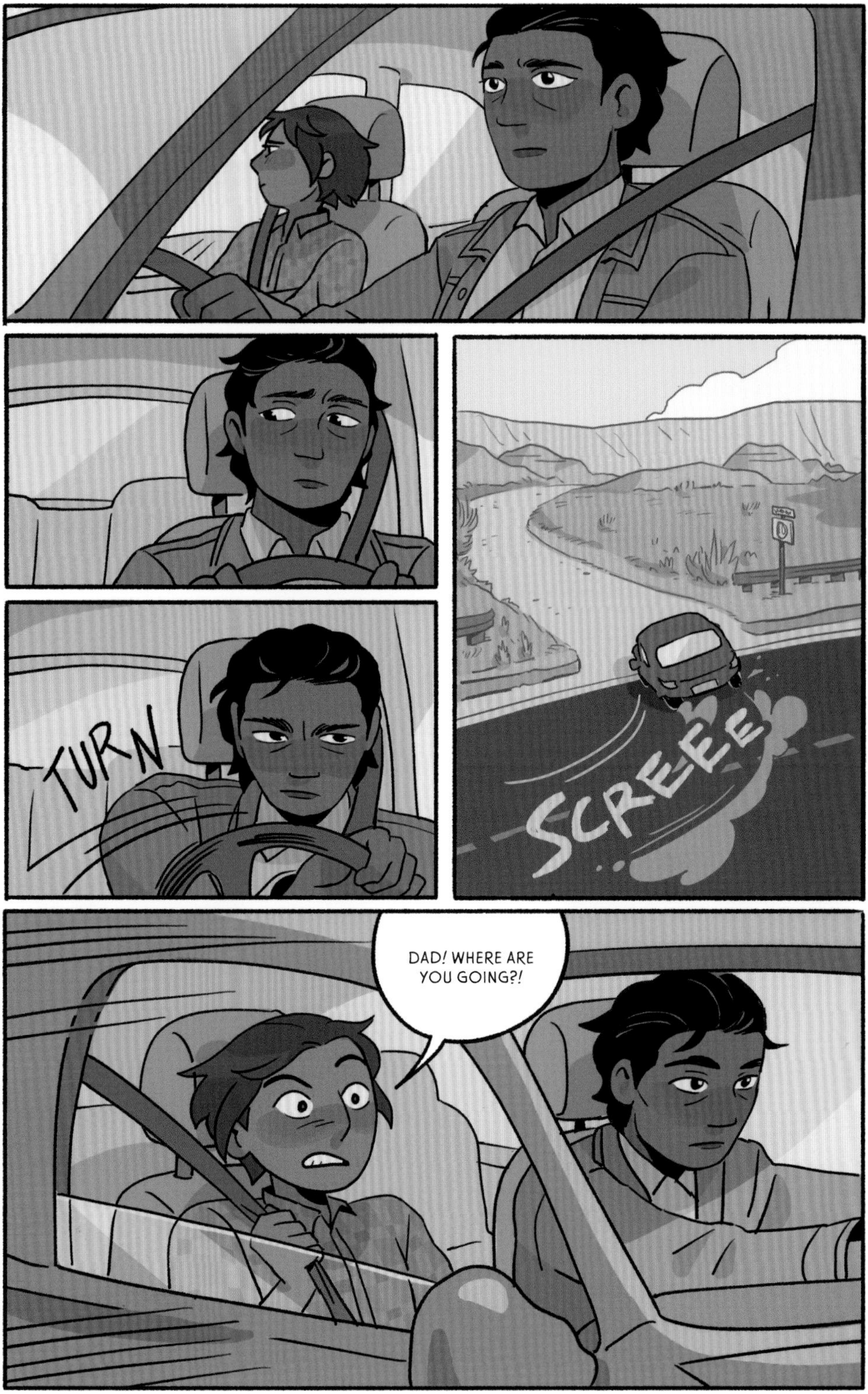
TURN
SCREEEE
DAD! WHERE ARE YOU GOING?!

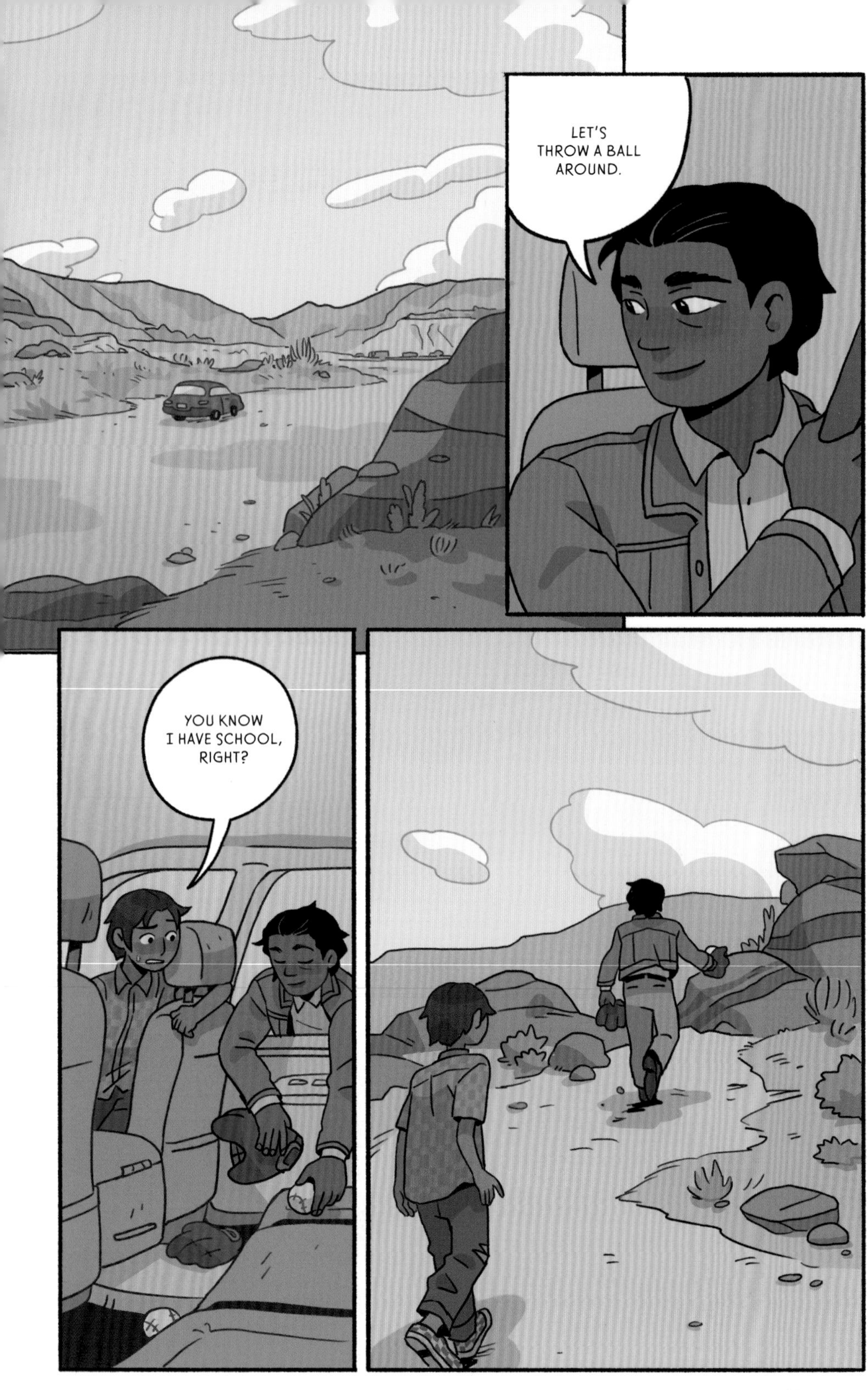
LET'S THROW A BALL AROUND.
YOU KNOW I HAVE SCHOOL, RIGHT?

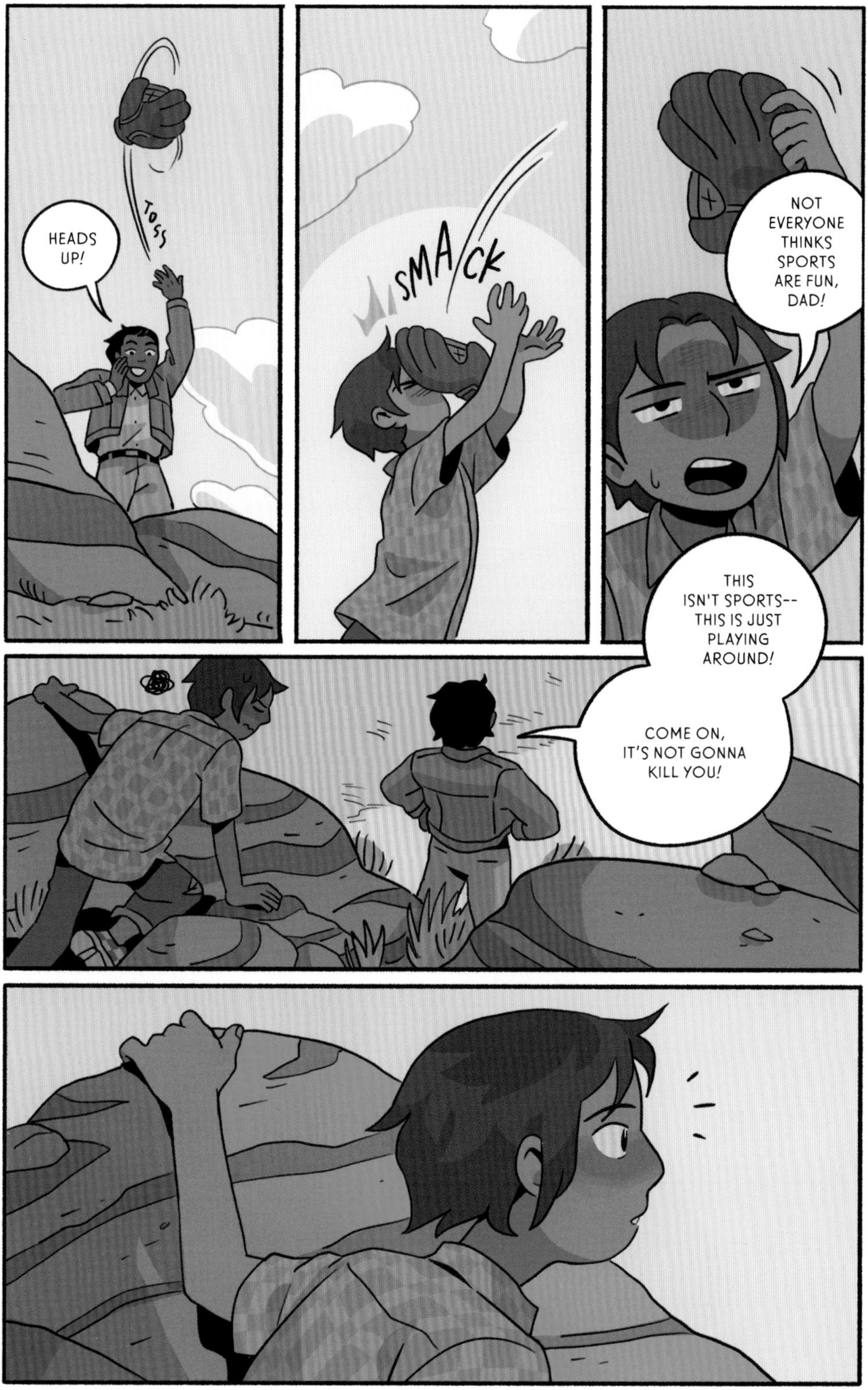
HEADS UP!
TOSS
SMACK
NOT EVERYONE THINKS SPORTS ARE FUN, DAD!
THIS ISN'T SPORTS-- THIS IS JUST PLAYING AROUND!
COME ON, IT'S NOT GONNA KILL YOU!

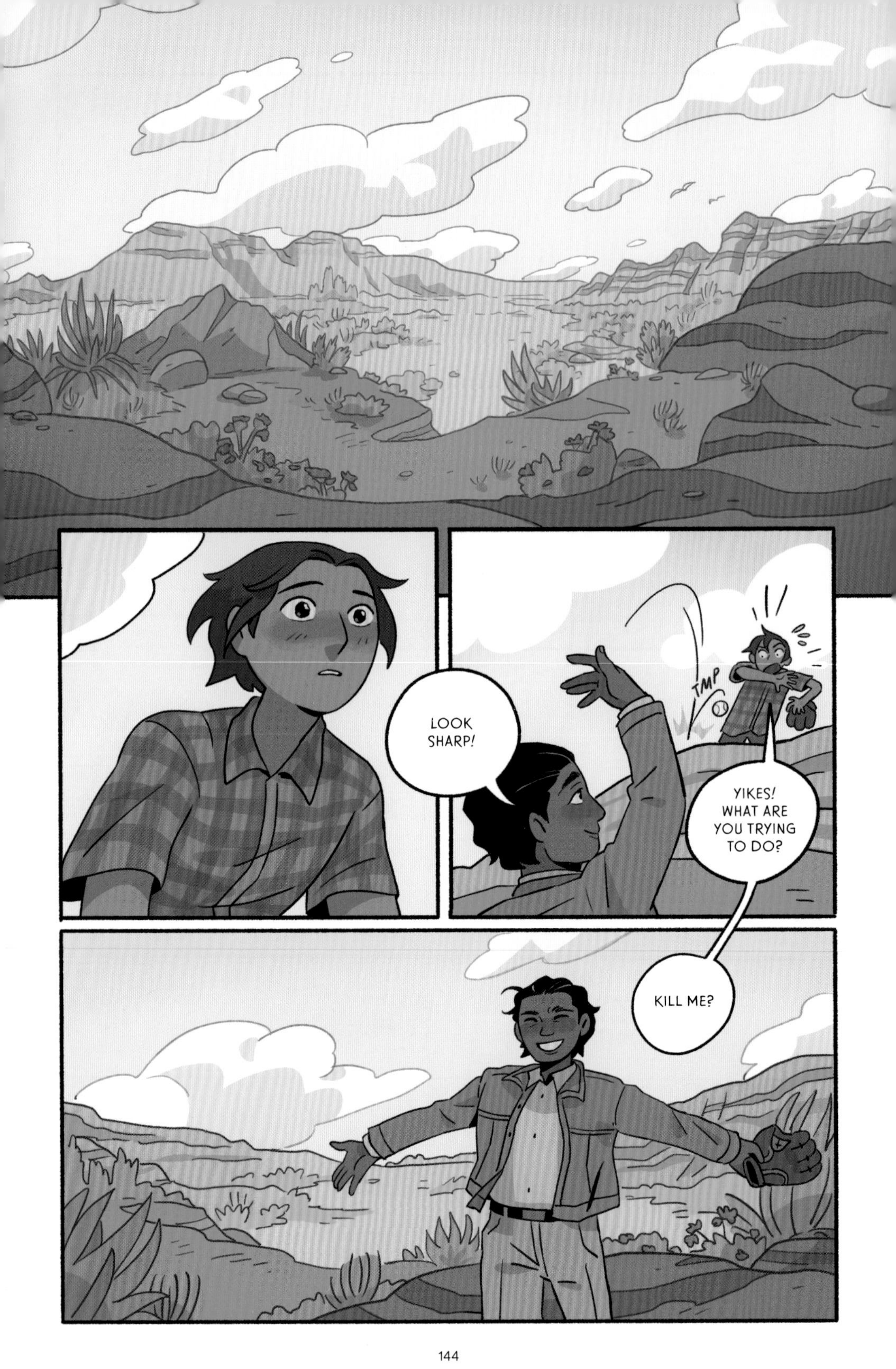
LOOK SHARP!
TMP
YIKES! WHAT ARE YOU TRYING TO DO?
KILL ME?

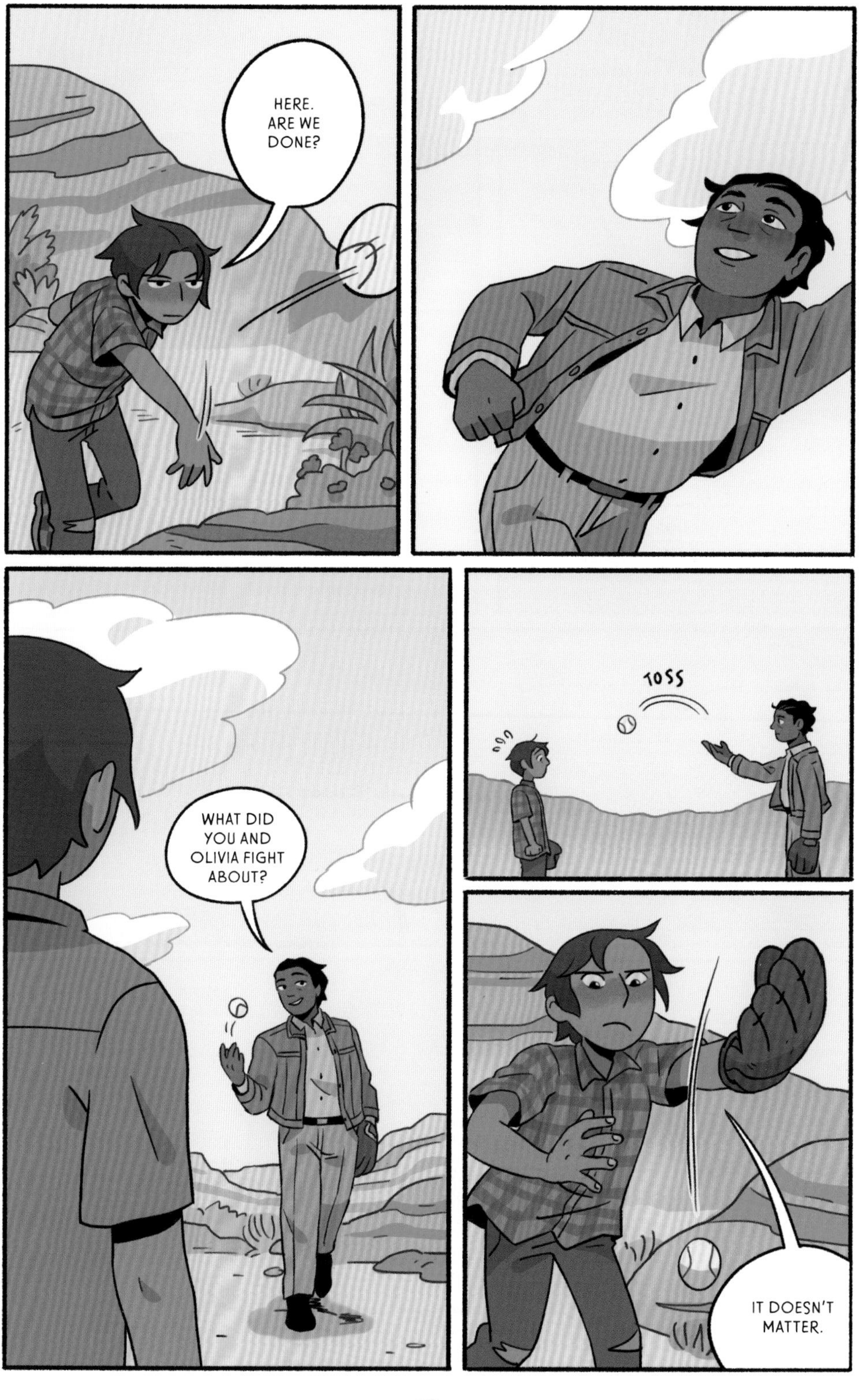
HERE. ARE WE DONE?
WHAT DID YOU AND OLIVIA FIGHT ABOUT?
TOSS
IT DOESN'T MATTER.

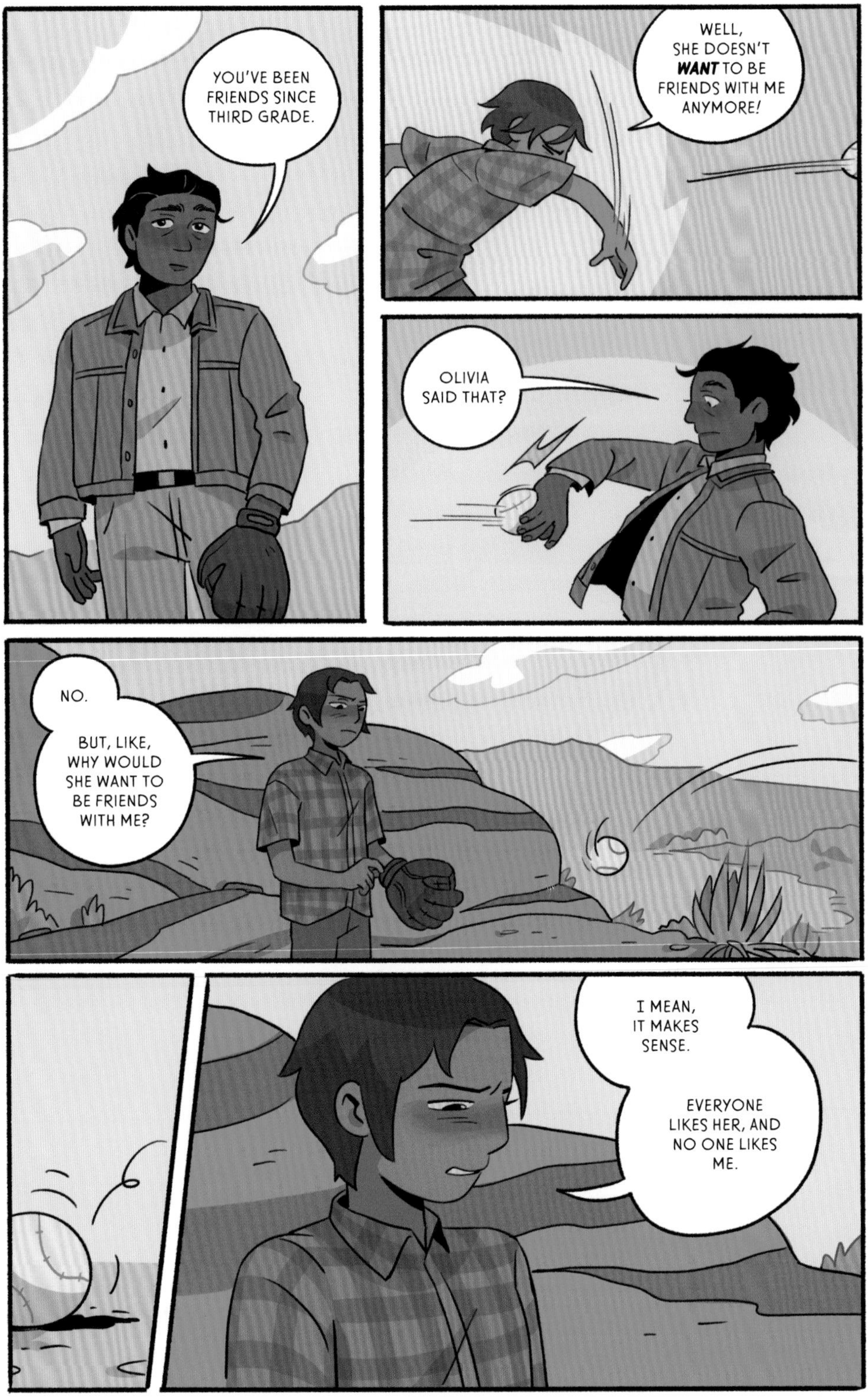
YOU'VE BEEN FRIENDS SINCE THIRD GRADE.
WELL, SHE DOESN'T **WANT** TO BE FRIENDS WITH ME ANYMORE!
OLIVIA SAID THAT?
NO.
BUT, LIKE, WHY WOULD SHE WANT TO BE FRIENDS WITH ME?
I MEAN, IT MAKES SENSE.
EVERYONE LIKES HER, AND NO ONE LIKES ME.

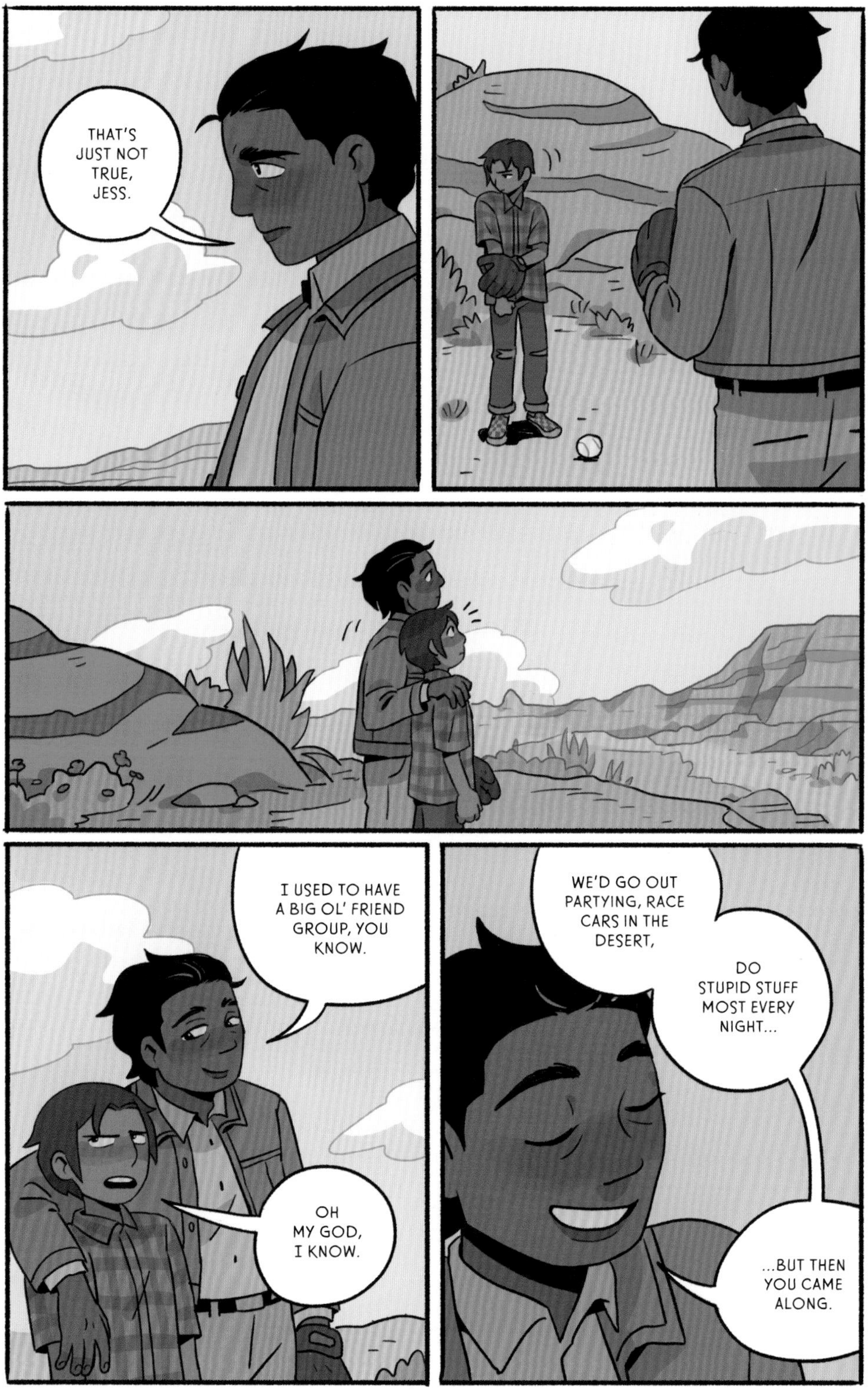
THAT'S JUST NOT TRUE, JESS.
I USED TO HAVE A BIG OL' FRIEND GROUP, YOU KNOW.
OH MY GOD, I KNOW.
WE'D GO OUT PARTYING, RACE CARS IN THE DESERT,
DO STUPID STUFF MOST EVERY NIGHT...
...BUT THEN YOU CAME ALONG.

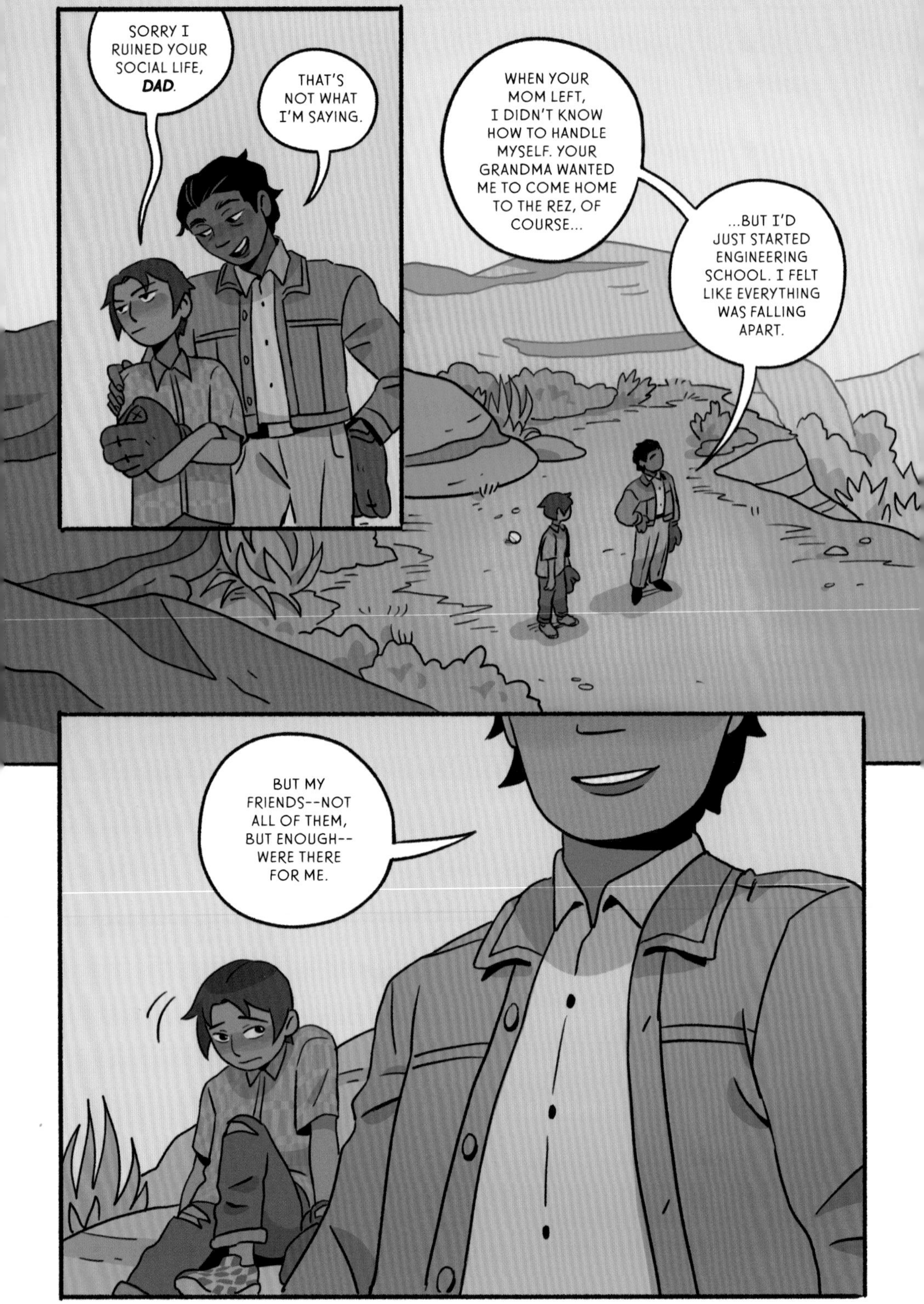
SORRY I RUINED YOUR SOCIAL LIFE, **DAD**.
THAT'S NOT WHAT I'M SAYING.
WHEN YOUR MOM LEFT, I DIDN'T KNOW HOW TO HANDLE MYSELF. YOUR GRANDMA WANTED ME TO COME HOME TO THE REZ, OF COURSE...
...BUT I'D JUST STARTED ENGINEERING SCHOOL. I FELT LIKE EVERYTHING WAS FALLING APART.
BUT MY FRIENDS--NOT ALL OF THEM, BUT ENOUGH--WERE THERE FOR ME.

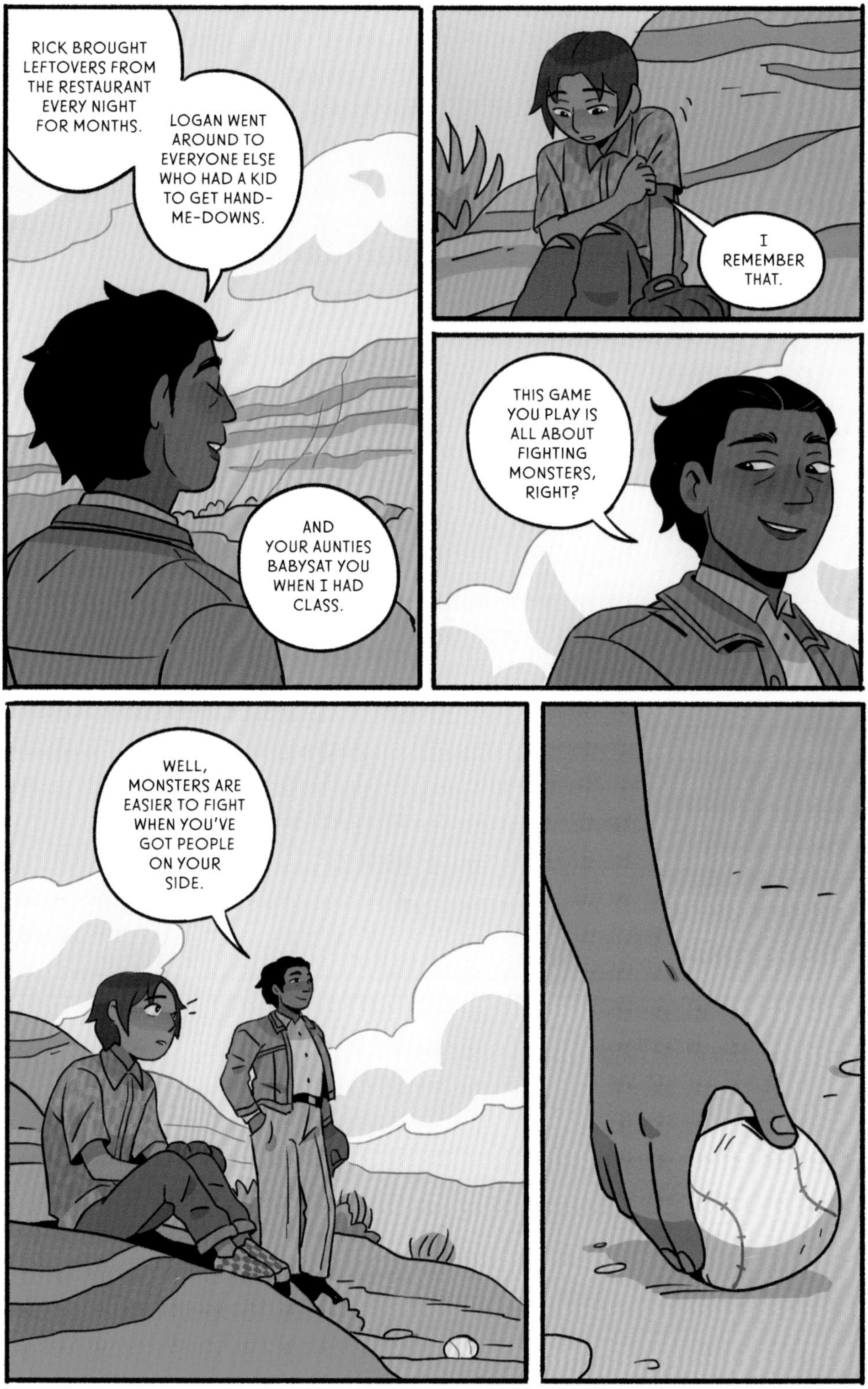
RICK BROUGHT LEFTOVERS FROM THE RESTAURANT EVERY NIGHT FOR MONTHS.
LOGAN WENT AROUND TO EVERYONE ELSE WHO HAD A KID TO GET HAND-ME-DOWNS.
AND YOUR AUNTIES BABYSAT YOU WHEN I HAD CLASS.
I REMEMBER THAT.
THIS GAME YOU PLAY IS ALL ABOUT FIGHTING MONSTERS, RIGHT?
WELL, MONSTERS ARE EASIER TO FIGHT WHEN YOU'VE GOT PEOPLE ON YOUR SIDE.

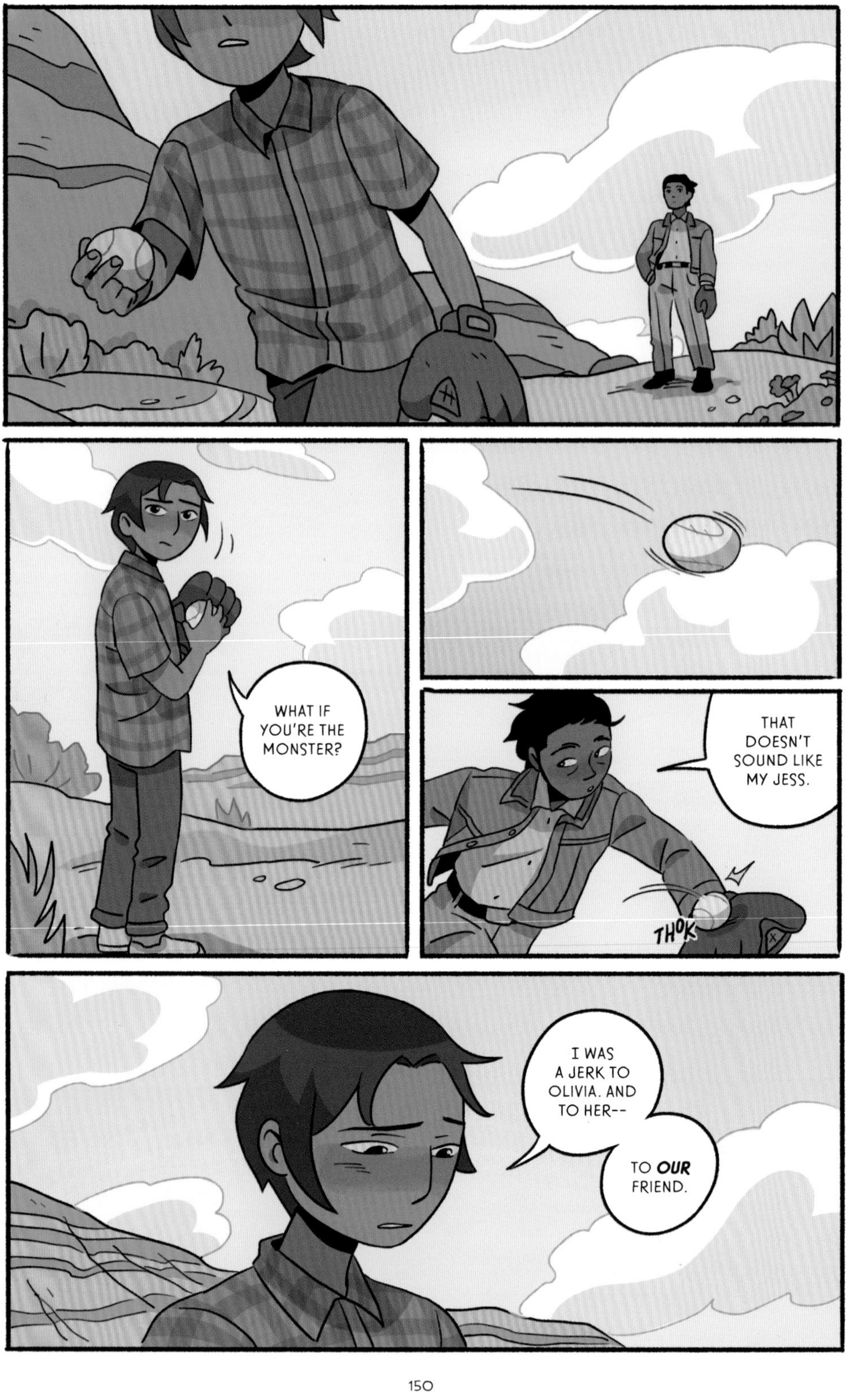
WHAT IF YOU'RE THE MONSTER?
THAT DOESN'T SOUND LIKE MY JESS.
THOK
I WAS A JERK TO OLIVIA. AND TO HER--
TO **OUR** FRIEND.

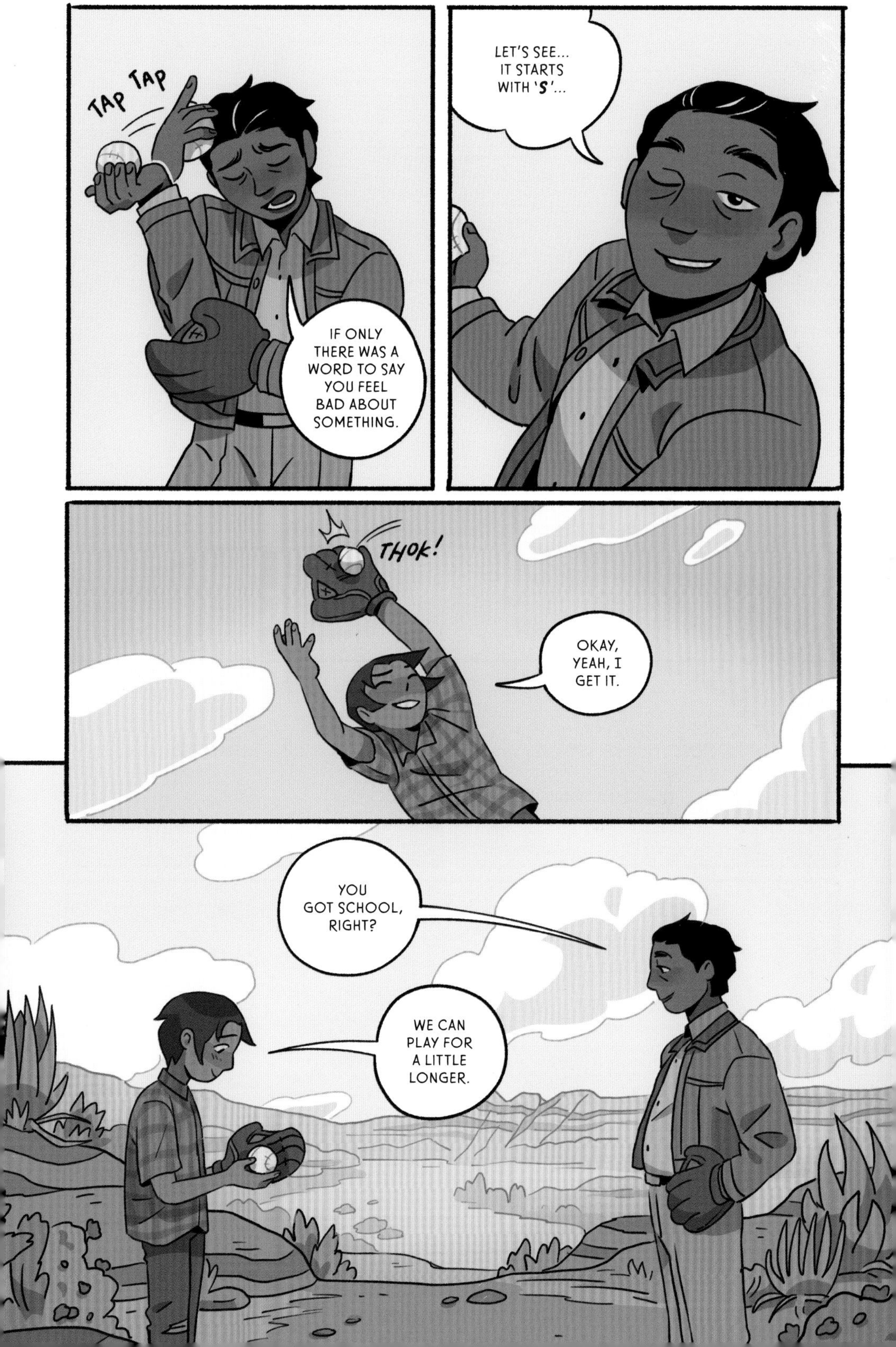
TAP TAP
IF ONLY THERE WAS A WORD TO SAY YOU FEEL BAD ABOUT SOMETHING.
LET'S SEE... IT STARTS WITH '**S**'...
THOK!
OKAY, YEAH, I GET IT.
YOU GOT SCHOOL, RIGHT?
WE CAN PLAY FOR A LITTLE LONGER.

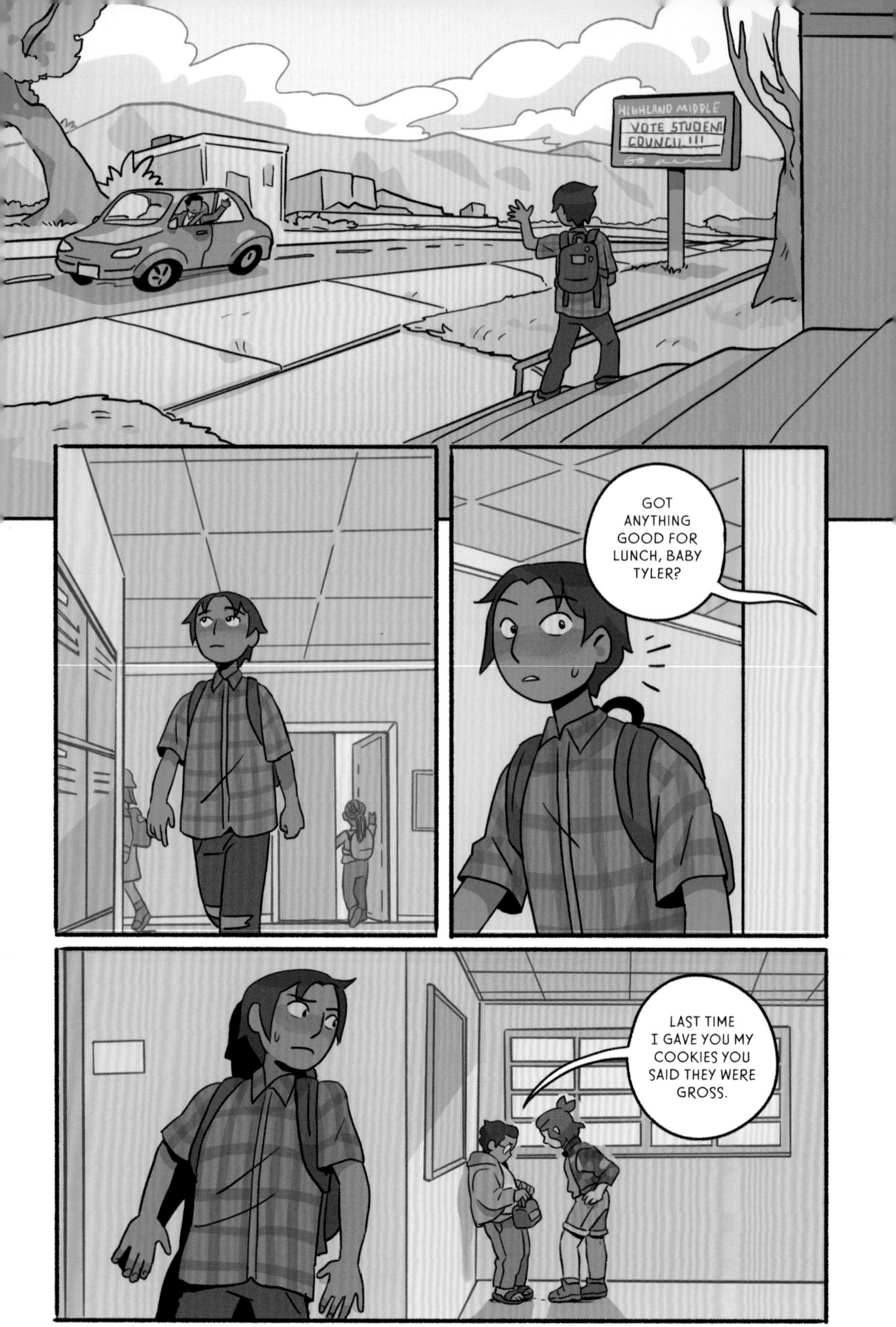
HIGHLAND MIDDLE
VOTE STUDENT COUNCIL!!!
GOT ANYTHING GOOD FOR LUNCH, BABY TYLER?
LAST TIME I GAVE YOU MY COOKIES YOU SAID THEY WERE GROSS.

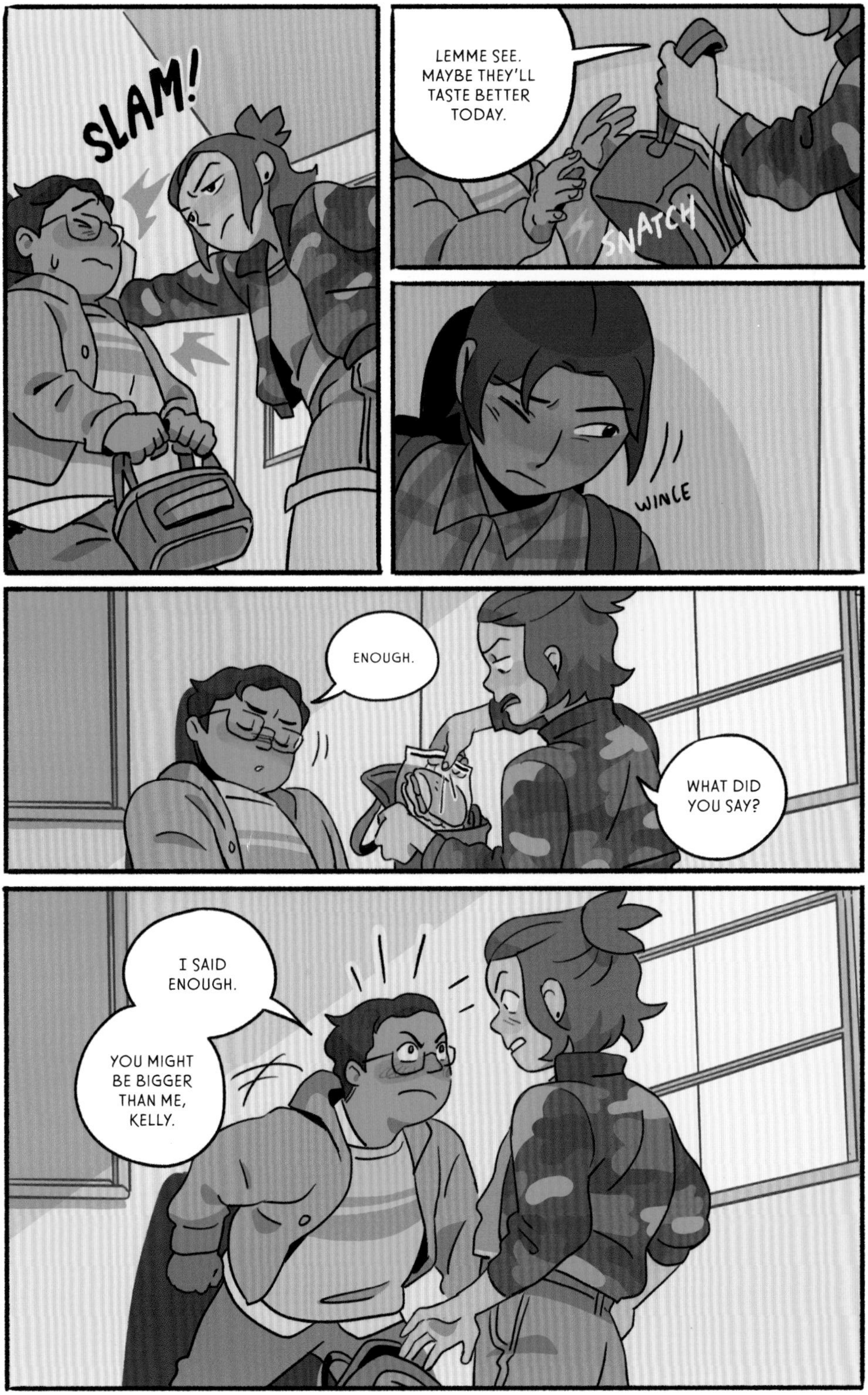
SLAM!
LEMME SEE. MAYBE THEY'LL TASTE BETTER TODAY.
SNATCH
WINCE
ENOUGH.
WHAT DID YOU SAY?
I SAID ENOUGH.
YOU MIGHT BE BIGGER THAN ME, KELLY.

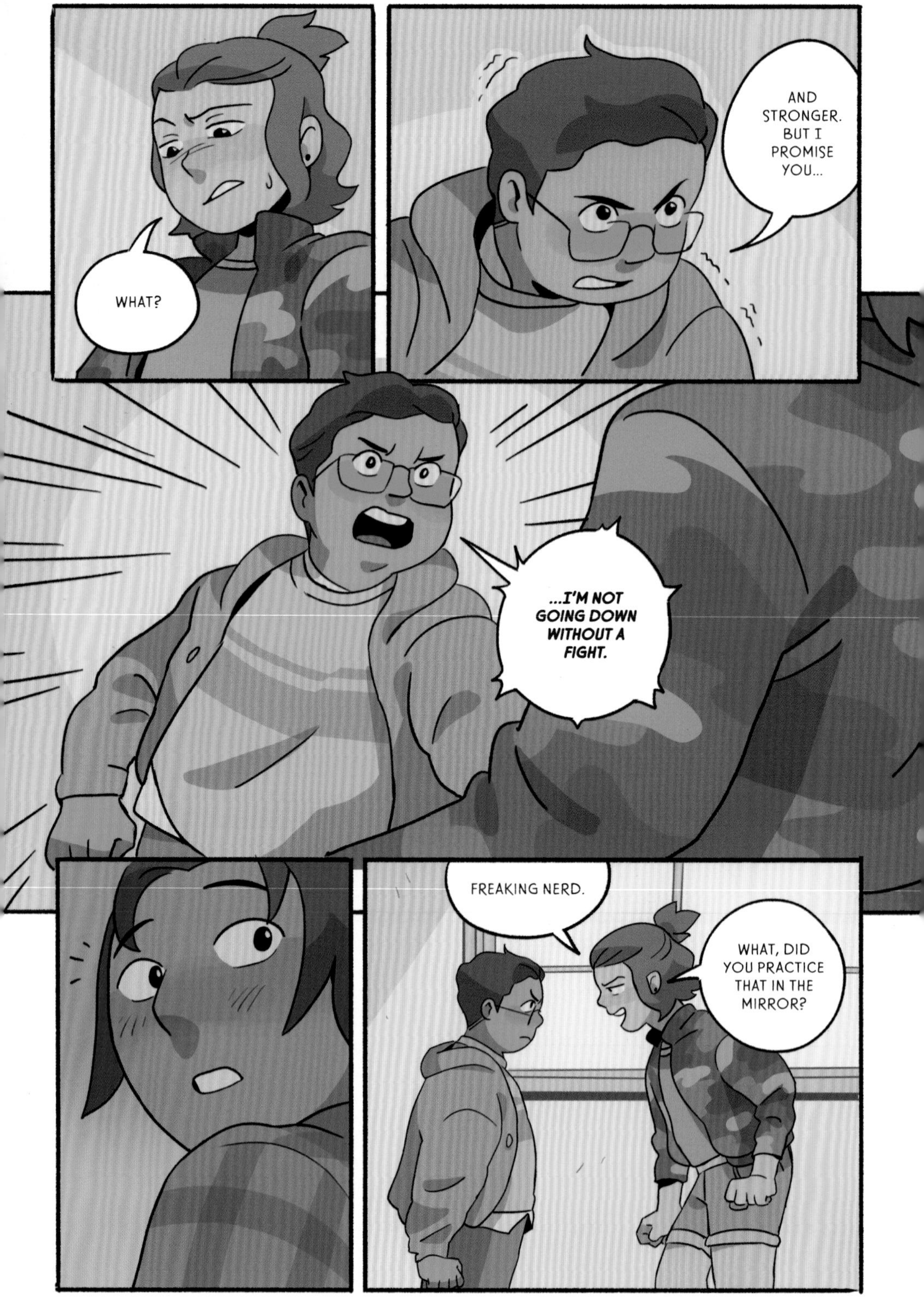
WHAT?
AND STRONGER. BUT I PROMISE YOU...
...I'M NOT GOING DOWN WITHOUT A FIGHT.
FREAKING NERD.
WHAT, DID YOU PRACTICE THAT IN THE MIRROR?

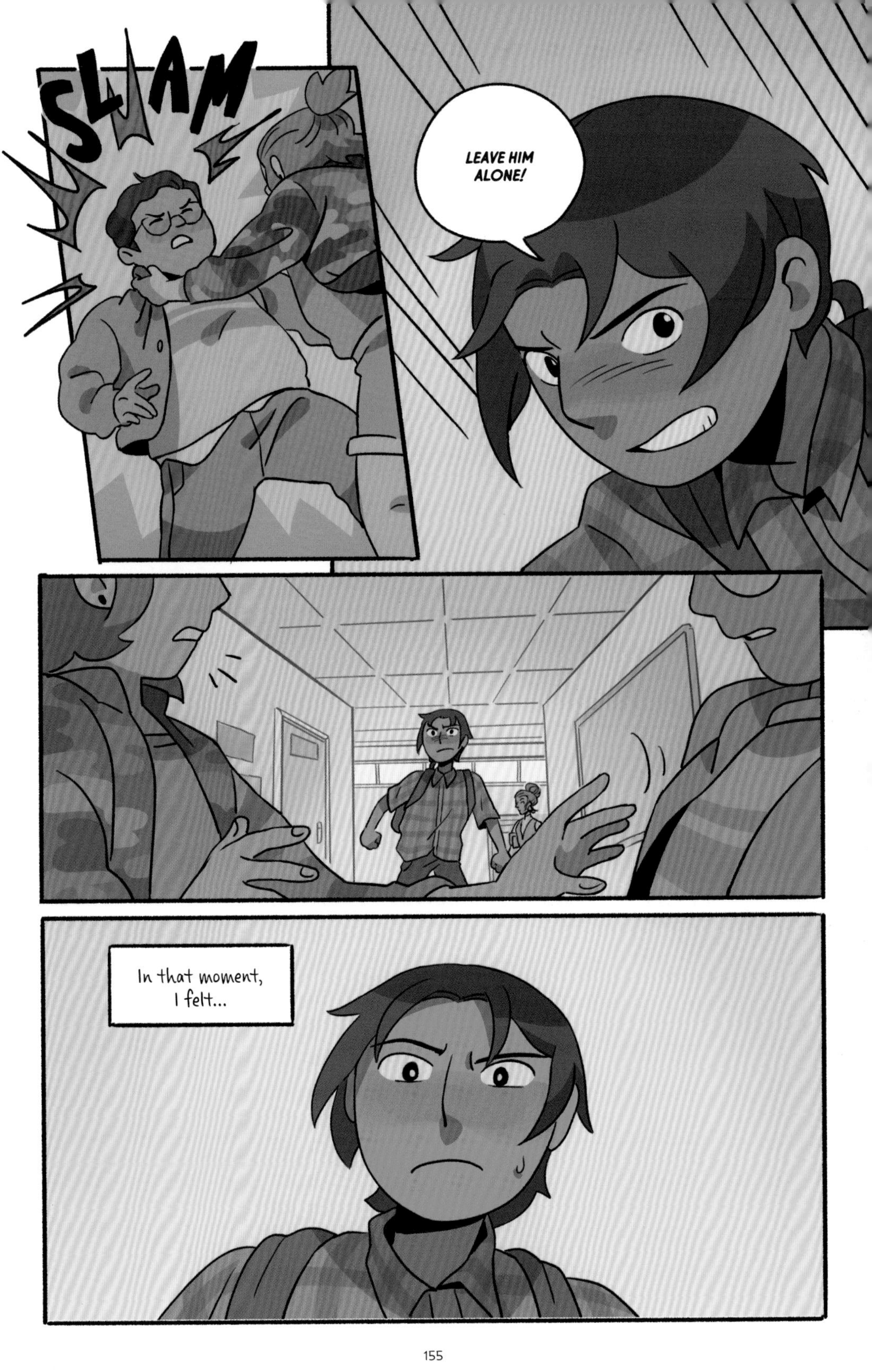
SLAM
LEAVE HIM ALONE!
In that moment, I felt...

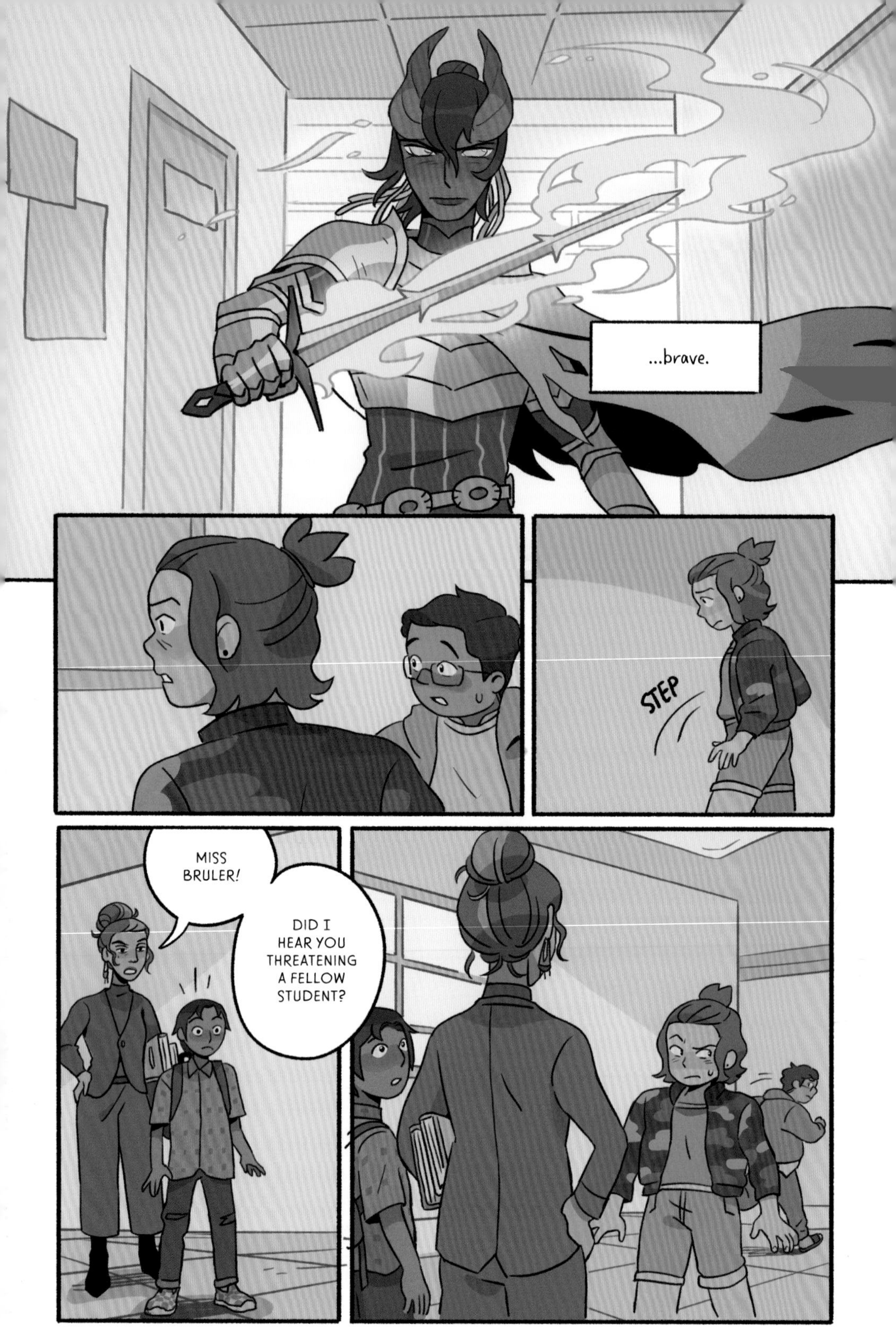
...brave.
STEP
MISS BRULER!
DID I HEAR YOU THREATENING A FELLOW STUDENT?

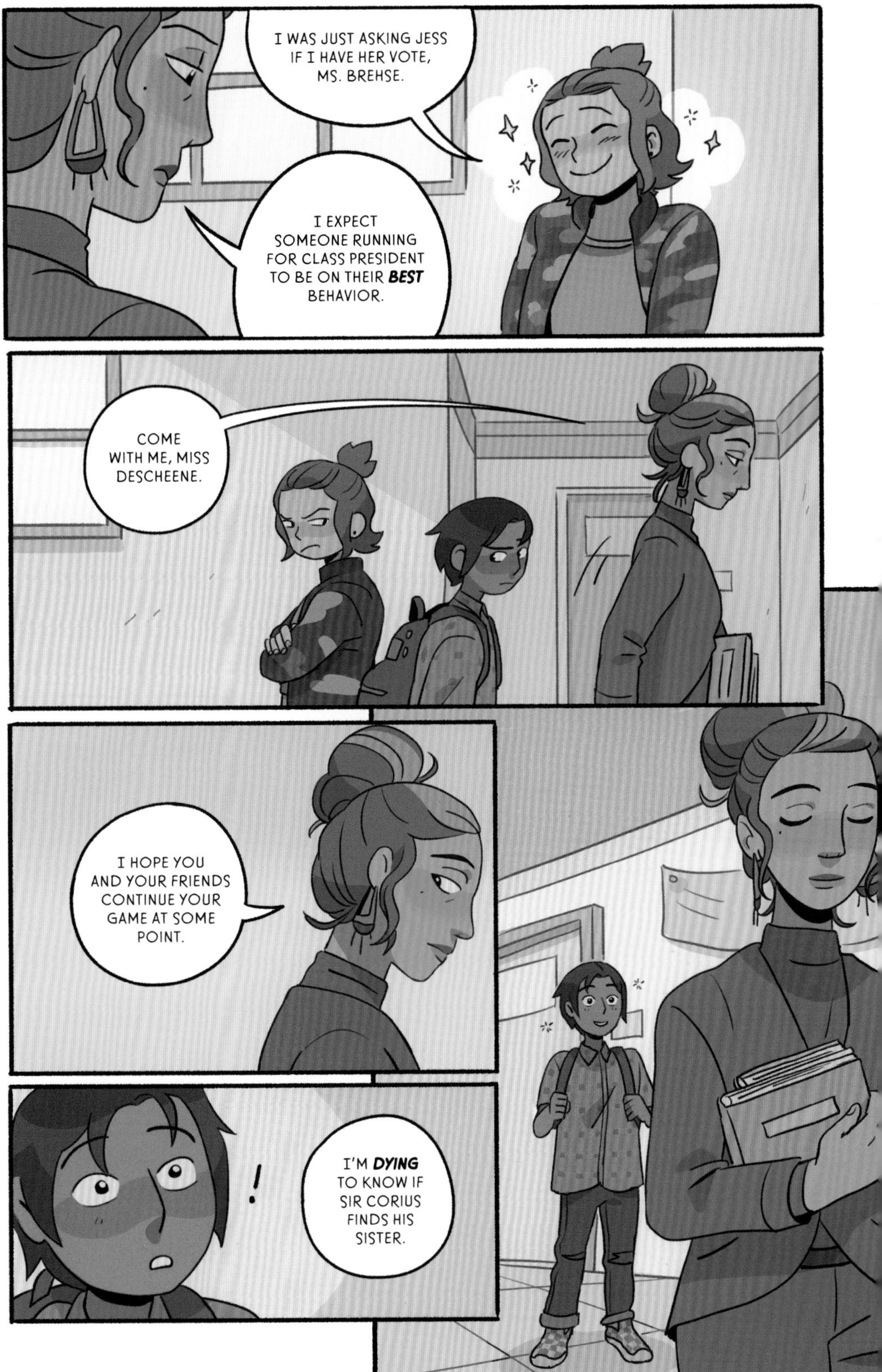
I WAS JUST ASKING JESS IF I HAVE HER VOTE, MS. BREHSE.
I EXPECT SOMEONE RUNNING FOR CLASS PRESIDENT TO BE ON THEIR **BEST** BEHAVIOR.
COME WITH ME, MISS DESCHEENE.
I HOPE YOU AND YOUR FRIENDS CONTINUE YOUR GAME AT SOME POINT.
!
I'M **DYING** TO KNOW IF SIR CORIUS FINDS HIS SISTER.

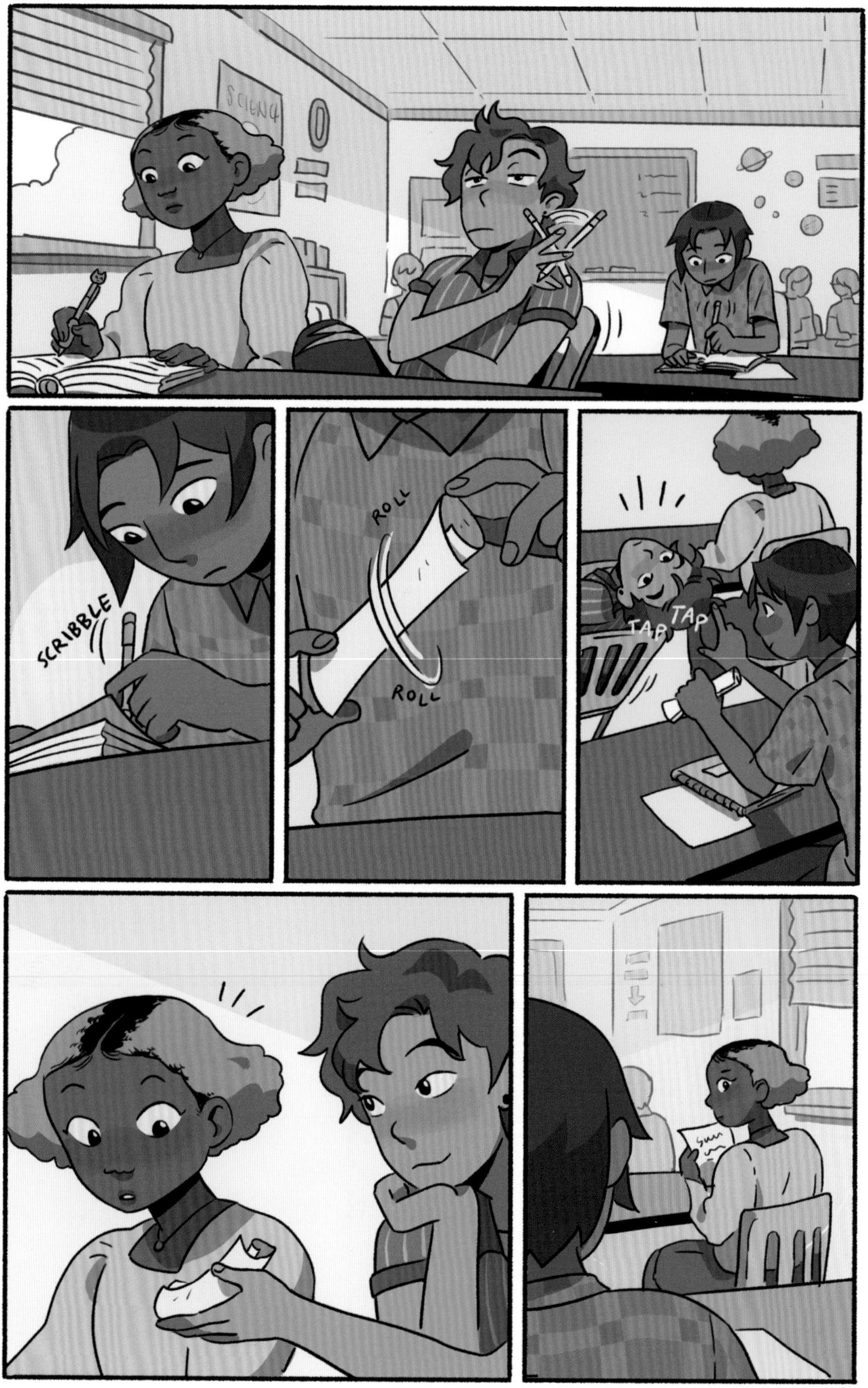
SCIENCE
SCRIBBLE
ROLL
ROLL
TAP
TAP

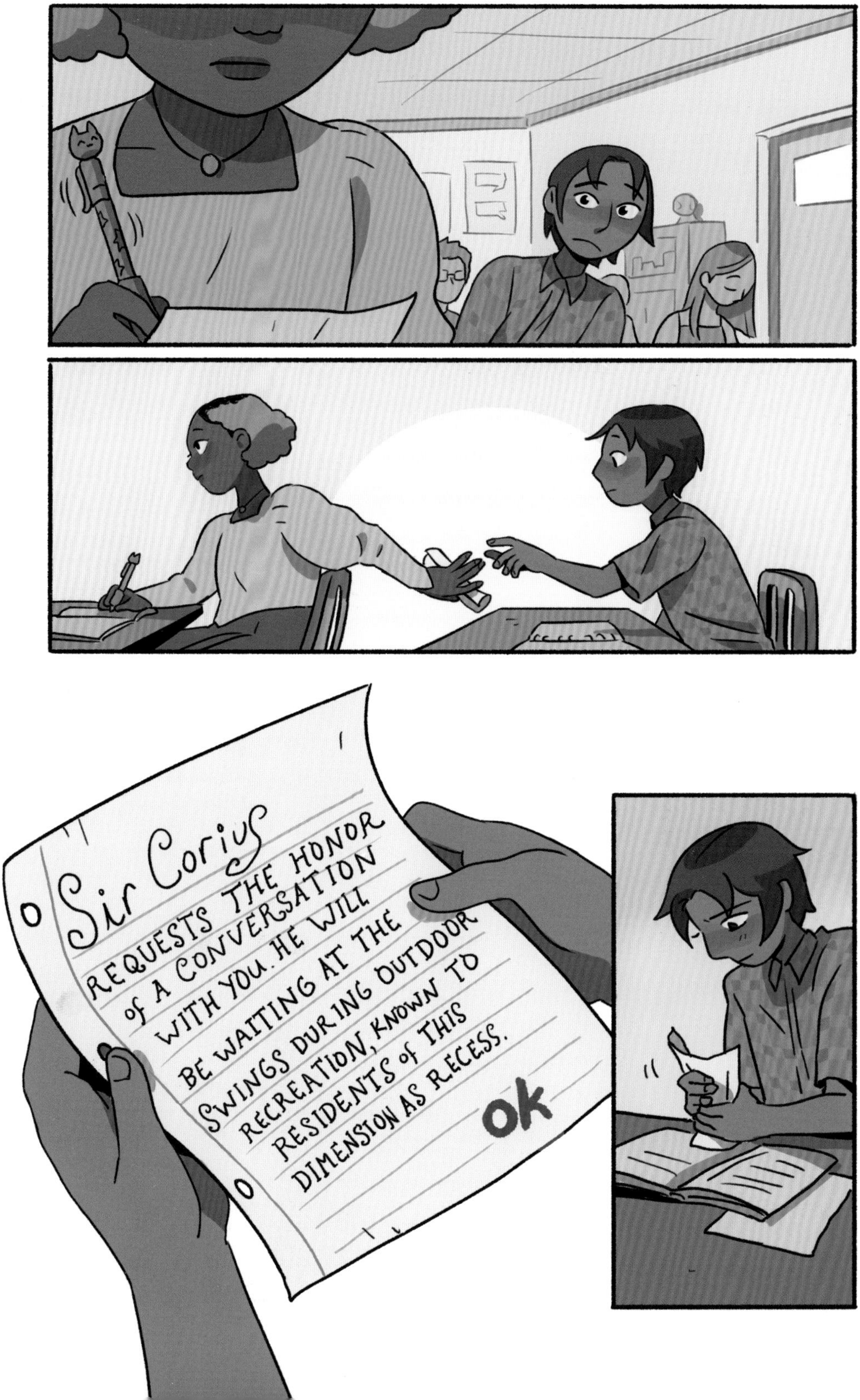
Sir Corius
REQUESTS THE HONOR OF A CONVERSATION WITH YOU. HE WILL BE WAITING AT THE SWINGS DURING OUTDOOR RECREATION, KNOWN TO RESIDENTS OF THIS DIMENSION AS RECESS.
OK

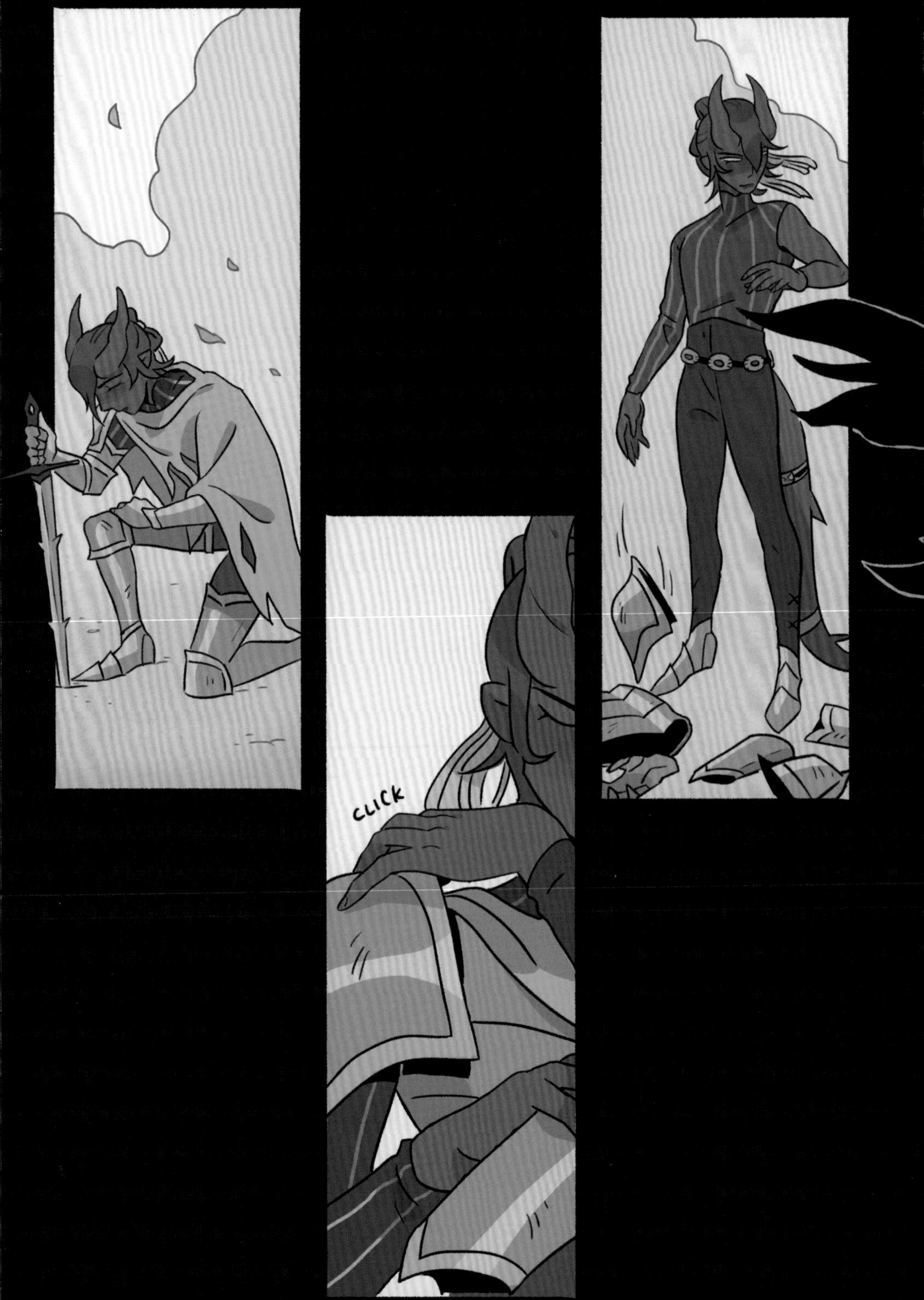
CLICK

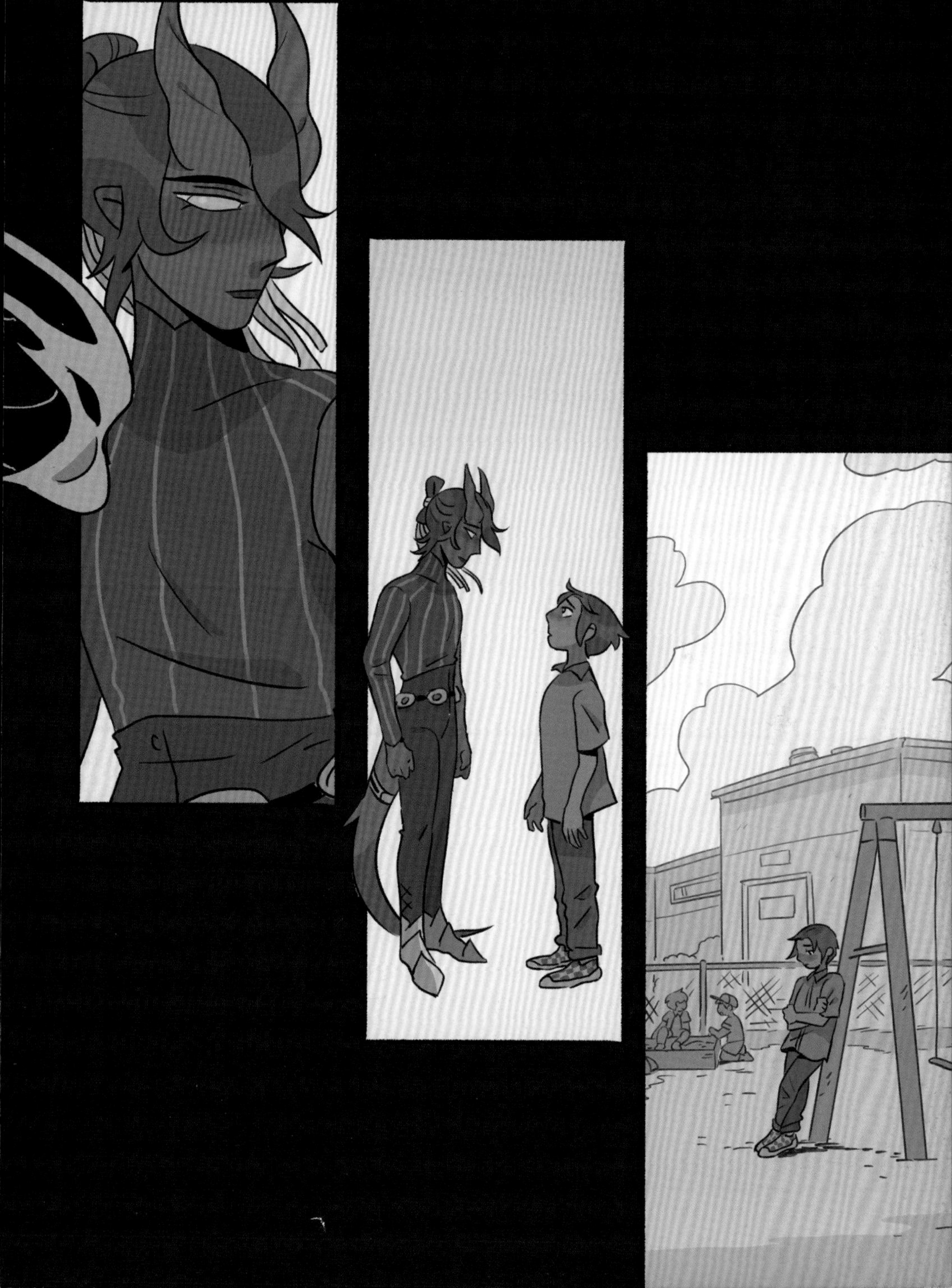

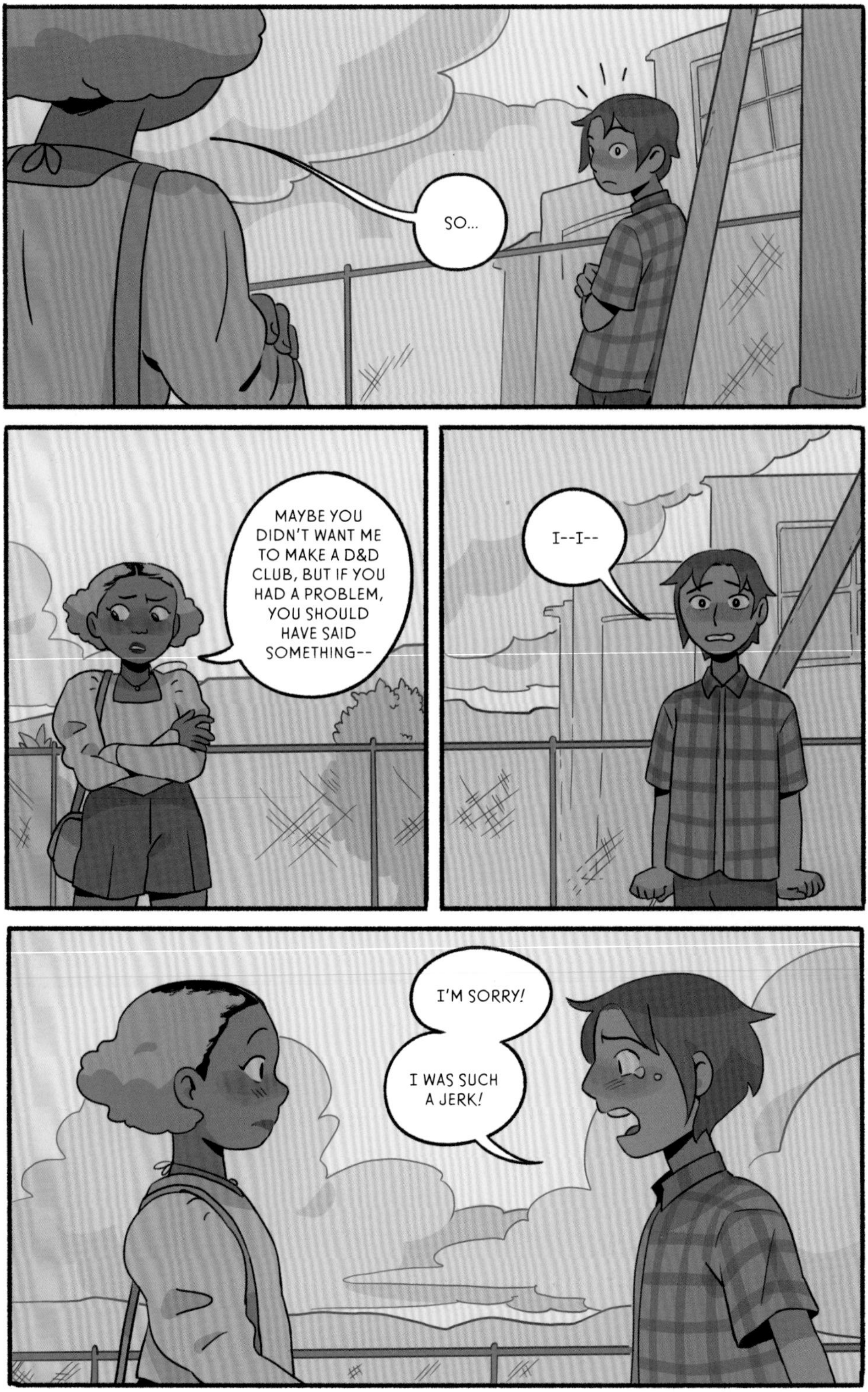
SO...
MAYBE YOU DIDN'T WANT ME TO MAKE A D&D CLUB, BUT IF YOU HAD A PROBLEM, YOU SHOULD HAVE SAID SOMETHING--
I--I--
I'M SORRY!
I WAS SUCH A JERK!

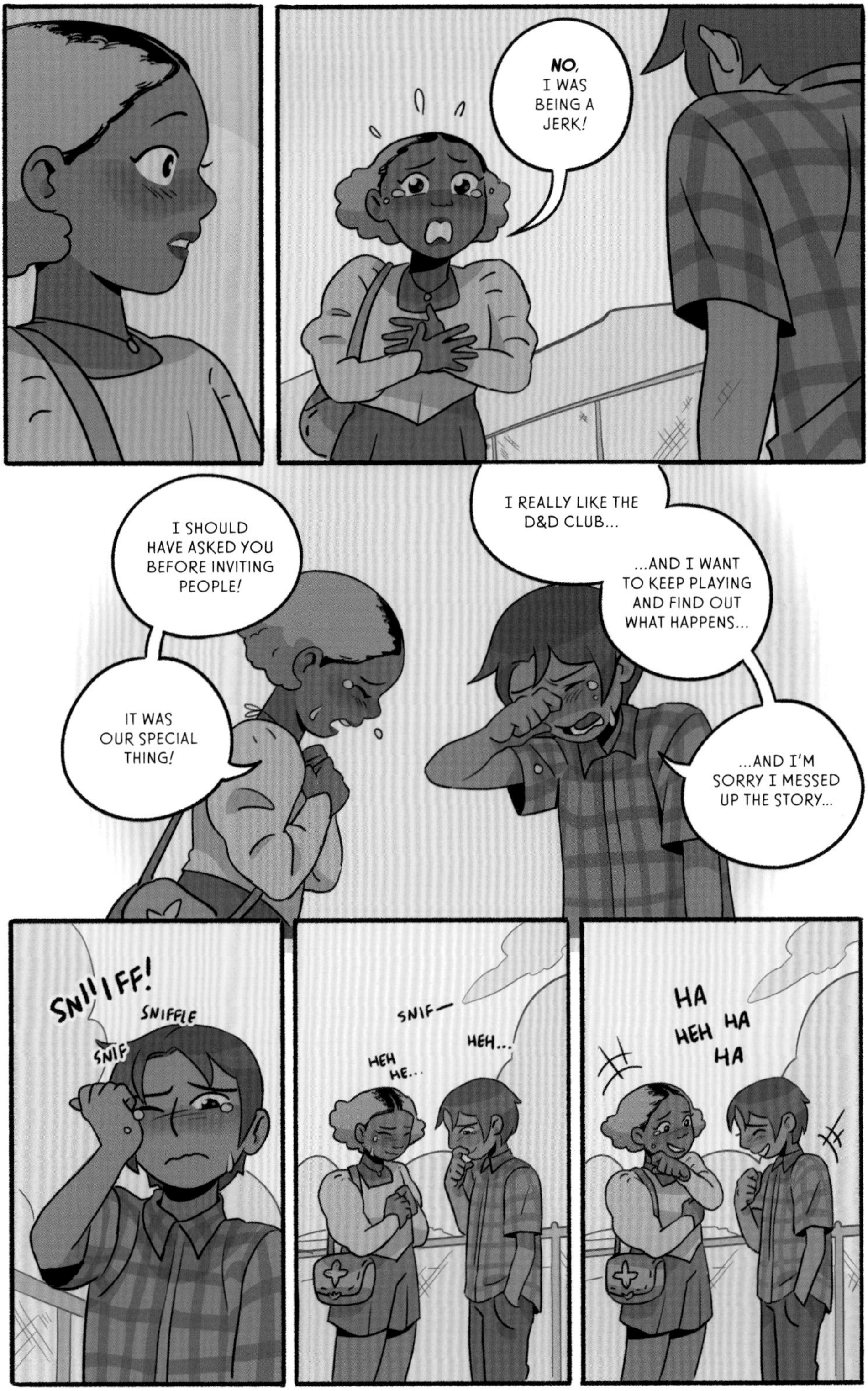
NO, I WAS BEING A JERK!
I SHOULD HAVE ASKED YOU BEFORE INVITING PEOPLE!
IT WAS OUR SPECIAL THING!
I REALLY LIKE THE D&D CLUB...
...AND I WANT TO KEEP PLAYING AND FIND OUT WHAT HAPPENS...
...AND I'M SORRY I MESSED UP THE STORY...
SNIIIFF!
SNIFFLE
SNIF
SNIF—
HEH HE...
HEH...
HA
HEH HA
HA

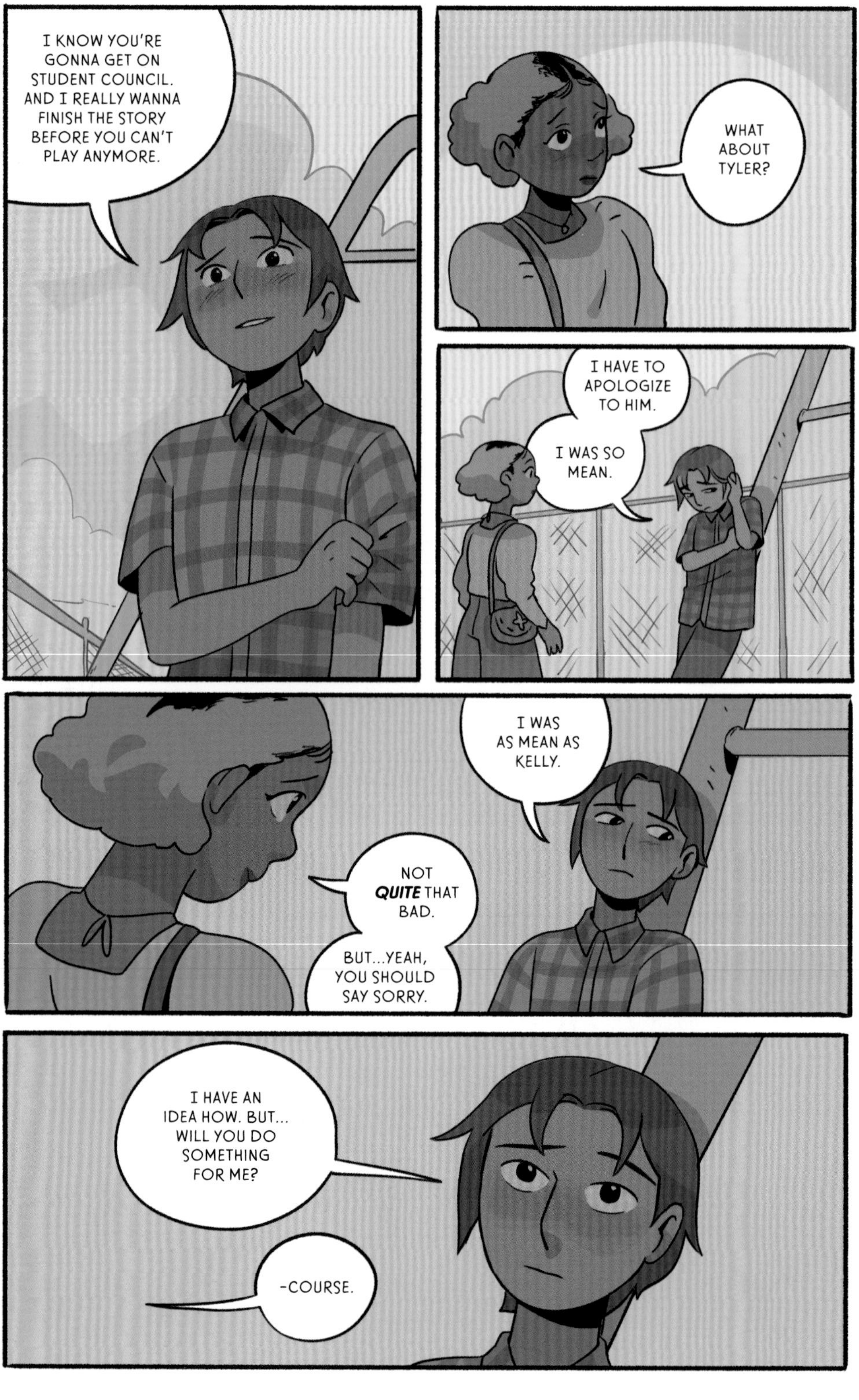
I KNOW YOU'RE GONNA GET ON STUDENT COUNCIL. AND I REALLY WANNA FINISH THE STORY BEFORE YOU CAN'T PLAY ANYMORE.
WHAT ABOUT TYLER?
I HAVE TO APOLOGIZE TO HIM.
I WAS SO MEAN.
I WAS AS MEAN AS KELLY.
NOT ***QUITE*** THAT BAD.
BUT...YEAH, YOU SHOULD SAY SORRY.
I HAVE AN IDEA HOW. BUT... WILL YOU DO SOMETHING FOR ME?
-COURSE.

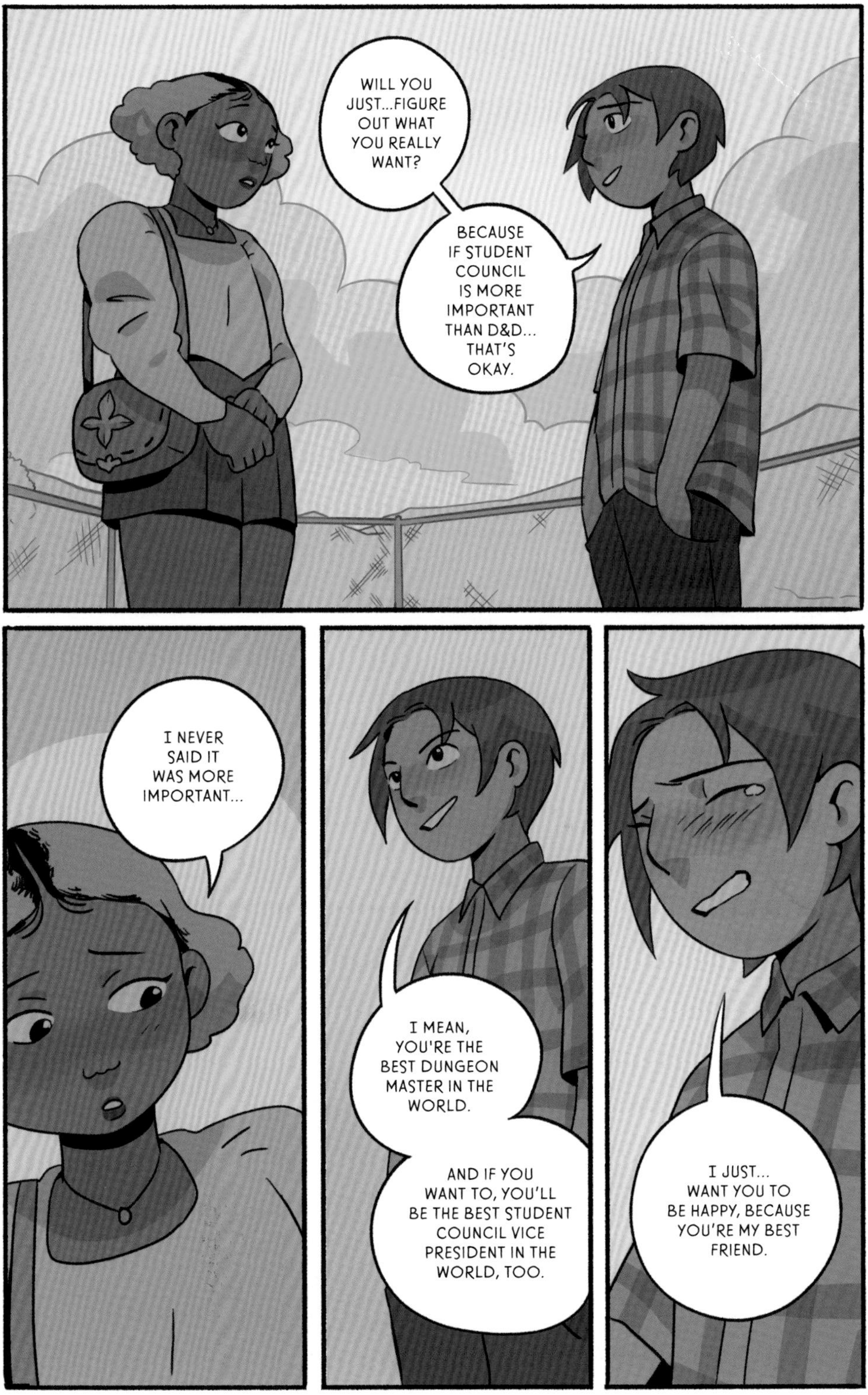
WILL YOU JUST...FIGURE OUT WHAT YOU REALLY WANT?
BECAUSE IF STUDENT COUNCIL IS MORE IMPORTANT THAN D&D... THAT'S OKAY.
I NEVER SAID IT WAS MORE IMPORTANT...
I MEAN, YOU'RE THE BEST DUNGEON MASTER IN THE WORLD.
AND IF YOU WANT TO, YOU'LL BE THE BEST STUDENT COUNCIL VICE PRESIDENT IN THE WORLD, TOO.
I JUST... WANT YOU TO BE HAPPY, BECAUSE YOU'RE MY BEST FRIEND.

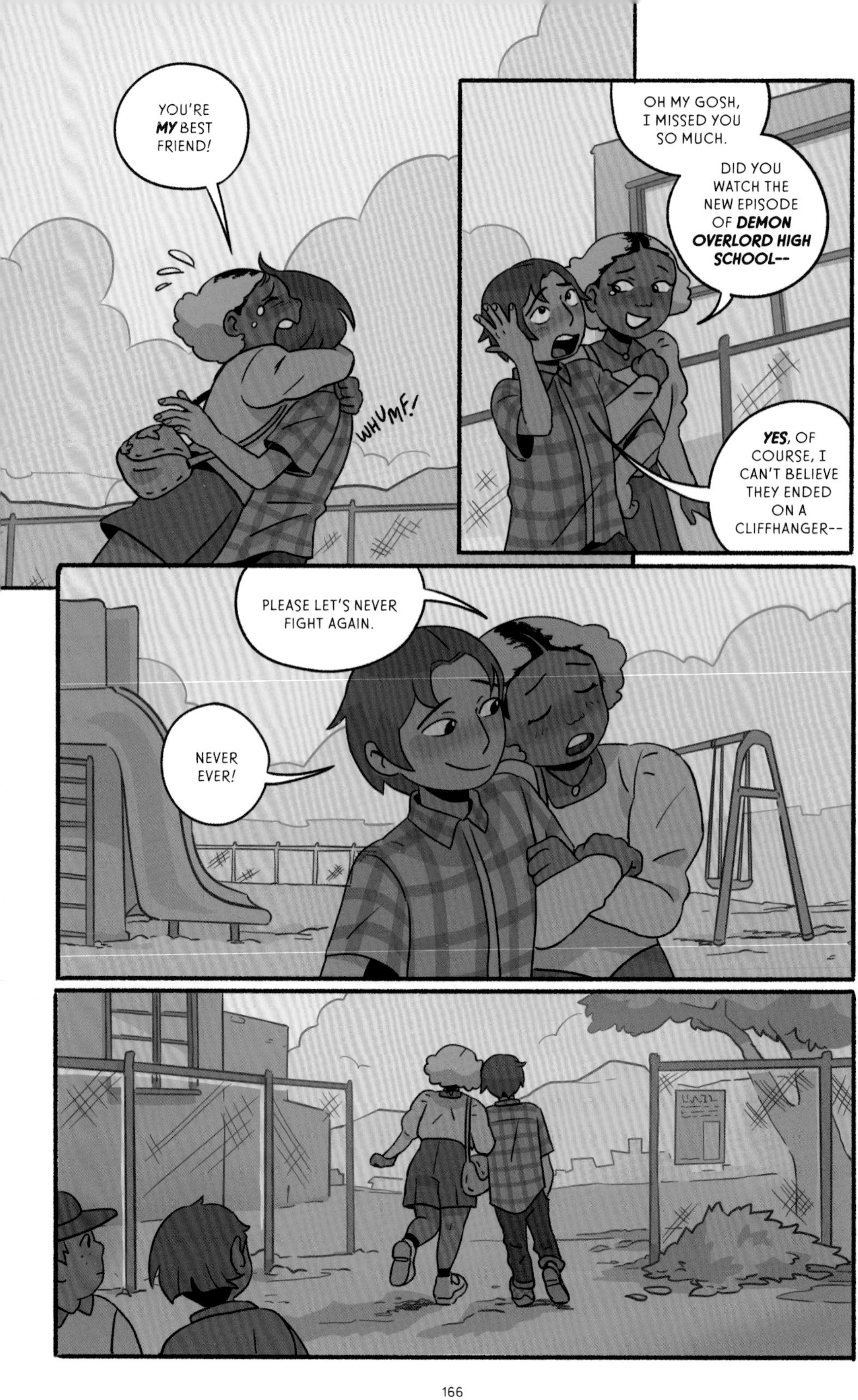
YOU'RE MY BEST FRIEND!
WHUMF!
OH MY GOSH, I MISSED YOU SO MUCH.
DID YOU WATCH THE NEW EPISODE OF DEMON OVERLORD HIGH SCHOOL--
YES, OF COURSE, I CAN'T BELIEVE THEY ENDED ON A CLIFFHANGER--
PLEASE LET'S NEVER FIGHT AGAIN.
NEVER EVER!

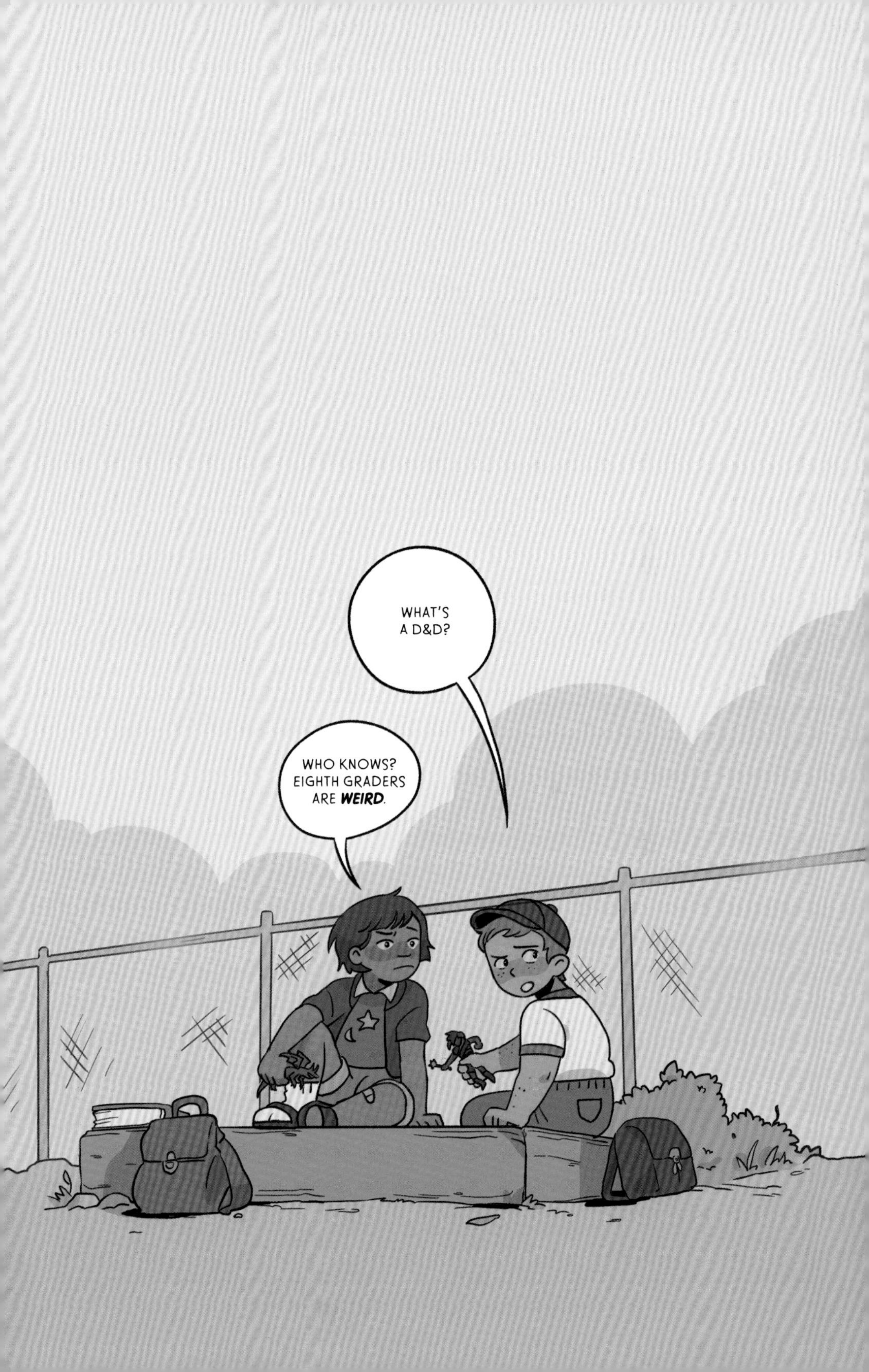
WHAT'S A D&D?
WHO KNOWS? EIGHTH GRADERS ARE **WEIRD**.

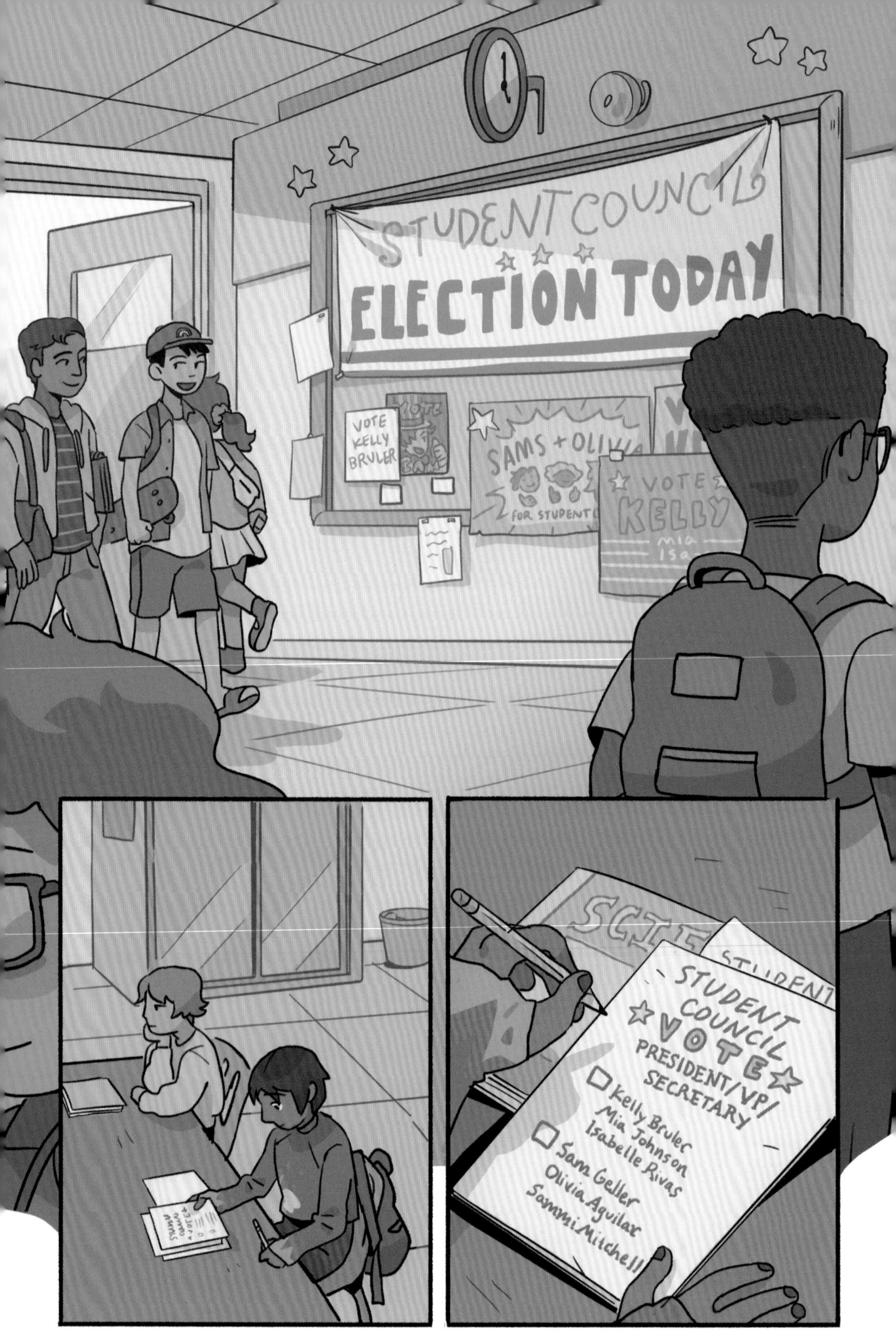
STUDENT COUNCIL
ELECTION TODAY
VOTE KELLY BRULER
VOTE
SAMS + OLIVIA
FOR STUDENT
VOTE KELLY
mia
Isa
STUDENT COUNCIL VOTE
PRESIDENT/VP/ SECRETARY
Kelly Bruler
Mia Johnson
Isabelle Rivas
Sam Geller
Olivia Aguilar
Sammi Mitchell

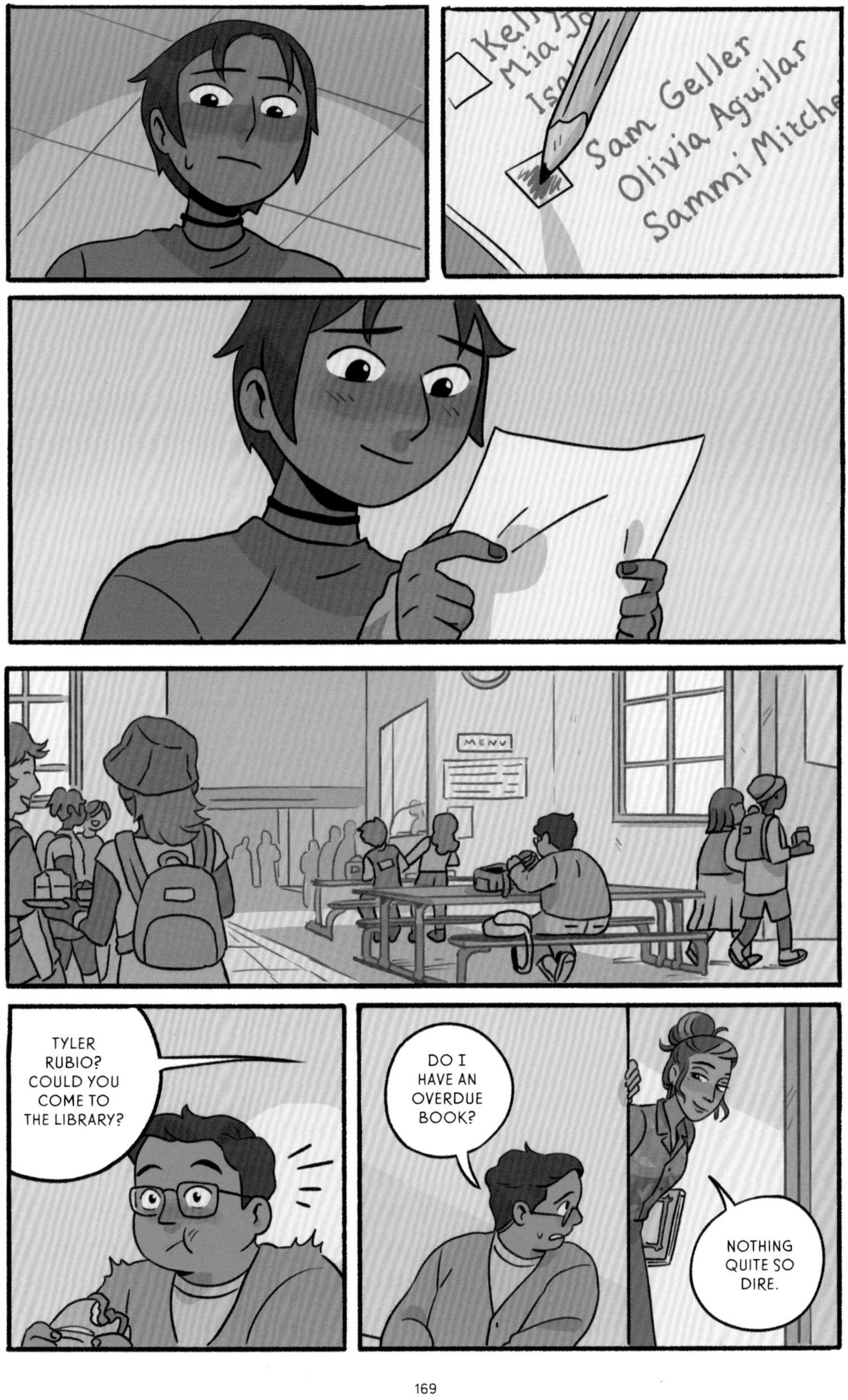
Sam Geller
Olivia Aguilar
MENU
TYLER RUBIO? COULD YOU COME TO THE LIBRARY?
DO I HAVE AN OVERDUE BOOK?
NOTHING QUITE SO DIRE.

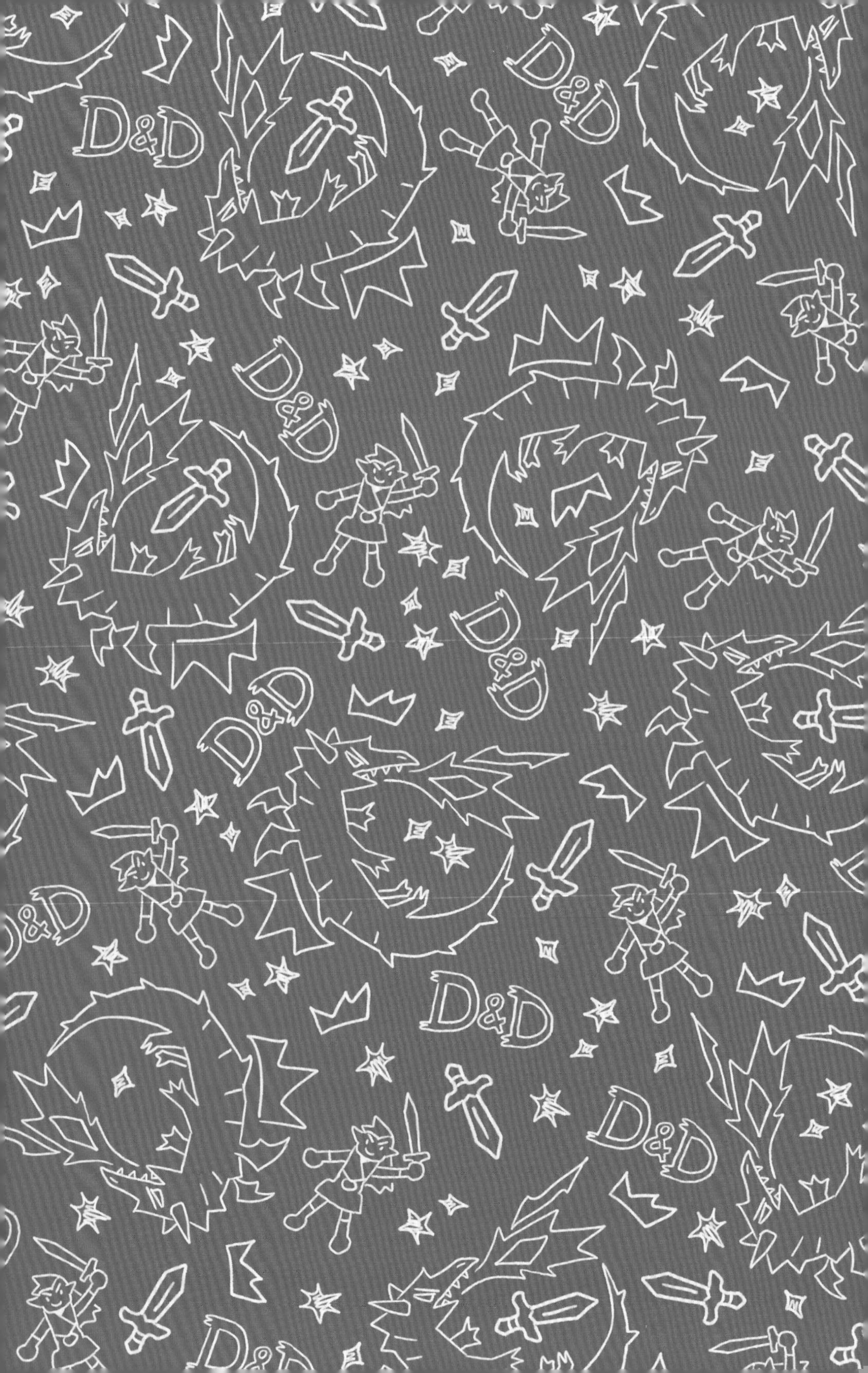
D&D

D&D DUNGEON CLUB

SESSION FOUR

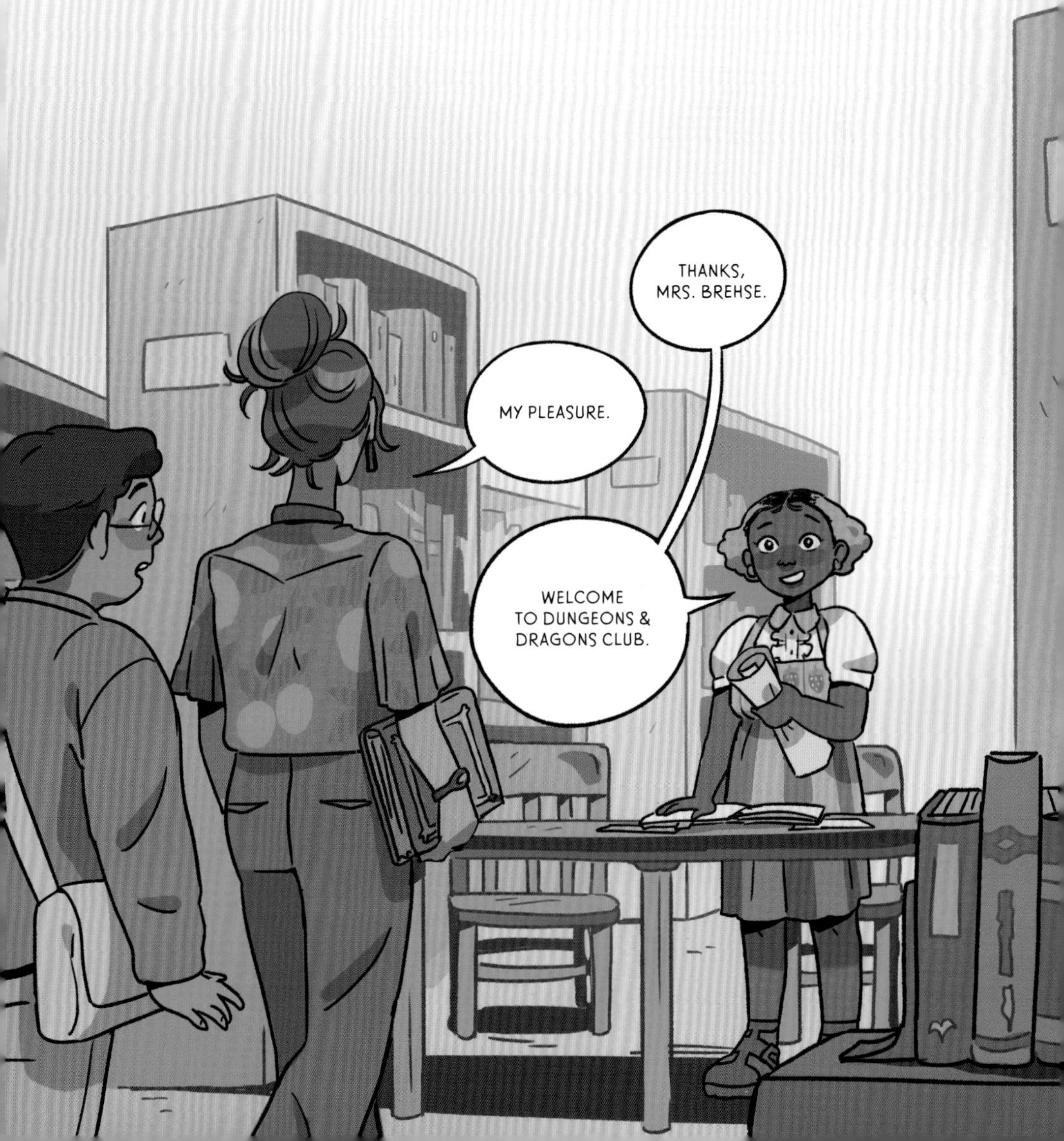
THANKS, MRS. BREHSE.
MY PLEASURE.
WELCOME TO DUNGEONS & DRAGONS CLUB.

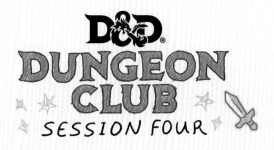

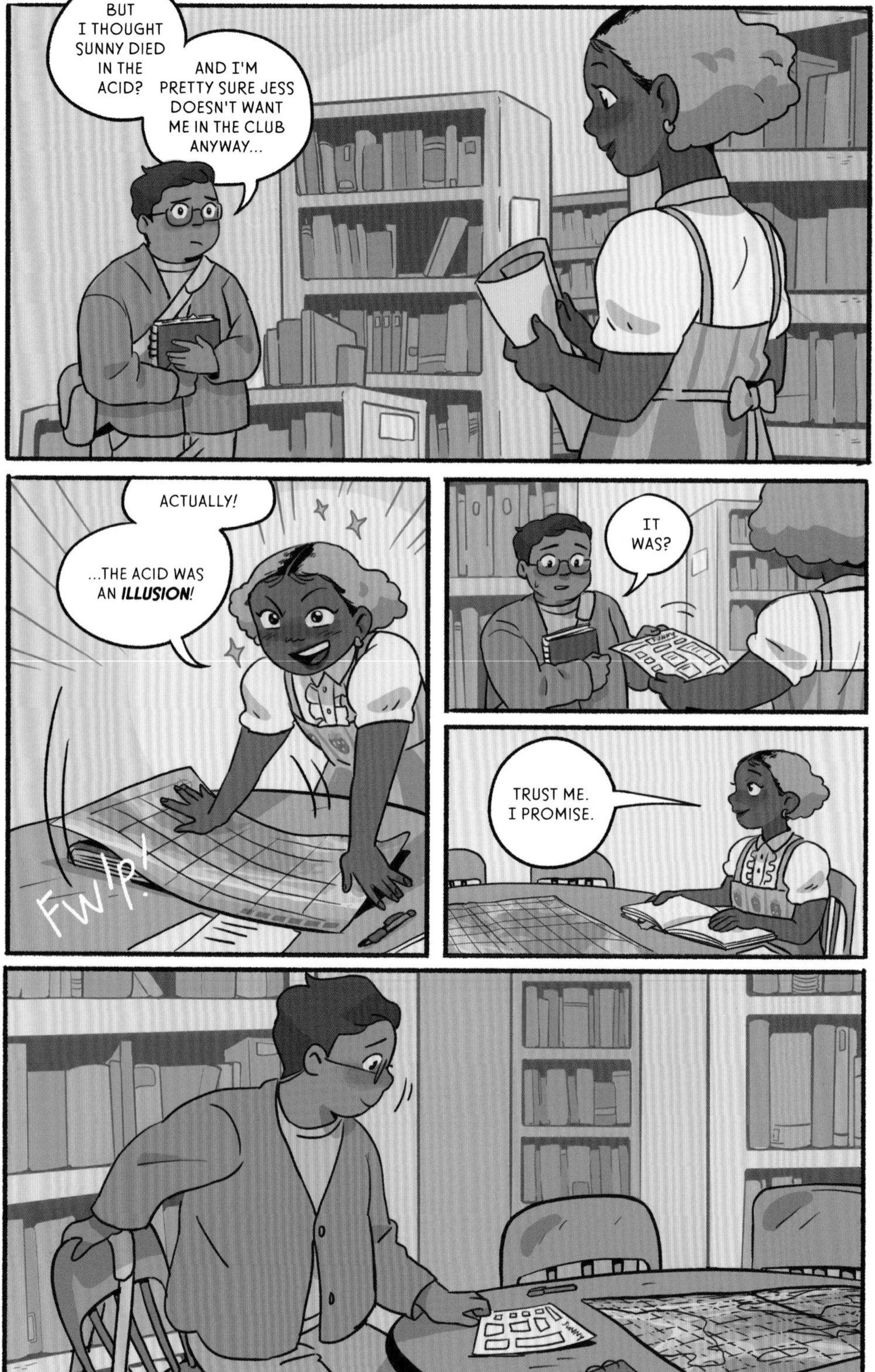
BUT I THOUGHT SUNNY DIED IN THE ACID?
AND I'M PRETTY SURE JESS DOESN'T WANT ME IN THE CLUB ANYWAY...
ACTUALLY!
...THE ACID WAS AN ***ILLUSION!***
FWIP!
IT WAS?
TRUST ME. I PROMISE.

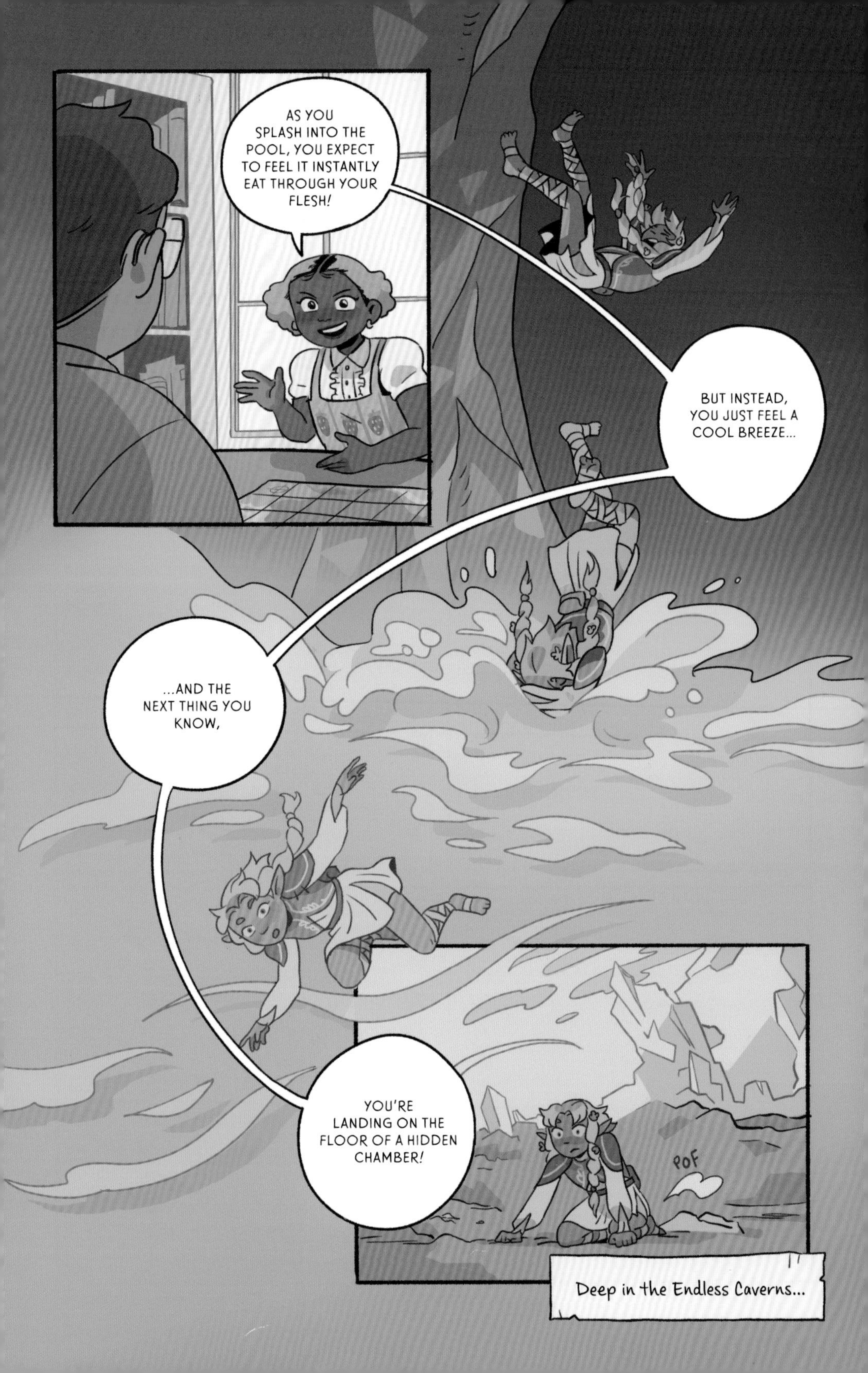
AS YOU SPLASH INTO THE POOL, YOU EXPECT TO FEEL IT INSTANTLY EAT THROUGH YOUR FLESH!
BUT INSTEAD, YOU JUST FEEL A COOL BREEZE...
...AND THE NEXT THING YOU KNOW,
YOU'RE LANDING ON THE FLOOR OF A HIDDEN CHAMBER!
POF
Deep in the Endless Caverns...

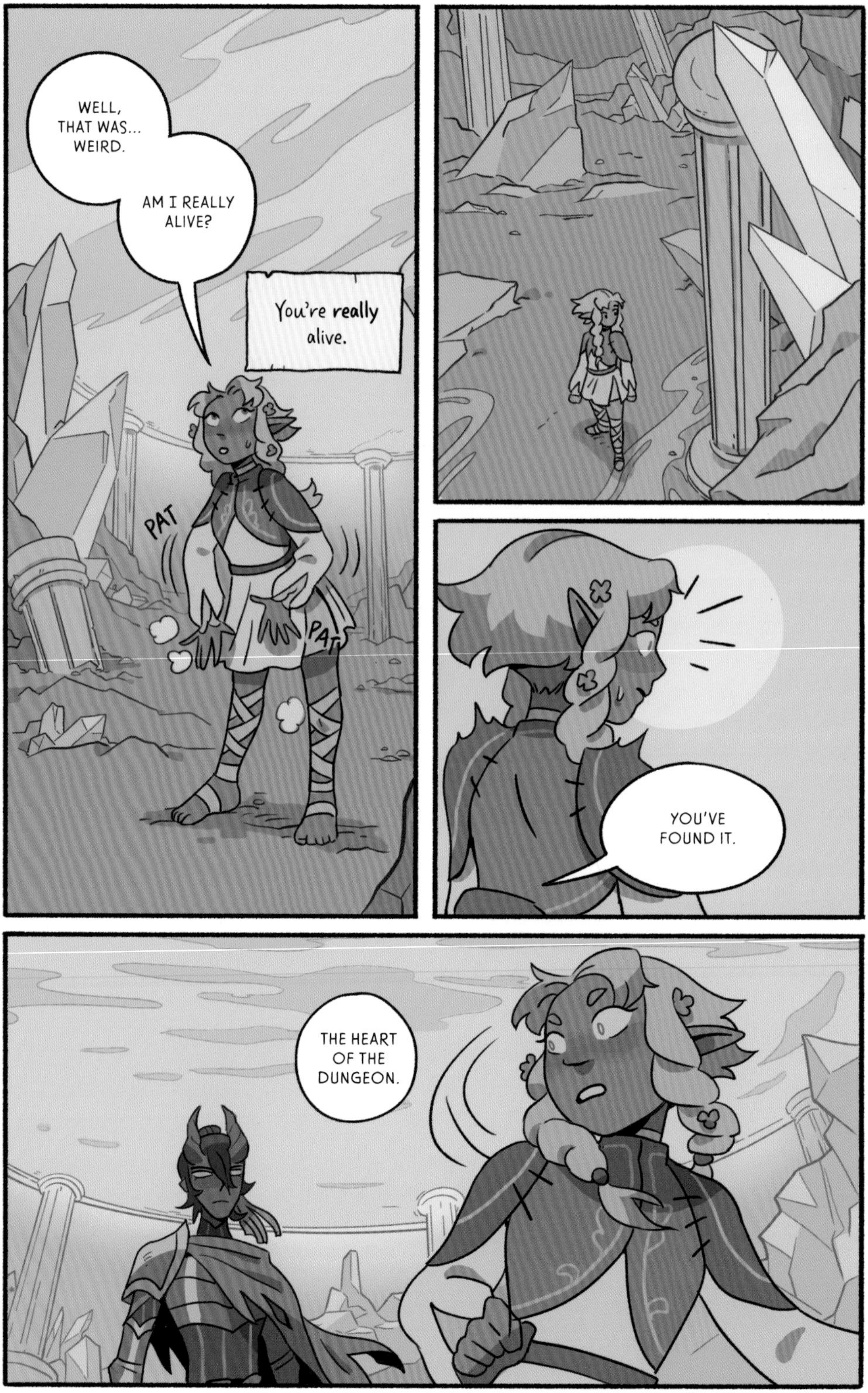
WELL, THAT WAS... WEIRD.
AM I REALLY ALIVE?
You're **really** alive.
PAT
PAT
YOU'VE FOUND IT.
THE HEART OF THE DUNGEON.

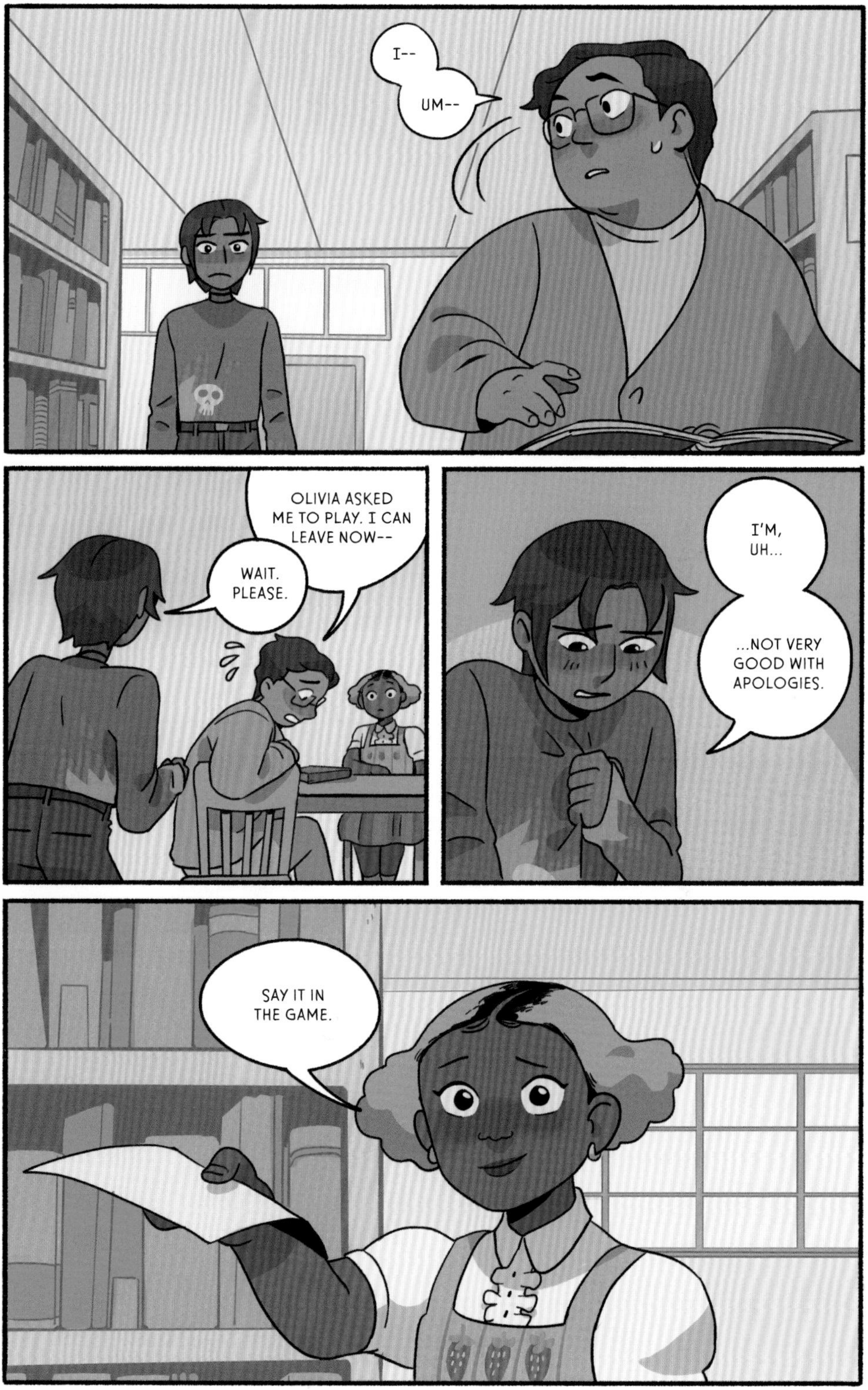
I--
UM--
OLIVIA ASKED ME TO PLAY. I CAN LEAVE NOW--
WAIT. PLEASE.
I'M, UH...
...NOT VERY GOOD WITH APOLOGIES.
SAY IT IN THE GAME.

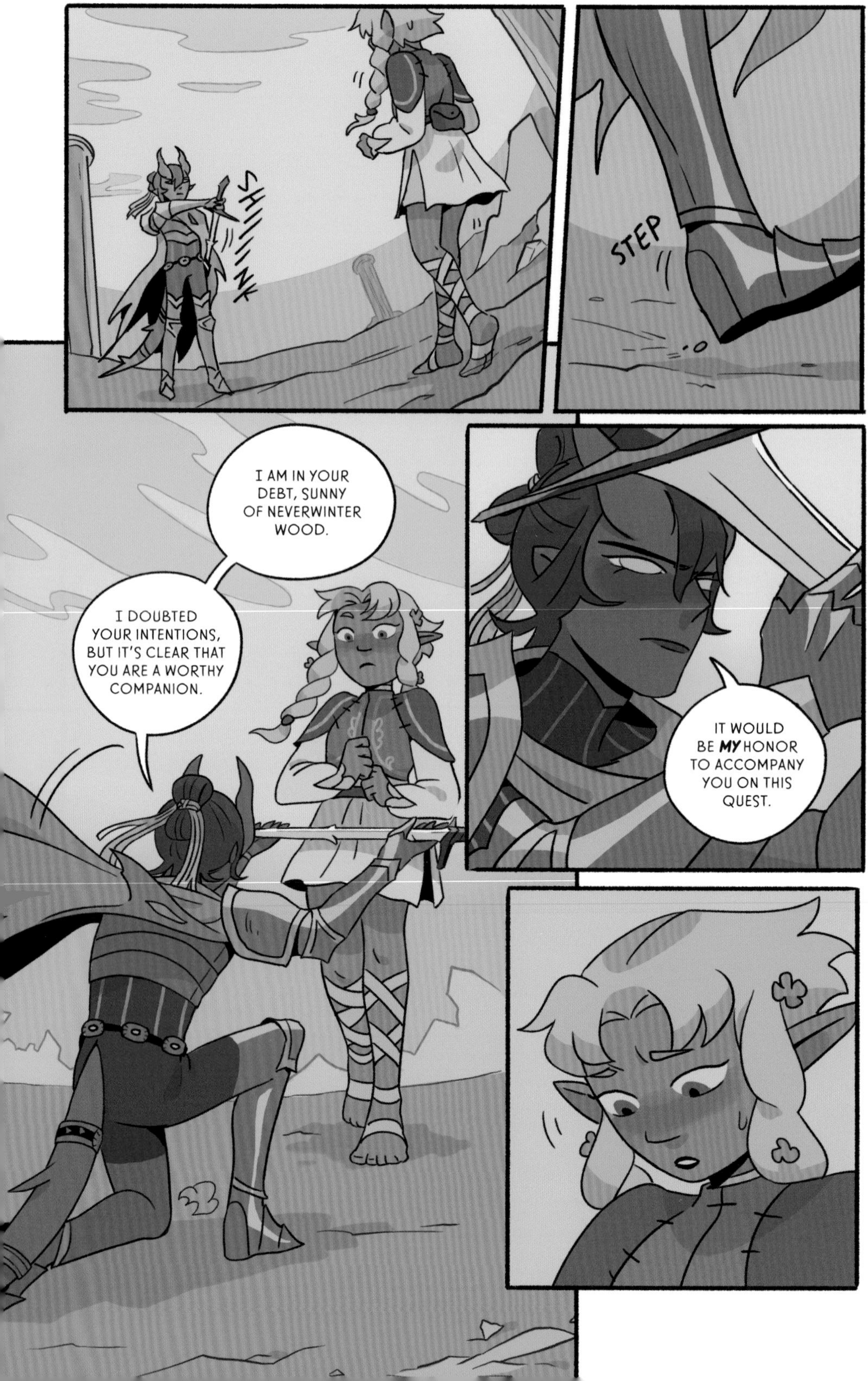
SHIIIIINK
STEP
I AM IN YOUR DEBT, SUNNY OF NEVERWINTER WOOD.
I DOUBTED YOUR INTENTIONS, BUT IT'S CLEAR THAT YOU ARE A WORTHY COMPANION.
IT WOULD BE **MY** HONOR TO ACCOMPANY YOU ON THIS QUEST.

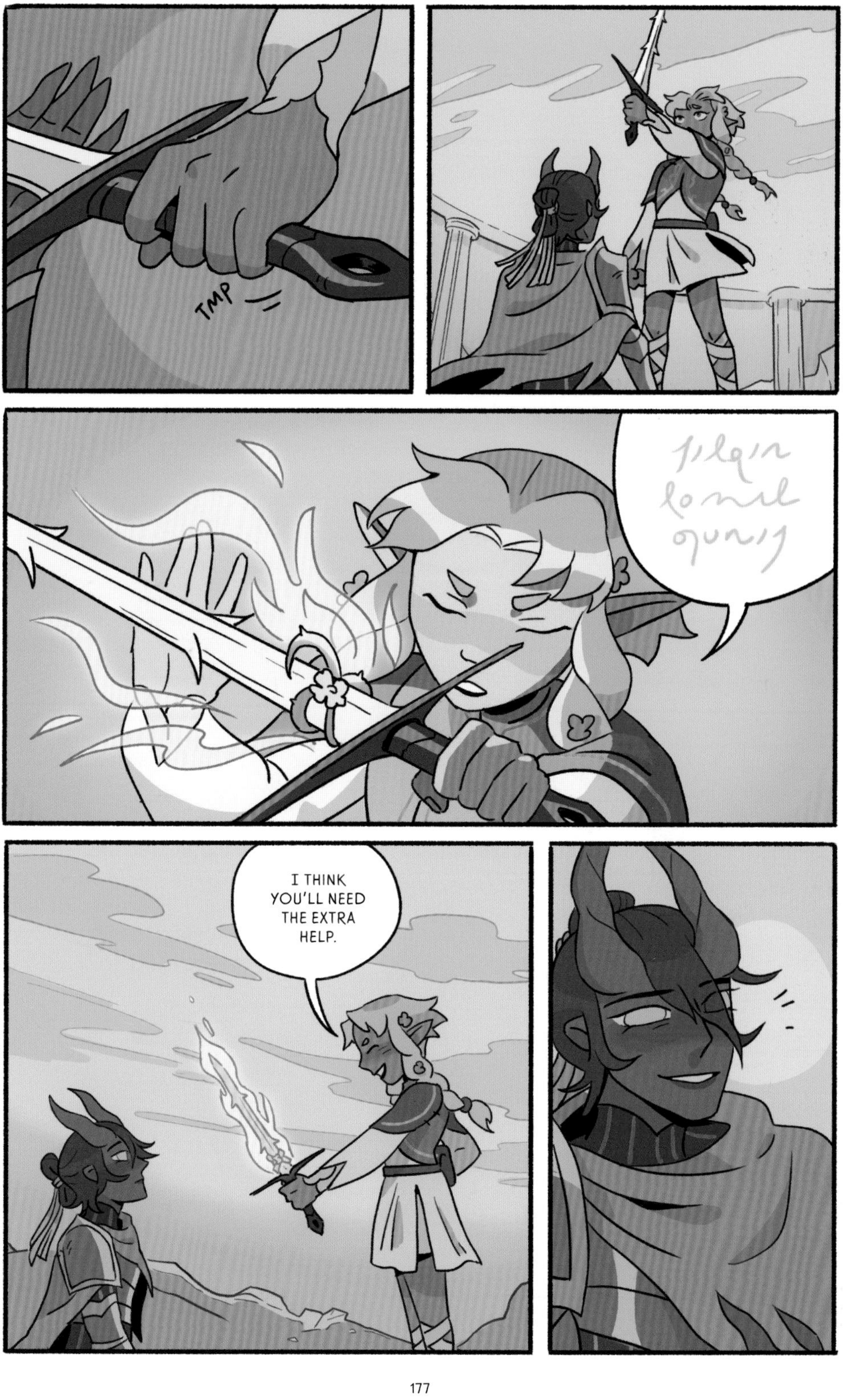
TMP
I THINK YOU'LL NEED THE EXTRA HELP.

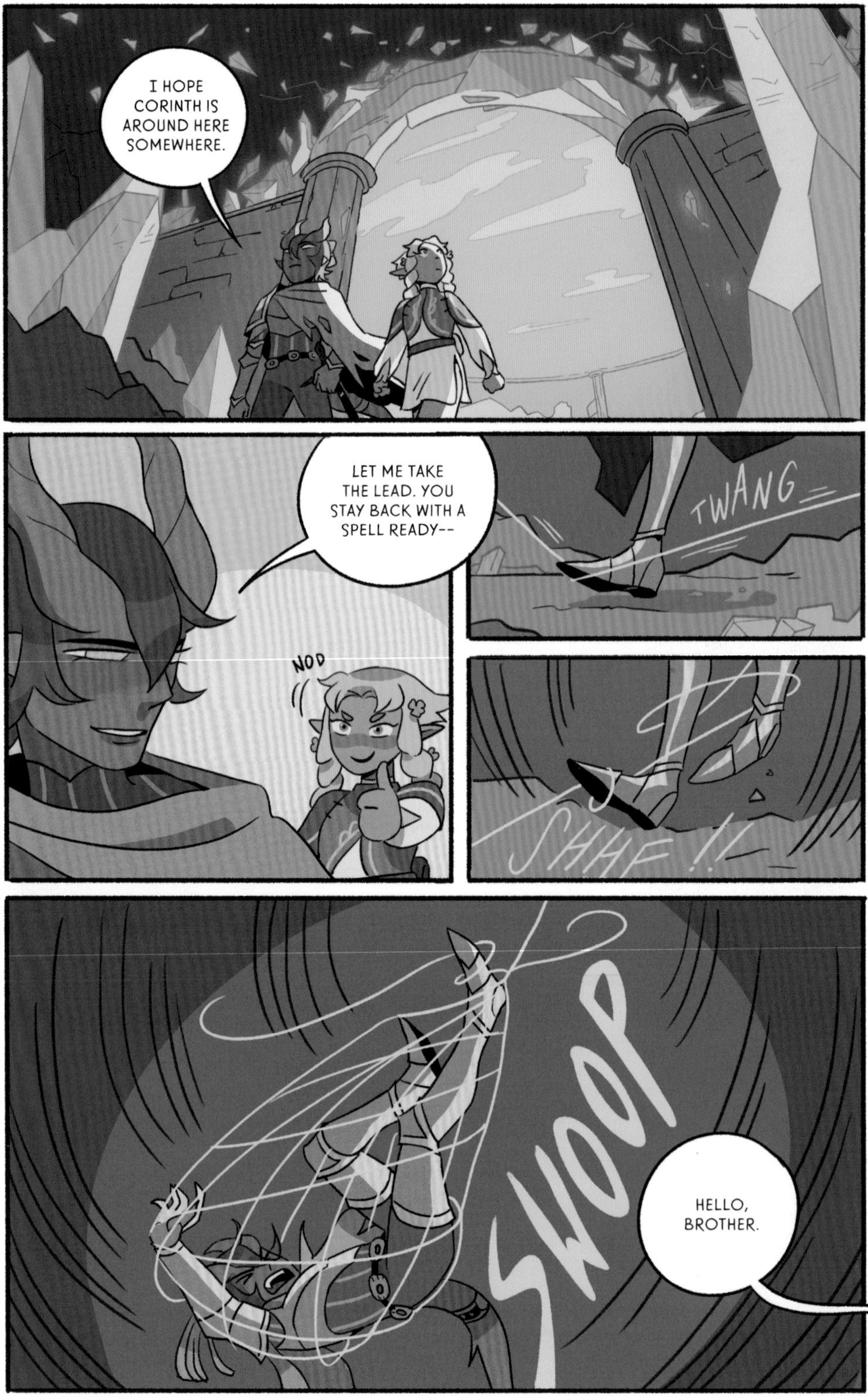
I HOPE CORINTH IS AROUND HERE SOMEWHERE.
LET ME TAKE THE LEAD. YOU STAY BACK WITH A SPELL READY--
TWANG
NOD
SHHF!!
SWOOP
HELLO, BROTHER.

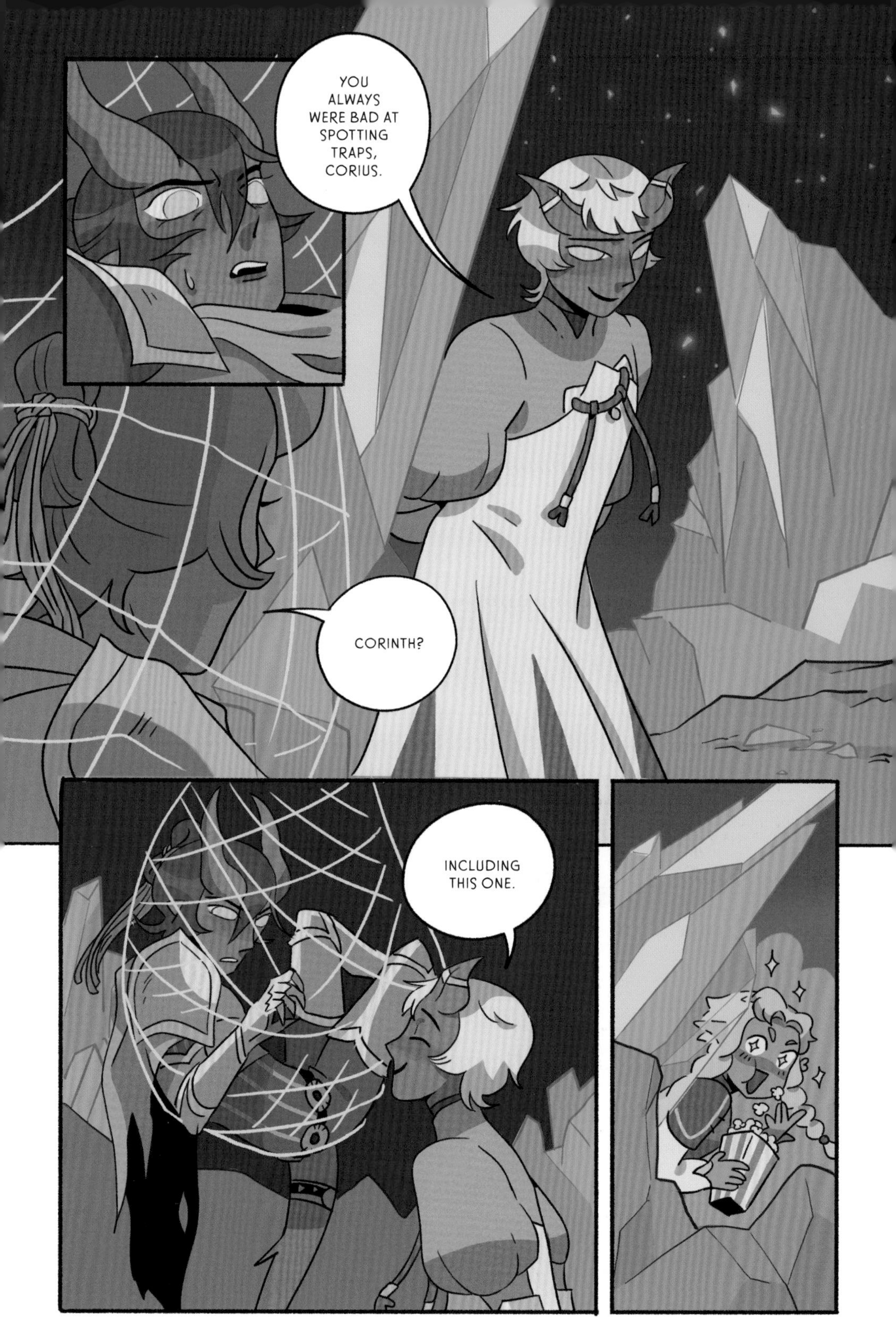
YOU ALWAYS WERE BAD AT SPOTTING TRAPS, CORIUS.
CORINTH?
INCLUDING THIS ONE.

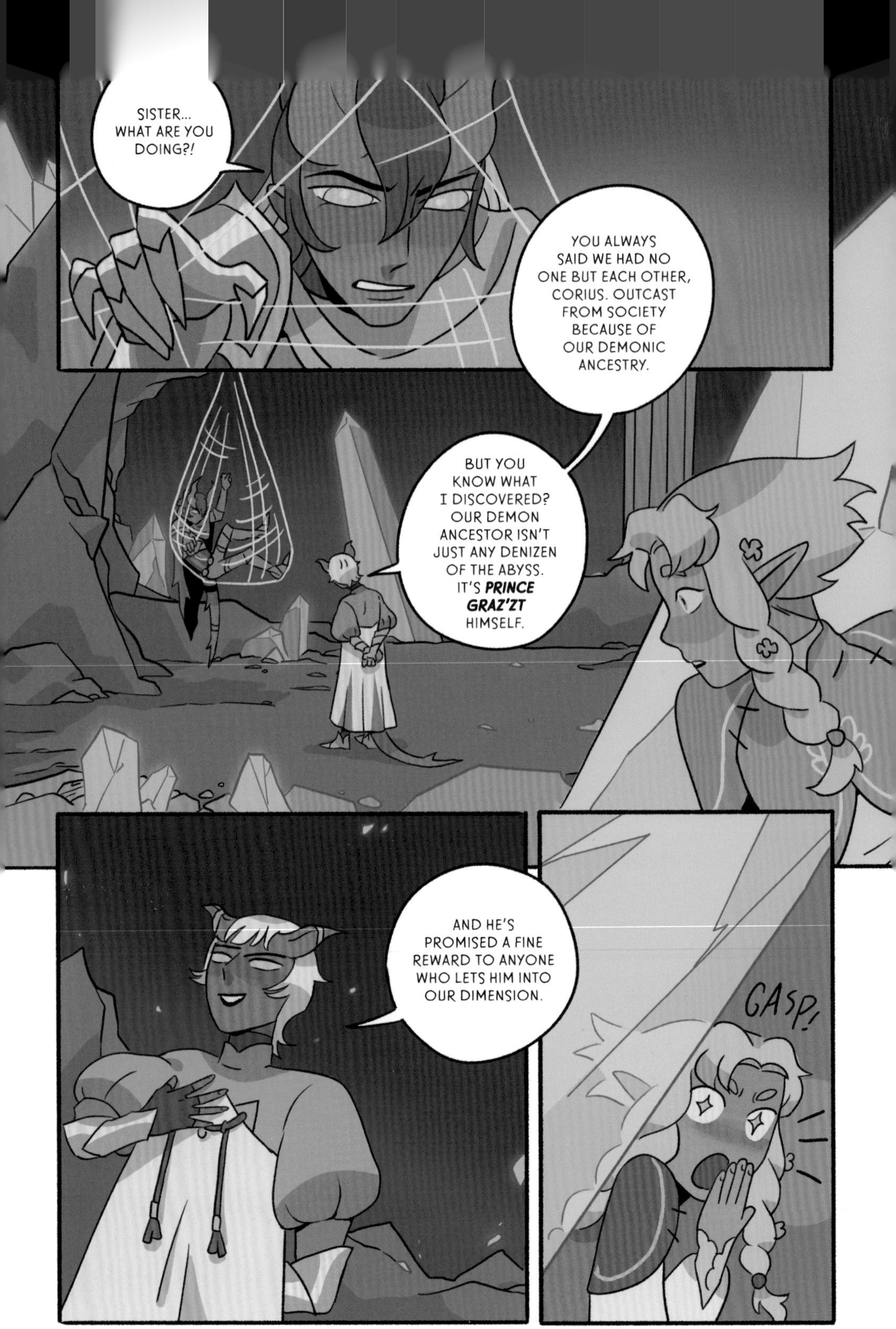
SISTER... WHAT ARE YOU DOING?!
YOU ALWAYS SAID WE HAD NO ONE BUT EACH OTHER, CORIUS. OUTCAST FROM SOCIETY BECAUSE OF OUR DEMONIC ANCESTRY.
BUT YOU KNOW WHAT I DISCOVERED? OUR DEMON ANCESTOR ISN'T JUST ANY DENIZEN OF THE ABYSS. IT'S **PRINCE GRAZ'ZT** HIMSELF.
AND HE'S PROMISED A FINE REWARD TO ANYONE WHO LETS HIM INTO OUR DIMENSION.
GASP!

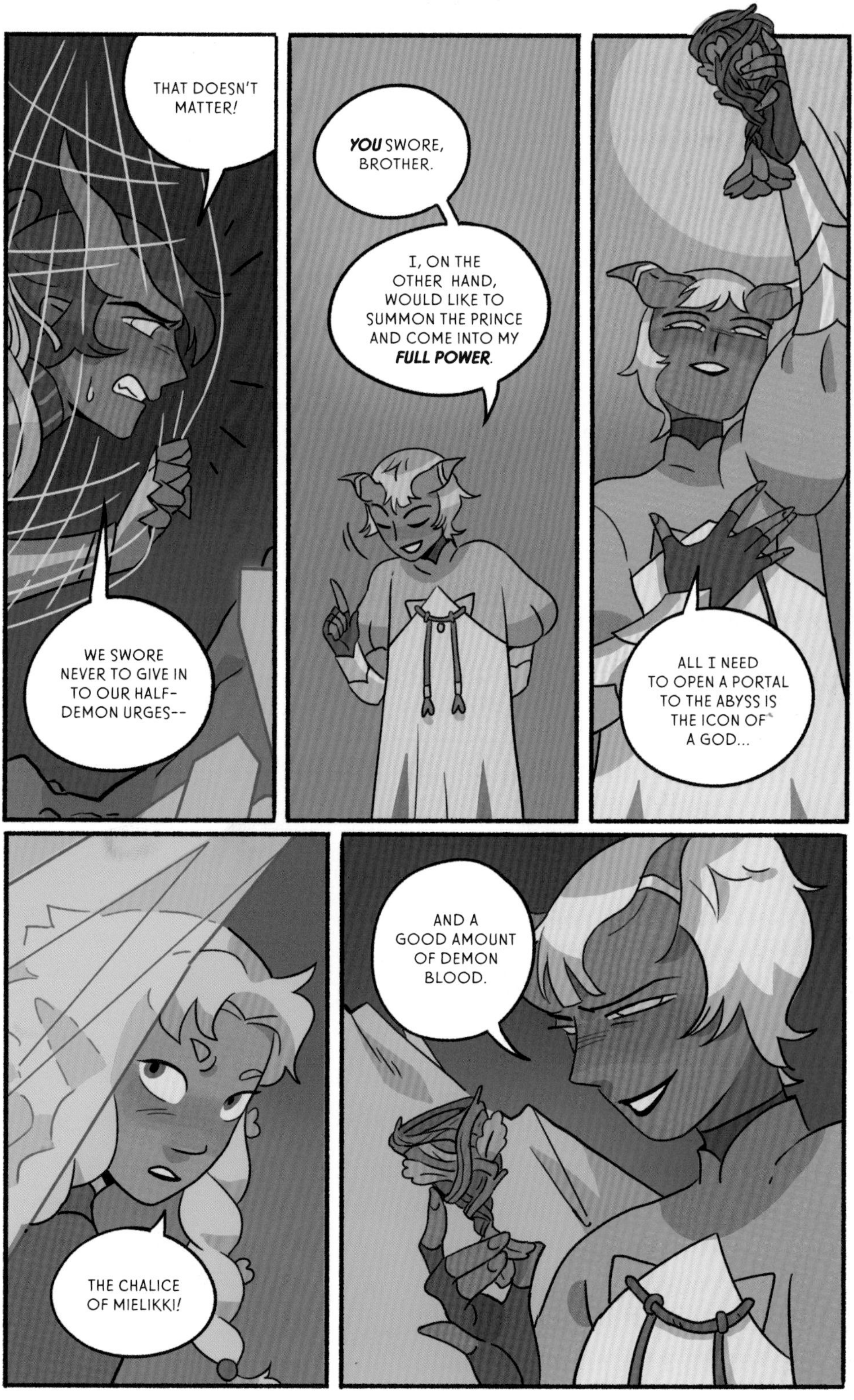
THAT DOESN'T MATTER!
WE SWORE NEVER TO GIVE IN TO OUR HALF-DEMON URGES--
YOU SWORE, BROTHER.
I, ON THE OTHER HAND, WOULD LIKE TO SUMMON THE PRINCE AND COME INTO MY ***FULL POWER***.
ALL I NEED TO OPEN A PORTAL TO THE ABYSS IS THE ICON OF A GOD...
THE CHALICE OF MIELIKKI!
AND A GOOD AMOUNT OF DEMON BLOOD.

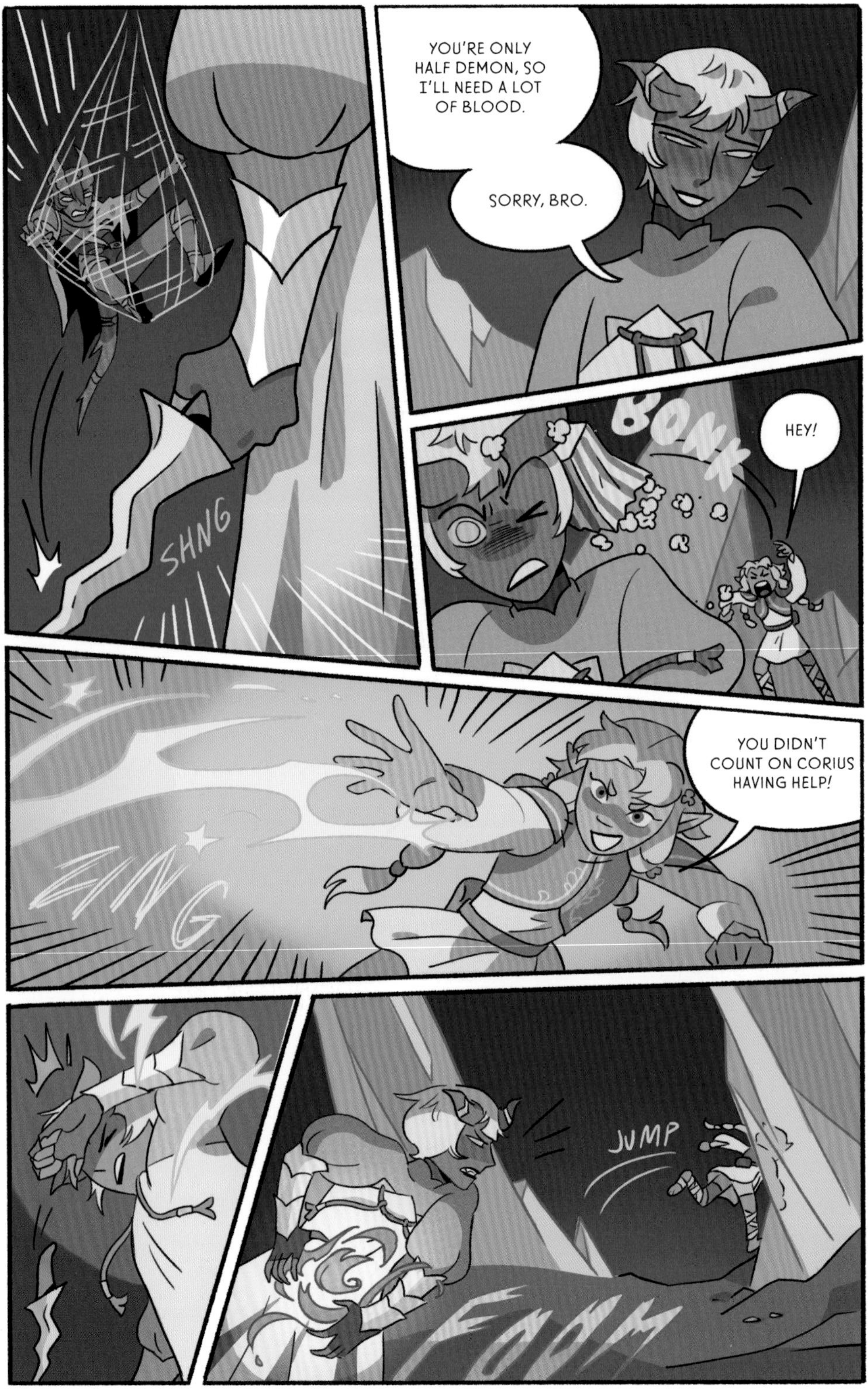
SHNG
YOU'RE ONLY HALF DEMON, SO I'LL NEED A LOT OF BLOOD.
SORRY, BRO.
BONK
HEY!
YOU DIDN'T COUNT ON CORIUS HAVING HELP!
ZING
JUMP

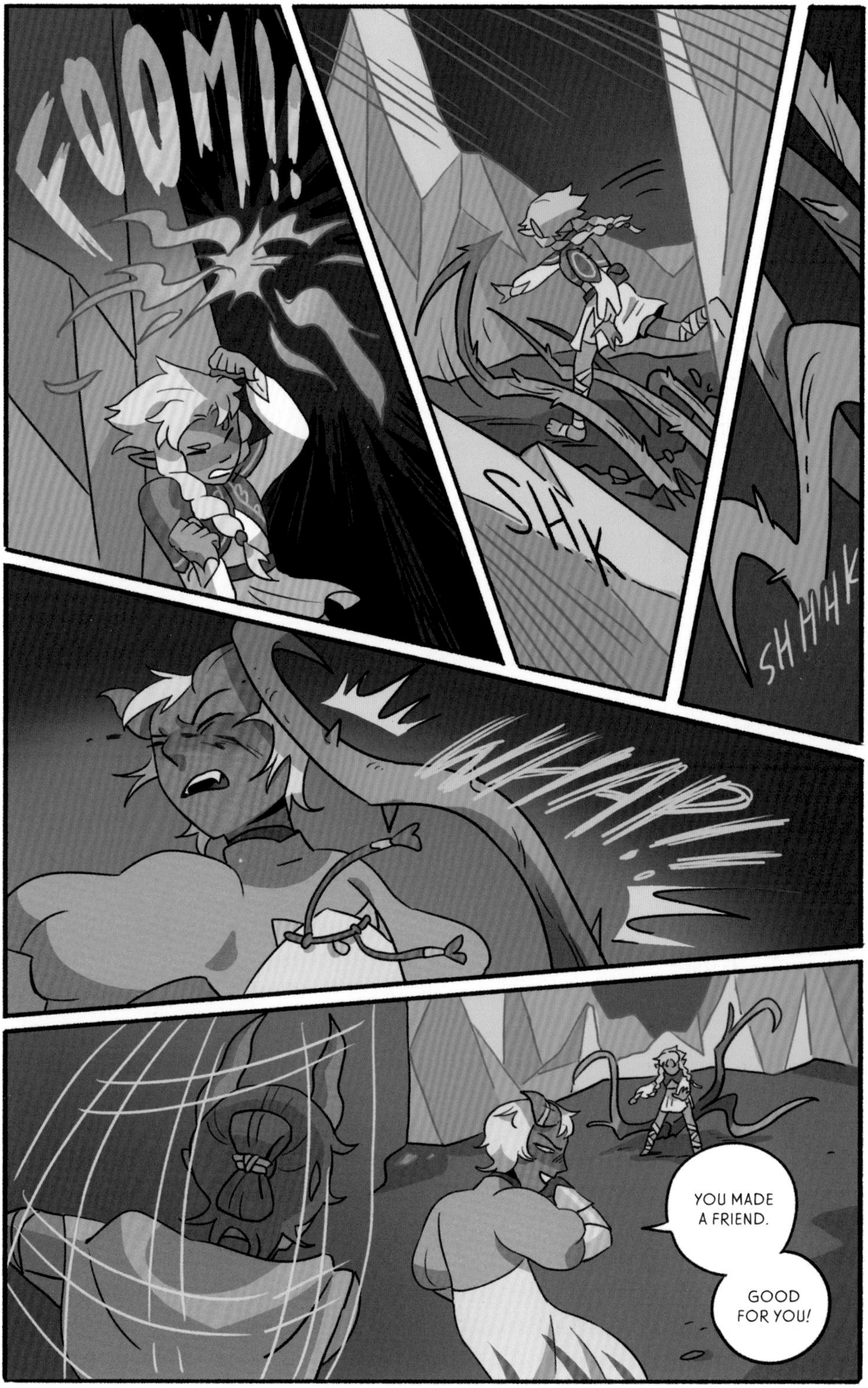
FOOM!!!
SHK
SHHHK
WHAP!!
YOU MADE A FRIEND.
GOOD FOR YOU!

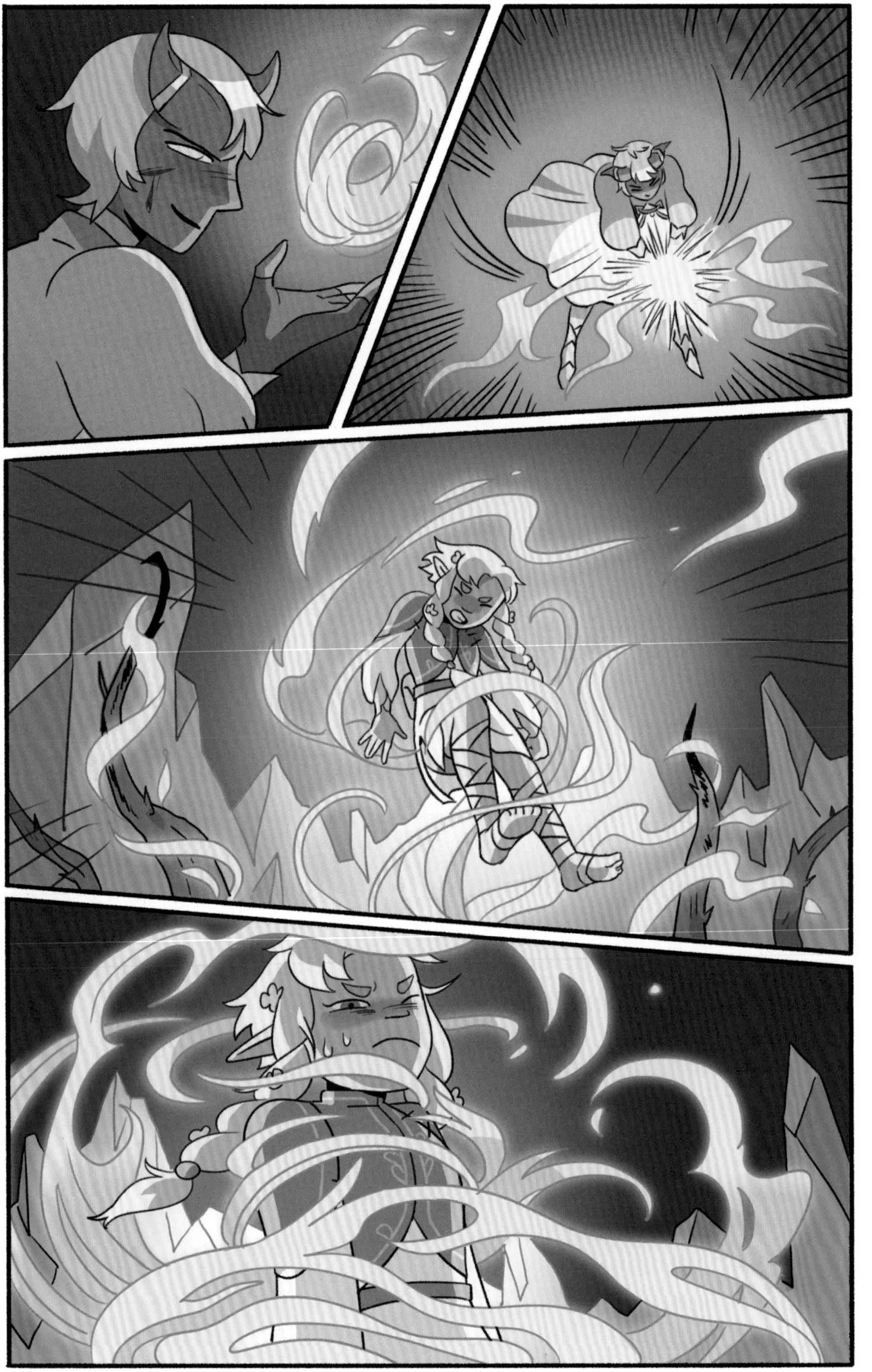

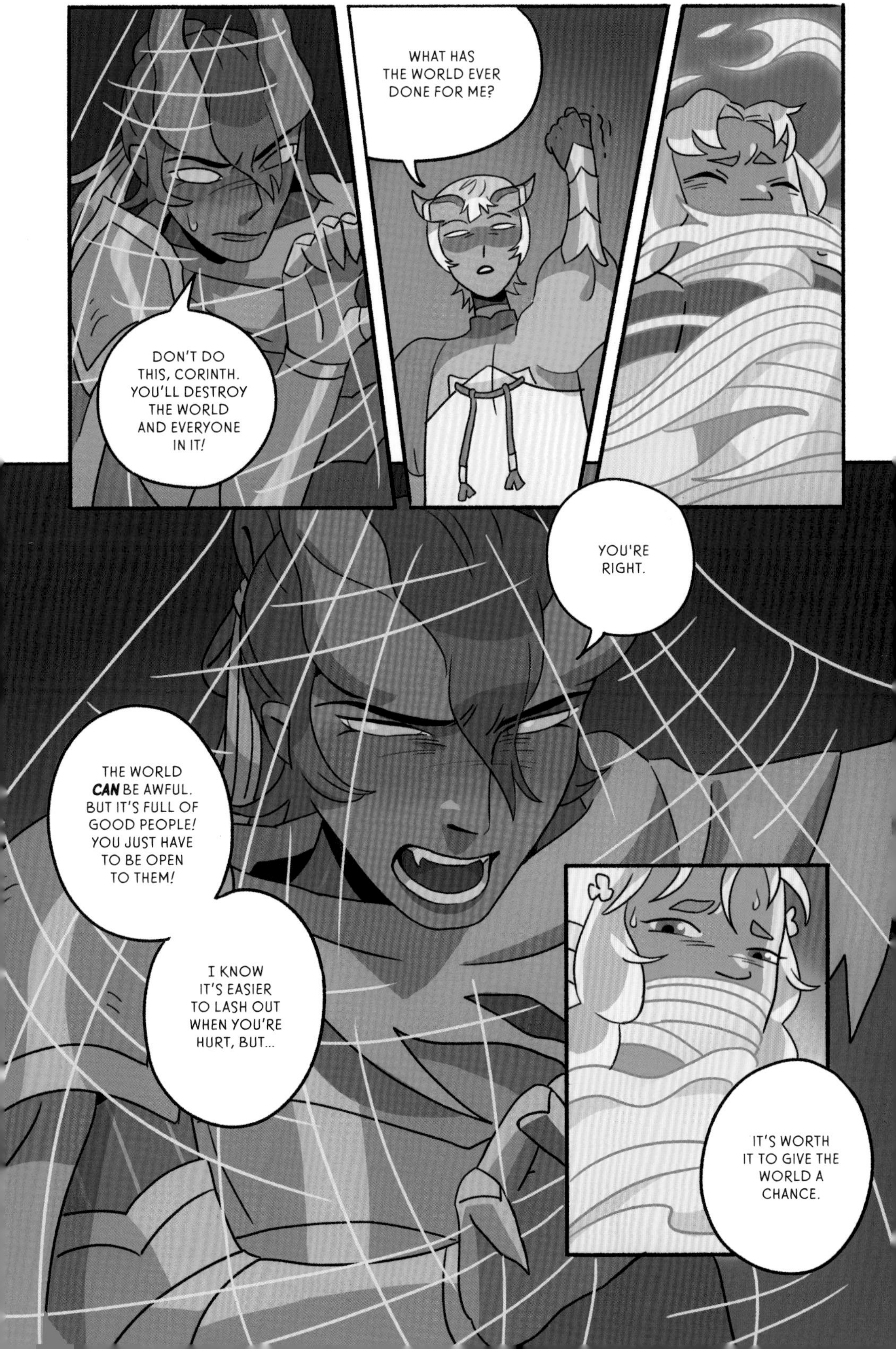
WHAT HAS THE WORLD EVER DONE FOR ME?
DON'T DO THIS, CORINTH. YOU'LL DESTROY THE WORLD AND EVERYONE IN IT!
YOU'RE RIGHT.
THE WORLD **CAN** BE AWFUL. BUT IT'S FULL OF GOOD PEOPLE! YOU JUST HAVE TO BE OPEN TO THEM!
I KNOW IT'S EASIER TO LASH OUT WHEN YOU'RE HURT, BUT...
IT'S WORTH IT TO GIVE THE WORLD A CHANCE.

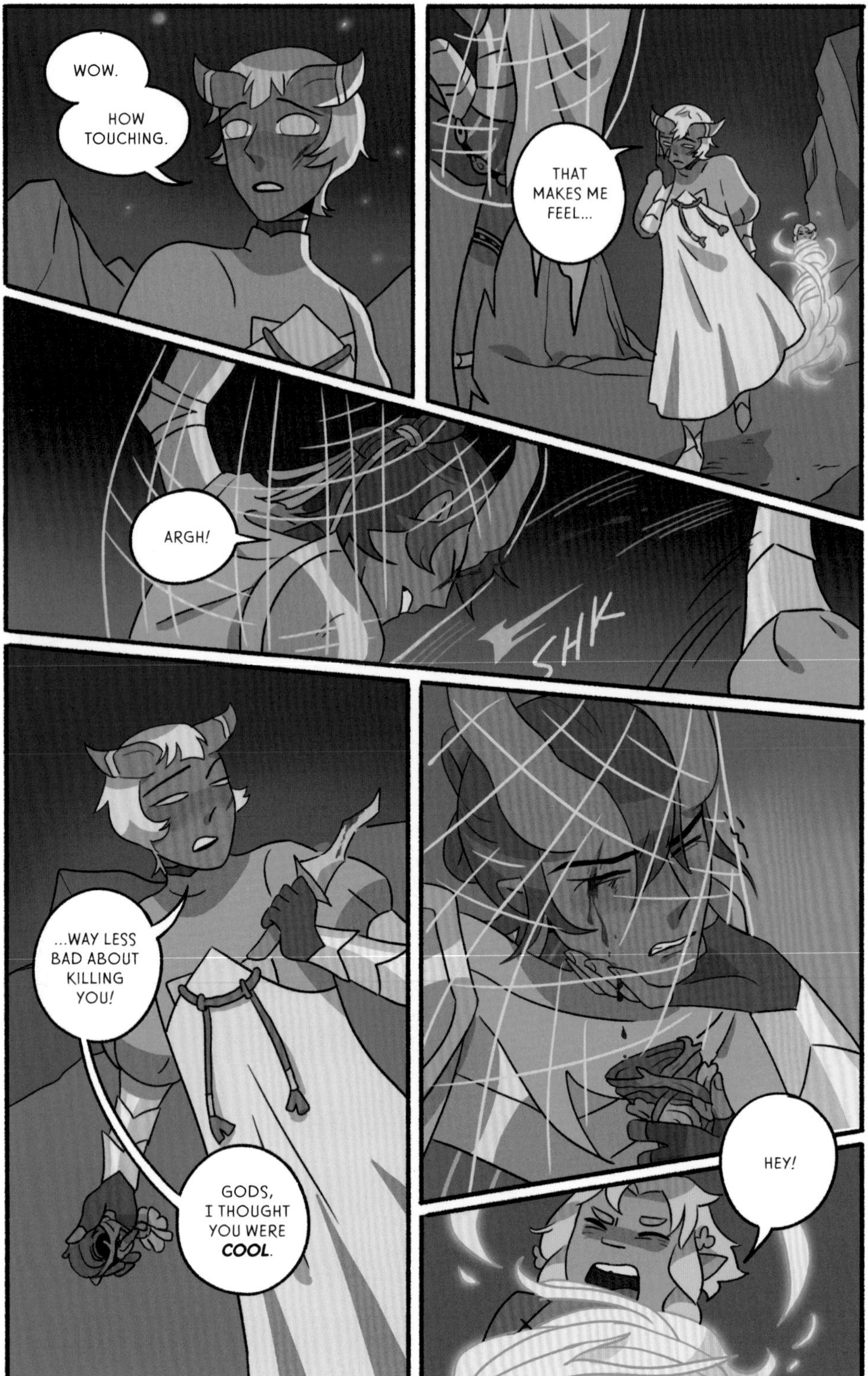
WOW.
HOW TOUCHING.
THAT MAKES ME FEEL...
ARGH!
SHK
...WAY LESS BAD ABOUT KILLING YOU!
GODS, I THOUGHT YOU WERE **COOL**.
HEY!

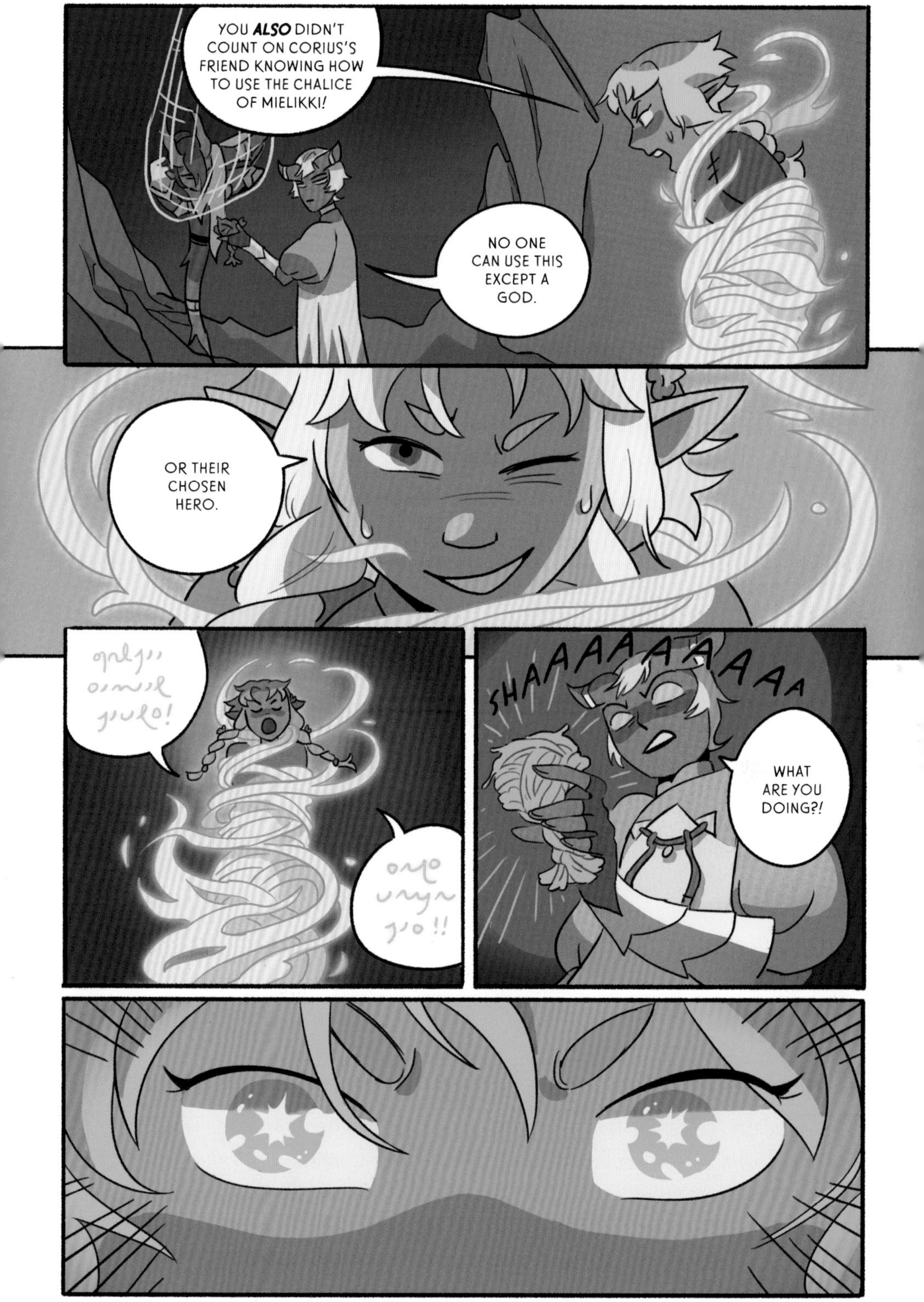
YOU ***ALSO*** DIDN'T COUNT ON CORIUS'S FRIEND KNOWING HOW TO USE THE CHALICE OF MIELIKKI!
NO ONE CAN USE THIS EXCEPT A GOD.
OR THEIR CHOSEN HERO.
SHAAAAAAAAA
WHAT ARE YOU DOING?!

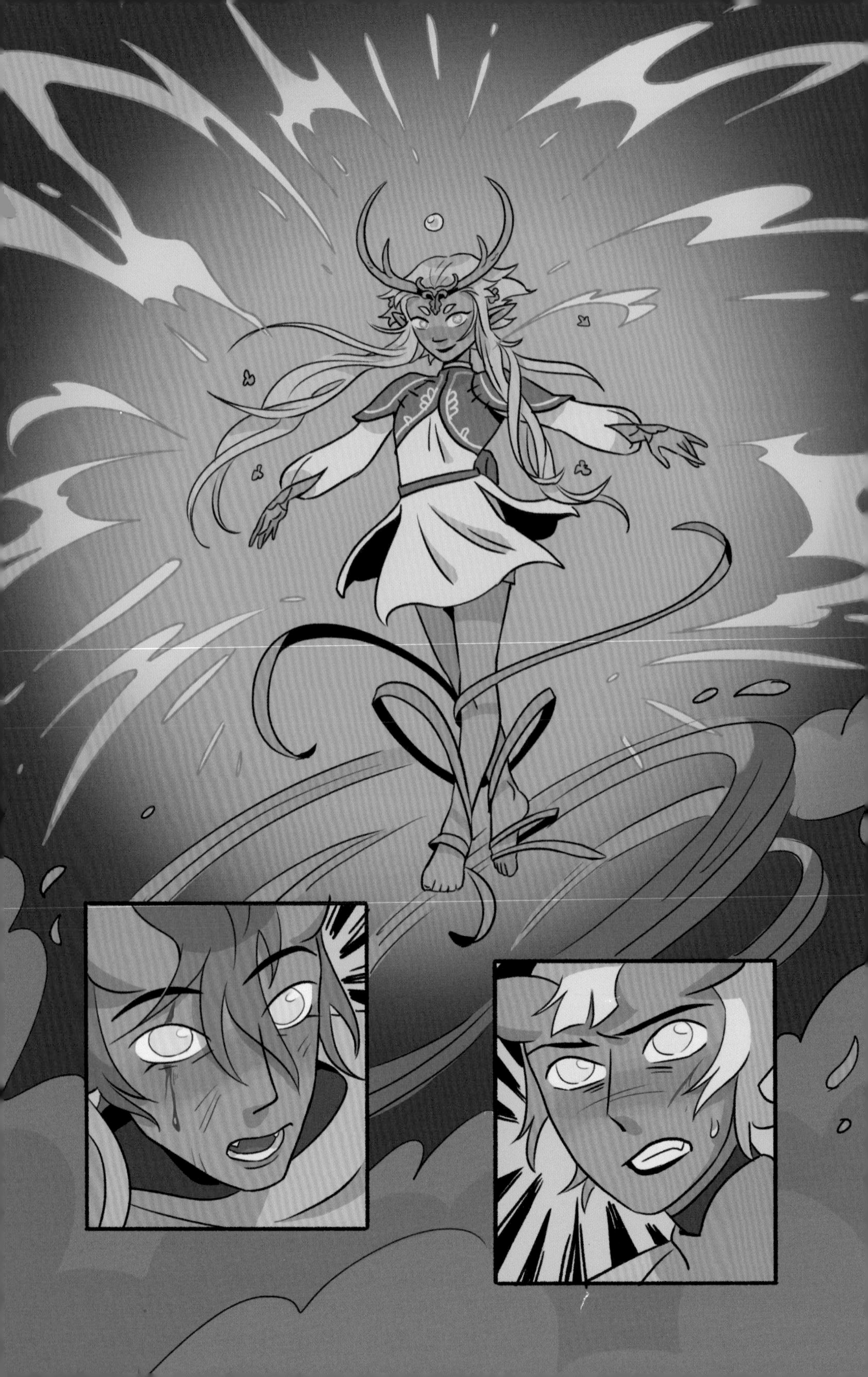

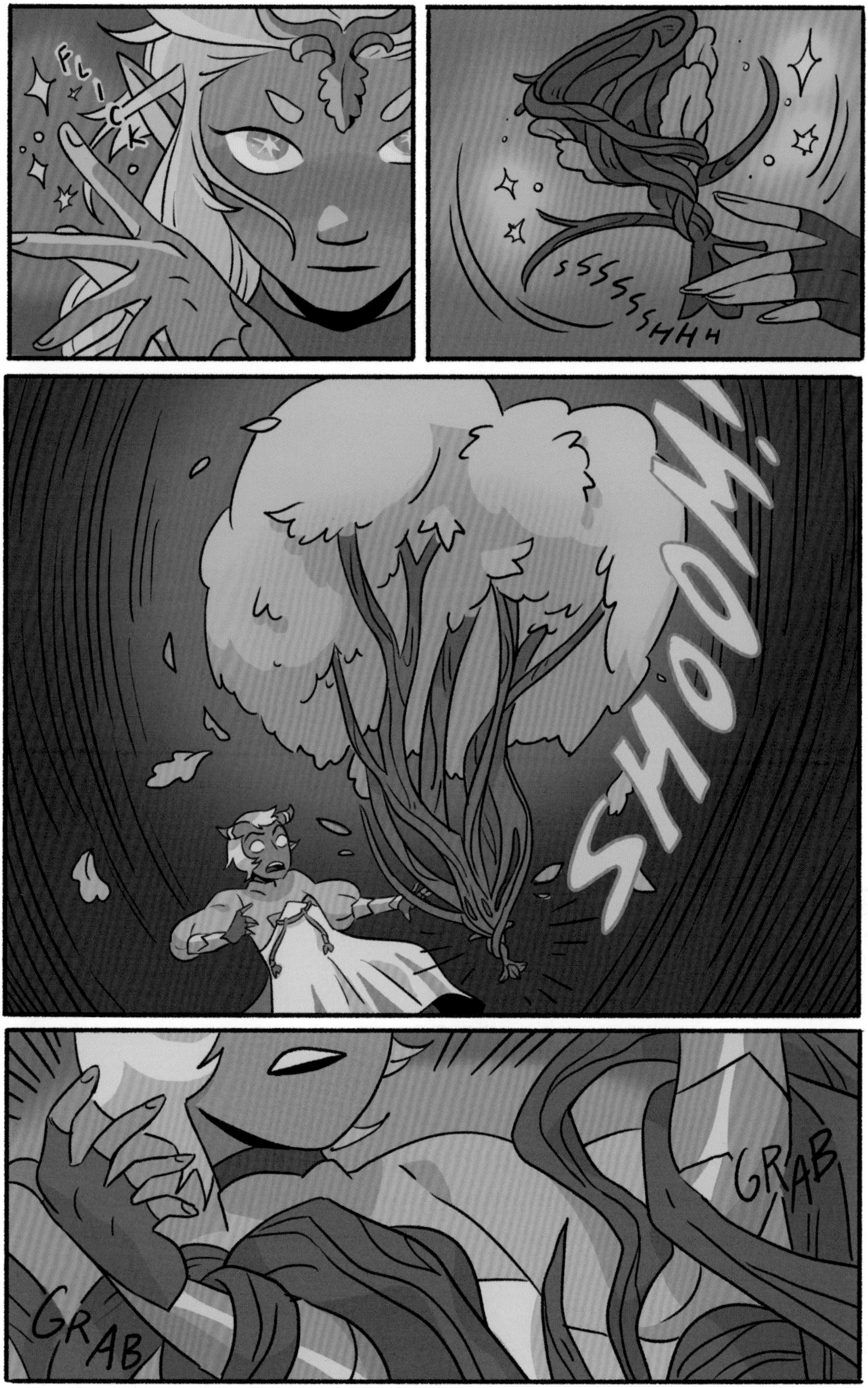
FLICK
SSSSSSSHHH
SHOOM!
GRAB
GRAB

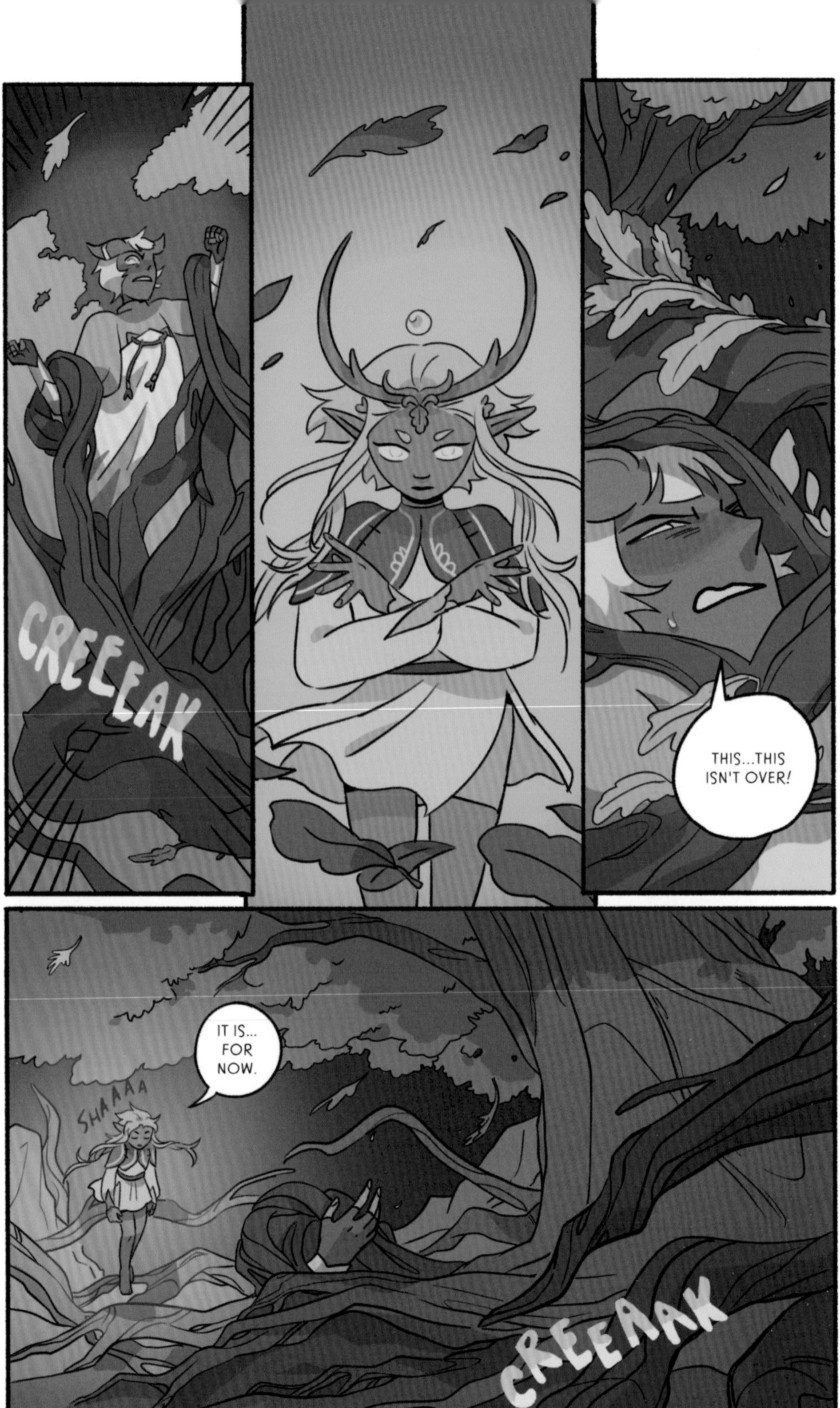
CREEEAK
THIS...THIS ISN'T OVER!
IT IS... FOR NOW.
SHAAAA
CREEAAK

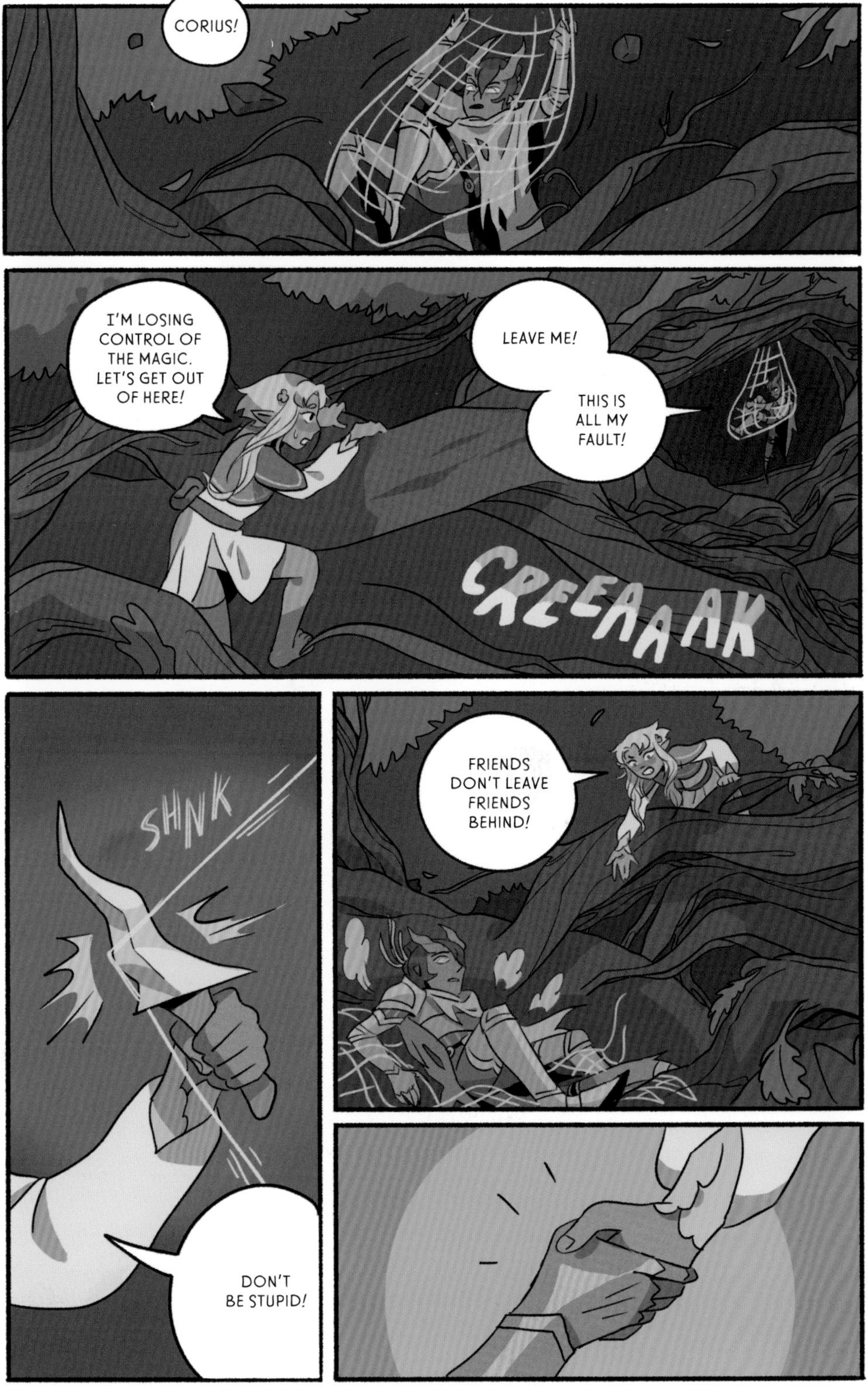
CORIUS!
I'M LOSING CONTROL OF THE MAGIC. LET'S GET OUT OF HERE!
LEAVE ME!
THIS IS ALL MY FAULT!
CREEAAAK
SHNK
DON'T BE STUPID!
FRIENDS DON'T LEAVE FRIENDS BEHIND!

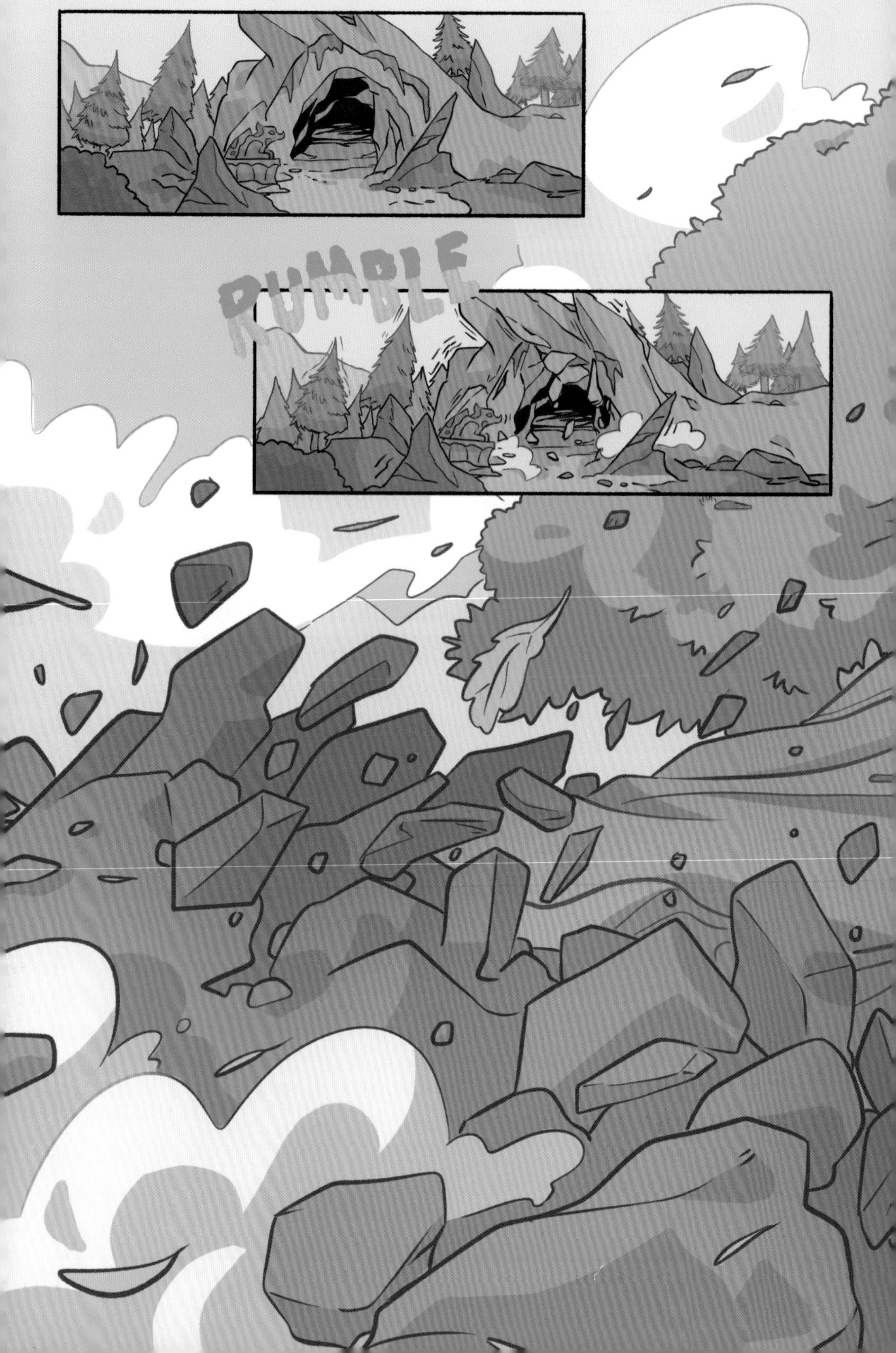
RUMBLE

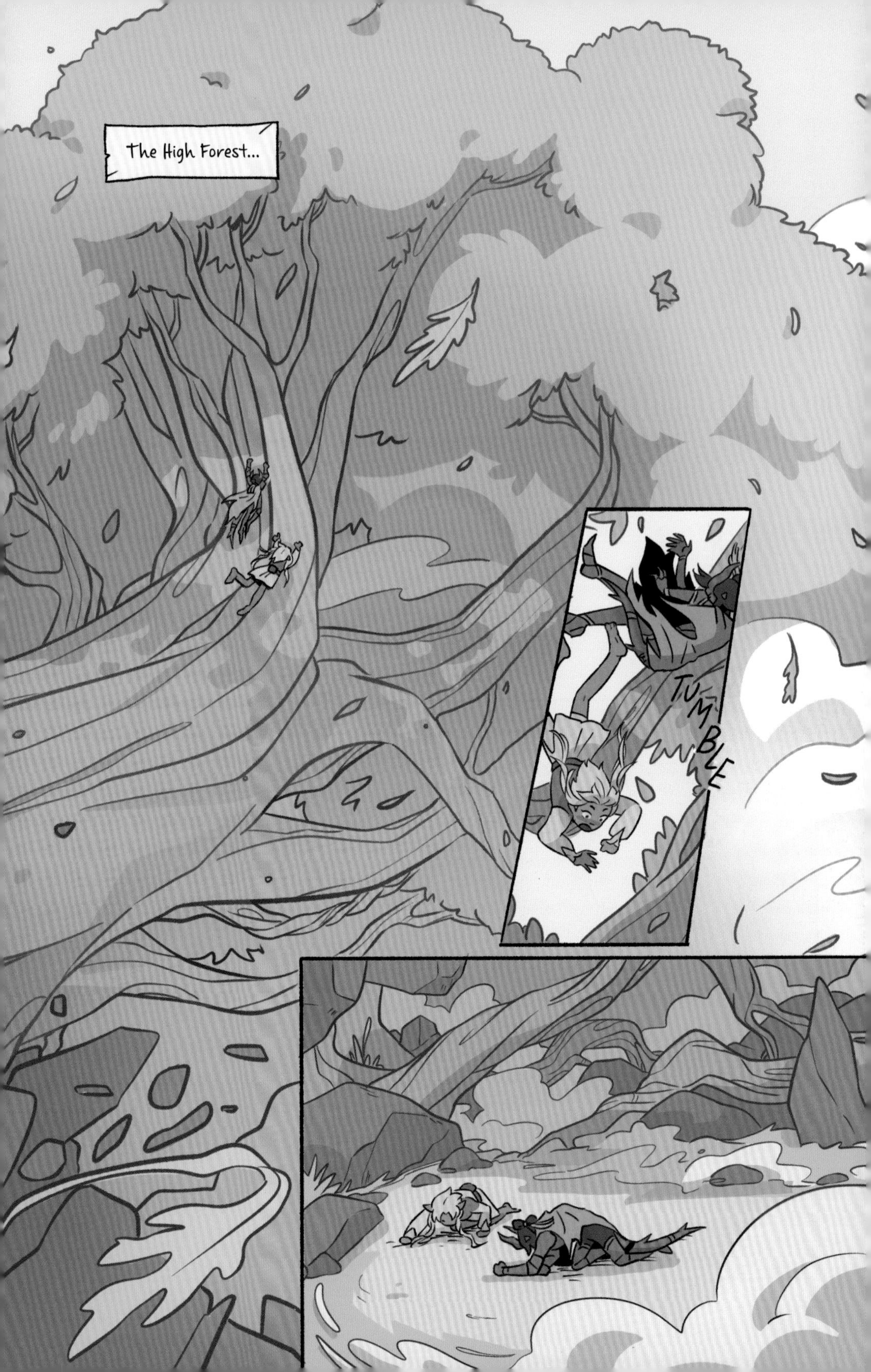

The High Forest...
TUMBLE

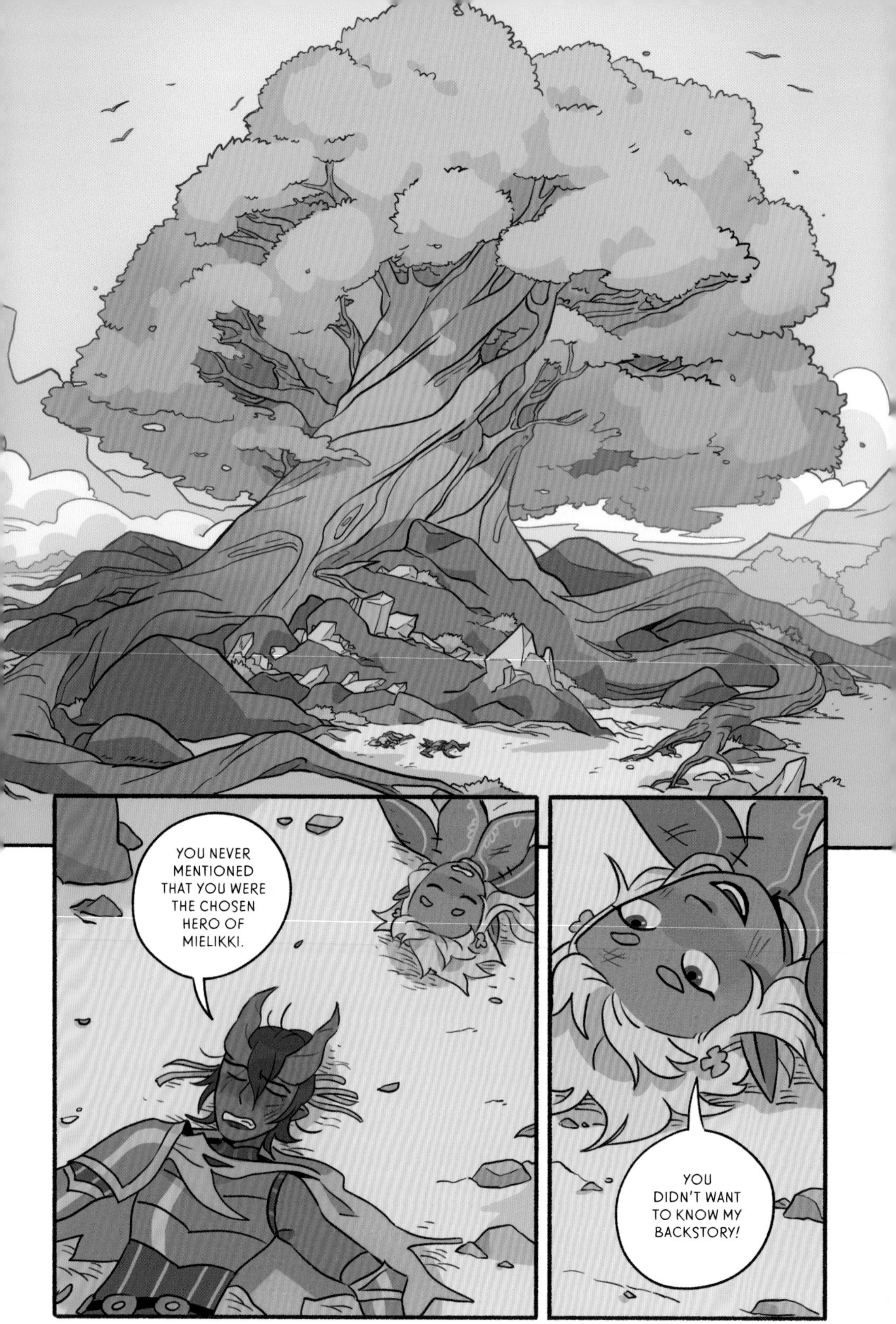
YOU NEVER MENTIONED THAT YOU WERE THE CHOSEN HERO OF MIELIKKI.
YOU DIDN'T WANT TO KNOW MY BACKSTORY!

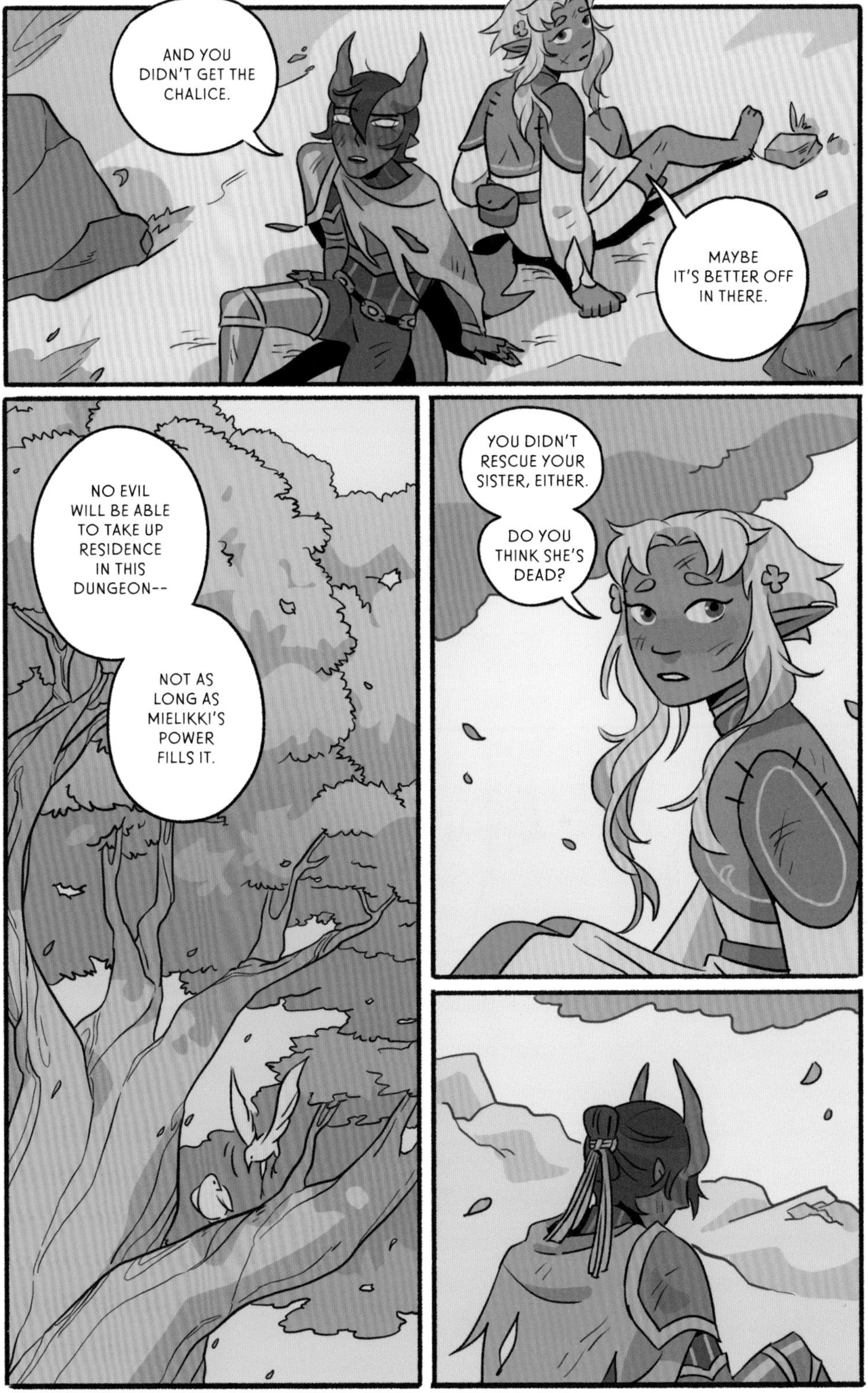
AND YOU DIDN'T GET THE CHALICE.
MAYBE IT'S BETTER OFF IN THERE.
NO EVIL WILL BE ABLE TO TAKE UP RESIDENCE IN THIS DUNGEON--
NOT AS LONG AS MIELIKKI'S POWER FILLS IT.
YOU DIDN'T RESCUE YOUR SISTER, EITHER.
DO YOU THINK SHE'S DEAD?

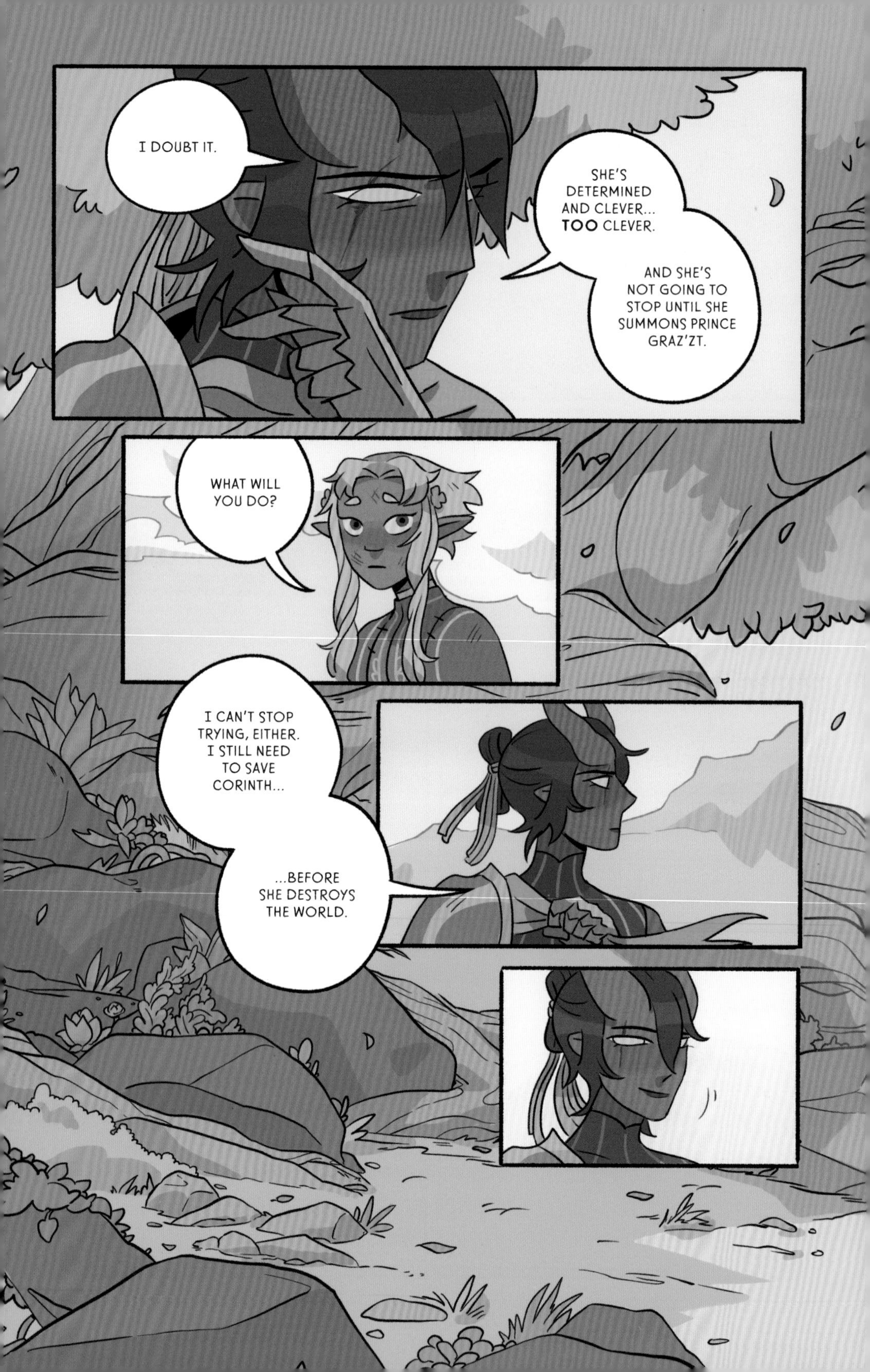
I DOUBT IT.
SHE'S DETERMINED AND CLEVER... **TOO** CLEVER.
AND SHE'S NOT GOING TO STOP UNTIL SHE SUMMONS PRINCE GRAZ'ZT.
WHAT WILL YOU DO?
I CAN'T STOP TRYING, EITHER. I STILL NEED TO SAVE CORINTH...
...BEFORE SHE DESTROYS THE WORLD.

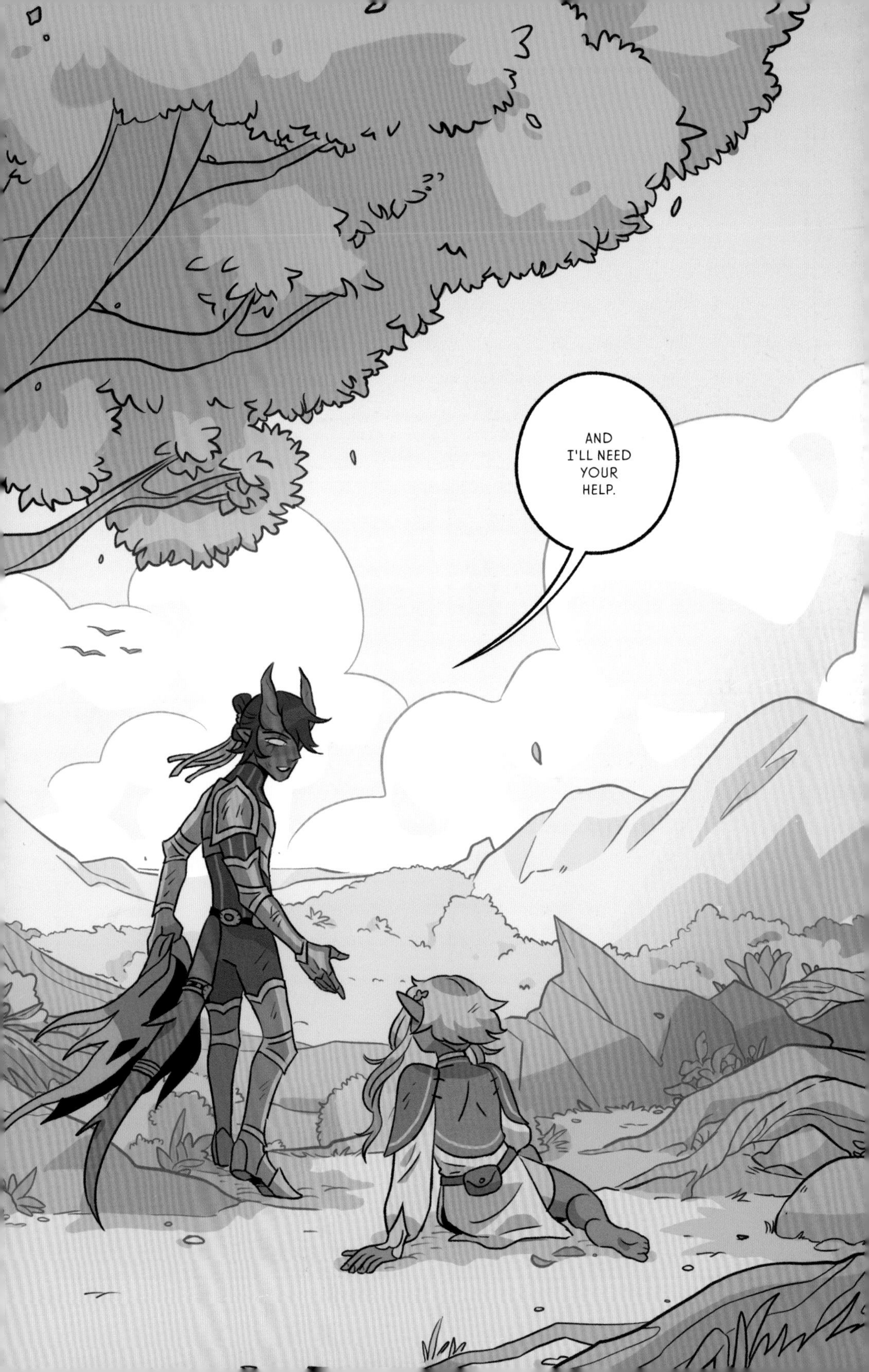
AND I'LL NEED YOUR HELP.

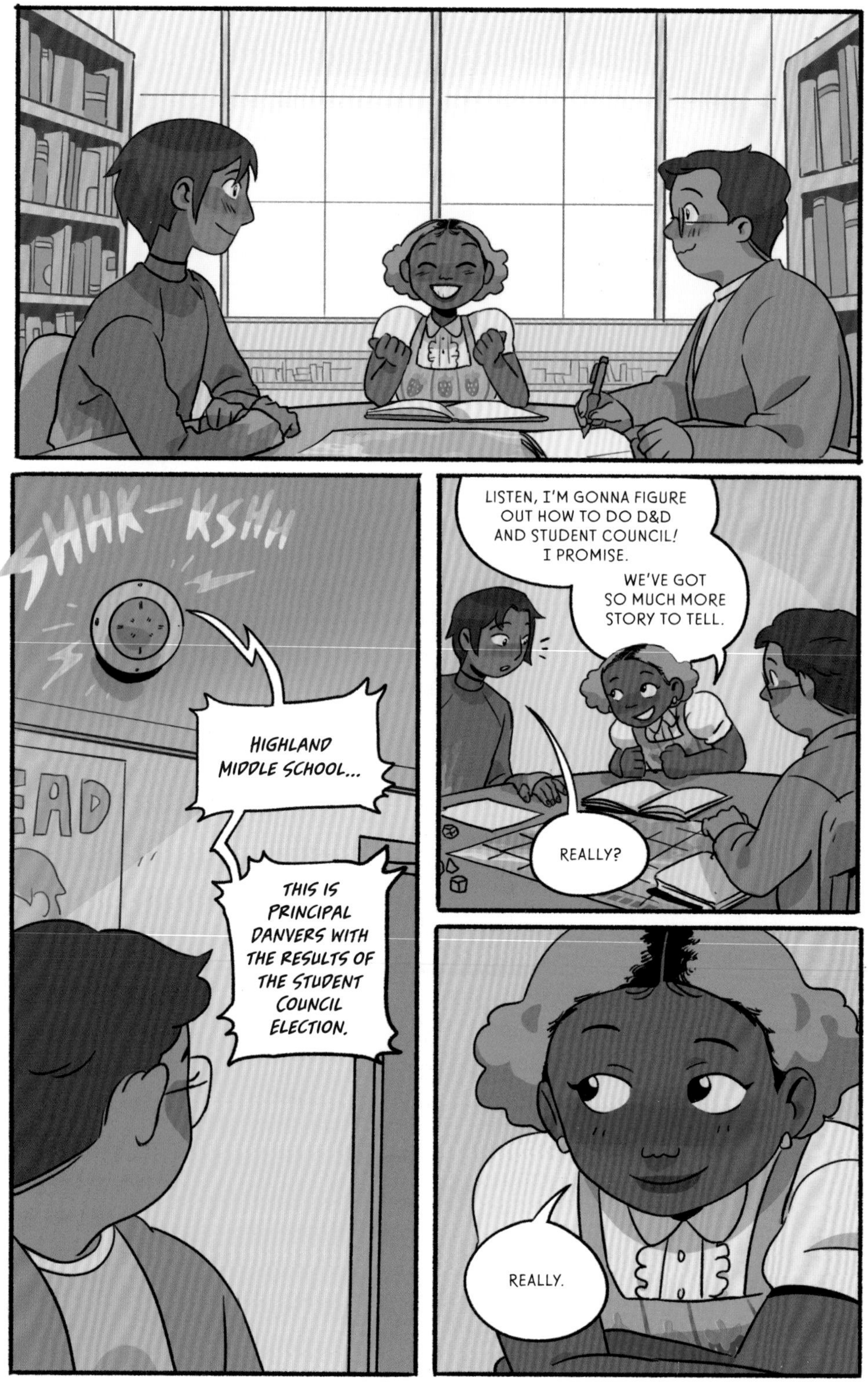
LISTEN, I'M GONNA FIGURE OUT HOW TO DO D&D AND STUDENT COUNCIL! I PROMISE.
WE'VE GOT SO MUCH MORE STORY TO TELL.
REALLY?
SHHK-KSHH
HIGHLAND MIDDLE SCHOOL...
THIS IS PRINCIPAL DANVERS WITH THE RESULTS OF THE STUDENT COUNCIL ELECTION.
REALLY.

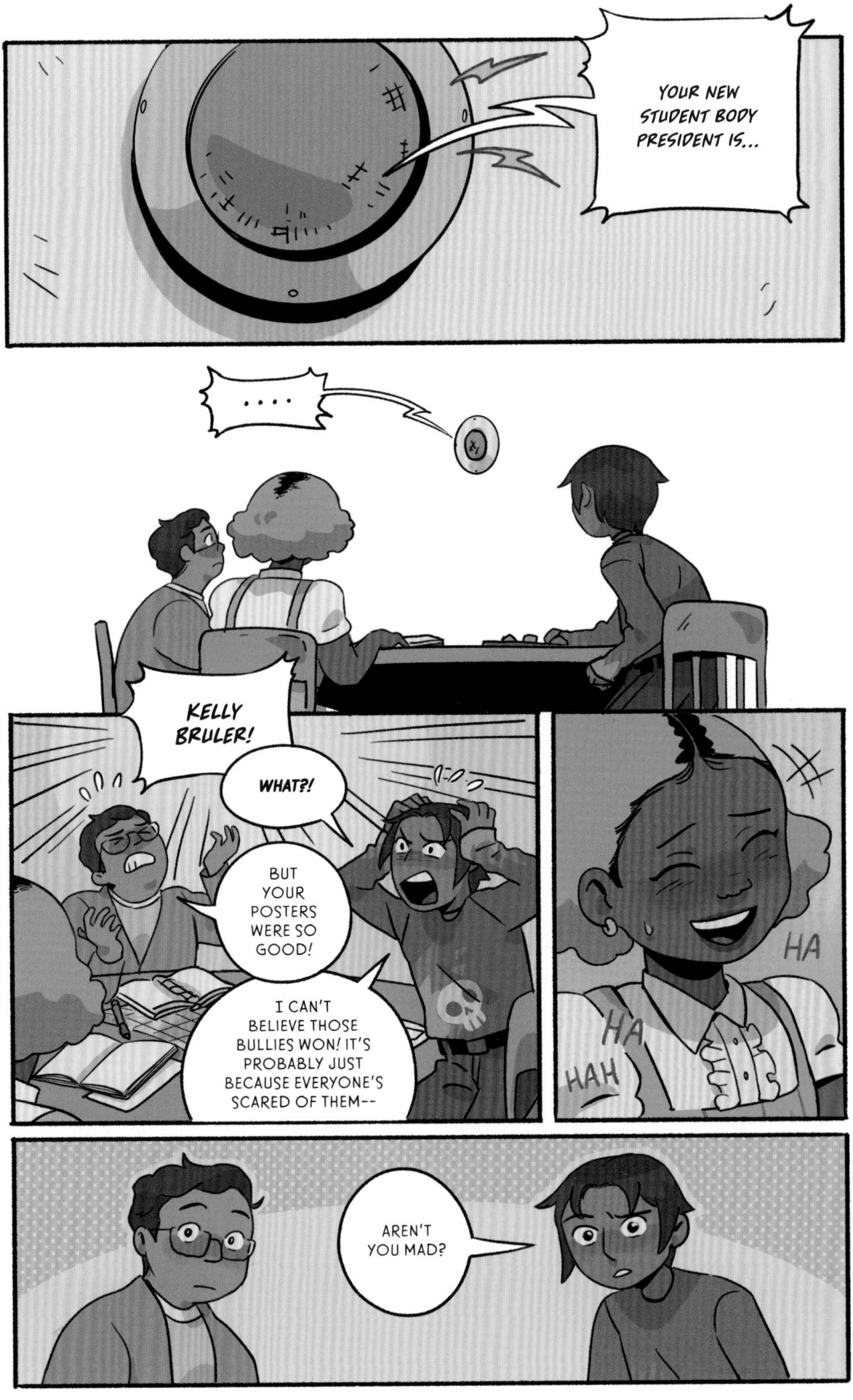
YOUR NEW STUDENT BODY PRESIDENT IS...
....
KELLY BRULER!
WHAT?!
BUT YOUR POSTERS WERE SO GOOD!
I CAN'T BELIEVE THOSE BULLIES WON! IT'S PROBABLY JUST BECAUSE EVERYONE'S SCARED OF THEM--
HA
HA
HAH
AREN'T YOU MAD?

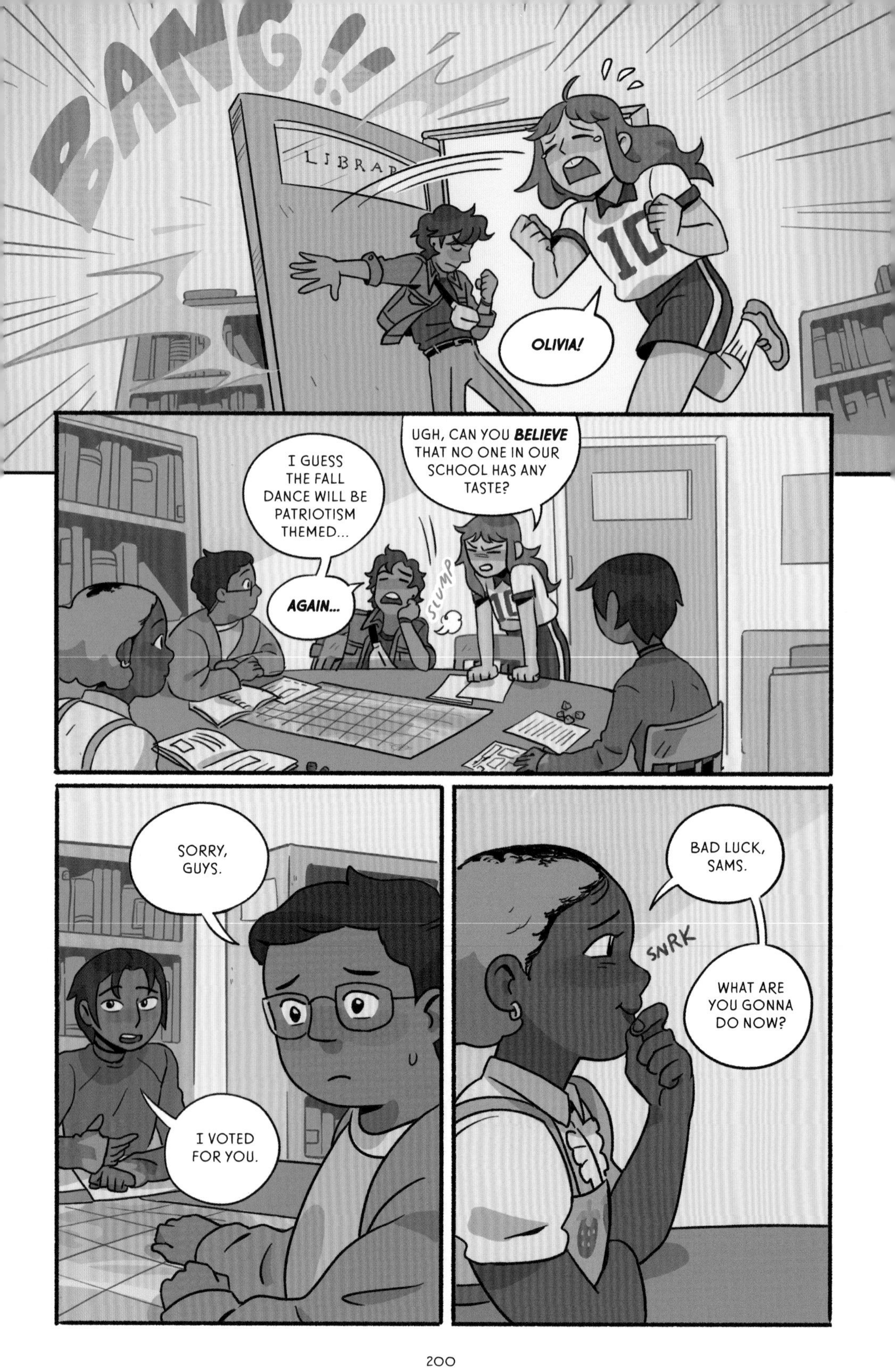
BANG!!!
LIBRAR
OLIVIA!
UGH, CAN YOU **BELIEVE** THAT NO ONE IN OUR SCHOOL HAS ANY TASTE?
I GUESS THE FALL DANCE WILL BE PATRIOTISM THEMED...
AGAIN...
SLUMP
SORRY, GUYS.
I VOTED FOR YOU.
BAD LUCK, SAMS.
SNRK
WHAT ARE YOU GONNA DO NOW?

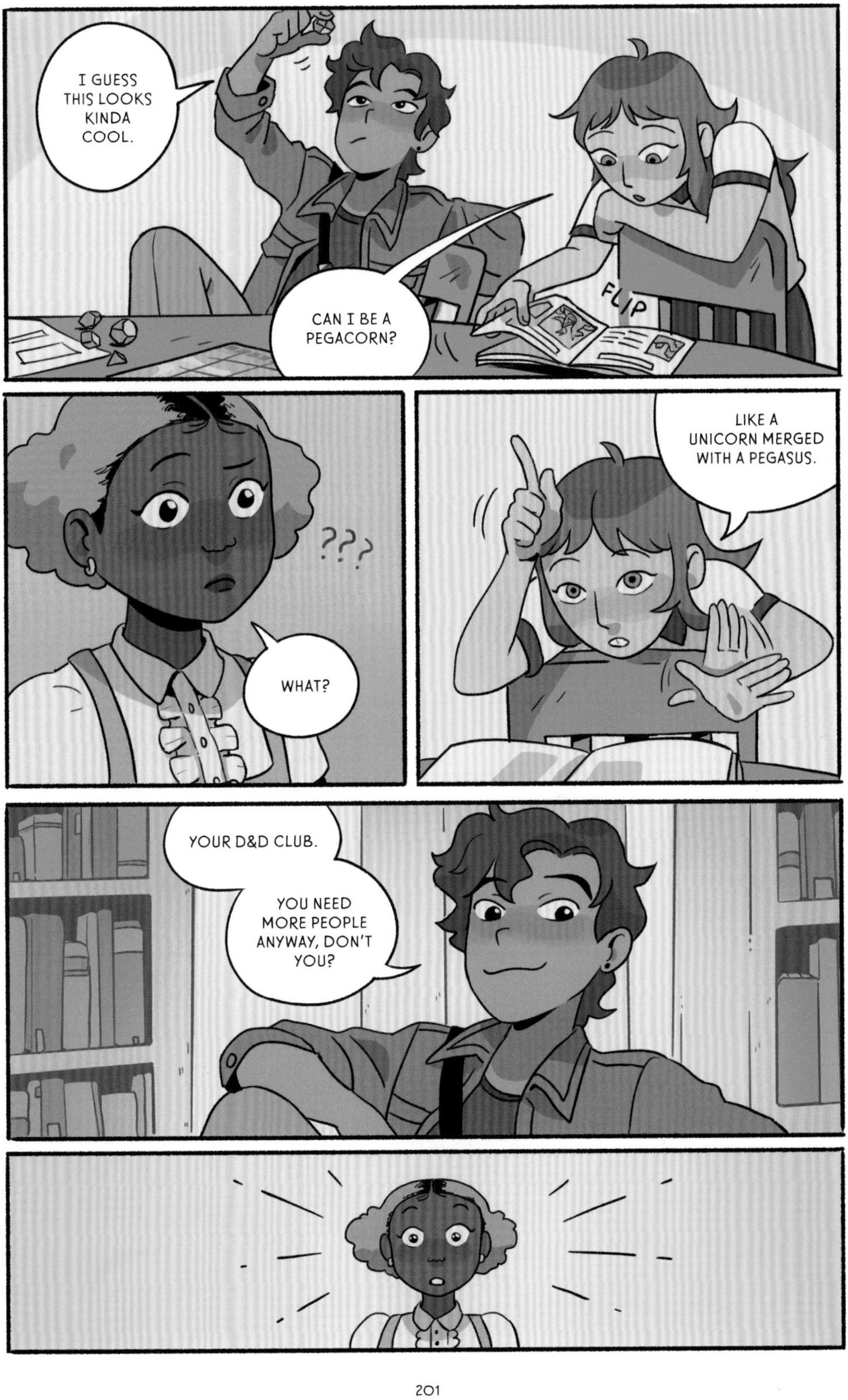
I GUESS THIS LOOKS KINDA COOL.
FLIP
CAN I BE A PEGACORN?
???
WHAT?
LIKE A UNICORN MERGED WITH A PEGASUS.
YOUR D&D CLUB.
YOU NEED MORE PEOPLE ANYWAY, DON'T YOU?

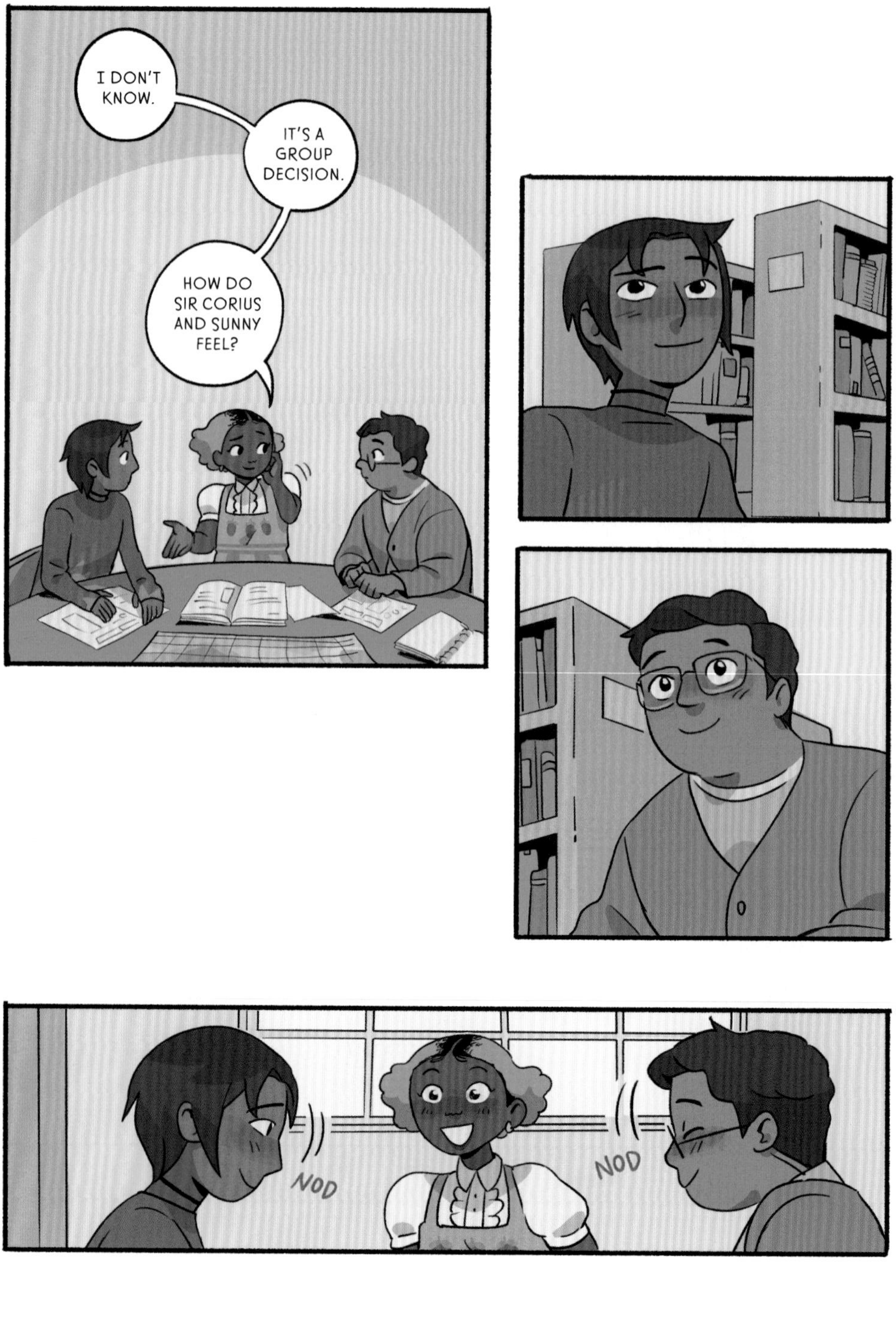
I DON'T KNOW.
IT'S A GROUP DECISION.
HOW DO SIR CORIUS AND SUNNY FEEL?
NOD
NOD

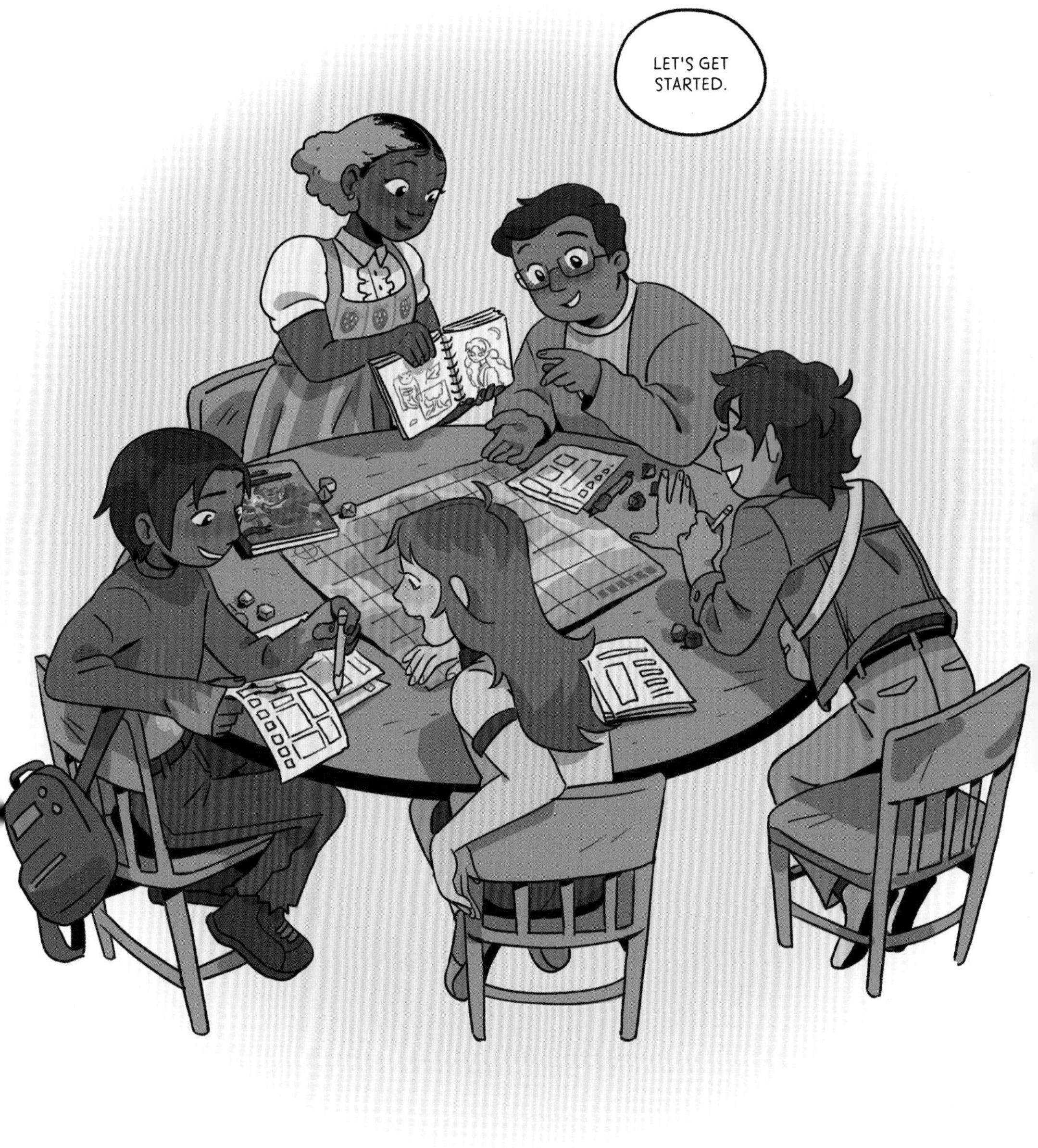
LET'S GET
STARTED.

Process for

D&D DUNGEON CLUB

ROLL CALL

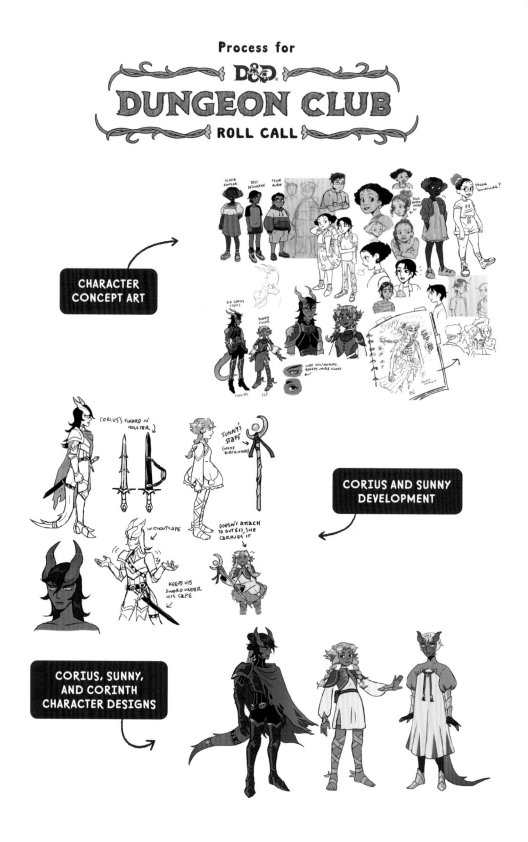

CHARACTER CONCEPT ART

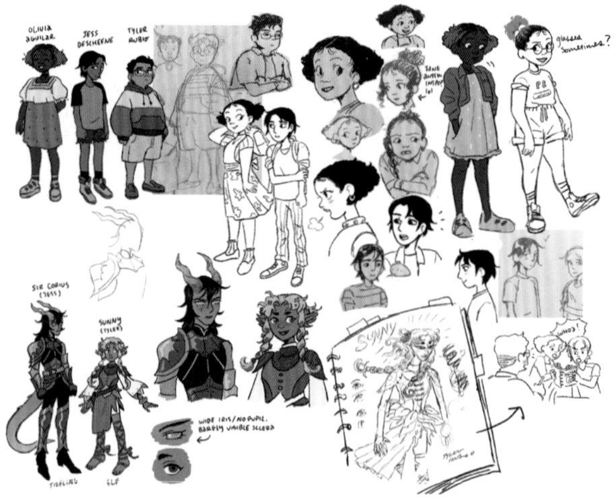
OLIVIA AGUILAR
JESS DESCHEENE
TYLER RUBIO
glasses sometimes?
SIR CORIUS (JESS)
SUNNY (TYLER)
WIDE IRIS/NO PUPIL, BARELY VISIBLE SCLERA
TIEFLING
ELF
SUNNY

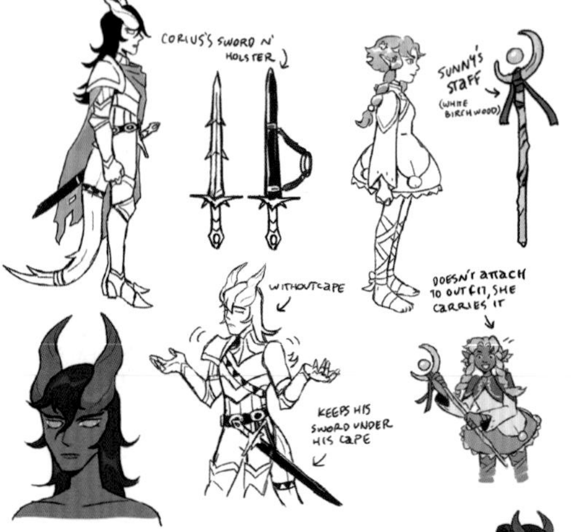
CORIUS'S SWORD N' HOLSTER
SUNNY'S STAFF (WHITE BIRCHWOOD)
WITHOUT CAPE
DOESN'T ATTACH TO OUTFIT, SHE CARRIES IT
KEEPS HIS SWORD UNDER HIS CAPE

CORIUS AND SUNNY DEVELOPMENT

CORIUS, SUNNY, AND CORINTH CHARACTER DESIGNS

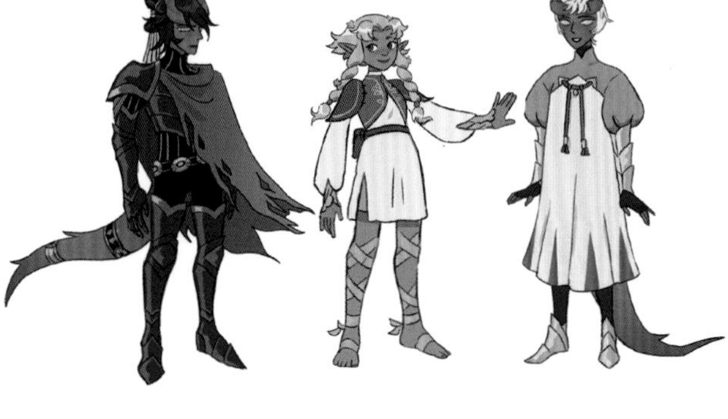

FROM **SCRIPT** TO **FINAL ART**

SCRIPT

PAGE 32

- Jess stares at the scene: **Sir Corius would fight them.**
- In Jess's imagination, the view shifts to a fantasy world. Kelly and her minions are gnoll creatures. Sir Corius steps in front of Tyler with his sword drawn.
- Sir Corius: **Her ears are pointed because she's an elf, which you would know if you'd ever picked up a book in your life.**
- **Assuming you can even read, Bruler.**
- In this fantasy, gnoll-Kelly looks terrified and Tyler looks grateful.

LAYOUT

32

PENCILS

INKS

FINAL ART

Sir Corius would fight them.
HER EARS ARE POINTED BECAUSE SHE'S AN ELF, WHICH YOU WOULD KNOW IF YOU'D EVER PICKED UP A BOOK IN YOUR LIFE.
ASSUMING YOU CAN EVEN READ, BRULER.

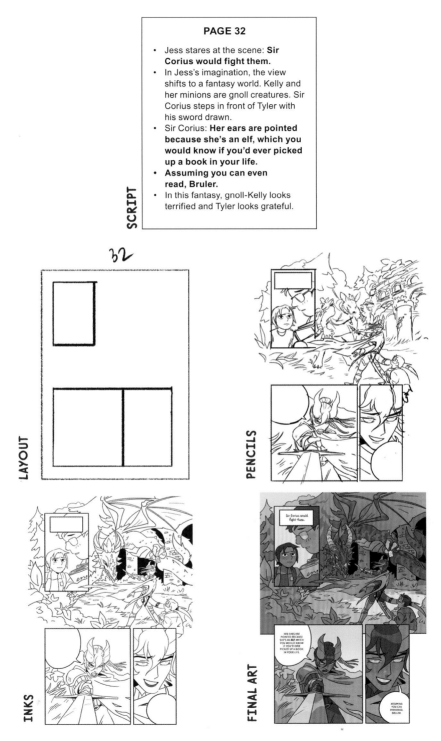

For all the friends I've made sitting at a table,
rolling dice and telling stories—you know who you are.

—Molly

For Dani, Sierra, Kami, Jessica, and Nicole.

—Xanthe

Special Thanks to:
Xanthe for being an absolute joy to collaborate with, and for bringing these characters to life,
ND for always talking through story with me...and for playing a certain angsty tiefling who ended up inspiring Corius, and
the Red Planet folks, L & N, for their notes on bringing Jess and their dad to life.
—MKO
Waleska "Waalkr" Ruschel for background ink and art assistance, and
Amelia Allore for her beautiful color work.
—XB

HarperAlley is an imprint of HarperCollins Publishers.

Dungeons & Dragons: Dungeon Club: Roll Call
Wizards of the Coast, Dungeons & Dragons, D&D, their respective logos, The Forgotten Realms,
and the dragon ampersand are registered trademarks of Wizards of the Coast LLC in the U.S.A.
and other countries. © 2022 Wizards of the Coast LLC. All rights reserved.

This book was illustrated digitally using Photoshop and
Procreate with a Cintiq and iPad tablet.

Book design by Maddy Price
Typography by Xanthe Bouma and Chris Dickey
22 23 24 25 26 RTLO 10 9 8 7 6 5 4 3 2 1
❖
First Edition

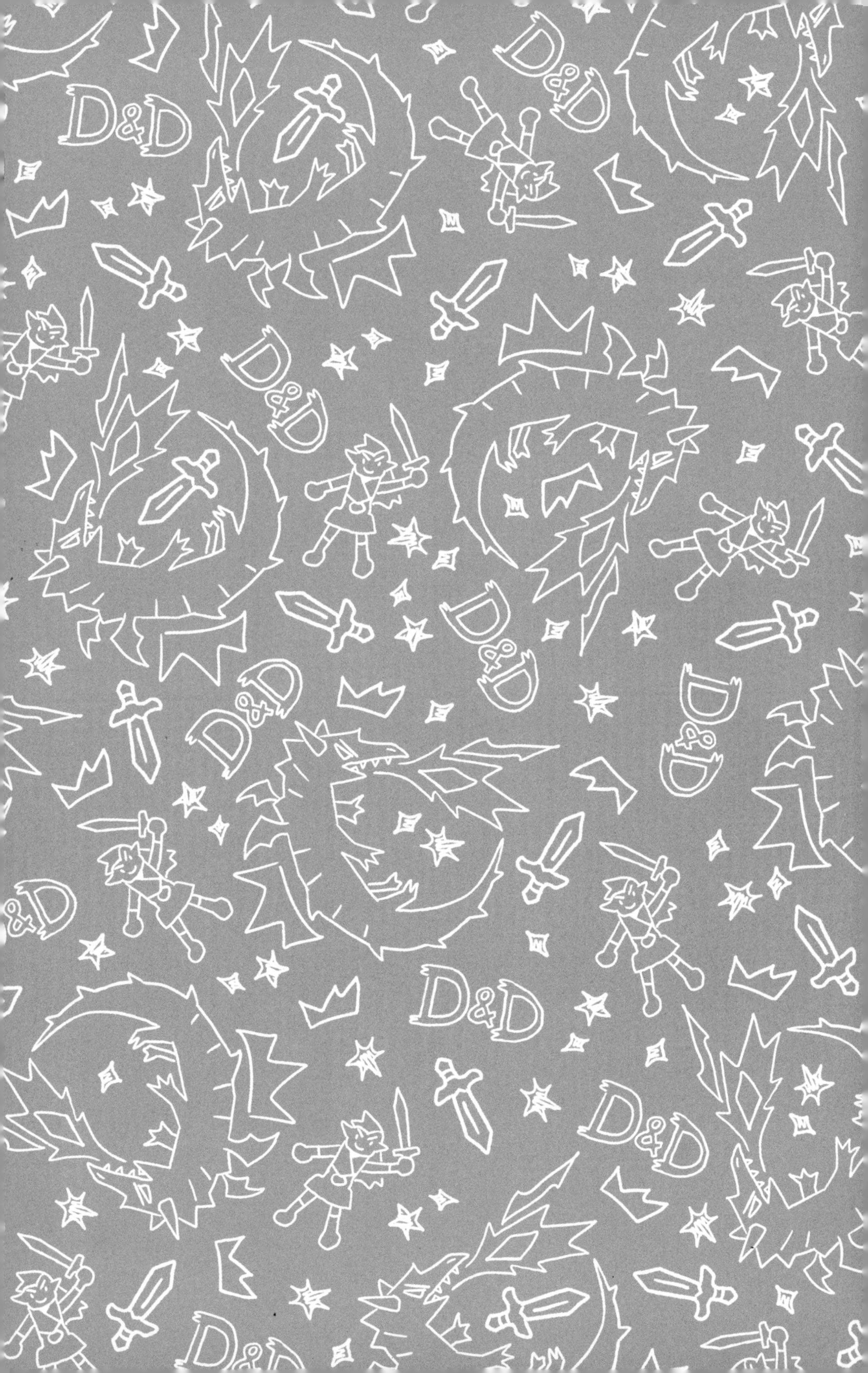
D&D

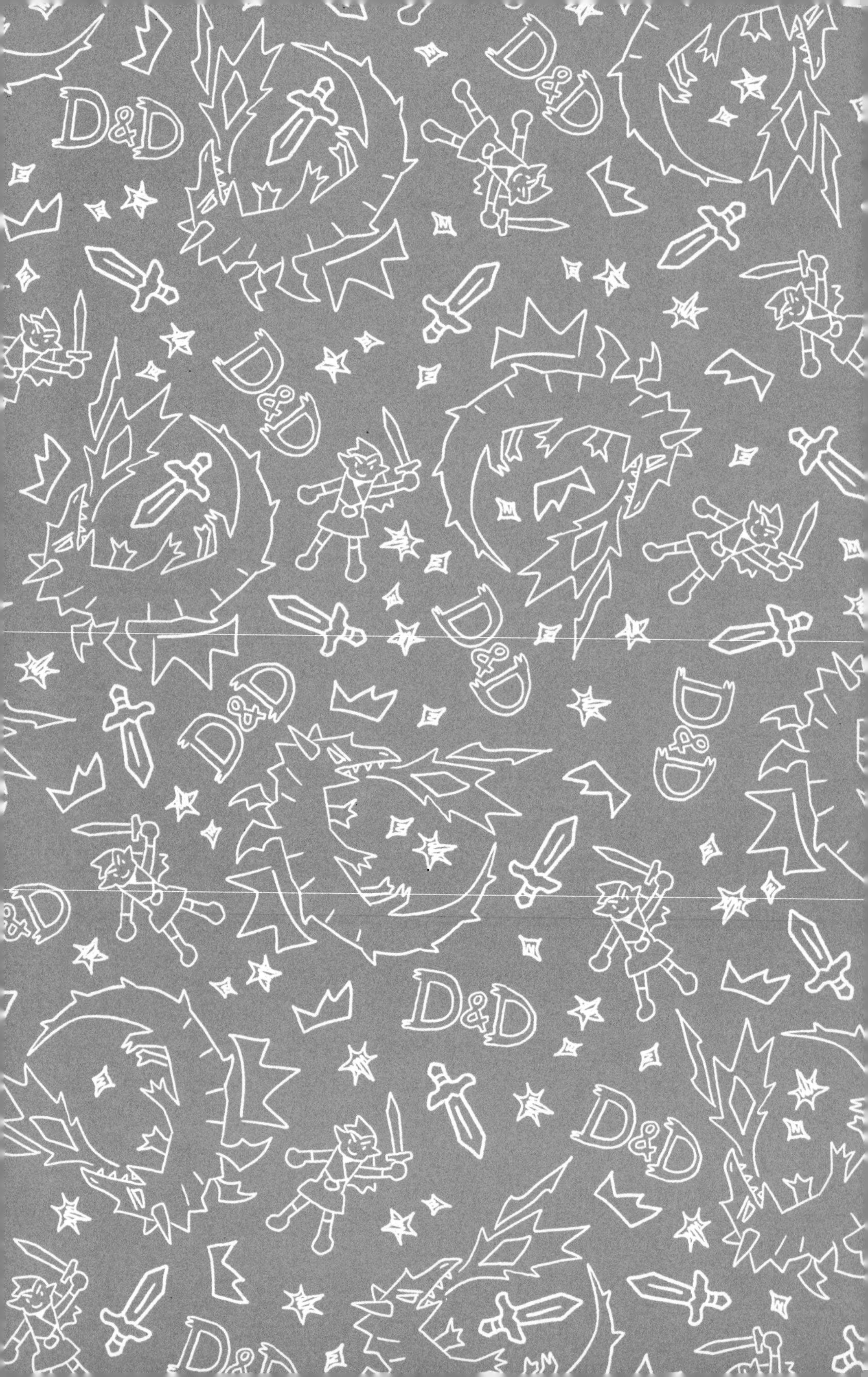
D&D